Praise for Shawna ... ...

GREEN
ISLAND

"Moving and suspenseful. . . . Full of compassion."
—*Richmond Times-Dispatch*

"An intricate, gracefully told tale that blends war history, suspense and a woman's coming-of-age and beyond. . . . The pages bloom with description, with a photolike sense of place." —*The Seattle Times*

"Gripping: a triumph of sustained focus. . . . *Green Island* is much more than an historical novel. It's also a family epic."
—*The Washington Times*

"A chilling, convincing picture of Taiwan during the years of authoritarian rule." —*Los Angeles Times*

"Sweeping . . . as epic in scope as the story is intimate."
—*The Arizona Republic*

"A moving and indelible story. . . . Ryan reshapes the immigrant tale in this precise and poetic work."
—*Publishers Weekly*

"As much a gripping narrative of an evolving Taiwan as an exquisitely crafted story of one family's devotion and compromises." —*Honolulu Star-Advertiser*

"Soaring." —*The Millions*

Shawna Yang Ryan

GREEN
ISLAND

Shawna Yang Ryan is a former Fulbright scholar and the
author of one previous novel, *Water Ghosts*. She teaches in
the creative writing program at the University of Hawai'i
at Mānoa. Her short fiction has appeared in ZYZZYVA,
The Asian American Literary Review, *Kartika Review*, and
Berkeley Fiction Review. She lives in Honolulu.

www.shawnayangryan.com

GREEN ISLAND

GREEN ISLAND

SHAWNA YANG RYAN

VINTAGE BOOKS
A Division of Penguin Random House LLC
New York

The Library of Congress has cataloged the Knopf edition as follows:
Ryan, Shawna Yang.
Green Island / Shawna Yang Ryan. — First edition.
pages ; cm
1. Taiwan—History—20th century—Fiction.   2. Taiwan—Social
conditions—20th century—Fiction.   3. Taiwan—Politics and
government—20th century—Fiction.   4. Taiwan—Social life and
customs—20th century—Fiction.   I. Title.
PS3618.Y344G74 2016   813'.6—dc23   2015002202

Vintage Books Trade Paperback ISBN: 978-1-101-87236-9
eBook ISBN: 978-1-101-87426-4

Book design by Iris Weinstein

www.vintagebooks.com

Printed in the United States of America
10 9 8 7 6 5 4

IN MEMORY OF TERENCE CHEUNG

這綠島的夜已經
這樣沉靜
姑娘喲妳為什麼
還是默默無語

This green island night
appears so peaceful.
Darling, why are you
still silent?

—"GREEN ISLAND SERENADE"
(TAIWANESE LOVE SONG/SONG OF RESISTANCE)

It doesn't matter what they will make of you
or your days: they will be wrong,
they will miss the wrong woman, miss the wrong man,
all the stories they tell will be tales of their own invention.

—JANE HIRSHFIELD,
"IT WAS LIKE THIS: YOU WERE HAPPY"

BOOK I
TAIPEI
1947–1952

IT WAS LIKE THIS.

1947

1

MY MOTHER LI MIN'S labor pains began the night that the widow was beaten in front of the Tian-ma Teahouse.

The first cramp was unmistakable. She leaned against the wall and pressed her fingers to the underside of her belly. All her previous children had taken their time, leisurely writhing for days before they finally decided to emerge. She expected the same with her fourth.

The children, freshly bathed and rosy from the hot water, their hair still damp, were upstairs in bed. She went outside and around the house to add more kindling to the furnace that would keep the water warm for my father's bath. A wave went through her, like a girdle expanding, pulled from the front of her pelvis to her back. She exhaled. Some women toiled up until the moment that they gave birth in a field, then went back to work while nursing the still-bloody newborn. This was women's lore. My mother, however, had given birth each time in her husband's clinic, with hot water and a midwife, and then appreciatively followed the prescription for a reclusive month indoors, hair unwashed, eating chicken soup, attended by a Cantonese woman her husband hired. No fields for her.

Across town, the widow, who sold black market cigarettes in front of the teahouse run by the popular silent film narrator Zhan Tian-ma, was about to become infamous.

She was just a young woman with a dead husband, sitting on her haunches behind a cheap makeshift stand on a busy road. She was a few years older than my mother, with two children playing in the waning light on the sidewalk next to her spindly-legged table. The lights on the street were coming up, and people—artists, writers, actors—the types who would drink, smoke, and laugh their way through the end of the world—drifted out of the teahouse. Often, they stopped at the widow's stand. She even sold American cigarettes. They tore open the pack right there, lighting up with a match she gave them.

The night was chilly, and smoke mixed with breath in the cold air. The widow's eyes settled on a pair of lovers who meandered down an alley, whispering, arm to warm arm. She was gazing in their direction, thinking of her dead husband, when the Monopoly Bureau agents approached. She knew only a smattering of Mandarin but did not need it to translate their haughty faces, or their greedy hands confiscating her cigarettes.

A shout of protest flew from her lips.

People turned.

One agent's face blazed, and he cursed the widow, reaching once more for her cigarettes. She grabbed his arm and he shouted, "Let go!" Ignited by his tone, the crowd drew closer, clamoring for the agent to stop. In a way, weren't they all widows selling black market cigarettes? And can shame—or pride—explain why the agent threw the widow to the ground, fumbled for his pistol, gripping it as if he would shoot, and then slammed the butt into her head? Was he merely saving face?

The bath was drawn and the room muted by steam. Dr. Tsai was naked, on a low stool, ladling water from the tub over his shoulders. Li Min hitched up her dress, settled slowly on another stool behind her husband, and began lathering the washcloth.

Another cramp knotted up. She gasped softly and exhaled. Her arm fell to her side as she waited for it to pass.

Dr. Tsai looked over his shoulder. "What is it?"

"It's begun."

"When?"

"Just a few minutes ago."

She watched her husband's shoulders relax. "I'll go for Aunty Cheung after we're done," he said.

But she thought the midwife could wait until morning, and she told him so. After her first child, she'd sworn not to have any more. One already required her whole self—absolute, daily devotion—but then there had been two, then three, and now four, like spirits forcing their way into the world, demanding life despite her precautions. She was ready to pray to the fertility goddess to take her blessings elsewhere, and deeply grateful that her husband agreed.

She moved the washcloth in slow circles and watched the skin on his back bloom pink.

Perhaps she'd end up like her neighbor's mother, having children into her late forties. The woman's breasts dangled like a street dog's teats beneath her thin shirt.

Four was already just shy of a litter, she thought.

"We're done," Dr. Tsai said. He rinsed himself, shook the water from his hair, and put a hand gingerly into the tub. He pulled back; it was bright red. "Ah," he said, pleased. He stepped into the water and sank down.

With effort, Li Min rose. Her face glowed with sweat and steam.

"It's too hot for me. I can't stand it," she told her husband.

The cigarette vendor clutched her head. Her fingers were greasy with blood. Pain rippled through her skull in slow waves. She imagined she heard her children screaming somewhere in the chaos.

The Monopoly Bureau agents, pressed to the widow's fallen body by the crowd rolling angrily toward them in a fog of cursing, kicked her. Eyes wild, the agents waved their guns and threatened to shoot, but the crowd's cries swallowed their words.

The people would not retreat; some fought to get to the bleeding cigarette vendor, while others surged forward in rage. The agents began firing and the crowd collapsed, fleeing, breaking into a hundred splinters.

Li Min paced the hall.

The midwife had told her it was natural to feel regret, but this did not stop her guilt. The worst was the months after each baby had arrived, when she wondered what curse she had visited upon this new thing by bringing it into the world.

Behind the bathroom door, water splashed occasionally, but her husband, resting neck-deep in the tub, was otherwise quiet.

Was it possible this one would be a son too? She hoped so, but not because she favored men. Her husband modeled the seriousness, the stoicism, that she hoped her sons would inherit, but she had nothing to teach a daughter. She could teach her to dream—say, to be a painter, as she herself had been trained—and then teach her to let it go. Teach her to cloister herself in dark hallways, admiring how the light fell through the rice-paper doors while knowing that there was no point in putting it on canvas. Already, her oldest child, a daughter, at ten years old could make simple meals, washed laundry, and cared for her younger brothers. Li Min did not know how to give her more.

Last time, the midwife had said castor oil would bring out the baby faster. But the shops were closed.

She concentrated on pressing each foot deliberately onto the floor, feeling the wood, cool at first and then warming to her skin. She concentrated her whole mind in her feet and tried to forget the pain.

The agents stumbled their way through the street and hid in a police box, where they waited while the military police were called.

A knot of people eased open. Among them, a man lay bleeding. Bystanders turned him over, saw the bullet hole clogged with blood. Shouting helplessly, pushing someone's shirt against the wound and feeling it grow heavy and wet, they watched his eyes glaze over, his mouth gape. Somebody beckoned to a rickshaw. When the driver saw the dead man, he shook his head and waved his hands in protest. "Oh no. No dead passengers." He cycled away.

Two Samaritans made a stretcher out of shirts and carried the body away.

The military police arrived and the crowd rushed them to demand a summary execution, on the spot, for the murderers, who cowered inside the police box. The MPs promised justice at headquarters.

Justice. That abstract word. Reluctantly, the crowd allowed the Monopoly Bureau agents to be escorted away. But the bystanders' fettered rage demanded release. They pulled open the doors of the agents' abandoned truck, ransacking the backseat, building a bonfire of everything they found inside. The crackle of the fire was hungry.

Still electrified, they turned their attention to the truck itself. They rocked it until it fell over and the windows on one side shattered.

. . .

Her husband slept but Li Min could not. Next to him, she sat up in the dark, feeling the weight of the baby pressing against her bones. If she had risen, gone downstairs, and soothed herself beside the radio, she might have heard the news.

The fire burned itself out, leaving a heap of ash on the pavement.

2

BY MORNING, Li Min felt her pelvic bones separating, opening up to greet the new baby. The creature shifted inside her, settled lower. It *is* a creature, isn't it? she thought. Some little monster feasting on her. Two months ago, she'd lost a tooth. In the palm of her hand, the tooth was translucent, almost gray. "Don't worry"—she could not help but notice the affectionate chiding in her husband's voice as he assured her—"the baby is not sucking the marrow from your bones."

Downstairs, the boys shrieked, and her daughter, good girl, hushed them. Far off, someone thumped at the clinic door. Chaos, muffled by the floor and walls, rumbled. Maybe the midwife had arrived. The woman was efficient, no-nonsense. A different kind of mind lay inside a person who was accustomed to seeing blood without injury and to thrusting her hands into that most private and miraculous moment.

My mother lumbered over to the vanity, pulled a sweater from the pile of clothes on the stool, and struggled into it. When the knitting cut into her, she realized how much her arms had swelled.

At every third stair, she winced with pain. At some point, the body became a boulder barreling toward the precipice: the cramps grew closer in time, harder; her heart quickened; and she would not be able to resist the impulse to force the baby out. An irreversible course. The clinic had quieted. She passed by the dining room, where the boys were splayed on their stomachs on the tatami, brows furrowed over a board game.

"Ah Zhay?" she asked.

"Kitchen," the oldest boy said. His eyes stayed on the game.

She found her daughter at the stove trying to stoke a fire. Hiccups broke her attempts. She was crying. She wiped her nose on her sleeve.

Mama stroked her daughter's hair. "What's wrong? Where's Baba?"

Ah Zhay cast her wet eyes toward the door that connected the clinic to the house.

"Did he scold you?"

Ah Zhay shook her head, but refused to say more. Li Min made it only two steps when her legs were suddenly drenched.

She hoped the other voice behind the door was the midwife's.

Inside the clinic, her husband was kneeling beside a man whose blood dripped through the bamboo mat of the clinic bed and spread over the floor, soaking her husband's knees. At the queer, metallic smell—worse than the bloodless pig heads in the market, with flies lighting on their eyelashes; worse than the far-off recollection of her thick menses blood—she fought the heaving in her throat. Her husband jerked his head, and his eyes, wild, met hers.

"What is—?" She could barely get the words out.

He snapped, "Not now."

She noticed a man standing in the dark corner, wedged between the microscope table and the bookshelf. He looked miserable, shocked and impotent. He glanced at her, then sank down onto his haunches and held his head.

Her husband's world encompassed the radius of an arm's length. He and his patient. Her husband's angry intensity alarmed her almost more than the blood. She stumbled back to the kitchen and found Ah Zhay struggling with the hot kettle.

"Is he dead?" Ah Zhay sobbed.

"Go look after your brothers." She grabbed the kettle, set it back on the cooling burner, and limped back to the clinic. Her husband had propped the injured man on his side. Keep the wound above the heart, she recalled her husband once saying. With the man now facing the wall, she could see that what had been just a black knot in his chest was an angry, ragged tear in his back. Her husband had snipped open the jacket around the wound, and the petals of ripped and stained cloth hung limply.

The wad of rags that had been stuffed against the bleeding was already soaked, and her husband took a thick fold of fresh gauze and pressed it against the old bandage. The blood seeped through quickly, flowering against the white. The man's eyes were closed, his lips blue. She was sure he was already dead. She noted the spent syringe, one last drop of liquid swelling at the tip, discarded on the tray beside the bed.

"He was shot in front of the governor-general's," the other man offered. Even without the worried twist in his eyebrows, he had a maudlin face, heavy jowled and droopy eyed. She realized that the splotches on his hands, which she first took to be freckles, were dried blood.

"Why?" She still had not left the comforting rigidity of the doorway, where post pressed to spine. She could flee easily into the kitchen and shut the door, and exist again in a world where life, throbbing and churning inside her, was primary.

Her husband hushed them. His fingers curled delicately over the man's wrist. His nostrils flared once, quickly, the only indication of what he'd learned. What good did it do to be so impassive? she wondered, then immediately reminded herself that a cool head—aloof even—was a doctor's talent.

"The bullet has broken into pieces," he said.

The man in the corner groaned, like a cat, then fell silent.

She couldn't help feeling that giving birth seemed almost an indiscretion at this moment. Quietly, without alarm, she told her husband that she was going to have Ah Zhay fetch the midwife.

Her pregnancy registered on the face of the man in the corner and fear lit up his eyes. "Your daughter? No, I'll go. They are shooting in the streets."

Her bones were widening, the baby insisting. She couldn't fit his words together.

"Who is shooting in the streets?"

He told her of the widow in the park, the morning's protests, the banners hung with the call for the "mainland pigs" to return to China—then the shootings at the railway station and in front of the governor-general's, where he'd been with his friend, this man who lay propped like a straw dummy in the mise-en-scène.

"It was inevitable," her husband said softly. Yes, she silently agreed. She thought of the slimmer and slimmer offerings in the market since the Japanese had left two years before, and how self-conscious she felt strolling past the wary gaze of the Chinese Nationalist soldiers. She had felt the tension of the city in her own body: her purse pulled close, her shoulders raised, her eyes averted.

Her husband wedged rolled towels beneath the man's shoulder to brace him. She could barely see the rise and fall of the man's chest.

"I'll go for the midwife," the injured man's friend said again, as if the errand was the only payment he could offer. Li Min saw how anxious he was to leave, and she wondered if he would return. Her husband gave him the address and the man slipped out.

Grimacing and impatient, she waited upstairs on her own bed. The man still had not returned and it was already afternoon. Finally, her husband appeared, his hands scrubbed and pink, but she swore she saw the injured man's blood dried, rusty, under his fingernails.

"Wash your hands," she said. She hoped her panic came off as annoyance. He nodded dismissively and pulled a chair to the foot of the bed.

"Where is he?" she asked.

"I think," he said, "that we are on our own, so let's move ahead." He was sure she saw the effort in his words; his confidence was halfhearted. He did not tell her that he had not planned for this, that he had been downstairs, in the clinic, thumbing through his old medical school text, taking a quick review course in obstetrics. He urged her knees up and lifted her skirt.

"Perhaps you should fetch your sister?"

He laughed. "We're better off on our own."

"You'll need my help," she said.

He pushed the hem to her hips and separated her legs.

"How big?" she asked.

He made a circle with his finger and thumb. "Like a—a date."

"A date?" She felt hysterical. "When it's a durian, we'll worry." He didn't smile at her joke. She carefully exhaled as another cramp clutched her and squeezed away her humor. Rage flooded in with the pain. The urge to urinate was strong, but she didn't trust it. When the tightening had relaxed again, she giggled.

"What?" His distracted question drifted toward her.

She didn't know why she was laughing. Just as quickly, the image of the injured man downstairs came to mind. Soon, she'd be drenching the bed with her blood as well. She willed the thought away, but it was stubborn and came back to her in black-and-white images.

Her first child—my sister, Ah Zhay—had been born the year Japan went to Nanjing. A victorious battle, the Japanese newspapers had said. Hardworking soldiers with nothing to eat but sweet potatoes, so many that they shit orange. Orange shit—this was the symbol of military sacrifice offered to the people. The Chinese Nationalists had arrived in Taiwan with a different version of events. They had thrust the photos, accusingly, in the faces of the Taiwanese: women speared through their genitals; breasts lopped off and tossed like baseballs; bodies stacked up along the riverside; severed heads impaled on fence posts as warnings. The Nationalists saw the ignorance of the Taiwanese as more evidence of their brainwashing under the Japanese and treated them not as rescued compatriots but like conquered adversaries. My mother tried to extract the memory of her daughter lying bloody on her chest from the other images. Some blood is good blood, she reminded herself. Then she suddenly remembered all the pain that had been sucked away by her last nursing child. She struggled: Don't think of it.

Her husband placed his hand on her knee. "Pay attention." She focused her eyes on the charcoal portrait that hung on the wall directly across from the bed. Her husband. She had done it herself one day, sitting as quietly as possible in the clinic, observing him, still perplexed by the man she'd recently wed. She'd come to know his habits—how he bit his cuticles while reading, how carefully he left his shoes facing out and perfectly aligned when he slipped them off at the door—and she could replay his routine between rising and bed like a film, down even to the schedule of his bowel movements, but he was still veiled to her. She liked it, she realized. That he remained, in some way, unknown made the thought of a lifetime together bearable.

Another contraction racked her; instinctively, she held her breath, and he reminded her to breathe, then glanced at his watch.

"Ask Ah Zhay to come up. You should check on"—she paused, as if unsure what to call the dying man—"your patient."

When he hesitated, she reassured him. "I've done this three times before. Don't worry over me, my husband. Go see your man."

.   .   .

The man was dead.

From the moment the stranger and the rickshaw driver had dragged in the injured man, Dr. Tsai had known that the man was doomed. He had already lost too much blood. His face was pale with shock. Dr. Tsai wished they had gone to the hospital and hadn't cursed him with this certain failure.

He would do nothing about the body until the dead man's friend returned. He pulled up his stool and inspected the man. Leave the bullet in. He knew that removing the bullet could damage the body more, the cure worse than the disease, but now that the man was already gone, he probed the wound and extracted a shard of the bullet. Was it as the friend had said—had the shooters really used hollow-point bullets? He knew little of guns except for the military books he'd read as a child. Hollow-points, he remembered, were forbidden by the Hague Convention. The way they opened up inside the body was inhumane. Dum-dum bullets, they were also called.

He reached into the man's pocket and found a silver card case. Inside, a dozen copies of the same name card. The man was a high school principal. At least he had an address if the friend decided never to return. Behind the cards was a hand-colored photo of a bright-cheeked woman. Her name was scrawled in watery ink on the back. He returned the case to the jacket and sighed. Though he didn't believe in the superstition that viewing a corpse was bad luck, he shook out a sheet and watched as it settled, like a bird alighting, over the body.

He heard, from the street, the echo of a loudspeaker. He left the clinic, crossed the gravel yard, and went through the wooden gate. The street was strikingly empty of traffic. A train of three military trucks, the insignia of the US Army barely disguised by a thin layer of paint, crawled down the road. The announcement came from them. He could not piece the words together until they came closer, squawking in Mandarin, Taiwanese, and Japanese that the military curfew would begin at six in the evening. Violators would be shot on sight.

Dr. Tsai slipped back into the yard and, feverish with dread, shoved the gate shut. The midwife, he realized, would not be coming.

3

"CLEAN MY GLASSES," Dr. Tsai ordered his daughter. When she pulled off his fogged spectacles, he was relieved to have the world blurred for a moment. His daughter's gestures were vague, her contours like a smudged sketch, but he heard her two quick exhalations and then the squeak of cloth against glass. She slipped the glasses back on him, and her flushed round face, expectant and obedient, greeted him. For a moment, he was startled. When did she start to look like a young woman? he wondered. Her limbs had shed most of her baby fat, and two modest bumps declared themselves beneath her blouse.

Li Min, sweating, half-coherently spoke. "Is the baby going back?"

"Going back?"

"Is it coming out? Is it going back?" A drawn-out groan floated through her clenched teeth.

Dr. Tsai squatted. The baby seemed wedged, its damp, warm head straining against his wife's body. He thought he might be able to slip his fingers in and urge it out, but her skin was stretched thin and had no give.

"Why aren't you doing anything, you worthless bastard?"

Dr. Tsai's textbook had mentioned nothing about his wife's horrific moans or the sheer anger she seemed to have at him and the baby who resisted inside her. Earlier, to calm her, he had given her a cup of whisky, claiming that his textbook had suggested it, then had guiltily watched her gag and spit it over the front of her dress.

"Snip it out. There's no room. Cut it; Aunty Cheung did it," she gasped.

The instructions came back to him as a block of text:

> When the infant's head no longer retreats this is known as "crown-ing." Now, it is in the mother's best interest to refrain from laboring any more. The physician should inquire about a "fiery" sensation, which signals that the mother should relax and allow the contrac-tions to complete the rest of the birthing process. At this point, the

doctor too may choose to cut the membrane to allow the infant to more easily pass through.

"My scissors. The small ones." While his daughter rummaged through his bag, his wife muttered, "Cut it, cut it," like a madwoman writhing in delirium. Ah Zhay finally found the scissors. "Wipe them down with that alcohol." The doused wad of cotton dripped as she cleaned the scissors. The damp blades in her small hand glittered in the lamplight. He saw no fear in her face. Dr. Tsai was nervously quiet, watching his wife grip the blankets as he palpated her stomach, cringing when she cried.

"Damn you," his wife hissed. Dr. Tsai took the scissors from his daughter.

I was born just after midnight on March 1, 1947. There was nothing spectacular about my birth. I was not born with my eyes preternaturally open, or oddly mute like the girl-goddess Matsu. Rather, I joined the street dogs in howling my way into that silent city.

My father laid me, still bloody, on my mother's chest as he sewed up the wound he had created. My sister held the lamp over his work. Careful, tiny stitches. His hands were steady.

One of my mother's breasts became infected and the vessels flared up, a red coral bouquet. The crackle of illness was more madness to the chaos. Fever sweat drenched her clothes. With the radio station under government guard, everything was rumor. The rumor of the shootings at the railway station and in front of the American consulate that had taken place on the day of my birth. The rumor that the railroad tracks had been dismantled by citizens to keep Governor-General Chen Yi's troops from moving north. The rumor that the soldiers had used forbidden hollow-tipped bullets. Rumors of indiscriminate shootings, of razor-wire barricades in front of the governor's office, and of Mainlanders tossed off moving trains by angry Taiwanese. Rumors whispered through the fence, by the rice seller on the back stoop of his shop, by the lone tofu vendor who dared pull his cart through the alleys. The only certainty was the loss of electricity, which caused the radio to intermittently sputter to life like a ghost awakened, then die down to silence with the lights.

Dr. Tsai, my father—*Baba*—had managed to keep the dead man a secret until the baby was born, but now my mother had the thought of the corpse stiffening downstairs to keep her company during her fever. She knew Baba had walked past the body when he went to fetch the pills for her infection, and she swore he was shrouded in death when he returned upstairs. She closed her eyes and turned away.

With my two brothers clinging to her skirt, Ah Zhay brought broth to our mother. The three children peered at the new baby. One look was enough for my brothers, who spent the rest of Mama's bedridden period reveling in my parents' inattention. For two afternoons, they rummaged through my mother's art supplies, wore her pencils down, drenched the paints in water, and tore the sketch pads until Ah Zhay, catching them, spanked them on behalf of our sick mother.

And then there was the matter of the baby—me—a stubborn girl who let the nipple tickle the roof of her mouth but did not latch on. Baba brought a bowl and helped drain Mama's breast by hand while I wailed with hunger.

On the second of March, the man with the hangdog face returned for his friend. In the doorway of the clinic, he muttered his apologies over and over, and Baba had only to gesture toward the covered body to silence him. The man shuddered and began pacing, frantic, crying out, "No, no, no." He stumbled toward the body, then staggered back, almost comically, as he caught the odor.

Baba didn't try to comfort him. He stepped outside and permitted the man his private grief, letting him cry until he was spent. Finally, the man, vigorously rubbing his eyes with his sleeve, came outside.

"When?" the man asked. Now, he could barely lift his eyes to the shrouded body, a lump of white in the dark office.

"Not long after you left." Baba offered him a cigarette, which he refused. Each breath ended in the exhausted sigh that follows violent tears. Baba took a long drag on his cigarette and exhaled. "Who shot him?"

The man shook his head, but began to speak anyway. He said that they had heard about the widow cigarette vendor on the radio, and a call had gone out for people to march to the executive office and demand punishment for the officers involved. He and his friend had been talking for months about the corruption on the island. At last, people were taking action; naturally, they decided to join the protest.

"Naturally," Baba echoed.

They thought they would crowd the plaza, shout, and maybe the governor-general would address them. They didn't expect the barrier of soldiers, all wielding guns. The crowd hadn't called for blood, and yet the soldiers had shot.

Baba continued smoking calmly, never revealing the anger rising in his chest. And he thought how stupid the authorities had been—didn't they realize an act like this would only inspire more people to oppose them? A massacre may incur silence, but a random shooting inspires ardor. This was the truth of human behavior, he decided. And it was true for him. The zeitgeist, he thought. Discontent was in the air; the explosion had only been a matter of when.

Later in the afternoon, the man returned with friends to carry the body away. They'd borrowed someone's truck, and they loaded the corpse in the bed and gently arranged the sheet around him.

The governor-general called a community meeting in order to find a solution to the unrest. The people, expecting nothing but honesty, were not suspicious of the suddenly conciliatory approach. My mother shook with chills and dampened the bedding with her fever sweat. My sister and brothers, who had not gone outside since the first day of rioting—five days—were restless in the destructive way of children; they'd already punched through one of the paper screens downstairs in their murderous chase of a poor gecko that had caught their eye. Despite the chaos under his own roof, Baba put on his coat and hat, told my sister to keep an eye on my mother, and left.

My father barely recognized the Taipei he stepped into that Tuesday morning. Once he exited the narrow, crowded lanes of our neighborhood— the windows pleading mute innocence with curtains or tacked-up towels and old shirts—he found that nearly half the buildings on the wide main boulevard were boarded up. Hastily painted signs—ragged banners fluttering from windows and over doorways—called out for justice or cursed the building's inhabitants as "mainland pigs." GO HOME! the posters demanded. The click of geta—Japanese wood-soled sandals that he'd not heard since Japan's surrender made its fashions suddenly suspect— sounded from the feet of women hurrying by, telegraphing the message to angry Taiwanese: *I am one of you, do not beat me.* Military trucks rolled by like pensive beasts.

At this moment, I want to call out across the decades, "Baba, turn around. Go home."

He kept walking.

Thousands of people, their stomachs ill with anticipation, filled the hot auditorium—the same room in which the Japanese, just a year and a half before, had signed over the island. Baba wedged himself among them. Flanking their leader, the governor-general's men sat on the stage like a row of grim judges, not even flinching as gunfire rattled in the plaza beyond the doors. Baba noticed that even when Governor-General Chen Yi was not smiling, his pudgy face looked amused. The men on the auditorium floor, stripping off their jackets and rolling up their sleeves, made their demands.

"Release the wrongly arrested!"

"End armed patrols!"

"Restore communication!"

"Negotiate in good faith: no more troops!"

Baba pushed his way toward the stage and demanded to speak too.

A man, sitting to the right of the governor-general, pointed at Baba. The auditorium quieted.

"Good afternoon. My name is Dr. Tsai." This was Baba at his best: his words loud and clear, his arms relaxed by his sides, standing centered as if integrity aligned everything inside of him.

With steady eyes and voice, Baba spoke about the friendship between Generalissimo Chiang and the United States. He said that since the money of democracy was helping to fund the war against the communists, it seemed only right that the Republic of China should apply those same principles on the island. Taiwanese, he argued, deserved representation in the new government. The rhetoric of American democracy was everywhere that week; there had even been a roaming truck that blared "The Star-Spangled Banner." The United States had run an impressive pro-democracy propaganda campaign after the war, and the island, fresh out of Japan's colonial clutch, had believed it all. A secret idealist, Baba had too.

In agreement, the crowd roared up around him again. Strange hands clapped him on the back. Men he didn't know thanked him. Amid the tumult, a voice sang out, "And the star-spangled banner in triumph shall wave . . . O'er the land of the free and the home of the brave!"

In a few days, Baba would discover the United States' response to the island's unrest: "This is *China* now."

4

BABA HAD PREPARED RICE, cold seaweed, and fried fish for dinner. Zhee Hyan, the youngest boy, cried out when my mother stepped into the room. This was the first time she had been downstairs since giving birth. Zhee Hyan scrambled over his oldest brother's legs to reach her.

"Be careful of the baby," she said.

Music played in the other room, an album by the singer Chun Chun. The record warbled from the lean years when my parents had only bamboo needles. Grinning to himself, Baba hummed along as he scooped rice for my mother.

My mother laid me in her lap. She was careful not to drop stray grains of rice on me. Ah Zhay put down her bowl and reached over to nuzzle my nose with her finger. "Little baby," she cooed. Just a week old, I was a snorting, wrinkly little rat with a puff of black hair. My aimless arms batted at my sister's poking fingers.

"Enough," my tired mother said. With her chopsticks, she gestured Ah Zhay away.

I was still nameless. My grandfather—my mother's father, for Baba's parents had died during the war—would determine the characters of my name by the date and time of my birth, my zodiac sign, and perhaps even any potential deficiencies that he noted as he held me. But the ceremony—sacred even to my pragmatic parents—would not happen until the chaos ended and the trains resumed. For now, I was "the baby" or, to make me seem unappealing to any malevolent spirits hoping to steal me away, "little monster."

Our house was just off the main boulevard that ran north-south through the city, the road that would one day be bestowed with the highest honor, the name of the father of the republic, and the road by which donated American Jeeps—hastily painted to hide their origins—now entered Taipei.

My mother hushed my brothers. My father looked at her, puzzled, then he too heard the sound of gunfire, the distinctive *rat-tat-tat* that even war virgins recognize.

"Ma—" my sister whined.

"Quiet!" my father warned. A long moment of silence engulfed the house and the city—and then shots again shattered the quiet. Unlike the indiscriminate horror of the early staccato firing, the quiet space between these singular gunshots revealed a frightening intention. Individual men were being targeted.

My father ran to the other room, lifted the needle off the record, and turned on the radio. Bach's *Die Kunst der Fuge* played. No news. He switched off the radio and returned to his family. Afraid and expectant, wife, daughter, sons gazed up at him. Their food, uneaten, appeared glazed and artificial. Wordlessly, he reached up and turned off the light.

In the dark, my father told my mother the rumors he had heard. He didn't want to recount them in front of the children, but he had no choice. The first one, from the governor-general himself, was that the governor-general had heard the demands presented during the meeting in the Civic Auditorium, admitted his flaws in managing the new province, and promised to address them. The other rumor, now brightening into truth, was that the governor-general had frantically begged Generalissimo Chiang Kai-shek for more troops to help control the "situation" on the island.

"Control what situation?" my mother whispered.

"Ah Bin"—Baba used her nickname, intimately—"they consider us more Japanese than Chinese. Two years ago, we were their enemy. We're still their enemy."

Despite my mother's warm hands and gentle rocking, I began to cry. She pressed me to her shirt and tried to shush me.

"Nurse her," my father urged. My mother opened her shirt and offered her breast to me. I cried even louder. Certain that the soldiers would now find us and kill us, my sister began to wail too.

"Stop." My father grabbed Ah Zhay's arm. "Quiet! Do you know what they'll do if—" He stopped himself. He turned toward my mother. "Give her to me."

My mother pressed me again to her bared breast. "No." Her voice trembled. "She'll eat."

Shots again rattled the night. I screamed. Ah Zhay curled on the floor and muffled her sobs in her arm. My oldest brother, Dua Hyan, now held Zhee Hyan and murmured against his cheek.

"Give her to me!" Baba tugged my blanket. My mother's soft protests threatened that she was close to tears. Again, she urged me to her breast. Finally, I took it and settled into hiccups and sighs.

The rest of the family sank into mute fear. The guns quieted by midnight; even soldiers need sleep. We fell asleep too—restless, uneasy, cold.

It was true: the Generalissimo had sent more troops from the mainland. He held the philosophy that it was "better to kill a hundred innocent men than let one guilty go free." Rumors claimed that the troops began strafing the shore before they even disembarked.

Perhaps the Generalissimo was also guilty of listening to rumors, like the one that said the protests of February 28 had been instigated by communist agents rather than unhappy citizens.

In any case, day by day and home by home, men began to disappear.

On the tenth of March, paper fell from the sky. Like giant snowflakes, they drifted into our courtyard, impaling themselves on the bushes and covering the gravel. My parents had forbidden my sister and brothers from going outside lest a stray bullet tear through the courtyard fence, so Ah Zhay looked on enviously as my father went out to gather them up.

My father dropped the sheets onto the table. Each page was exactly the same: the Generalissimo's official account of what had happened since the last day of February and explaining the presence of the new troops:

> I hope that every Taiwanese will fully recognize his duty to our fatherland and strictly observe discipline so as not to be utilized by treacherous gangs and laughed at by the Japanese. I hope Taiwanese will refrain from rash and thoughtless acts which will be harmful not only to our country but also to themselves. I hope they will be thoroughly determined to discriminate between loyalty and treason,

and to discern between advantage and disadvantage; and that they will voluntarily cancel their illegal organizations and recover public peace and order, so that every Taiwanese can lead a peaceful and happy life as soon as possible, and thus complete the construction of the new Taiwan.

Thus only can Taiwanese be free from the debt they owe to the entire nation, which has undergone so many sacrifices and bitter struggles for the last fifty years in order to recover Taiwan.

That day, giving the Generalissimo's words their due, Baba taught my siblings how to make folded paper boats.

A few days later, a soft knock at the door startled my parents. The delicate sound of knuckles on wood told my parents that the visitor was friend, not foe, but Baba still herded the family upstairs before he opened the door.

The visitor was the nephew of my father's very good friend Su Ming Guo. He was panting. His sandals lay in the dirt, apparently kicked off in hasty respect before he had stepped onto the porch. He shared with his uncle the same drooping eyes and dark circles, even though he was likely no older than thirteen.

The boy said he had no time to come in. "A wanted list has gone up at the train station; my uncle says to tell you that your name is on it." The words were too urgent to be softened.

My mother eavesdropped from the top of the stairs. She waited for a moment longer as the boy told Baba that many of the men who had been at the meeting had already escaped, but even more had been arrested.

"My uncle is leaving too. He says you must go. He says wait a few days at Mount Kuanyin and then leave from Tamshui."

My mother went to the bedroom, pulled down Baba's suitcase from the wardrobe shelf—the same suitcase he'd carried back from Tokyo at graduation—and began to pack. Her hands moved, her mind planned, but her eyes, darkening, watched scenes that my father had not yet conceived as he climbed the stairs to tell her what the boy had said.

"What are you doing?" my father asked as he came into the room.

"You're leaving." With studied care, she laid one of his shirts in the suitcase.

Baba closed the dresser drawer with a jerk of his knee. "Stop packing."

"You're leaving. They are already looking for you. I heard him." Unable to face him, she opened the drawer again and began yanking everything out. "Where are your gray pants?"

"Stop packing. I've done nothing. They'll ask me a few questions and be done with it."

She stopped. Yes, this too was Baba's flaw: the belief that the world was as sensible as he was. She stepped over the mess of clothes, wrapped her arms around his neck, and put her mouth against his ear. "Not this time. Not anymore." She felt his body tense in her embrace.

Baba pulled down her arms. "Get your gold necklace and the jade earrings. Sew them into the hem of one of my white shirts. I must find . . . something." The drifting sentence betrayed my father. My mother heard it. She knew him too well to not see the vagueness in his eyes and the tiny tightening around his mouth that revealed his fear. He had looked like this the very first time they had argued; early in their marriage, she had made a self-deprecating comment about how wan her face looked, coyly hoping he would counter with a compliment, and was livid when he had agreed with her.

Now, her hands shaking as she stitched the jewelry into his shirt, she regretted that ridiculous fight. What did a misunderstood word matter in the context of everything else about their life? How many times had he told her she was beautiful? She regretted all of their arguments. From a distance, every single one seemed petty. She held her breath, trying to suffocate her heart to stillness. She whispered prayers into the seam, hoping to imbue the necklace, the earrings, the shirt with protective magic. "Keep him safe. Let him pass through unharmed." She did not know which god or goddess she spoke to—she'd be satisfied with any that would listen.

Somehow, she cooked dinner, using the last of their fresh vegetables and a final tin of fish, hoping the meal would convey what she could not bring herself to say. The whole family ate together. Neither Baba nor my mother told the children that he would be leaving. Zhee Hyan climbed in and out of my father's lap and drifted over to pet my head as I slept in my mother's arms. Ah Zhay chattered on about a pirate story she had made up that afternoon.

Dua Hyan earnestly questioned her. "Mean? How mean?"

"He kept ten samurai swords on his belt from all the samurai he had killed. And when he cut someone's head off"—Ah Zhay pretended to gag as she hacked her throat with the blade of her hand—"he did not even bother wiping the blood off. He just used a new sword for his next victim."

"How big was his ship?" Dua Hyan's chopsticks hovered midway between the bowl and his mouth.

"Oh, I forgot to tell you! He hated little boys the most. The blood on his swords was all from little boys. Eight-year-olds were his favorite victims." She raised her eyebrows at him.

My father smiled at how solemnly she delivered this information, but my mother saw the faltering corners of his mouth. Who knew what pirates would pursue him, and if they craved his blood too. She saw, in his glistening eyes, that he was etching every detail of each of their faces to his memory. To hide her own tears, she brought her sleeve to her mouth and pretended to cough.

As they continued their banter, my brothers and sister never noticed that our parents' food remained untouched.

Since February, the nights had grown longer as the fearsome dark threatened to repulse day indefinitely. Except for this night, which passed too quickly. Once it opened into tomorrow, my mother knew, it would be as if the night, and all that had passed before it, had never existed.

The police arrived before Baba could leave. The knocking, too early to be considered polite, woke my parents.

A stunned breath passed between them. My mother said she would answer the door. "They'll be kind if they see the baby," she said.

"Or they will think I'm a coward." Shaking with adrenaline, Baba struggled into the clothes he had prepared for his escape. My mother wrapped herself in a robe. She tried to look as disheveled and helpless as possible. Who was more naive—my mother for thinking she could manipulate these men, or my father for believing the administration was not deranged enough to consider his criticism of it a "crime"? He told himself it would take only five questions for the investigators to discover his innocence and let him go.

The knocking grew more insistent.

"Go out the clinic door," my mother pleaded. Baba refused. He kissed her, felt the worried pulse in her temple beat against his lips, and hurried down the stairs. With the baby cradled in her arms, Mama scrambled after him.

Baba threw open the door. Three men. Mama would recall three men clustered at the door, their dark figures blocking the faint morning light, and when she could talk about it again, she would note the same thing over and over: "They were so young. Just boys." Boys who tackled my father at his first words and dragged him away as my mother stuttered her protest.

She ran after them. Across the yard, through the gate. Babe squalling at her breast, her robe falling open, she chased them down the alley until one of the boys finally turned and, with no sign of hesitation, leveled his rifle at her. She stopped running; her screams faltered into gasps. At the end of the alley, framed by two houses in shadow, more soldiers lifted Baba into the bed of a truck. Only then did the boy lower his rifle.

On March 14, 1947, my father disappeared.

5

WHEN BABA HAD NOT RETURNED by the next morning, Mama broke her postpartum confinement. Staring up at the railroad station's wanted poster, Mama met another abandoned wife, not ready to call herself a widow, who shared a protocol for finding their missing husbands.

The first stop, she advised, was the police station.

A line of dark-eyed women dribbled out the door, continued past the sundries shop next door, and folded around the corner. They waited politely despite every impulse to rush the police station, leap over the desks, and tear at the files. After each unsuccessful query, they whispered down the line that the man in question could not be found, but each woman still believed her husband would be the exception.

Three hours passed. My mother had left me at home in Ah Zhay's care. She had lied to the children: *Baba went on a trip.*

Where? Ah Zhay had asked.

The answer came without thinking. *Tokyo.*

Why didn't he tell us?

All she could say was *I don't know.*

Ah Zhay pressed on, Baba's absence already incidental: *Will he bring us a souvenir?*

Yes, I'm sure.

Mama's hips ached from standing. Finally, she crossed the threshold into the station and faced a weary young officer who made a superficial search of the rolls and told her they knew nothing. They had no record of my father.

"I saw him taken away with my very eyes," she said firmly.

"Your name again?" asked the officer. His tone chilled my mother back to sanity. "I might have made a mistake," she murmured.

She let the next distraught wife step forward in her place.

Some of the wives also claimed the American consulate could help. My mother stood outside the gate, among other women, pleading with the guards. "Think of your own mother. Think of your own wife. My children are missing their father." Sympathy flickered over the young men's faces; only this consulate fence kept them from being one of the missing. As if realizing misfortune could taint them too, the guards blotted out any mark of concern and stared past the women. My mother glanced up; figures stood at the windows—she knew the men inside must have seen the women down below wailing at the gate—but then they passed again into the building recesses.

Our aunt, Baba's sister, came to our home with a bundle of incense wrapped in paper and a tiny carved god.

"How can they do nothing?" my mother cried to her.

"What do they care? Like everyone else, they just want to save their own skins." She dragged a table against the wall and set the god on it. She lit the incense, then threw herself to the ground and begged her dead parents—my grandparents—to watch over their son. Dua Hyan and Zhee Hyan clung to the doorway and gaped at my aunt heaped on the floor, hiccuping with tears and prayers. My brothers had never seen such a display.

Finally, she sat up. Bedraggled and exhausted, she said, her voice hoarse, "Why didn't I think of this sooner? I know a fortune-teller; he can answer our questions."

"A fortune-teller?" my mother scoffed. She jiggled the baby. "You've lost your mind. I don't have money to throw at charlatans."

"Mere men can't help us now. There's nothing else left to do."

My mother thought again of the long line of women in front of the police station and of the women clamoring at the consulate gate. What did hope cost? A few coins? My mother shook her head as she said yes.

The fortune-teller kept a table on a small street near the river, revealing fates until sundown. My aunt and mother took a rickshaw to the place. As my mother trudged up to his table with her dirty hair and clothes, the fortune-teller noted her fading spirit. She was just like the other women who had come to him in those weeks as a last resort, hoping for some clue about their missing husbands.

He said, "You have darkness in your face."

He reached across the table and held one of her hands palm up, flat and open to the gray sky.

He covered her hand with his and closed his eyes. A cluster of calluses grated against her skin.

"He's alive," he croaked.

My aunt gasped. My mother lifted her head and finally looked at the old man. In a loose cotton top and pajama pants, he dressed like a coolie: he was a specimen from the last dynasty. What could he know? He'd found a simple way to make money when a tender hip and weak shoulders no longer allowed him to work.

"Where is he?" she asked wearily.

The man looked at the sky. The city stank of death, a sudden breeze relaying from far off a reminder of unclaimed men. Or maybe the odor simply wafted out of the earth on warm days to deliver the message: *This is not a dream.*

"I don't know."

My mother nodded. Of course he didn't. Thousands of husbands disappeared in those weeks. Sons as young as twelve. Brothers. Friends. What better way to remake society, my mother thought, than to eliminate the teachers and principals, the students, the lawyers and doctors—truly, anybody who had an opinion and a voice? Beyond the river, execution grounds, field after field irrigated with blood, waited to be discovered. Buildings would crush the bones.

Yet the fortune-teller was only my mother's penultimate hope. The very last resort was the harbor at Keelung, which, rumors claimed, had become a watery graveyard.

No clouds marred the clear blue sky; there was nothing to diminish the strong March sun. Sweat ran down the channel of her spine. The stench of decay, like a ghost in the humid air, assaulted my mother before she even saw the water. The executions were supposed to be secret, but the tide had carried the bodies back toward land, where they clogged the port, wedged along the hulls of ships. The doors of the normally busy quayside warehouses were shut. The majestic cranes, long necked and gangly like prehistoric creatures, were still. Even the giant ships seemed to slumber. Enterprising fishermen offered their dinghies for a small fee. My mother beckoned one over and the boatman held her hand as she stepped in. He wore a peaked straw hat, like a farmer, which cast his face in shadow, and a bandanna masked everything below his eyes. She huddled in the boat, holding me to her chest and a handkerchief pressed to her nose and mouth. Her blouse was damp with milk.

With a long pole, the fisherman carefully negotiated their way around the bodies. Down here, drifting among the monstrous ships, the port seemed larger than it had the day she had sailed in on her return from university in Japan. That day, she had leaned on the deck railing and, with a bittersweet pain in her chest, waved at the waiting crowds. She had not yet spotted her family, but she knew they were there. Japan was behind her now, a phase of her life forever gone.

On that day, daydreaming of her future, she had not imagined this. My mother scanned the water as if one swollen corpse could be distinguished from another. She swallowed the nausea that rose up her throat. She ignored the faces, which, waterlogged, had become alike, and looked for a telling glow, a chain of gold revealed through the translucent wet seam of a shirt. She cried out a few times, and each time the fisherman stopped and nudged the body, but something would be wrong: the hair was too long, the watch had a square face not round, the pants were brown not black.

They searched all afternoon, until the fisherman finally said, "He's not here."

My mother curled over me and, in relief and fear, cried into my blanket.

AS MY FATHER STUMBLED alongside the three young soldiers, he realized he had misbuttoned his shirt. This upset him. He could not stop fingering the orphaned button at the bottom and the empty buttonhole at the top. He imagined the neighbors secretly watching and how they must have pitied him, taken so quickly and foolishly without time to properly dress. With a hand under each armpit, the soldiers hefted him into the waiting truck. There, finally, he could rebutton his shirt.

The canvas cover arcing over the truck bed hid four other men and two soldiers to watch them. Baba sat between one young soldier and an older man who wept into his hands, exposing the haphazard tufts of white hair atop his otherwise bald head. The man was even less prepared than my father—he wore only his pajamas, which consisted of a frayed white singlet and cheap hand-sewn cotton pants with a gaping fly. Mud flecked his bare feet.

The other three men were just as pathetic, startled too quickly out of sleep into an entirely new world. Two wore formal coats as if apprehended en route to an early-morning appointment. A folded piece of paper poked out of one man's sock, supporting my father's suspicion that the "early-morning appointment" was only an alibi for their getaway. The third man huddled against the cab, his face completely concealed by his upturned coat collar and lowered hat brim. He could have been crying, sleeping, or dead.

The young soldiers didn't bother to hide their boredom. Their heads nodded along as the truck rattled over the lumpy road.

"No breakfast again," one complained. He coughed free something from his throat, lifted the canvas panel, and spit.

"Why ruin your appetite when we'll be having cabbage again tonight?"

"Cabbage. Shit."

One of the prisoners pulled a leaf-wrapped rice dumpling from his pocket and held it out. "Mister," he said in heavily accented Mandarin.

My father snickered at the useless gesture. They were being carted to the gallows—why be kind?

The soldier glanced at his friend. Was it a ploy? Poison? He grabbed it, tore off the twine, and peeled the leaves back as if it were a banana. The aroma of pork and rice made Baba's stomach cry. The soldier took a bite, then held it out for his friend. They took turns and finished it with boiled egg yolk, the dumpling's savory center, powdered across their mouths. Like a little rat, the first soldier gnawed across the open leaves, cleaning off the remaining bits of rice.

Perhaps bribery was not a bad strategy. Perhaps it would buy time, freedom, life. Baba felt the hem of his shirt, where my mother had sewn in the gold necklace. He was often surprised at the treasures she pulled from her jewelry box. Most of it had been given to her at their wedding. She told him that she really did not own much, but each time she wore earrings or a necklace to dinner or another wedding banquet, he swore he had never seen it before. This gold chain too, weighing down the edge of his shirt and resting heavily on his thigh, had been seemingly conjured, just the right thing for the moment. If a dumpling could buy kindness, what would gold buy? They could let him out right here. He wouldn't say a word. But if it didn't work—if they kept the gold and kept him—he would feel he had wasted his wife's gesture. It was too risky. He would wait for a more powerful man to bribe.

The commanders held the soldiers on the edge of hunger to keep them angry and sharp, like dogs snapping at the ends of their chains; the food offering had subdued them, lulled them into sated puppies ready for a nap. One of them closed his eyes and rested against the tarp's hard frame and his teeth rattled as the truck jittered along.

Finally, the truck stopped. The crying old man had fallen asleep and, with a grunt, he jerked his head up. Baba had not slept. Every minute on the road had worried him more. Any thoughts of a proper arrest were gone. The farther from the city that they went, the more likely death was. No police station or courthouse lay out here.

Brighter and brighter threads of light had pierced through the seams and tears in the canvas as they had gone on, but Baba was still startled when the soldiers threw back the flaps. The sun was high. Half a day had passed. The soldiers ordered them out and Baba leaped to the ground on stiff legs. The older man needed help from the truck. Like a child, he clambered down in the arms of the soldiers.

Baba was surprised to see the curled-up man, with the high collar and hat, stir. He was not dead, feeble, or sad. He sprang from the truck without hesitation. As he came toward the waiting group, he lifted his head and glanced at my father from under the brim of his hat, raising an eyebrow to acknowledge him. It was Kai Hsiang, a fisherman whose children Baba had treated. My father offered a barely perceptible nod in return. He knew better than to say anything.

"I need to . . . relieve myself." The old man pleaded in such polite, pathetic terms that Baba cringed.

"Shit," the first soldier, the hungry one who hated cabbage, said. "Hold it."

"Let him go," the second one said. "I gotta go too. Anybody else?"

At the question, the urge suddenly struck my father.

"Over there." The second soldier waved his gun at the wall of sugarcane that ran alongside the road. On one side, the hill rose up in a tangle of brush; on the other, the sugarcane extended down the hill as far as they could see. A small gutter of mud ran between the field and the road. How naive would they have to be to line up, all together, with their backs to the road in the perfect formation for execution? Baba declined. He waited beside the truck as the rest of them arranged themselves before the cane.

The cicadas clicked incessantly like seeds in a rattle, and from somewhere deep in the field, birds cried. All of a sudden, someone yelled, "No!" Baba saw the second soldier disappearing into the shaking cane field. The old man was making his escape. The field swallowed up predator and prey and the outer stalks trembled to stillness, but the stunned audience tracked the path of pursuit by the birds bursting out of the cane. A shot rang out, followed by a final cloud of birds.

Saliva flooded my father's mouth. So this was how the game would go.

"Line up!" shouted the first soldier. He thrust his rifle toward them as if he were herding an unruly group of pigs. The remaining men arranged themselves in front of the truck.

The second soldier returned. Sweat darkened his armpits and his face glistened. He was alone. Baba and Kai Hsiang exchanged glances. Show nothing, Baba told himself, and hoped Kai Hsiang was still alert enough to think the same. Do not blink, grimace, or nod. He thought of the old man's body melting into the ground, changing the taste of the cane, and the only witnesses soon dead too.

7

THEY MARCHED UPHILL through the forest for another hour, passing a single brick farmhouse that appeared abandoned despite the plump chickens scratching through the courtyard and the carefully tended melon vines. Nobody dared ask for water or a break, even though their mouths had long gone dry and the only food had been sacrificed as a peace offering hours before. In any case, the soldiers carried no water bladder and shared their thirst. Baba had missed his usual morning tea and his head felt hollow. He unbuttoned his shirt down to his singlet, yet he was still hot.

Weariness depleted his fear. His shoes were made for city streets, not root-strewn mountain paths, and blisters erupted in three different places on his feet. Perhaps they planned to kill them via exhaustion.

Occasionally, however, panic reared up again and he forgot his discomfort. What would they charge him with? What would be his defense? Was it the man who had died in his clinic? Had he given succor to an enemy of the state—or, worse, a hero to the people? Or was his crime shaming the authorities with his critique? But they were just words from a simple, unknown doctor. He had not inspired a revolution. He had simply pointed out the hypocrisy of their rhetoric. He'd stated only facts, not opinions.

They seemed to be traversing a range of hills, no longer moving up now but sideways, and the path, lightly trampled, drifted in and out of sunlight. Fog covered the valley, and my father thought of his wife and children somewhere down there among the thousands of ignorant people. He realized he would not see his children's faces harden into maturity. What childish habits would they drop and which would linger in adulthood? Would Ah Zhay—who had ventured out as his assistant after Taipei was bombed by the Americans, and had not flinched at the dead birds littering the ground and the body parts hanging in the trees—end up a brilliant doctor? And solemn Dua Hyan—what profession would suit him? Was Zhee Hyan's scampering silliness simply a four-year-old's innocence, or an inborn, everlasting trait? And, finally, his youngest daughter, just a couple of weeks old—what would be her first word—or even her name?

And his wife. He'd heard her screaming behind him as the soldiers dragged him away, and he had hoped for her to stop. He wanted to turn around and tell her that he would be fine, tell her that the children needed at least one parent to be safe, but one of the boys had growled, "You're already dead. Just keep walking." He could still hear the echo of her racing footsteps.

He fought the urge to throw himself down the hill.

Finally, the group came into a clearing of brick houses and meticulous gardens.

The soldiers ushered them into one of the homes and ordered them into a bedroom. A Japanese-style half-curtain hung in place of a door.

"Stay here. We'll come back for you."

The four men (unlucky four, Baba thought) arranged themselves around the room: two men on the bed, which was piled with blankets; Baba on a chair; and Kai Hsiang on the dirt floor.

No one spoke. Mind exhausted, Baba became entranced by his shirt. A long black strand of hair caught his eye. He pulled it off and examined it. He remembered a novel he had read at university in which a doctor recognizes his daughter because he has saved a strand of his wife's hair throughout his imprisonment. What was the book's name? He could not remember. Baba wrapped the hair around his finger like a ring. It went around six times. At the moment, it was his most precious possession.

After a while, he spoke. "Is it you?" he asked Kai Hsiang. He didn't dare say his name aloud. The other two men could not pretend to not hear in the small room, so they watched with open interest.

The man straightened up and revealed his face.

"Doctor," he said. So it was Kai Hsiang.

Kai Hsiang caught fish for a living. His hands were salt burned. He had seven children. What on earth could have been his transgression?

"Why are you here?" Baba asked.

"They say we're communists."

Baba looked at the other two men. They looked like bankers. Communists? He thought of the strident, ruddy-cheeked Chinese peasants he saw in the newspapers. These men had soft pale hands. If anything, they looked more like the "capitalist running dogs" whom the communists seemed determined to wipe out.

"You two—are you communists?"

"We're just professors," one of them protested.

"Someone lent me a copy of Marx, but I never read it. I tossed it on a shelf and forgot about it. I swear," said the other.

"Shut up," Kai Hsiang said. "You're not on trial yet."

"Communists? How do you know?" Baba asked Kai Hsiang. Since Ming Guo's nephew's warning, nothing had made sense. "Why you? You're just a fisherman," he blurted out.

"And you're just a doctor." Though Kai Hsiang's tone was matter-of-fact, Baba flinched. "It'll all come out in the trial. You'll find out then what kind of criminal you are."

Like the hero of some Russian epic, my father wanted to cry out, *I'm innocent!*

"Listen"—Kai Hsiang leaned forward and lowered his voice—"they have a plan and if you stand in the way . . ." He hissed as he drew his finger across his throat.

One of the professors stood up and paced the room. "We should be in Tamshui, on a boat heading to sea," he muttered. He stopped at the window and peered out. "Not a soul. What is this place?"

"Tamshui? You should have kept your mouth shut," Kai Hsiang said. "You should have been a good, docile subject."

The day passed. The room turned dark. The four men did not speak. My father had not eaten since the night before. For a few hours, his stomach burned, then his hunger faded to something clean and light in his veins. A man could fast for days, weeks. He was not worried.

Eventually, they heard footsteps in the other room and an unfamiliar soldier poked his head in.

"Eat," he said in thickly accented Taiwanese.

In the front room, brightened by a lantern, a young woman scooped boiled mountain yams and cabbage into bowls and poured cups of lukewarm tea. All the men watched her flat and impassive face, wanting recognition: Did they still live? She did not look at them. She was feeding ghosts.

Baba's fast had sharpened his tongue. He thought he could detect the faint saltiness of dried shrimp in the cabbage. The boiled yams were pale and slimy, but all of it was satisfyingly warm in his belly. The young woman stood off to the side while they ate. Baba wondered if there would be seconds, but she took their empty bowls and piled them into her aluminum pot with a clatter.

"Sleep now," the soldier said in Mandarin. "Tomorrow will be important." Carrying the lantern with him, he escorted the young woman out of the room.

After he left, Kai Hsiang asked what he had said.

"Tomorrow," said one of the professors. "Tomorrow, they shoot us."

In the dark, the four men arranged themselves around the room with the blankets. Baba curled up beside the empty wardrobe. The blanket was full of musty ghost odors. He wondered who else had lain beneath it, sweating anxiety. He thought of how much a single life could hold. The breathing of the others slowed as they finally slept. The blue moonlight in the window reminded him of the restless nights he had spent during the Pacific War.

The war. He had departed with soldiers, and the memory he had carried away from Taiwan as the ship set sail was the fading call of voices: *Rippa ni shinde kudasai, rippa ni shinde kudasai,* please die beautifully . . .

On the war front in Burma, among Japanese doctors, he once again was overcome by the childhood feeling that had chased him through his segregated elementary school education in Taipei, stalked him when he was questioned in the streets by Japanese police, and clung to him, hissing in his ear, when he had discovered that his favorite high school teacher, Mr. Sasaki, had served on a colonial policy committee dedicated to formulating a grisly plan for how to handle the island aborigines. Hundreds took the medical school entrance exams, but only dozens of Taiwanese were accepted. Sometimes, he could still conjure up the elation he felt the day that he found his name on the list of those who had passed. A kind of relief, as if he had escaped the grip of some banal destiny by the skin of his teeth.

However, skill and education could not erase his second-class stigma. The Taiwanese doctors ate separately and endured snide comments on their fluency in Japanese.

He tended to all sorts of ailments brought on by the hot, damp conditions. Illnesses of the mind, which were more prevalent, were outside his realm and ignored. He did not believe in the war, or in Japan's project—the Greater East Asia Co-Prosperity Sphere—but the job put rice on the table, even if back home in Taipei patients suffered from the shortage of doctors.

And then dysentery hit the camp and my father realized that death would not be by British bullet, or wild cat, or even starvation. It would come through the simple economics of a body's need for water. This was the noble death the war recruiters had promised when they had lured Taiwanese boys into fighting for the glory of the Japanese empire? The majestic death of wrinkled skin, a parched throat, blinks that no longer moisten the eyes? He might have been angry had he the energy.

In the Burma camp, he became ill too. He curled up on his bunk beside a growing puddle of his own stink. He would die there. He understood that fact, even as everything seeped from his brain. Anything beyond that simple meditation was enough to call up the nausea that he was trying desperately to keep at bay. He fought off images of his family: his oldest child, a daughter, flicking the abacus beads with her chubby fingers; his oldest son, who had just started school, marching off to class in his school cap and tidy navy shorts; his youngest son still toddling around in diapers. And his wife. He recalled the day he had noticed a paint stain on her finger, a deep jade she had been unable to wash away and that he had first taken for a bruise. He realized that she was still painting in secret. He didn't say anything to her, but remembering how carefully she had hidden her passion, his throat clenched with pity.

He pitied himself too, because he would not see any of them again. He was certain he would die here. His pants were damp with filth and he could not even bother to button them.

A nurse stripped him down and bathed him. In the warm tent, beneath the caress of the wet rag, the shit stink of his body was unleashed. She wiped the terrible pungency of fear from his armpits. She made him new. His lids grew heavy. Finally, for the first time in days, he slept.

He supposed she expected a miracle. He did too, but the next time he awoke, it was from the urgency that rushed out of him in a torrent of shit and blood and mucus. Still crouched, sweaty, he bowed his head, now sick with realization. He cried, but had no water left for tears. He closed his eyes and dry sobs racked his bare chest until he faded to sleep.

Light slanted through tall windows. He turned his head—neck aching—and his gaze unfurled over an endless row of beds.

"Where are we?"

The man in the bed to his left turned toward him. His head was encased in bandages and one bright black eye blinked at him. My father saw the blood seeping through the gauze as the man answered: "Bangkok."

From the jungles of Burma to a hospital in Bangkok.

He had survived. He thought, wryly, he could recover and fight yet for the empire—demonstrate the Yamato spirit of a true Nihon citizen. He scanned the long columns of men with hunks of torn flesh, decaying limbs, missing eyes, and scorched skin surrounding him. The odors that wafted up when the nurses changed the sheets of the man to his right—a bullet had torn through his back and exposed his spine—or the bandages of the man to his left—an eye, part of his cheek, and his ear were gone—intensified his sickness. Amid these wounded, a quiet illness like his was forgotten.

His body had expelled every ounce of strength. He had absolutely nothing left. This was the most inglorious sort of death, and he wished for some proclamation that might redeem it. An utterance like *Tenno Heika Banzai!* to indicate that his last thoughts were, loyally, on the empire. Instead, he closed his eyes and willed himself to sleep.

Startled by a gunshot, Baba woke up in Taiwan, the intervening years gone. He was still in the village house surrounded by his fellow prisoners. Another shot rang out. He pressed against the side of the wardrobe and could not move. On the bed, Professor Wu lay on his side, frozen, one glazed black eye staring at him.

"It could be anything," Baba whispered to him, but then the hard crunch of boots stomped past the window, and before they could sit up, a voice from the front room demanded them.

Baba felt for the lucky talisman of my mother's hair, but his finger was bare. He looked among the dust on the floor and found nothing but grit and what appeared to be their own detritus. Suddenly, life and death seemed to depend on finding that elusive and fortunate strand of hair.

After all, in the novel, the doctor with the same lucky charm had eventually been freed.

"Dr. Tsai, let's go," Kai Hsiang urged.

He couldn't. He was now a man with a single possession and he needed it.

He crouched over his blanket.

"Dr. Tsai." An unfamiliar worry trickled into Kai Hsiang's voice. From the other room, the unseen man commended the professors for their punctuality and again ordered the rest of them out. The blanket was filthy—nubby and speckled with many long strands of anonymous hair. He didn't want to think about what had happened to the woman who had once slept beneath it.

"Dr. Tsai," Kai Hsiang pleaded.

It was a lost and insane cause. Baba scrambled to his feet and joined the others.

They walked by the freshly executed men who lay facedown in the dirt road, their hands bound behind their backs. Heat still rose off the blood seeping from them. Out of the corner of his eye, Baba saw women moving quietly between houses. Only women.

The group turned off the road and traipsed past a tidy garden and then along a narrow dirt path. Soon, a temple came into full view—somehow, in this remote, godforsaken little place—painted red and green with touches of gold leaf. The thick round columns, lacquered red, gleamed. However, boot prints dulled the carefully varnished wood floor.

Their guard ordered the four to sit in a line at the center of the room. Baba stared up at Matsu's incense-blackened face. She, like them, had been silent; her muteness had been the first sign of her immortality. The final sign—legend claimed—was the day that she, at the age of twenty-eight, walked up a mountain where she'd seen the light lancing the earth and disappeared into the clouds. Her wordless arrival and departure sealed her legend. Fishermen adopted her as their patron saint. Men carved her face into wood and stone and carted her on palanquins down village roads, arraying her in firework and incense smoke. Her best likeness was set into a special temple and worshipped for so many centuries that her face blackened from the smoke. And now Baba prayed that the goddess of compassion would open her eyes to them.

A soldier stood before them and beckoned their attention with a spool of wire. "We need to make sure that you all stay together. Hands clasped behind your backs."

Why not handcuffs? Baba thought. The soldier began with Professor Wu, and when he screamed, Baba understood why not handcuffs. They were being strung together like fish for market. Professor Wu sobbed as the soldier moved on to Professor Hsiao, who had already begun to pant with worry.

"I can't. I can't," he cried.

"Shock will set in and you won't feel it." My father tried to comfort him, but the professor squealed through his gritted teeth, and the tendons in his neck swelled. Matsu continued to gaze placidly upon them, not a flinch in her expression. The demon guards on either side of her, stern faced, betrayed nothing.

"Endure it for a minute," Baba told Kai Hsiang, who was next. "And then you will feel nothing."

Kai Hsiang took deep, heavy breaths as the soldier pierced his palms. The wire now had the blood of three men. Despite his own assurances, my father's heart was pounding. Even though Kai Hsiang resisted crying out, tears streamed down his clenched face.

Just endure, Baba reminded himself, advice difficult to follow now that he sat beside three weeping men. When the wire broke through his skin and slid through his flesh, worming past the metacarpal of his index finger, his heart began beating so quickly that he could not swallow his spit. His brain flooded and his ears throbbed and went deaf with pain.

He gasped and cried despite himself.

The soldier stabbed his right hand. He gnashed his teeth. Sweat rolled down his face. He waited for the nothing that he had promised. No, he had been wrong. The pain pulsed in a searing heat that made him twist his back. The others protested every time he twitched—each shiver echoed down the line.

Three higher-ranking men—Baba did not know what ranks the various colored bars and plum flowers signified, only that these men had a well-fed luster, like the infamous concubine Yang Kuei-fei, creamy as sculpted lard—took seats at a table set up between the prisoners and the Matsu idol. They sat like triplets of varying plumpness. Other soldiers began to fill the room: surrounding the men, sitting cross-legged on the floor, slouching against the lacquered columns, fiddling with bits of wood or string or detritus from their pockets.

The man on the left, whose shirt held the fewest flowers, said languorously, "You are on trial for sedition and challenging the status quo." He rolled his eyes as a soldier translated into Taiwanese.

"Sir." The plea broke between Kai Hsiang's pained breaths.

"What?" The word echoed from the soldier's mouth in Taiwanese.

"I'm just a fisherman. Please use plain language."

The words traveled back to the men behind the table, and their mouths curled into sneers. The man on the left smacked the table. "You're spies!"

The accusation fell without any reaction from the audience, whose purpose Baba did not understand. This was clearly not a court but a farce, perhaps played out every day at this time. Guilty shot in the morning, newly accused sentenced after that, and then repeat, day after day between breakfast and lunch. All of it done in the secrecy of little villages. *So no one can count the bodies,* Baba thought.

The man in the middle, swollen, with jowls like heaps of white dough, clearly suffered from decadence. Too much rich food. Baba knew that if the man stripped off his shoes, his feet would be fat with gout. Indeed, beneath the table, the doctor could see the man's laces were very loosely tied. He also was the highest-ranking man at the table.

He grunted in impatience. "Read the charges."

The pain in my father's hands subsided for a moment, then howled back. Without it, he might have thought more about how his knees ached on the hard floor. As the soldier-secretary began to recite their crimes, Baba felt the trembling of the others through the wire.

Professor Hsiao was accused of reading Marx and sympathizing with Mao. Professor Wu was named a collaborator with Professor Hsiao. They were both enemy agents because they had spent time at a Chinese university during the war.

"I was there because I didn't support the Japanese!" Professor Wu cried.

"Your colleague on the mainland is a known communist. He has rebuked his position and forsaken academia. He now works for the communists. He is a hero."

Professor Wu's eyes widened. "I had no idea," he said.

"Is ignorance an excuse?" the man on the right, a deflated version of the other two, asked the one in the middle.

"The professor knows too much to be ignorant."

"I am an admirer of Chiang Kai-shek," Professor Wu protested.

The central man dragged his finger down a sheet of paper. "Did you not write a newspaper editorial claiming that the decadence of Governor-General Chen Yi's regime is draining the island of much-needed resources? You say, 'This is not the time for more war. This is the time for recovery. We must first heal the island before healing the mainland.'"

Professor Wu hung his head.

"I believe this is a criticism of Chiang's plan. What did you expect people to feel when they read this?"

"This clearly incites discontent." The man on the left nodded. "Obviously."

"Also, while buying soy milk from the street vendor, two neighbors report they heard you express doubts about the ability of our republic to control the mainland. You have been extremely careless. What do you say to the charges?" asked the man on the right.

"I'm not guilty." Desperation made his voice shrill.

"Unfortunately that's not an option. I will note that you admit you are the author of these statements." The only sound in the temple was the scratching of his pen. "And you, Professor Hsiao?"

"I tossed out the Marx. I never opened it." He was firm, assured.

"Hand him the book," snapped the man on the left.

A soldier placed the book on the floor before Professor Hsiao.

"I'm sorry." The man on the left laughed. "Hold it for him." The soldier lifted the book before Professor Hsiao's face. "Is this your copy?"

"I never looked closely at it. I can't say. These are mass-produced. How can I say if it's my copy?" Baba was shocked at the insouciance in Professor Hsiao's voice. Did he not yet comprehend their situation?

"And has the binding been broken?"

The soldier opened the book and everyone heard the binding snap, fresh pages cracking like eggshells. "The binding is broken," the soldier said.

"So it has been read," the man on the left proclaimed.

"It hasn't!" shouted Professor Hsiao. He strained and the wire tugged at Baba's hands. All four men cried out.

"I will take this as evidence of guilt." Again, the loathsome scratch of the pen.

"Next, Fisherman Liou Kai Hsiang. Despite your innocent face, you are the most insidious of them all. We have a copy of a handbill that you printed at your cousin's shop. You quote Marx: 'Therefore, we should not say that one man's hour is worth another man's hour, but rather that one man during an hour is worth just as much as another man during an hour.' What do you say?"

"It's true," Kai Hsiang replied simply. A murmur of surprise disrupted the temple.

"The words are true or the accusation?"

"Both. I believe democracy is part of the journey to communism. I am not a spy, but I believe in revolution. We have nothing to lose but our chains. You!" He nodded toward the soldier who had been jogging back and forth, delivering evidence. "You!" He looked at the one who had strung together the men, who'd had to bite back his humanity in order to not flinch. "Why do you clean their boots and pick stones from your rice while these men eat fresh meat? Don't you work harder? Suffer more? And when it's all done, what will be left for you? A pathetic pension and a tin medal?"

"Stop him!" roared the man in the middle. His hands shook and his pale face turned red. "Shut up!" But his lackeys were frozen. How to stop a man already bound and bleeding?

"I admit all charges! I am proudly guilty!" Kai Hsiang settled onto his heels and his linked compatriots had no choice but to follow suit.

Kai Hsiang was both stupid and brilliant. "Please, stop," my father pleaded. Could it be true? Did Kai Hsiang really believe what he said? The communists were abominable; Baba felt it. Yet Kai Hsiang was not.

The man in the middle sneered. "You're a poison to the Republic of China, an admitted traitor. I'll shoot you myself. Did you think that honesty would buy leniency?" His pen slashed across a piece of paper. "Now, the doctor."

Baba closed his eyes. As the charges against him rang out through the temple, he relived the moment of his alleged crime. He recalled winding his way through the anxious crowd to the spot in front of the auditorium stage that was set aside for public comment. Another time, he might have been nervous about talking in front of a large group, but the memory of the man who had died in his clinic superseded any fear. This abysmal government's policies were personal now.

"*Traitor*," the man in the middle proclaimed. Other words followed, but this one dangled in the air like a noose. Baba clenched his teeth. It had required genuine loyalty—real faith, not treachery—to have said what he did in front of the community meeting that day: considering the political maturity of the island, they deserved a locally led civilian government. He had spoken for—not against—the interest of the people.

Why bother defending himself? What he said did not matter. They were already dead. He could admit or refute and it would not matter. He could say he was a spy. He could say that he had already telegraphed his mainland compatriots and ships were due to land at any minute. None of the four accused men would make it to the next week. They would all bleed red before April.

Evening brought a death banquet, and when the condemned refused the liquor they were offered, they were forced down on their knees, their mouths pried open and wine poured down their throats. Despite themselves, they got drunk. My father believed that alcohol brought out a man's true character. Indeed, Professor Wu became belligerent. The soldiers egged him on, teased him, and brought him to tears once again. His face swelled up and turned red from the wine. When he began to sweat, the soldiers forced him to strip down to his bare chest. A lightning bolt of red flushed down his pale, slim torso. His two limp hands bore the stigmata of the afternoon. The soldiers formed an arena of men around him, and then one marched to the center, threw off his own shirt, and lunged at the professor. Professor Wu's glasses fell to the floor and in the tussle were kicked to the side, where someone picked them up and wore them atop his head.

Clasped in the soldier's arms, Professor Wu groaned and cried. His blood smeared across the young man's bare shoulder.

The room tossed back and forth like a ship. Baba slipped off his own glasses and wiped them. With his eyes closed, the room went bright with the panting of the fighting men and the shouting from the spectators.

Baba fumbled his glasses back on in time to see Kai Hsiang pull Professor Wu from the soldier's grasp. "Stop it! Try me instead," Kai Hsiang declared. The professor crawled to the edge of the circle and lay down.

The new foes circled each other, two suspicious predators with bared teeth. Kai Hsiang, who was stocky but not tall, barreled toward the young man, knocking him over. His fist broke across the young man's cheek once before the soldiers pulled him off. They held his arms behind his back—restrained him for the young man, swaggering and offended, to beat like a dummy. My father's mouth filled with spit every time Kai Hsiang gasped for air. Both men were bathed in sweat. Kai Hsiang's nose cracked and blood flowed from one nostril. Finally, his legs gave out and they dropped him.

"Doctor!" they called. Baba realized they meant him. He squeezed his eyes, trying to will himself toward sobriety.

Kai Hsiang's ear was mangled, his lip split against a broken tooth, his nose smashed. Both eyes were so swollen and purple that his lashes disappeared into the flesh. Blood ran down his neck and soaked his collar.

A bubble rose in the blood streaming from his lip and Baba knew that he still breathed, but the doctor had no tools besides his pierced and swollen hands. He removed his own shirt and used it to wipe the blood from Kai Hsiang's eyes, his nose, and his ear. He couldn't bring himself to promise comfort.

"He'll be fine, Doctor." The—sergeant? colonel? general?—from the trial, the portliest one with the loosened laces, beckoned my father to stand. "Come with me."

8

You are a Taiwanese. The Taiwanese sky hangs over you and your feet tread on Taiwanese ground. What you see are conditions unique to Taiwan and what you hear is news about Taiwan. The time you experience is Taiwanese time and the language you speak is Taiwanese. Therefore, your powerful pen and your colorful paintbrush should also be depicting Taiwan.

IF MY FATHER HAD CHOSEN literature or art as a path, he might have heeded these words from the writer Huang Shih-hui. Instead, he had chosen medicine.

The body, unlike a poem, is tangible. Flesh is a real thing; often, illness and health are visible—the pale fingertips or slack skin, or even a shine in the eye. We prod at a poem by testing its metaphors, finding the heartbeat in the scan of a line, and looking for meaning in the white space. My father needed touch. Needed the sweetness of a diabetic's breath, or the murmur of a faulty valve. Needed to see the jaundice in the skin. His world was concrete.

In the seized house that served as the officers' quarters, he found his hunch had been right: the man's tender feet revealed gout.

"Without my medicine bag, there isn't much I can do." He was glad to have an excuse not to treat the man, who insisted that my father call him Big Brother, a nickname—my father noted—more appropriate for a gangster.

"The pain keeps me up. Can't you make some herbal solution?"

"My training is in Western medicine," Baba said evenly. He tried to soften the Japanese accent that sometimes seeped into his Mandarin.

"We have aspirin."

"A high dosage might help you clear out some of the uric acid, but it might make it worse too. What about ice?"

Big Brother laughed. "Ice? I haven't seen ice in months."

Baba slipped the sock back over the man's swollen foot and sat back on his haunches. "I can try to offer you some relief from the pain, but you will really need to watch what you eat if you want to avoid this in the future. These are the symptoms of an indulgent lifestyle."

Baba's stomach seized with worry when Big Brother said nothing. Would his advice be considered a critique of the entire administration? He would be shot in the morning anyhow. He vowed to speak his mind. This was his last freedom.

"I understand." Big Brother's voice was cold.

"Strawberries may help. They aren't common, but your men may be able to find some in the city. May I stand?"

Big Brother indicated his permission with a jerk of his chin.

They were supposed to meet the executioner's gun too drunk to fear it, but even though my father was still a little drunk, he felt a sobering nausea coming on. He burped. An idea—an old home cure—came to him, but he asked himself why he should help this awful man. He should let him limp along in pain. He wished kidney stones upon him.

However, after a long moment of debate, Baba spoke again. "My grandmother used to soak her swollen feet in warm charcoal water. I thought her feet were just tired, but now that I think about it, she likely had gout."

"Charcoal water. We can do that."

Big Brother ordered my father to supervise the man who made the charcoal bath, then asked the doctor to sit with him as he soaked his feet. Through the wooden shutters, Baba heard the bacchanalia in the temple continue.

He was fully sober now. The wounds in his hands throbbed; the infection had started. If the bullet didn't kill him, tetanus would.

The water in the bucket burbled as Big Brother shifted his feet. "It's charity."

Baba reluctantly lifted his eyes from the jumble of scrolls piled on a shadowed shelf. "What is?"

"The liquor. The men meet their fates half giddy. They barely know what is happening. Didn't the Japanese do the same?"

"They didn't have firing squads." My father couldn't keep the sneer out of his voice.

"The pilots. The kamikazes. They spent the whole night drinking before their final flight. True?"

"There was absolutely no honor in survival," Baba murmured. During the war, he'd spent a few weeks with young men preparing for their flights and that was what they had been taught. American soldiers were trained to kill; Japanese soldiers were instructed to die.

Big Brother laughed like a bird choking a fish down its gullet.

A flurry of gunshots woke my father. He had fallen asleep in the chair. The bucket of charcoal water remained, but Big Brother was gone.

The window revealed nothing but the muddy alley and the neighbor's wall.

A soldier posted at the door stopped him, but another waved him through. He ran down the hill, past the temple, and through the garden. In the quiet morning, his breath smacked in his ears. He burst onto the main road. Three bodies lay there.

Professor Hsiao was facedown in vomit and blood. Professor Wu's finger twitched. His guts leaked out of his torn stomach. Kai Hsiang's eyes were glassy, but a heartbeat, like the faint flicker of a hiding moth, still pulsed in his neck.

Baba touched Kai Hsiang's damp head and felt the heat seeping from it. He held his palm there until Kai Hsiang's skin went cool.

The young pilots had been naive but right. Survival carried no honor.

9

ONE MORNING, screaming drew my mother to the window. Soldiers dragged our neighbor's bedding into the rainy street. The neighbor, a drenched and disheveled woman, shouted for help, but the loose rifles and bored gaze of the soldiers had stigmatized her as untouchable. My mother saw hazy faces in the windows of the neighboring homes. One by one, they turned away and closed the curtains.

A few weeks later, my mother found a letter nailed to the gate. The grim black ink declared our misfortune to every passerby: we were to be the neighborhood's third eviction. The soldiers now claimed that our beautiful house—with its blond tatami and white paper screens and dark halls—was to be requisitioned. My family had two days.

Fighting an urge to claw the letter to shreds, my mother tore it from the nail and brought it inside. She gritted her teeth, determined to not amplify her children's misery with this latest insult, but Ah Zhay saw the rage in my mother's face.

"What is it, Mama?"

My mother found that she could not speak. She shoved the letter into her pocket and looked squarely at her oldest daughter. *Tell her everything is fine,* she thought, but she knew that if she opened her mouth, only tears would emerge.

She shook her head at Ah Zhay, then went upstairs to the room in which she had become a wife and then a mother.

From the doorway, she surveyed her wedding trousseau. The beautiful carved wardrobe and the matching vanity table. All of it to be left to the Nationalists. She cursed them. I, lying swaddled on the bed, began to cry. "Squall" is a word often used to describe the sound. The noise rises up violently, stormy and sudden. Babies know nothing of modulation; everything is the cry.

My mother lifted me up and hushed me. She agreed with my complaints in a low voice, repetitive and soothing, like a groove revolving and rasping beneath a stylus. "We will leave," she whispered to me.

Her parents lived south in Taichung, a few hours by train. We would go there—"home," my mother called it—and leave this godforsaken house, "this cursed city," she cooed. She went home at least once a year; now she would stay, protected by her parents as she had been when she was a girl. Still, I wailed. Finally, in the shade-drawn dark of a house that she would never see again, she lay down on the bed and nursed me.

On the floor of the bedroom were books Baba had read and stones he'd collected on the eastern coast. The frustration boiled up—so many things he had touched and made, scents still lingering. My mother felt like an archaeologist, excavating proof of his existence.

After the war ended and the Japanese gave up the island, the homes abandoned by the Japanese were reproduced in the secondhand markets of Taiwan: table and chairs, cupboards full of dishes, chopsticks and sake cups, beds draped in neatly smoothed bedspreads. A dirty joy swept through the people as they brought their children to bounce on these beds, as they snapped up fine European umbrellas, as the paper collector came for the kana schoolbooks to sell to the pulping plant.

Two years after the end of the war, my mother too was humbled as she dragged a cart filled with Baba's belongings to the secondhand market. My mother gathered up Baba's books, his equipment, and his clothes and dumped them into Dua Hyan's play wagon. Before my mother left the house, Ah Zhay hung on her arms, trying to slow her with deadweight. "No, Mama! What will Baba wear when he comes home?"

My mother tried to shake her free. "Let go." Her cold voice hid the heat in her chest.

"You don't love him! Don't you love him? Baba won't have anything when he comes home!" Ah Zhay's voice rose to a hysterical squeal. My mother wanted to slap her and then complain of her own misery and guilt, but her daughter was still too young to understand.

"How about this." She tried to soothe Ah Zhay's panic with her calm tone. "Why don't you and your brothers choose one thing to keep safe for when Baba comes home? He will see how much you love him."

Ah Zhay kept Baba's extra pair of glasses, Dua Hyan took a box of glass slides, and Zhee Hyan grabbed a little booklet on obsolete politics that had a fanciful cover.

Mama went from stall to stall, offering, bargaining, assuming novel voices. "The doctor retired," she lied. "This was imported from France before the war—look how well kept it is," she said to another stall keeper. When that pitch failed, receiving only a skeptical glare, she tried a different tack: "My four children will eat on this money. Don't let them starve. I could sell this for so much more, but we need rice."

The equipment went first: the microscope, slightly bent from a police raid, but easily fixed; the stethoscope, still gritty with Baba's earwax; his battered leather medical bag; even his wheeled stool. His textbooks, in Japanese, were more difficult, but finally a shrewd stall owner calculated the price of selling them to the paper collector and purchased them. Lastly, then, went Baba's clothing.

As far as mementos go, clothing is curious. The shape of the body, but no body. The touch of the skin to this cloth. And then the smell. My mother had lined the bottom of the wagon with Baba's neatly folded pants and shirts. Owner after owner shook his head; they all suspected where these clothes had come from: one of the unlucky missing. The last stall was run by a woman who might have been a little dull in the head from the way she slowly ran her eyes over the modest clothing and then listened to my mother speak while looking only at her right ear. She nodded and, in a voice as slow as her gaze, uttered a price.

My mother began to protest. "I bought this just a few months ago for five times—" She made a quick calculation of the value of hope against money. "Yes, that'll be fine."

She emptied the clothes from the wagon. The last item was a shirt. The lightly stained strip that had caressed his neck, the seams that had brushed against his armpits when he picked up a book or measured out a prescription, the tinged cuffs that had dragged against paper as he updated his records. The front panels, along the buttons, seemed to contain the heat of his chest. Briefly, without the other woman noticing, my mother pressed it to her nose. She inhaled him. For a moment, he was there.

Then she put the shirt atop the others on the rickety bureau that made up one side of the woman's stall and Baba was gone.

My mother gave her paintings and vases to the neighbors. She packed our birth certificates, her marriage certificate, photos, and clothes for summer and winter. With an ax, she destroyed the bedroom set and dragged it downstairs piece by piece.

While Dua Hyan and Zhee Hyan watched, frightened, from the base of the stairs, Ah Zhay scurried up and down the steps behind her. "Stop it! Mama, stop!"

"Hush. Help me carry this." Half a headboard thumped its way down. My mother was pleased to see a deep scratch in the floor tracing its path.

Ah Zhay screamed—a frustrated and crazed ten-year-old girl's howl— and tossed a dismembered vanity table leg down the stairs. It clattered to a stop next to Mama's foot. She kicked it away. "Bring down the others too."

My mother gathered nearly all the paper in the house—the journals she'd kept since girlhood, her sketchbooks, the medical records the police had missed in their raid, Ah Zhay's and Dua Hyan's school compositions— and piled it atop the destroyed furniture in the courtyard. She surveyed the heap and readied herself to turn her life to ash.

A woman pushed through the gate clutching a small boy's hand, and my mother froze. "What are you doing, Li Min?" the woman demanded. "Dr. Tsai is gone? Li Min, give me." She beckoned for the matches.

My mother reached out and dropped them into the woman's outstretched hand. "Naomi," she began. "I . . . They . . ." She covered her face. She breathed deeply. She would not cry again. Despite herself, the tears came. She kept her hands pressed to her eyes, trying to hide her sobbing. The woman spoke to her son: "Wei, go inside and find Ah Zhay." After he had scampered inside, the woman embraced my mother.

When my mother's tears were spent, she wiped her face with her bare hands and asked, "And where is your husband?"

Baba had met Naomi's husband, Uncle Lin, when they were children in the Twa Tiu Tiann area of Taipei that was then called Daitotei by the Japanese. When my father went to Tokyo for university, he had roomed with Uncle Lin, who studied medicine as well. Being Taiwanese in Japan was like being a guitar-playing monkey: their fluent Japanese elicited awe from the people they met, yet they were considered not-quite-whole people. Uncle Lin fell in love with another student at the university, Naomi, a Japanese woman, whose parents disapproved, and my eloquent and reasonable father spoke to them. They reluctantly agreed to the match. For the first year of the Lins' marriage, the three of them had lived together.

"He is home. He did not think it was safe to come, so he sent this." Naomi lifted her blouse and pulled a pouch from her waistband.

"I can't," my mother protested.

Naomi was soft-spoken, yet forceful. "You must. This is not for you but for your children. You know that you must take it." She pushed it into Mama's hand and folded Mama's fingers closed atop it. "You've had the baby. Is it a girl or boy?"

"A girl."

Naomi smiled. "Wonderful. You must take the money. Four babies."

"We've been evicted," Mama whispered. She looked over her shoulder at the mound of papers and hacked furniture.

"So you will burn it all."

"My life is over."

"Four babies. Your life is not over. But you can do it if you feel you must."

They looked up at the children gazing at them from the second-story window.

Naomi handed Mama the matches. My mother lit one and touched it to the corner of one of the books on the pile. For a few seconds, it threatened to die out, but the flame caught and soon it roared, surges of fire anxiously gulping air.

She burned everything.

South of Taipei, headed toward Taichung, three children slept on a hard wooden seat, their heads nodding with the sway of the train. Across from them, their exhausted mother cradled a baby. The car was nearly empty. The land outside was dark. Only the cigarette of the man sitting across the aisle glowed, its reflection doubled in the window.

From the train station, a taxi brought us to our grandparents' house. They lived outside of Taichung, in an old-style three-sided brick country home with a courtyard, accessible by one lone road, or—for those on foot—by the narrow levees that separated the paddies and fields. Through the silent countryside, the taxi growled like a demon. Lights flickered on in each of the houses that we passed.

The driver stopped right in front of the courtyard gateway. The boys tumbled out and trudged through. Ah Zhay held me while my mother unloaded the car.

Hastily dressed and toting a lantern, my grandparents burst out of the house. My brothers erupted in happy cries: "Ah Ma! Ah Gong!" My grandfather crouched and patted each boy on the head before helping my mother with the bags.

My grandmother clicked her tongue. "What's this? Come, give me." She took me from Ah Zhay's arms. "Look at this one." She nuzzled my cheek. "This baby is too young to travel. Boy or girl?"

"Girl, Ah Ma," Ah Zhay said proudly.

"Marvelous! Lucky baby—she has such a good older sister." My grandmother squeezed Ah Zhay's arm. "My sweetheart. So tall already."

My mother and grandfather dragged the luggage through the gate and the taxi rumbled off.

"Where's your husband?" My grandmother's eyes darted between my mother, my grandfather, and our meager belongings. She had heard about the trouble in Taipei; Taichung had been racked by its own violence and arrests.

Ah Zhay declared, "He went to Tokyo to visit his friend."

My mother choked out the words, "Yes, Tokyo." She managed a weak smile and my grandparents saw that this was a lie. My mother was their only daughter. When she fell in love with the young doctor, my grandparents had been pleased. They still remembered the world before the Japanese had come, and they liked this young doctor's politics, his ambition, his sober manner.

Understanding amassed in the silence.

My grandmother said, her voice too bright, "Have you eaten? What an adventure. And now you are tired and probably hungry. I'll fix something for you." She urged the children inside.

Once the children were out of earshot, our grandfather put his hand on my mother's shoulder. "Where is he?"

My mother bit down her lip and shook her head: *I don't know.*

MY FATHER SPENT TWO MONTHS with Big Brother at the execution station in the mountains. His original impression had been correct: trials at midmorning, drunken banquets in the evening, and dawn executions on nearly a daily basis. He saw close to a hundred men killed, and every day he wondered if he would be next.

By the end of the second month, he started to think that he might be freed despite what he had witnessed. He had become Big Brother's confidant and adviser and had begun to understand the man. Under his supervision, Big Brother slimmed down, and his gout subsided. Baba told himself that the word "betrayal" had no significance when it came to medicine. His only loyalty was to his patient.

Loyalty had a different meaning to Big Brother, however, because in the middle of May, Baba was once again ordered into a truck and driven back down the mountain.

The village seemed almost quaint once he met the damp prison walls. Perhaps prison *was* a kind of leniency, the only loyalty Big Brother could have offered in this new world. Daily fear was replaced by a long-term tenacity.

In the interrogation room, shackled by a rusting leg iron that chafed his skin, he was shown twenty-eight methods of torture and asked to choose the one he preferred. Hung by the arms bound in front or bound in back? Four limbs strung up? This could be avoided for the time being, however, with a bit of writing.

"For your sake, let me be brief: half a dozen witnesses heard you demand independence and accuse the KMT of not adhering to democratic values. Your unfounded accusations are extremely damaging to the government. We want the whole story. We want anything else you might be hiding."

Baba's skin felt scorched. It took all of his will to stay stubbornly quiet.

He knew he'd never be able to stand the smell of green menthol oil again. The guards reeked of it while the prisoners were tormented by dozens of mosquito bites, scratched to blood, irritated by the humidity and dirt, that took weeks to heal. It was among the smallest of the indignities, but that they managed these insults big and small demonstrated how much thought went into cruelty.

"Oh, Dr. Tsai. Silence is a luxury you can't afford. You aren't anybody. You're a ghost. A ghost. You think you're dead now? Just wait. I am going to leave you this pen, this paper, and my chair. Take your time. Tell me the entire truth."

The interrogator, as ageless as a recurring nightmare, left. Outside, sunshine caressed the window and teased Baba.

Truth. "Sincerity," "honesty," and "accuracy" were all synonyms, but with different connotations. Which kind of truth did they want? What kind of truth—if any—would set him free?

Truth is in the details. *Yes*, Baba thought. *Details, minute and exact, weave a fabric of truth.*

He did not want to betray anyone, yet if he hid a name, he was sure the men reading his account would know. He understood their strategy: it was a test. He was to write the truth as his captors knew it, and if he happened to reveal a previously unknown name along the way, they would think it all the better.

Each day, he thought of new people to add to his story. He listed his fellow overseas classmates in Tokyo who had worked with him on *Tomorrow's Hope*, a simple newsletter where they railed against home politics. The empire, benevolent and secure, could bear talk of autonomy from its visiting Taiwanese students. In Japan itself, encouraged by more liberal leaders, dreams of Taiwan's self-rule burst open in blossoms of possibility. On Taiwan, however, these conversations could happen only in whispers, lest they trigger the government's alarm. Punishment was swift.

He recounted conversations that damned his acquaintances—he noted who had nodded in agreement with his complaint about the KMT's corruption, or even blinked in a way that said yes.

He wrote about the strangeness of hearing the emperor's voice as he announced Japan's capitulation (the emperor would not—did not—use the word "surrender"). The emperor had *a voice*. Divine beings spoke in some platonic ideal—whatever one heard in his head as the growl of ultimate authority—but these were the words of a real man, middle-aged and trim.

Let the entire nation continue as one family from generation to generation, ever firm in its faith in the imperishability of its divine land, and mindful of its heavy burden of responsibilities and the long road before it.

Baba described witnessing the arrival of the KMT troops in the fall of 1945 on American ships after Japan was forced to give up its colonies as part of its surrender. Eager onlookers crowded the roads from Taipei to the port of Keelung. Banners rose over the boulevards: welcome signs with earnest, heartbreaking Nationalist flags accidentally drawn backward. The schoolchildren were pushed to the front of the crowds that crammed the port. His daughter stood among them in a white dress with a starched collar. Her white socks folded over into lace cuffs. As her mother had instructed, she smiled and waved a tiny Nationalist flag. The gangplank had already thudded to the ground hours before, and it taunted, empty before the murmuring masses.

When the men finally disembarked, they looked nothing like the laudatory terms that the newspapers had used, nothing like liberators. Their uniforms were dirty; some wore shoes so ill fitting that they had to be bound with rope. They carried their own cooking pots, their own sad sacks of rice. They were kids and old men with creases seared into their ruddy faces. They smiled for the cameras that archived the event.

Beneath the cheers, disbelief churned its way through the crowd. These coarse men—the ones who smiled like bumpkins hitchhiking through the countryside, the ones who now stood beside the ship and relieved themselves—these junkyard soldiers had defeated the emperor?

Yes, he had wanted Taiwan to rule itself. Yes, he had uttered thoughts disloyal to the KMT. But these were only ideas, only words. Baba did not believe himself guilty, but he wrote himself so.

My father confessed it all.

.   .   .

A year after he had last seen his family, Baba received a ten-year sentence. The judge assured him that it was a generous punishment. He would come out still a relatively young man. He would see some of his children become adults.

Even at the jail, the dawn gunshots continued. The cells were emptied and filled weekly. My father wondered if there would be anyone left on the island. History was—as the interrogator would have said—scuttlebutt, dribbling into his world via each new prisoner: the war with Mao's men was—no, not *lost*—it was . . . *on hiatus* . . . Chiang Kai-shek had brought all his men and their families to Taiwan—more than two million people had fled China and now crowded the streets . . . Chiang Kai-shek claimed they would stay just long enough to regroup and retake the mainland . . . Chiang Kai-shek had a multiyear plan . . . Baba tried to imagine what the world outside the prison now looked like: the sidewalks teeming with soldiers and buildings crammed with haphazard shops, beggars in the streets, ladies strolling by in high-necked, frog-button gowns. And he tried to imagine us, his family.

11

HERDED OUT OF THE PRISON, the prisoners—accused communists, thieves, and rabble-rousers—crowded the train cars, sharing seats and cramming the aisles. The windows were pulled down and those nearby pushed their faces toward the hot air rushing past. They were going east, my father noted.

Somebody said they were heading to sea, somewhere far from land where they'd be left to fight out their last few hours in the warm salty water with nothing to cling to but each other.

Indeed, there was a ship.

Baba thought of the last time he had seen the sea: 1934. The year he had returned from Japan. The sun had been so bright that whiteness blinded him. They had approached *Kiirun*—Keelung. Lush green hills sloped gently toward the town that embraced the water—he imagined that Gauguin, if he'd only known, might have chosen Taiwan over Tahiti. *Ilha Formosa*. Instead, it had been claimed by Chinese fishermen and pirates, by the Dutch and Spanish, and then finally by the Japanese. He could almost smell the camphor distilleries and sugar mills. Long warehouses with large green corrugated sliding doors, not sandy beaches, lined the cement quay that greeted the water. A variety of boats crowded the harbor: ocean liners, ferries, cargo ships, and slim fishing canoes. Coolies in their pajama uniforms hurried about, moving freight. Where Baba's ship was set to berth, waiting pedicabs crowded into a jumble of wheels and canopies. Under the carefully spaced trees along the water's edge, food vendors had settled next to their carts.

He had edged himself between the people clustered at the railing to watch the ship slide, like a tamed beast, into its slip. After four years, he was finally home. Among the crowds gathered to greet the ship, no one was waiting for him—he had planned on taking the train to Taipei on his own—but the group's enthusiasm caught him. Tears brimmed in his eyes and he had scoffed at himself for crying at nothing, for nobody, not understanding that his joy was for exactly this: the chaos of cranes, ropes, and cargo in the harbor; the black coal smoke gusting from the trains heading south, deeper into the island; the cities with their overflowing bushels of goods spilling into the walkways; and the marble gorges and bamboo forests and craggy mountains and grassy plains enfolding all of it.

Now, in the rags of a prisoner, and in an unknown year, he made the opposite voyage from Keelung to a new destination.

A pale, bony parade of men limped down the gangplank before the scrutiny of the Ami tribe. Baba stumbled on the porous volcanic ground and knew where he was. The Japanese had called it Kasho-to, Fire-Burned Island.

"Welcome," shouted the guard, beckoning them toward land, "to Green Island." As if the new cool, verdant name could hide the rocky black ground and the sun blazing without relief. It was unbearably hot. Baba rubbed his face against his shoulder, trying to blot the sweat. The guard called it New Life Camp, the sweet sound casting irony over the cluster of sheds and bare ground begging to be broken and cultivated.

The prisoners made a new life out of the barren earth. Breaking stones shaped the doctor's arms; reeducation classes shaped his mind. Mornings in the garden browned his skin. He raised chickens and pigs. He hiked into the hills and chopped wood. In narrow rooms, the prisoners slept in shifts, propped along one side: arm, rib, and thigh. Sitting in perfect columns and rows, they took exams on the beach and pretended to not notice the photographers lauding these perfect pupils who readily recited their anticommunist lessons. In hot examination rooms, they sat for tattoos bearing slogans of revolution, the ink transforming blood: *Retake the Mainland!*

Solitary confinement is an old concept, a practice meant to elicit introspection and remorse. Absent of outer light (save for that small dribble, that melting glow oozing through the tiny window, that minuscule hint of God), my father is meant to find inner light.

On Green Island, the solitary cell is padded, the size of a wardrobe, a psychological effect that implies insanity while simultaneously encouraging it. At first, he panics within the soft walls that threaten to swallow him and the dark humidity that sits like layers of dirt piled on a coffin. He runs his fingers along the ledge of the small window to reassure himself.

The light dribbling through the shoe-box window fades to darkness then brightens to day and then fades to darkness and brightens to day then fades to darkness and then the slot in the door screams open and a plate shoots into the room followed by a cup of warm water. My father has traveled past hunger, but the smell of the rice and salt and wilted, blackening vegetables awakens his stomach again and he scoops it up with his hands, shoveling it in until his belly aches and groans. He picks up the cup and drinks carefully so as not to lose one drop, and then he continues the dance of the last few days: standing, pacing, sitting, curling up, sleeping, touching the window ledge, singing, sleeping, jumping. He won't talk to himself—that's the first step toward separating self from self, the first step toward the fracture that makes one unfit for any post-cell life. He reassures himself so often that it becomes a circular thought, and he forces these thoughts away lest this too is a path toward insanity's seductive call. The slop gurgles inside him and he feels it churn through his intestines. He rushes to the soil bucket. He has no paper and he pulls up his pants still dirty. Now he lies on the floor, stretches out his arms and touches either side of the cell and begins to whistle.

He fears he is losing his mind.

And then—through the magic of sheer hope—she's right here. He stands in the center of the cell, the moonlight through the window just touching the top of his head, and looks at her. It is really her, not some idealized hallucination: sweat beads on her forehead and her thick makeup is turning to milk. He drops to his knees and crawls toward her, collapses his face to her feet and sniffs. He smells her shins, her knees, dragging his nose up her warm body to her neck, her hair. Her first touch, fingertips pressed to his neck, hurts. Thank heavens for the dark—to add color to smell and touch and sound would devastate him.

Her hands drift down his back and he moans.

"What is it?" she asks.

Wordlessly, he turns around and strips off his shirt, and her hiss tells him all he needs to know about the weeping cuts on his back.

"Animals," she says.

He sinks down to rest his head on her inner thigh. She smells like the world: like soap and streets and restaurants and traffic lights and parks and people, and he muffles his cries in the thick of her flesh.

1952

12

FIVE YEARS PASSED. Rumors—airy, vague, unsubstantiated—blew through those years. One whisper put Baba in a prison in Taipei, where a friend of a friend of a friend had seen him, his face obscured by a philosopher's beard, sitting broken against a cell wall. Another placed him in a shallow grave, his body atop others, turning to dirt. Yet another claimed he was in Naha, passing as Okinawan and treating American servicemen.

March 1947, according to official history, had not happened. My father had not disappeared. Nobody in my family spoke of him. My father did not exist. But the arrests that had been set in motion in 1947 continued. Martial law had never really ended.

The disappearances were an island-wide secret. My father was not the only man who had evaporated. It seemed everyone knew someone, and it was simply unspoken: this way we could not count the missing; we would not know for decades that the dead measured in the tens of thousands.

Five years packed with the struggles of life pass quickly; five years of longing drag on. Mama was tethered between the two extremes. On bad days, she would spend an hour listening to the clock, as if each tick was a mark on a scroll of time measuring the space between his leaving and his return. On good days, hours would pass in which her husband did not cross her mind; then suddenly she would remember, and she would punish herself for forgetting.

My grandfather was reticent about my missing father, but my unsentimental grandmother urged my mother to move on.

"It has already happened. Thinking won't bring him home." My grandmother understood my mother's obsessive mind. Mama almost believed that she could will time backward and worry her way to another path. Over and over, she reinvented the story of that last day.

She was lonely too.

When I close my eyes, the market rises up and I see her winding her way among the crowd, tilting her parasol as she moves among the other shoppers. She has discreetly mended the dress she wears. Her posture, her skin, and the way she speaks declare the height from which she has fallen. Can observers detect in her patrician gait the folded newspaper that shields the hole in the bottom of her shoe?

She still loves books, and she lingers at the bookseller's booth. She drags her finger down sooty spines and across yellowing pages. The books are piled atop tables and amid shelves in a little maze that leads into the alley, where the bookseller sits in the shadow of a torn awning.

"What are you looking for?" he asks.

She names some French authors she read at university, when it was sexy and exhilarating to read in the park or a café and utter French names aloud. Or perhaps, really, it had been tedious, just a class requirement inspired by a vague promise from her professor that these books would help her become a better painter. Is it only nostalgia that recalls the flecks of paint on her fingers as she turned the pages, and the little craving in her mouth for a cigarette, which seemed outrageous and bohemian? She has trouble distinguishing her real memory from her fantasy of it.

The bookseller rises from his perch. He's younger than his gray hair indicates, and his shirt is clean. He reaches into a box beneath one of the tables and pulls out three clothbound volumes for her.

"*Pour la belle dame.*"

"*Mais, vous parlez français? C'est inattendu.*" She blushes. She has not spoken since college. Most of her classmates had studied German.

"I've been to Paris. It's a lovely city. I learned French reading Proust," he says.

"I haven't spoken in such a long time."

"Your accent is perfect."

My mother modestly deflects his compliment. The flutter in her stomach surprises her; she has felt nothing like it for years. Guilt quickly replaces the moment of flirtatious joy. Her husband, she reminds herself. Her poor husband. She quickly asks how much the books cost.

"No one else will buy these. I'm not even sure how I came across them. So, please, take them. *Un cadeau.*"

My mother protests. She must pay. She rummages through her purse and finds a few bills, probably much more than the books are worth.

"I insist. Please, mademoiselle." He begins to bundle the books with string.

"Take the money." She is frantic now. She thrusts the bills at him, and when he ignores her, she drops them on the table.

He looks up at her. Is he perceptive enough to see that this is more than mere manners? Does he notice the alarm in her gestures?

The thought will not leave her head. Desire counterbalanced by shame. The bookseller is determined to win her over. He tucks the money into the knot of string that binds the books and presents the package to her.

"No," she says. The gift feels like a promise and an obligation.

What happens next is childish but imperative. She runs. She leaves behind both the books and the money and turns her back to the bookseller's shouts and runs out of the alley and through the market until she is sure that he will not follow.

She must be vigilant against forgetting, she tells herself.

She stops in front of the sundries stand, beside stacks of chairs and hanging brooms, and composes herself, worrying at the talisman of memory as if her pain will lessen her husband's.

She was still young. She felt young as well, but was also aware that a certain phase of life had irretrievably passed. She had four children to remind her every day that she once had a husband. At the same time, my sister, Ah Zhay, could not walk down the street without men stopping her to ask the time or her name.

Before I began school, I had to memorize the rules. My sister lectured me on these as I helped her scrub the kitchen floor or as we tossed peelings to the pigs. My brothers reminded me of them when we waded in the creek and tried to catch pollywogs.

"No Taiwanese" was the first rule, which Zhee Hyan, my second brother, had learned slowly and painfully. Under the government's plan to unify the people with a national language, every syllable of Taiwanese spoken at school brought punishment from the teacher. Taiwanese was for home; Mandarin was for the world. My brother's hands turned purple with beatings until he finally learned to reflexively clench his mouth before a Taiwanese word slipped out.

The second rule I knew already. "Our business is our business," Ah Zhay said, dipping a rag into a bucket. "Do you understand? Whatever we say here, you can't tell anyone. Or they might come take Mama away. Do you want Mama to go away?" She pushed the rag across the floor and did not look at me.

I did not want Mama to go away. I promised to be silent.

For school, my mother cut my hair to my ears and declared me a big girl. I proudly wriggled in my seat. I wore a navy skirt and a white shirt. She tucked rough brown paper in my pocket for the school outhouse. I rode to class on the back of my sister's bicycle. My classmates lined up outside to salute the flag and practice our morning calisthenics. I carried my lunch in a metal bento box, which the class captain collected each morning and returned to us at lunchtime, warmed in a large steamer. I learned to write "mountain," "fire," and "water." I learned the history of our country, the Republic of China, which carried on a five-thousand-year legacy. One day, according to Chiang Kai-shek, we would "recover" the mainland and the nation would again live happily united. Cheerful, obedient, I was shaped into a good girl and a good citizen.

When I began school, Zhee Hyan was nine years old: good-natured, prone to practical jokes, and grinning his way through our mother's scoldings like an idiot. On the other hand, Dua Hyan and Ah Zhay were solemn—even grim—teenagers. I feared both of them. Every afternoon, they waited for me at the school gate, aloof amid the chaos of the street and the tumultuous blur of small children scrambling out of the school.

They remembered Baba's destroyed clinic; they dreamed of our mother's admonishments for silence. The government warned against the communist spies who lurked among one's family and neighbors, in the marketplace, in the theater and temple—for which the only antidote was to be a spy oneself. Dua Hyan and Ah Zhay lived in fear of all these watchers. Dua Hyan, already thirteen, still wet the bed.

In the fog of my early memories, my gaze is often on my sister: she is the luminous figure negotiating a crowded street, picking her way among the sidewalks teeming with displaced bachelor soldiers from the mainland under the wary eye of her younger brother. She was fifteen. Like me, she wore her hair in an ear-length bob, standard for schoolgirls. Her navy skirt and white blouse gave her away as a student, despite her height. Like my mother, she was tall and slim. She walked as if she had nothing in mind but her destination—or something beyond it—staring ahead with Mama's elongated black eyes, glossy with a kind of circumspect longing.

On the island, late May is thick with heat and every gesture is a chore. I fidgeted in the classroom, yearning for the fan to swing back toward my side of the room. We'd made little paper fans as well, but mine, damp from my hands, collapsed limply. I waggled it at my best friend, Hsiao Yen. She giggled and the teacher snapped at us. Finally, we were dismissed, and, arm in arm, Hsiao Yen and I trudged out into the early summer glare.

Ah Zhay waited at the school gate, shielding the sun from her eyes with her arm. Dua Hyan and Zhee Hyan had gone to cram school to continue their studies after regular school hours, and Ah Zhay had promised me shaved ice before we rode home. I said good-bye to my friend and took my sister's hand.

The shop was a tiny, dark place, its walls packed with shadowed jars of candy and tins of crackers, sucking light and smelling of candy haw flakes and powdered ginseng and burned mosquito punk, the proprietor lounging behind the counter listening to Taiwanese opera and chewing an old toothpick. A huge, hulking iron ice shaver sat behind the glass counter, barely illuminated by the light drifting in through the open storefront.

At a tiny rattan table on the sidewalk in front, we dug into red bean shaved ice topped with condensed milk and tried to eat faster than the ice could melt. I danced in my seat as the ice cooled my mouth and the sugar bathed my teeth. I decided there was no food I liked better and declared that when I grew up, I would eat this every day. The sun burned the top of my head. I prattled on about school, retelling each of Hsiao Yen's silly jokes, while my sister nodded and hummed. The other tables filled. Three soldiers took the table next to us.

At that time, every soldier was also a refugee. Most of them had come to the island owning only what they carried. Fleeing made them orphans

and bachelors. In the panic of the end of the war, when the Nationalists retreated hastily from China, they had been separated from their
families—their children, their wives—and the chilled cross-strait relations meant that they could not send even a letter home. Though homesickness lingered among them, in 1952, a flutter of optimism still ran
through the island, some hope that the Nationalists would again rule the
mainland, in fact and not just in name.

Our mother had warned us about these bright-faced men. Among the
horrors of the castrated schoolboys left for dead on the mountain roads
and the bodies in the Keelung port during the '47 massacre were the
misfortunate women, caught in the streets or home alone. Even at five
years old, I was leery when one of the soldiers dragged his stool toward
our table.

"Can you finish that, little sister?" In the heat, he had unbuttoned his
shirt, exposing a white undershirt. I dropped my gaze.

"Don't be rude," Ah Zhay urged me. A minute twitch of fear flashed
across her face, and she tried to assuage the soldier with a smile. "She's
shy."

I refused to lift my head and watched his feet shift. His white laces
glowed against his black boots. The leather was shiny and looked like
licorice.

"Don't worry, I won't eat your ice." He wasn't the monster I was expecting. Ah Zhay saw it too. She cast a sideward glance at him and smiled
again, not to pacify him, but out of genuine friendliness.

Then Ah Zhay snapped her eyes toward me. "Don't be rude. Answer
him."

Her reprimand embarrassed me, and it seemed purposeful, as if she
could shame me into courteousness. My chagrin quickly flashed into
anger. I elbowed her and stomped my foot. "I'm not worried!"

When I glared at them, Ah Zhay and the soldier laughed. I didn't understand what was so funny. Couldn't they see how cross I was? Shouldn't
they care?

"Look at me," the soldier said. "I want to see if you are as pretty as
your sister."

Ah Zhay coughed in embarrassment. I again flashed him my dirtiest
look. Delighted and surprised, he chuckled, but Ah Zhay gasped and
kicked me under the table. "Brat! Apologize! How embarrassing."

"Don't worry about it. She's plucky." He stood up. "Wait a moment. Don't leave." He disappeared into the shop's shadows.

"Behave yourself, you little monster." Ah Zhay withdrew a tiny compact from her book bag and squinted into it. She licked away a fleck of red bean caught on her tooth.

"You look ugly."

"What do you know?" she hissed back.

The soldier returned and placed a roll of candy next to my plate. "This is for you. You remind me of my little sister."

Ah Zhay shrank away and waved her hands. "No, please, we can't."

The colorful wax paper wrapping teased me. I decided I would refuse to eat it, but I could not resist poking at it.

"Take it. It's just candy." His chair leg skipped across the pavement as he pulled closer to Ah Zhay.

Ah Zhay's breath warmed my ear. "Say thank you."

I moved my mouth but refused to let a sound pass through my lips.

I despised the soldier even more when he smiled warmly at my ingratitude. "She's just like my little sister. She was about six when I last saw her. Spunky like her."

"She's a brat," Ah Zhay said as she pushed the candy out of my reach.

I saw the red beans spoiling in the sun. I saw my sister give a sideways glance to the soldier, binding herself to him with her betrayal. Her cheeks were flushed and sweat glistened on her upper lip.

The soldier winked at me. "I doubt that."

"She is," Ah Zhay insisted. She seemed to think throwing me to the dogs would save her face. We fell silent. I slouched and dragged my spoon through the tiny pebbles of ice floating in the milky water. Ah Zhay tucked her hair behind her ear and stroked the back of her neck. An almost imperceptible sigh slipped out of her.

The soldier's smile lingered on Ah Zhay too long. My annoyance flared up again. She was *my* sister. She belonged to me, not this strange man. He touched her arm. His thumb pressed her flesh. She lowered her chin and gazed at him from under her lashes. I jabbed at the bowl, again and again, taking pleasure in the hard, cold clack of metal against ceramic.

One afternoon, my mother shut me in the bedroom for my nap. I lolled on the bed, tugging at the mosquito net, clapping it in my sweaty hands and blowing on it so I could watch it flutter and billow. Through the hazy cloth, I watched a mosquito land. I was just beyond its bite. A puff of breath sent it buzzing away. Thin voices drifted in from the rest of the house. I resented the loneliness of this part of the day. I raked my nails across the bamboo mat and, humming softly, pretended that I was playing the zither. I pressed my face to the mat and then examined the damp, oily mark left on the wood.

Finally, I thought of the suitcase in the wardrobe that I had first glimpsed a few days before. As my mother rummaged through, a disturbed hem had revealed it in the shadow. I crept under the mosquito net and hopped down before the wardrobe. It opened without a squeak.

I tugged the suitcase out and rubbed the taut leather, which glowed with age. A sticker, still firmly glued, shouted a series of English letters that were gibberish to me: TOKYO.

Inside, I found a small sheaf of stamped papers. These too were indecipherable and I tossed them to the side. Beyond the papers was only a little coin purse of soft, flaking brown leather that sat like a drooping fig in my palm. I unclasped it and was delighted to find a roll of bills and some unfamiliar coins. I flattened out the bills on the floor around me. I'd never seen any money like it.

I thought of the tempting, beautiful bowls of mitsumame: a rainbow of fruit and sweet red beans and translucent cubes of jelly quavering in the sun. I wouldn't have to wait for Ah Zhay's generosity; I could buy my own bowl. I could have it whenever I wanted. I tucked a couple of bills into my waistband and crammed the rest back into the purse. I looked over the papers once more—still, I recognized none of the characters except for our surname—boring and useless to me. After fumbling with the suitcase buckles, I gave up and shoved the suitcase back into the wardrobe.

Once again under the gauzy mosquito net, I pretended to sleep, and when I awoke, the sun was already low and my mother was pulling my arm, softly calling my name and clicking her tongue in disapproval at the mosquito bites on my face.

I asked the shop woman for a bag of dried plums. My mouth watered as the lid popped off the jar and the sour-sweet smell of licorice and plum drifted out. Despite the cramped display—the narrow shelves precariously full and more boxes piled on the floor, jars of sundry dried goods taking up every speck of counter until a heavy dusty odor mingling fish, fruit, and wine spilled long ago filled the room—I yearned to spend hours here, perusing every illustration on each cookie tin, memorizing the colors of every box. Ah Zhay and I had come so often that I called the shop woman Aunty. At that moment, I wanted to caress her ruddy wide cheeks like a babe reaching out for its adored mother's face. Bouncing on my toes, I watched as each wizened plum tumbled from the scoop into the bag.

"I got money," I declared, and slapped my stolen money onto the counter.

As if I'd smacked her, the red in Aunty's cheeks deepened. "What's this? Your mother give you this?"

I wondered how my guilty fingers had marked up the bills. I masked my shame with defiance. "Yes!"

"Little monster. What kind of trick is this?" She dumped the plums back into the jar. "Take it! Go!"

I shrank back below the lip of the counter.

She leaned over. "Bad girl. I'm going to talk to your mother."

"Mama gave it to me."

Aunty turned her back to me and began some trivial task behind the counter, muttering to herself. I grabbed the bills and crunched them in my fist. The plums, crammed back into the jar, taunted me.

"Bad Aunty!" I shouted as I left the shop.

I was lying in bed, telling a story to the moon framed in the window, when I heard footsteps through the courtyard gate. Like dogs sounding an alarm, the pigs in their pen snorted. I stood on the bed and peered out.

Silvered in moonlight, the shop aunty lumbered across the yard. She called out my mother's name. I humped into a ball on the bed, squeezed my eyes shut, and prayed to dissolve into darkness. I had hidden the stolen money in a small gap beneath the wardrobe. In the shadows, it grew eyes and watched me. My mother called out Aunty's name. I gripped the hem of the mosquito net and fiddled with it. The explosion of greetings softened to a low crackle of conversation.

I had fallen asleep—my fists squeezed and folded beneath me—when my mother brought in the lantern and flipped back the mosquito net. Fleeing the light, I nuzzled my face against the mat.

"Where did you get the money?"

I thought she might leave if I kept my eyes closed and didn't answer.

Her hand drifted across my back in a thoughtless caress. "Sweetie, I'm not mad. I don't know why I kept it. It was Baba's. You don't remember him, of course. You were just a baby. The money is so old, just junk now; having it makes us look like . . ." She paused, then said carefully, "Bad people. That's what scared Aunty. I know you didn't know. I should toss it but . . ." She didn't finish her sentence.

Baba. My mind snagged on the word. Baba. He was a myth, a legend, just a name that could have any person behind it. His name whispered like a demon we were afraid to conjure. But the purse made him real, not a god or ghost. A man who dealt in earthly matters like money. The crumpled bills glared at me from their exile beneath the wardrobe. I was still afraid. A taboo paralyzed my mouth; "Baba" sat on my tongue like a stone and I could give no comfort to my mother.

She crawled in beside me and nestled her head against mine. "Your hair stinks," she said, but her tone was tender. Her fingers raked through the tangles. Every so often, I could feel a knot come loose and hair tearing out with it. I uttered an unhappy grunt of pain.

"Such a silly thing to keep, isn't it? A silly little coin purse," she murmured into the top of my head. "Why didn't I burn it with everything else?"

BOOK II
TAICHUNG
1958–1972

1958

13

MAMA SAT BESIDE THE RADIO, her hands fisted in her lap. The announcer repeated the same news he had all morning. His patriotic voice, spirited and cartoonish, billowed.

"We are prepared to make great sacrifices in this opportunity to reclaim the mainland! Right now, troops fight valiantly as we attempt to liberate our Chinese brothers and sisters. Your families are waiting for your return!"

Promising to "liberate" Taiwan, our beloved Republic of China, from Chiang Kai-shek and the KMT, China had bombarded Kinmen, a tiny island claimed by Taiwan off the Chinese coast. The night before, I had overheard a neighbor, Uncle Owyang, talking to my grandparents about it.

"What China doesn't understand," he had said, "is that the Republic of China is the rightful ruler of China. We carry the banner of the republic. We are a government in exile!"

My grandfather slapped the table. "You're brainwashed! Taiwan belongs to Taiwan!" He refilled Uncle Owyang's wine cup. "Come, have some more."

Mama explained to me later that night that my grandfather was drinking out of worry, not jubilation. His adored grandson Dua Hyan was there, on Kinmen, serving in the air force, and we'd had no concrete news of the casualties.

I opened my mother's fists and climbed onto her lap. I hung an arm over her shoulders. "Is that true, Mama? Are we a government in exile?"

"Hush. I'm listening for news." She wrapped her arm around my waist. "My goodness. You are heavy. You're much too big to sit on your mother's lap." Then she sank forward again, her eyes mindlessly scanning the far distance as she listened.

I rested my head against hers. "Is Dua Hyan going to die?"

"No!" she snapped. "Don't even say such things. It's bad luck."

I bit my lip, worried that I had just redirected a bullet toward my unfortunate brother.

In another part of the house, my niece wailed. Ah Zhay, her husband—whom I called Jie-fu, *older sister's husband*—and their year-old daughter shared a room in the left wing, sleeping together on a giant canopy bed carved out of black wood that had been my great-grandmother's.

"Mei Mei is awake. Go get her." My mother gently pushed me off her lap and turned up the radio.

Mei Mei stopped crying when I came in. Her cheeks were bright red and her hair was plastered to her forehead with sweat even though she wore nothing but a diaper. I lifted the mosquito net and called her to me. She crawled over.

"Yi!" she called, as close to ayi, or aunt, that she could manage. She grabbed my shoulder and pulled herself to her feet.

"What a good baby!" I kissed her flushed cheek, then patted her bottom and found that her diaper was wet.

"You poor baby. Ayi change your diaper, okay?"

She cried, "Yi! Yi!" and squirmed as I struggled with the pins and powdered her with talcum. Finally she was dry and clean. I put her on my hip. "Let's go see your grandma."

When we came out of the bedroom, we found my brother-in-law home early. "Ah! I was just looking for my two favorite girls," he said. Mei Mei squealed as her father took her from my arms.

I patted her diaper. "I changed her," I told him.

"You are the best aunt. You're such a good girl." His smile was bright. Feeling modest, I pushed my cheek into my shoulder.

Not long before graduating high school, another day, over another bowl of shaved ice, Ah Zhay had met another soldier. She immediately noticed his smooth brown forearms, his fine cropped black hair, his strong cleft chin, and the way he said her name with a Shanghai accent. And then the things she would not admit: he was older, an outsider, and forbidden.

His name was Deng Yan. He was twenty-five years old, a mechanic in the air force. His shirts were always bleached and pressed and his shoes shiny. He smelled nice, not like the sweaty boys at school who jostled her and catcalled and pulled at her book bag. With him, she felt like a woman.

She barely knew him; she had no idea of what he thought or had seen. She could not imagine the American trooper ships gliding across the gray sea carrying hundreds of seasick men, Deng Yan among them, in a final escape from the communists, who had no navy. Men crowded onto the deck in their sweat-stiff uniforms; they wrapped their arms around ropes and railings; they filled the hallways and bunks. For Ah Zhay, it was enough that he was handsome.

Ah Zhay's marriage was more proof that my mother had dissolved into a shadow; she had barely protested the union, despite the gossip among all my grandparents' friends, who believed that the match between a Taiwanese girl and a Nationalist veteran could happen only if the girl was very poor, very ugly, or very stupid. The marriage cast doubts on my sister; the rumor was that she must have had some secret ailment, some birth defect or undisclosed mental issue. To my family's chagrin, my sister had disregarded her husband's lack of a family or history and married simply for love. I adored Jie-fu. Sometimes, I accidentally called him "Dua Hyan." And after he had come into our lives, I realized that all the warnings we'd been given about the soldiers were not always true, and that good or bad was a matter of perspective.

Days after the 8-23 Bombardment of the small island of Kinmen began, a typhoon swept through. The warning arrived between radio updates on the bombardment. We immediately went to fetch the pigs, which we boarded in one of the bedrooms. Tied into baskets, the chickens joined the pigs. We shoved our biggest pieces of furniture in front of the windows. By the time we closed the front door, the sky had turned black. We stuffed rags against the doorsills and waited.

Zhee Hyan and my grandfather began a game of chess by lamplight. I curled up on a chair near the lantern and read a comic book. The wind knocked at the doors and windows, and unknown objects clattered against the roof. My mother brought out the mah-jongg set and convinced Ah

Zhay, Jie-fu, and my grandmother to play. The clatter of the game tiles and their exclamations—my mother's semiserious complaint that my grandmother was winning—were comforting against the unseen chaos outside.

In thick, noisy sheets, the rain began. With a lack of crowing admirable for a fifteen-year-old, Zhee Hyan won the chess game and my grandfather settled down next to me to prepare his pipe. My grandfather's pipe was made of a long, thin section of bamboo with a gnarled end.

"I have a story for you," he said as he pressed the tobacco into the small, carved bowl. "Better than what you're reading." He lit the pipe, briefly puffed, then said, "This rain reminds me of when I was young and the Japanese first arrived in Taiwan."

Not taking her eyes off the mah-jongg tiles, my grandmother clicked her tongue and said, "What does that have to do with anything? You were too young to even remember it. Don't bother her."

"I'd like to hear the story," Jie-fu called over his shoulder.

My grandfather nudged me. "See, he wants to hear it. What about you?"

I reluctantly put down my comic. "Okay."

"See. And you?" he asked my brother.

"Of course," Zhee Hyan said. He had rearranged all the chess pieces back in their ranked spots.

"Of course. See, he says of course."

"Ba, please," my mother protested. "Don't. Not now." She laughed as she grabbed a tile. "Pong!" She tipped her row of tiles, revealing her win.

"Did they teach you this in school?" my grandfather asked me.

"No," I said.

He held the pipe elegantly with three fingers and smacked his lips, popping out a circle of smoke. "Of course not. This is not *national* history."

In May 1895, he continued, he was five years old. Word had come that the Empress Dowager Cixi, a concubine who had risen to queen after boiling her rivals in hot oil, had given Taiwan to the Japanese under the terms of the Treaty of Shimonoseki. Islanders feared that the Japanese would make slaves of them all. Their solution was to declare Taiwan an independent republic and rally people to fight their new invaders. Traitors were beheaded and their heads hung by their queues.

"Ba!" my mother exclaimed.

I was intrigued by the image of heads swinging by their long black braids. "Go on."

The newly recruited army of the Republic of Taiwan would meet the arriving Japanese at Keelung. Men of all ages and sizes took the train there. Old men and women and children eager to board and escape quickly replaced the crowd of would-be soldiers that clambered off the train. Flotsam exploded outward along the ballast: a mess of abandoned suitcases and bedding and toppled furniture and songbirds crying in cages. Two flags of the new republic, yellow tiger on blue background, flapped limply.

My grandfather's father, my *great*-grandfather, joined the stream of men drifting to the fields near the sea. They were sorted into regiments and practiced drills in the rain with imaginary guns. The battle, when it came, would be fought with unearthed rusty old cannons that had been left by the Dutch. Afterward, the men filed into muddy barracks and ate slop that had been boiled in large kettles. My great-grandfather broke from the line and, with his cousin, went into town to see what they could find among the abandoned shops and buildings. The villagers had left so hastily that in some homes, pots of still-warm food sat on the stoves.

My great-grandfather and his cousin fell asleep in one of these abandoned homes, in a bed that smelled of strangers and under a soothing canopy of rain. Later, a drum called them back into the storm. Japanese ships had been spotted. At camp, they sorted themselves into unsteady, sodden lines.

My great-grandfather and his cousin received rifles with dulled bayonets and small chipped knives to keep in their waistbands. Regiments marched to the hill forts that were better equipped with Armstrong and Krupp cannons and bright-colored flags.

The rain stopped. The cousins were ordered to patrol the village. Debris from the previous day's looting was strewn through the streets. They walked up and down the main road, then stopped at the damp, broken shutters of a looted shop and shared a pipe they found inside. They discussed the reward for dead Japanese soldiers—one hundred and fifty taels—versus the reward for an officer, which was double that. They'd have to bring in a head as proof. A hundred and fifty taels was enough to live on for a year, and my great-grandfather and his cousin, in their bravado, swore their first piece of business would be beheading an officer.

. . .

The firefight began the next morning. Energy swept through the town of wet, bored men, but the gunfire stopped before noon. My great-grandfather and his cousin wandered nervously up and down the streets and through the haphazard alleys, always with an ear cocked toward the sea.

Silence.

No messengers passed through.

My great-grandfather and his cousin took out the pipe and took turns gnawing the stem. They would fight today. The gunfire had confirmed it. It would be upon them like a flash of lightning; they had nothing to do but wait.

The rain began again. Mist obscured the hills. His cousin cleared his throat and hawked and suggested that they return to the house they had slept in the day before.

My great-grandfather knew battles were bloody and dirty and sweaty, but rain had not appeared in his dreams of glory. They hugged their guns to their chests and hunched over. The already soaked ground quickly turned to mud. The peels and skins and guts that people tossed behind their homes came washing up into the streets.

A noise like a cry of surprise or maybe of warning startled him. He saw a line of dark figures advancing through the driving rain. His cousin grabbed his arm and they stumbled into an alley. My great-grandfather fell to his knees and fretted with his gun. Amid the clatter of the rain, his breath was loud. A gunshot rang out, then another. He crept to the corner and peeked. The column had turned loose a detachment of dispersed soldiers gliding down the street with their guns cocked. They shouted in Japanese. They did not look like dwarfs or barbarians as he had been warned. They even wore cream-colored knee-high gaiters over their shined black shoes.

"They're coming," he hissed to his cousin. They ran. They followed turn after turn as alleys bled into one another without pattern. They turned again and caught a glimpse of a surprised Japanese soldier. They quickly backed up to the corner. My great-grandfather blindly fired. The man yelped.

My great-grandfather peeked around again. The soldier leaned against the wall fiddling with his gun. His eyes searched around in wild panic.

Before him, a sheet of water poured from the roof. This time, my great-grandfather aimed. The man howled. My great-grandfather had missed his head, but the man clutched his arm. He drew his limbs in tight, trying to make himself as small as possible.

My great-grandfather crept forward with his gun pointed at the man. His cousin called his name.

One hundred and fifty taels for a head.

The man wailed in pain. When he saw my great-grandfather, he dropped his hand from his bleeding arm and fumbled for his gun.

"Don't!" my great-grandfather cried. The gun made him brave, but the man's unpredictable fear, like an animal ready to chew off its own trapped limb, scared him. He warned him again. The man did not understand and he fired. My great-grandfather fell back, stunned, and fired again. The shot obscured the man's sobbing gibberish.

Once more, my great-grandfather had missed. Insanity flashed in the man's eyes and my great-grandfather suddenly understood that it was suicide to go any further. He could not bring back this man alive or dead. He turned and began a wildly erratic escape, ricocheting from side to side down the alley in an attempt to evade the man's aim. His head throbbed and blood rushed up and down every vein and artery. He made the corner and he felt ice sear across his leg.

The ice turned into an incredible heat. He kept running. Air burned in his lungs. He could not get enough.

He ran until the sound of bullets was behind him. He ran to the railroad tracks that led back to Taipehfu. He saw other men limping along, their jackets torn or lost.

Rain diluted the blood that ran from his wound. He stumbled into the grass where he dropped to his knees and twisted around to look at his injury. He could not see how deep it was. He wiped the rain from his face. He felt faint. He collapsed elbows out to the muddy ground and covered his face with his hands and screamed into the earth.

At that primitive scream—which my grandfather re-created for us in blood-chilling accuracy—a loud crash, punctuated by bellowing pigs, interrupted the story. Jie-fu and Zhee Hyan leaped up and ran toward the bedroom where we had boarded the animals. I hopped up too, and my mother yelled at me to sit down. I ignored her.

Behind the door, pigs cried and chickens squalled. Jie-fu waved us back and slowly opened the door.

The wardrobe that we had used to block the window had fallen over, crushing a basket of chickens and frightening the pigs that milled in the tight space. One had sought refuge on the bed. Wind and rain swept through the broken window and a small cyclone of leaves whipped around. Jie-fu pulled Zhee Hyan into the room and I slipped in behind him. The churned grit stung my face and I could barely open my eyes. While my brother and Jie-fu heaved the wardrobe off the unfortunate chickens, I herded the pigs out of the room. The pigs scattered, upset the mah-jongg table, knocked into the ancestor altar and toppled the incense pot. My sister shrieked and rescued Mei Mei from her playpen. My brother and Jie-fu shoved the chicken baskets into the hallway and slammed the door. The squawking chickens—a few among them dead— joined the pandemonium.

I scrambled onto a chair and started giggling. My sister laughed too as she jiggled my crying niece. My grandmother was angry. She blamed my grandfather.

"Why talk about the dead?" my mother cried as she gathered up the fallen mah-jongg tiles. "Look what you've done."

The next morning, we opened the doors to a cool gray sky. The storm had driven away the heat. The trees were a vibrant green. Branches littered the courtyard. One wall of the pigpen had collapsed. We found roof tiles from a neighbor's house.

While Jie-fu and Zhee Hyan began rebuilding the pigpen, my mother and sister swept the house. My sister tied my niece, Mei Mei, into a sling on my back, and then I began clearing the courtyard. I spoke to Mei Mei as I worked, talking about typhoons and explaining where rain came from. She gurgled back an appreciative stream of "Yi's."

The radio was dead, and in our attention to the mundane, we momentarily forgot about the bombardment in Kinmen. Zhee Hyan raked out the pigpen. Mama and Ah Zhay bickered while my grandmother banged around the kitchen. Grandfather was somewhere silent and unseen. The comforting hum of labor filled the day.

Eventually, loud, pained lowing distracted me. I scanned the fields.

In the distance, three water buffalo, more victims of the storm, trudged through a drowned field in aimless circles. I thought they might belong to the Owyangs, who farmed the land to the right of us. I marched toward the levee between the paddies to see if I could identify them.

I hadn't bothered with shoes, which I saved only for school days. My feet sank into the cold mud. Disgust and delight snaked up my spine. Mei Mei whined.

"Let's go see the cows," I cooed.

On either side of me, lucid, still water glimmered amid the lush rice grass. A waterlogged slipper floated in the paddy. Though the water was not deep, vertigo chilled me. I saw myself tumbling over, Mei Mei with me, lost among the grass, suffocating on mud. "We're okay," I said to reassure myself. I reached back and squeezed her little bare foot.

From the other direction, a man stepped onto the levee from the road.

I gestured toward the animals. "Uncle Owyang!" I shouted. "Are they yours?"

The man stopped. I realized I had made a mistake.

He was a stranger in clothes that belonged to a different city, perhaps even a different time. Black pants, a white button-down shirt. His face was dark, his eyes sunken into a squint. And he wore shoes. Even from here, I could see they were black patent leather and he did not mind the mud. He was not a farmer. The bag hanging from his shoulder began to swing as he picked up his pace.

I considered turning around and running back home. When he passed me on this narrow slice of land, only inches would separate us. I would smell his sweat, the odor of his unwashed scalp. Cigarettes in his clothes or yesterday's wine in his skin.

He came closer. His brown cheeks were wet with tears. He wiped his face, rubbed his nose against his sleeve, and smiled at me. Then he called me by my sister's name—not Ah Zhay, *big sister,* as I called her, but her formal name. "Tsai Li Ka?"

An itch overtook my leg, and I rubbed at it with my other foot, leaving smears of mud.

"I'm not Tsai Li Ka," I said.

Water spots dulled his glasses. His hair was too long and going white above his ears.

"Do you know Tsai Li Ka?" he asked. He spoke Taiwanese without an accent. My posture softened in response. I squeezed Mei Mei's foot for reassurance. She batted my head. "Yi!" she shrieked.

"She's my sister," I said softly. "Tsai Li Ka is my sister."

"Your sister." The question dissolved into a statement. "Who is this?" He jerked his chin at Mei Mei.

"My niece."

"Your niece." He echoed me again, adding awe to the words, and I began to wonder if he was an imbecile.

His eyes met mine. The whites of his eyes were threaded with veins. His gaze traveled my face: my eyes, then my hair, then my nose and mouth.

"Stop," I pleaded.

"Please take me to your mother."

We walked single file along the levee. Mei Mei wriggled in the sling. I didn't dare turn back to look at the man who followed me, but I listened carefully for the suck of the mud on his shoes. I worried my mother would scold me for bringing this stranger to the house. I considered leading him to the Owyangs' place, calling Aunty Owyang "Mama," then running off to let them disentangle the lie. Or I could desert him and warn my family.

But I did none of this. We came to the courtyard. Jie-fu and Zhee Hyan halted at the sight of us. I saw the wary curiosity in their eyes, so explained, "He's looking for Mama."

Jie-fu greeted the stranger, took Mei Mei from the sling, and told me to get my mother. I found her mopping the floor.

"Ma."

"You're getting the floor dirty." She shooed me back toward the doorway.

"Somebody came to see you." My stomach tingled with fear and pride: a stranger had come to see Mama, and I had brought him.

She jerked her head up and looked at me. "Who?"

"I don't know. A man." I did not mention his damaged glasses, or his new shoes. Or how he had repeated my sister's name with wonder.

She dropped the rag into the bucket and went to the kitchen. I followed her.

"What does he want?" she asked. She washed her hands, and the pink bar of soap spinning around and around in her grip mesmerized me.

"Didn't say."

Thin, milky bubbles ran down the drain. She shut off the water and looked into my eyes. "What's he like?"

"He has black shoes."

Mama paused. "Did he mention Dua Hyan?"

"No."

A small mirror hung over the sink. She glanced into it and swiped water along her hair, then, checking the result, snorted and shook her head. "A mess. It'll do."

"I don't think it's about Dua Hyan," I said, trying to reassure her though I was not sure. We had heard nothing about the impending battle in the strait since before the storm.

When we came out, Jie-fu was still talking to the man, who sensed our presence and turned.

"Ah Bin," the man said. In his mouth, my mother's name sounded like a broken plate, the shards of it lacerating his throat.

My mother raised her eyebrows in hope, but it quickly darkened to a frown. She clenched her hands. She spoke as she approached him. "Who are you?"

The man repeated my mother's name like a plea: "Ah Bin."

"Leave," she said. "Leave."

"It's me."

She stood right in front of him now, and her closeness was intimate even though her face was hard.

"Prove it. What's his name?" She pointed at my brother. "Or hers?" She gestured toward me. "Your uncle's name? The one who ran the printing shop? The cousin who married the Japanese doctor?" Her hope—and disbelief—mutated into an anger that brought her close to tears.

Ah Zhay stepped through the dark doorway into the bright and cool morning. Something glimmered through her body, turning her into a young girl again.

"Baba," she said. And then she stopped, as if she feared coming closer would dissolve the ghost. She blinked, puzzled, her mouth indecisive, quivering toward a smile and tears. *Baba?* I thought. *Baba?*

Zhee Hyan, who had been only four years old when my father left, repeated the word, two unfamiliar syllables, and then I turned toward the stranger and said it too.

"Baba."

My mother exhaled. Her chest seemed to cave. A decade of tension dissipated on the breath, and, finally, my mother touched his—my father's—sleeve.

14

I IMAGINE THE TIME before Baba left, before my siblings and I existed, when my parents were just a family of two.

It's an August evening in 1935. The sun has set and the street glows with neon signs and lit apartment windows. Occasionally, car headlights slice the dark.

They are newlyweds. My mother's wedding dress—white lace and a delicate birdcage veil—is folded into a box in the wardrobe and still smells faintly of her perfume. They had honeymooned at Alishan, welcoming the cool morning mist of the mountains, the giant cypresses and cedars that contrasted the palms dotting the rest of the island. This was how my mother had imagined Europe to be. Alishan had been significant in another way too: here my parents had shared their first intimate night together. But my mother had not been a blushing bride. Art school had already accustomed her to nude bodies. My father was taken aback by her insistence to leave the lamp on and wondered briefly about the woman he had married. Of course, this is what he loved about her: her modernity, her dismissal of the giggling, coquettish ways of other women her age.

They come to the restaurant. A huge ceramic fish sculpture bursts from the center of the room, tail curled to the floor, head pointed to the ceiling, a red electric light glowing in its gaping mouth. Their friends wait at a round table behind the fish. When they spot my parents, they erupt with greetings, waving them over, exclaiming hello, asking about the honeymoon.

These are the best and the brightest of the colony: two doctors, a school principal, a book editor. The wives are university educated; one is a doctor too. They talk loudly, laugh without self-consciousness, make raunchy puns, tease each other, and gesticulate with the confidence of youth who are destined to inherit the world.

My mother watches my father speak about the recent agreement to demilitarize Chahar and she wonders how she ever had the good fortune to marry this man. He is not the most handsome man at the table, but he is eloquent and intelligent. She has always had the sense that some central, purely moral thing lies inside him. She doesn't know if it is his certainty when he speaks, or the steady way he holds one's gaze when he listens, or just some intangible she can't quite articulate—something below language: the tiny gestures, blinks, tones barely registered—that coalesce into this impression. She laughs along with them, her chopsticks darting into the communal dishes, at a glance appearing to be as fully invested in the conversation as the rest of them. Do they admire him as much as she does? Do they notice his smooth skin and neatly combed hair, his clear enunciation? She *feels* moral for having been chosen by him.

She puts food into his bowl; he flashes a look at her, *stop* on the edge of his tongue, then says nothing.

Of course. Of course. A spike of heat burns her neck and jaw. None of the other wives do this. She must seem so provincial, so Confucian. She returns to her own bowl. No one can see her embarrassment: my mother quiets her emotions beneath a placid mask. Anxiety looks like grace; she doesn't know that it's precisely this quality that attracts my father. Even now, feeling reprimanded, she betrays nothing, doesn't hang her head or blink meekly.

They walk home arm in arm, my mother's heels clicking on the macadam. The night is hot and the air pungent with the odor of ripe fruit. The rickshaw drivers pedal by. Their white uniforms and white hats glow in the night. Out of other restaurants comes the mechanical whine of music spinning out of record players. They turn down their alley, which is empty except for a cat lapping at a puddle beneath the communal spigot.

Upstairs, among the new bedroom furniture that still smells like fresh varnish, they undress. My father sits on the bed and pulls his socks off his damp, pale feet. My mother wipes the powder off her face with a cotton ball dipped in cold cream.

"The way the administration is dealing with the savages is completely misguided."

"What?" my mother says. She drops the cotton ball into the trash and picks up her hairbrush.

"Assimilation is the solution. Otherwise, we'll always have a population ready to chop off our heads at any provocation."

"Indeed." My mother realizes he is responding to a conversation from dinner. She wants to talk about what motivated Mrs. Lin, a Japanese woman, to marry Mr. Lin, one of them. Why she gave up her country and citizenship to come here. But my father's mind, as always, is on much loftier topics.

"And then they numb them on drink. Generations from now, this will be a problem. Wu Ming is wrong. Completely wrong."

She can't remember what Wu Ming said, but she hums her assent. She watches him in the vanity mirror. He strips down to his undershirt and underwear and pauses to wipe down his glasses with his shirt hem.

"The issue is we shouldn't even use the word 'savage.' Aren't we as Formosans in the same boat? How are we any different from them? All of us are second-class citizens. Looking down on them doesn't turn us into first-class citizens." He holds the glasses close to his face and squints, then scratches at something on the frame.

"You believe everyone is equal. That's your flaw," she says, half joking.

"It's true." He puts his glasses back on and notices for the first time she is wearing only her negligee. "Wear that," he says, desire tightening his jaw.

"To bed?"

"Yes."

"But it's my slip." She self-consciously touches her shoulder. "I've been wearing it all evening."

He walks over and kneels behind her. Gaze meets gaze in the mirror, then he kisses her shoulder and bites the strap. She reaches back to touch his cheek.

It was like this. In the beginning, it was like this.

Another city, another era. Taichung, 1958. No longer wide, spacious streets or cool, lush parks. Everywhere now were cars and bicycles, trains crying out of stations, and people chatting under the teeming arcades, driving up the temperature by a few degrees. My mother regretted wearing stockings.

She was fixated on the sweat tickling her calves and the phantom feeling that her nylons were slipping. In the heat, her lipstick began to feel thick and gaudy. Elbows, purses, and sacks jostled her, driving her into my father, who stared straight ahead, charging through his own nattering thoughts.

My father had been home for two weeks and my mother had planned this dinner in order to vanquish rumors—for some, his return was an intimation of disgrace: What price had Dr. Tsai paid? What deviled deal had he made? She tried to forgive those who begged out, citing other plans; she knew they feared that Baba's trouble was contagious.

As they strolled to the restaurant, Baba imagined he was a time traveler. He'd been set inside a time machine—this one more simple than the kind in books—made of concrete and iron and moving no faster than time or light, and had emerged into this strange world where even the palette had changed. His children grown, his wife another woman with a tentative smile. The streets had been so open and empty that they used to walk in the middle of the boulevards. Now, seas of people surrounded them. Military police in white helmets strode past. Mountains of trash swept up from the morning market waited for the garbage collectors. Drivers pounded their horns at this weaving bicyclist or that careless truck. What kind of world was this? Again, the force of the crowd pushed her into him. He could tell her about the time machine. Speaking things made them less real. But already, planning out the words, he heard how absurd they were. He would stay quiet.

If only he had spoken. His silence poisoned the dinner. The mood began to sour, my mother thought, when the women—my aunt and a few of my mother's middle school friends—rushed forward, exclaiming over my father as if he were a sweet-smelling newborn.

"Dr. Tsai! You haven't changed a bit."

"Ah, good old Dr. Tsai. Glad to have you back."

My mother suspected that they had decided to save face for my father and pretend that the eleven missing years had been nothing more than a business trip gone awry. My mother returned their enthusiasm, but my father uttered his greetings in an unsmiling monotone: grunts that passed for hello and nothing more. A tendril of worry unfurled itself in my mother's chest. She had insisted he bathe and had dressed him in a new shirt, and, for the first time in days, he had complied. But what was he doing now? Was he reneging on the promise, unspoken but so clear to her?

"Still the same serious doctor," Aunty Chu teased. "Sit down so we can order." Her hand at his back, she guided him to his seat.

Once everyone was settled again, and after Aunty Chu had given the waitress the order, an uneasy silence fell over the table. Someone remarked on the flavor of the bean curd and a chorus hastily agreed. My mother decided that since she and Baba were the reason for the awkwardness, she had a responsibility to warm up the conversation. Directing the question to no one in particular, my mother asked how the children were.

With care for my mother, Aunty Wong leaped on the opening. "Wei Shin passed the university entrance exam."

"Wonderful!" my mother said. "She was always such a smart girl." She waited for my father to echo the sentiment, but he was staring into his tea.

"Will your son be home for the Mid-Autumn Festival?" another aunty asked my mother.

"We hope so. Everything is so uncertain now."

"I bet he can't wait to see his father," Aunty Wong said. Her husband immediately touched her arm. She had called the elephant into visibility. It lumbered out of the corner and sat on the table.

"And we can't wait to see him, right?" My mother's hand landed gently atop my father's. He jerked and said, "Yes."

Uncle Wong spoke up immediately, some comment on the recent cross-strait fighting, which carried the conversation into the realm of current events, a topic on which everyone could express some outrage and concern. My mother was grateful.

Blinking like a man stumbling out of a cave, my father emerged into the moment. His eyes darted among the dinner guests, gaze tracking the conversation. My mother poured more tea for him. She muttered, "Drink."

"I want to go home," Baba said just loud enough for my mother to hear.

"We just got here. Wait for the food."

"I want to go home."

"Wait."

My father stood up. "I'm going to have a cigarette."

"Need a light?" One of the uncles proffered a lighter. My father shook his head.

"You don't have to go outside. Here's the ashtray," Aunty Wong said, but my mother noticed how her eyes moved around the table, searching for shared judgment.

My father lit the cigarette. "I'll go outside."

A bas-relief of a goddess swirling among clouds hung on the back wall of the restaurant. It was the gaudy type of art that my mother hated. "Art." It didn't even deserve the label. The sort of thing pressed out by a machine, swabbed with glue and paint, and then sold in a cheap sundries store. As my father left the restaurant, my mother kept her eyes on the gold-leafed goddess. She sipped her tea, which was weak and cold. The tendril in her chest had bloomed, full leaves and blossoms, snaking around her heart, choking her throat.

When the food arrived and my father still had not returned, she went out to look for him. He was not in front of the restaurant. The garbage trucks had come through and cleared away the trash, leaving damp circles. She hurried to the corner, expecting to find him squatting on some overturned crate and surrounded by cigarette butts. He was not there. She went one block farther, hoping to catch him in front of a closed shop, idly staring through the window. Still no sign. She went another block. Maybe he had decided he was in the mood for noodles.

Returning alone to the restaurant was too shameful, so my mother caught a bus.

The open windows rattled and exhaust thickened in the humidity. My mother watched for my father on the street below. Dozens of men, dressed similarly, sauntered down the streets, smoking, toting parcels, holding their children's hands. She felt like fainting. Afraid that she might vomit out the window, she gripped the seat in front of her and hung her head. Waiting had been easier. Guilt overcame her and she chastised herself. What a terrible, terrible thought. She remembered those days of uncertainty and potential. All those daydreams of his return, family completed. She had never considered this. The bus stopped, exhaled, then shook back to life. All those naive canvases she'd painted of reunited families against idyllic landscapes. She had considered only happy endings.

. . .

He was not home. She waited at the table in the dark courtyard. This was too familiar to all of us. I came out and sat beside her. She put her arm around me.

"I'll stay with you," I declared.

"You should go to bed. He'll be home soon. He'll come home."

I am thinking of that moment. I am thinking about the texture of skin, the particular clamminess of my mother's arm on my bare shoulder and her hand pressed to my hip as she leaned over to kiss me.

When I got older, I still thought I could write life. I didn't understand, as my mother had just realized that evening, that it is the other way around. And yet, here I am, still trying.

15

IN ALL WAYS, he was a stranger.

With a wary eye, my mother continued to watch my father. When she hung clothes in the courtyard, she would glance over her shoulder as he helped her. He squeezed water from a shirt with the intense and clumsy concentration of a child learning to thread a needle. Or her gaze would drift down the long hall, from kitchen to front room, where my father sat in awe of the newspaper. Reacquainting his eyes with the look of words, he read article after article, then began again when he had finished. As he read, he rubbed at the paper until his fingers were black and the surface pilled.

At dinner, we watched his shaking hands as he brought his bowl to his mouth, the chopsticks clattering in his fingers. I stared at his damaged teeth until my mother snapped at me to keep eating. For days, Baba refused to leave the house. He would not bathe and he carried his stench through the rooms behind him, like the shadow of a shadow.

I hated baths too. One evening, when my mother ordered me into the water, I pointed out her hypocrisy.

"But *he* doesn't have to," I protested.

"*He* who?" Her eyes brightened, an ebony rage sliding over her irises. "*He* who?"

Through gritted teeth, I muttered, "Baba."

I didn't even see her lift her arm; the smack of her hand on my cheek was loud and painful and left a memory of burning splinters on my skin. When I cried out, she hit me again.

"Stop!" I caressed my cheek with both hands.

"Don't ever talk about your father that way. *He?*" Tiny glitters of sweat arose along the bridge of her nose. "You don't want a bath? Fine." She crouched beside the tub and grabbed the handles.

"No, Mama! I'll wash."

"Ungrateful child." With a rasp of effort, she overturned the tub. The water burst out, an errant wave consuming the floor. It lapped the wall and swirled around the bristles of a broom. It crept under the feet of the stove. Dried bug carcasses floated back out and spun in sluggish circles.

"*He* is your father," she reiterated as she surveyed the flooded kitchen. "Your *Baba.*"

One afternoon, a month after his return, I toiled away on my homework at the courtyard table beneath the shadow of the banyan. My father brought out a stool and settled across from me.

"What are you doing?"

I was practicing my multiplication tables. I offered the same cool politeness I would have given a very distant cousin. I did not meet his eyes.

He continued to watch me work. I had not yet memorized the times tables and I resorted to drawing little clusters of hash marks. But under his gaze, my pencil dragged on the page; I felt I had even forgotten how to draw a line.

"This is not the way to learn."

I lost my place counting and began again.

"Where is your abacus?"

"I don't know." It was under my bed. If I did not look at him, he might leave.

"Forget it. You should memorize this. Look at me."

Finally, I raised my eyes. His chin was dotted with dried blood from his morning shave.

"You should be able to recite it without thinking."

I nodded.

"Give it to me." Without waiting, he took my homework and folded it in half. I uttered a tiny note of protest, but quickly swallowed the sound. I looked into his eyes. Dua Hyan had Baba's eyes: heavy lidded and sparsely lashed, and I found comfort in thinking of my brother.

"Three times five."

I counted by fives silently. "Fifteen."

"Good. Three times six."

I added three to my last answer.

"Good. Three times eight."

Feeling confident, I answered quickly. "Twenty-eight."

"Wrong. Three times eight."

"Twenty-seven."

"Wrong." The word cracked in the air. I flinched.

The correct answer receded. I held out my fingers and counted upward from eight.

"Stop. Stop. Does anybody else in your class count on their fingers? Does your teacher let you count? How old are you?"

"Eleven."

"Eleven! And you are counting on your fingers like a five-year-old?" His eyes widened, ringing his irises in white. It was a look of madness.

I dropped my limp hands into my lap.

"Follow me." He began to recite the times tables, pausing after each one to let me repeat. My voice dropped to a drone. I watched a bird hop from branch to branch in a tree. I watched the pigs snuffle against one another in their pen. I thought about Cheng Ping, a boy in my class, and how I might impress him with my math smarts.

"Pay attention!" Baba's voice startled me. "You aren't listening."

"I *am*." My voice was meek. Mama often got frustrated and let me be. However, Baba seemed to be having the opposite reaction. I felt squeezed tighter and tighter. *Go, just go,* I silently pleaded.

He unfolded my homework and erased my afternoon's worth of work. "You won't eat until you can recite it perfectly."

"What?" Fear of my mother kept me from kicking this stranger and shouting my refusal.

"No dinner until you can do this without mistakes."

I looked at him. I no longer saw a trace of anyone familiar in his eyes. No echo of Dua Hyan or hint of Ah Zhay. His eyes had clouded over, as if he conversed with another person in another time. I didn't want to listen to him. I scrunched my nose up in disgust at this injustice.

Luckily, he did not catch my impertinence. He stood up. My homework lay before me, smudged, creased, and littered with eraser ash.

While my family ate, I murmured numbers over sheets of homework fanning across the floor. The fragrance of fried pork, the glistening creamy fat, the salty cabbage, and the steamed rice made my stomach burn. My head felt empty. I felt abandoned and pitiful, like a poor foundling suffering at the windows of the rich. Every once in a while, I cast my disgusted eye at the source of my misery.

"Let her eat," my grandmother said.

My father did not look up from his bowl. "No."

"She's worked for hours."

My mother tried to hush my grandmother. She dropped food into my grandmother's bowl, attempting to appease her with filial piety.

My grandmother was not swayed. "This is the way you treat your daughter?" Her chopsticks, stabbing the air, emphasized each word.

"Ma," my mother murmured.

My father glared at my grandmother. "This isn't your business." A blade slid through his words.

No one said anything. My brother-in-law found something fascinating in the surface of the table while my sister fed my niece. My grandfather concentrated on flicking grains of rice off his vegetables. Zhee Hyan searched the communal bowl for a particular slice of meat. My grandmother threw down her chopsticks and left the table with such force that the chair legs skidded across the floor.

My mother pushed more and more rice into her mouth, more quickly than she could chew it. Her cheeks swelled and the food crowded her tongue. Tears fell off her chin. No one acknowledged my grandmother's departure or my mother's crying.

"Baba, I'm ready." My mastery would save dinner.

"Come here."

I stood before them. He told me to start. I enunciated carefully, trying to think past my hunger. Numbers. Numbers twisting around each other into bigger numbers, numbers marching in troops. I tried to visualize the sheet I'd been staring at since the afternoon.

I got to the nines. And even though I knew the nines table merely repeats multiples that have come before, but in reverse order—nine times six rather than six times nine—I stumbled.

"No," my father said. His wooden face declared his duty: enforce the rules, don't pity the suffering.

My mother whispered, "Please, just let her eat."

"She's wrong. Keep working."

"Darling, come eat. Mama will fix you some food."

"No!" Rice flew from my father's mouth and his bowl cracked against the table.

"I don't want to eat," I said.

I wanted my father to watch the suffering he'd created. I wanted to grow light-headed, waste to white, topple over so that guilt would seize him, so he would cry out, curse himself, and want to die.

"Try again when I'm done," he said, returning to his dinner.

"Yes, Baba."

I fell asleep on the floor, crumpling my homework. My mother woke me. She held a bowl of cold food, hushed me, fed me like a baby.

Baba kept his vow that I would work harder. Every afternoon, after I'd fed the chickens and had a snack, Baba sat with me at the courtyard table and watched me do my homework. After I was done with that, he brought out the lessons he'd created while I was at school: pages of math problems, sheets of characters to copy, classical poems to memorize.

On some days, he kept me at the table until dark. He would bring out an old lamp and set it before me and I had to write through the dancing shadows it cast. I glimpsed Zhee Hyan inside reading a comic. Ah Zhay marched through the halls clasping my giggling niece. Darkness swam into my eyes from so many hours by the yellow light.

This was how I learned that I was his favorite child.

16

WHEN BABA WAS NOT SUPERVISING my education, he spent most days in his room. Ah Zhay would lean against the doorframe with the baby on her hip and tell Baba little frivolous things: that Mei Mei had just put together a sentence—*just three words, but nonetheless* . . .—or a piece of gossip that her husband had heard at his construction job. At the table, she put meat in his bowl, and she brought back cigarettes for him when she went to town.

He nodded at her stories, ate the meat, smoked the cigarettes, but his eyes looked at the wall or the floor, anywhere but at her coaxing, anxious smile.

"He's not well," she'd whisper to me as we prepared dinner. Feeling guilty, I nodded. I plunged bean sprouts into a basin of cold water and she drove a cleaver through a slab of pork. The knife stuck for a moment in the damp wood, and we both ignored the dirt in the creases of my neck from the long afternoon I'd spent with Baba looking for frogs to supplement my science lesson.

Ah Zhay was the oldest. Of the four of us, she had known him best.

She knew his hand on the back bar of her bicycle when she learned to ride, the look of his brushstroke spreading across a scroll, and the sound of his voice reading the paper aloud at dinner. Her memory, unlike mine, contained whole narratives: incidents with beginnings, middles, and ends.

We awaited Dua Hyan's visit home for the Mid-Autumn Festival. If Ah Zhay could not bring Baba back to normal, perhaps the sight of his oldest son would. We scrubbed the floors and cleaned the windows. Mama aired out the bedding in Dua Hyan's old room.

I expected Dua Hyan to be different after so long away, that he would have become as cheerful and easy as the soldiers I saw in town, but beneath his sunburn and the train odor lingering in his wrinkled uniform, the usual wariness still knotted his shoulders. When he stepped off the train, he ignored Mama's smiles and my exclamations, set down his duffel, and bowed deeply as he met Baba again, his body reaching back to the gestures of a defeated culture. I thought of the man with amputated limbs who dragged himself through the market: he'd set his bowl before us and violently knock his head against the ground, as if only the most debased self was worthy of a spare coin. Dua Hyan too looked only at the ground and, like the beggar, he could not see the wincing face above him.

To celebrate Dua Hyan's return, we went to Café Paradiso, a European-style restaurant with red vinyl chairs where they served coffee in white porcelain cups rimmed with gold. Mama said it was like a café they used to go to in Taipei where artists and writers gathered before the war.

"It was just like being in Paris: people fighting over art, arguing about surrealism, defending Picasso, hating Magritte. I studied French at university. Did you know that?" She flashed a full smile at Baba. She was so giddy that she spoke while chewing. I half listened, bored by the list of foreign names. I was more interested in blowing the steam off my coffee and watching the vapor fade away. My father's knife broke through a tendon of meat and squealed against the plate.

Mama stopped for a moment, glanced at my father, then continued to tell us about a theater director they'd known who had chosen to move to Japan when the war ended. The director had once been a silent film narrator, a benshi, one of the most famous in Taipei.

"They put his name at the top of the marquee," she said, "above the title of the movie."

"Watch your voice," my father warned. He glanced around and returned to his steak.

We fell silent. His hands trembled as he lifted his fork. That afternoon, my mother had finally coaxed him into a haircut, and a ring of pale skin traced his trimmed hairline. He looked like an overgrown schoolboy.

"I haven't been to a movie in a long time," Dua Hyan said.

"Let's go," my mother said. "The place near the airfield."

With his mouth on his coffee cup, my father muttered, "We'll talk outside."

"Ah Lu's mom sells peanuts there," Zhee Hyan said. Ah Lu was a classmate whose name came up often enough to reveal Zhee Hyan's feelings for her.

I taunted him with the tines of my fork. "Ah Lu, Ah Lu, *Ah Lu.*"

"Shut up."

Dua Hyan dug into his food and talked over us. "I'm starving. I feel like I haven't eaten in months." He laughed. If we were loud enough, if we said enough, maybe we could erase Baba's fear.

"You do look thinner," Mama noted for the tenth time that day.

"You have more muscles," I declared.

Dua Hyan smiled. "Check it out." He pushed up his sleeve and flexed his arm.

"Ooh," I teased. I reached over and squeezed his biceps. "Like Popeye."

"So what was it like? Did you kill any commies?" Zhee Hyan asked. I leaned in. Even my mother shifted, betraying her curiosity about the battle Dua Hyan had just witnessed.

Dua Hyan began to speak but my father interrupted him. "Be quiet. People are listening." I glanced at my mother to see if this was true.

The usual restaurant din rang around us: clinking silverware, waitresses shouting at the kitchen, and a rumble of intersecting conversations. The lovers sitting in the booths across the aisle smiled and cooed and self-consciously wiped imagined crumbs from their mouths. Two men talked over coffee and pastries. Other families loudly coaxed their sullen children.

"You're here now," my mother said. This was how she soothed my father during his nightmares, or when he imagined men outside our windows. It was what she had quietly said when Dua Hyan had first bowed before Baba in his Nationalist uniform.

"I know you don't believe me," Baba said.

The cheer vanished from my mother's eyes. She arched her neck, feigning dignity as she did when she felt humiliated. I wished my father would go away again, then quickly pinched myself for my evil thought.

Dua Hyan tried to distract us. "A movie is a great idea."

Baba glanced around the restaurant. A boy, reprimanded by his mother, had begun to cry. At another table, a woman left a stunned man staring at her empty lipstick-marked cup. Baba's gaze lingered on the two pastry-eating men, who now pored over a clipped newspaper article. I found everyone utterly boring; I wondered what Baba's critical eye saw.

"Ba?" Dua Hyan said. "What do you think?"

Baba kept his eyes on the two men as he uttered his agreement.

"Hurray," I chirped. "Let's go. Hurry, Mama." I gulped down the rest of my coffee and coughed on the silt.

.   .   .

The theater near the airfield was actually just a sheet tacked up in a fenced lot that lay beneath the airfield's flight path. The night was warm, and the film, *Old Yeller*, dubbed into Mandarin, was occasionally interrupted by the roar of descending planes. The screen family mirrored ours: a missing father, two brothers and a sister. But Dua Hyan had never had a dog—some loyal, scrappy thing, but regal—and become some hobbled-together combo that dummied the missing father.

If only we'd had a dog, I thought. Not some mean street dog that nipped at your heels when you rode by on your bike, though maybe he'd start off that way. I'd feed him clumped old rice and gristle I hid in my sleeve during dinner, and coax him closer and closer until he was tamed.

Behind me, my father whispered to my mother. She said, "You're losing your mind."

The family lived in a house made of logs, but like us, they raised their own chickens and pigs. They had a cow with horns like a water buffalo. Though I'd seen American faces on cosmetic boxes in the drugstore and on advertisements, this was my first sight of moving, talking Americans. The mother was lovely and bleached out, like a shirt left too long in the sun. Her eyes were the color of marbles.

"We're not going," my mother whispered so loudly that the woman in front of me turned around.

I pretended I didn't hear them. If we just didn't listen to him, maybe he would stop.

My father gripped my neck. His hand was clammy, the heat throbbing against my skin: "Let's go."

"Let go of her." My mother's voice was firm.

"Ba," Dua Hyan said.

If we left, I swore I would never forgive him. I crossed my arms and hunched over. "Don't touch me," I hissed.

"Come."

People on either side of us glanced over.

"I don't want to go!" I shouted.

His grip tightened. "Stand up."

With his hand on my neck, I had no choice.

"Sit down!" a man yelled. A chorus of agreement joined him. My mother grabbed at Baba's sleeve, but he yanked it out of her grip and urged me out of the row, accidentally overturning our stools. My mother and brothers scrambled after us.

I was yoked in my father's pinch. My face prickled with hot anger; I felt no pain. He led me through the gate. The rest of the family trailed us in a tumult of protests. "Baba, slow down," Dua Hyan called, while Mama cried, "What's happening?"

"They've seen us now," he snapped. "You made them see us."

I didn't care. I wanted to know how the movie ended. I began to cry, frustrated that I would never know what happened to Travis and Old Yeller. Much later, when my daughters were small, I would finally see the movie to the end and learn what I had missed: Old Yeller locked into the corncrib, snarling, sick with rabies, and Travis's tears when he raises his rifle.

"They've seen us now," Baba repeated.

"Because of you!" I cried.

In the alley, my mother and brothers talked over one another, urging my father to calm down.

My father glanced around. "The men from the café. They're here."

"What men?" Dua Hyan asked.

Still sniffling, I pressed my face into my mother's arm. As I peeked back at Baba through my tears, I saw the wildness in his eyes. He had nothing for them. He was not important; he could barely even bathe himself. He was nothing.

"In the café. They were there. Let's go." Baba looked over his shoulder at the ice pop seller, who was wiping condensation from the top of his cart. "Come now."

As we walked home, the night snack vendors looked up from their stands and the bare bulbs that hung above their heads cast long shadows, turning their eyes into dark hollows and stretching their noses. The late-night lovers who strolled the gloomy streets had no faces. Cats darted out from black alleys, winking neon green eyes before they disappeared again. No one said a word.

I perched on a chair, my knees folded to my chest, mindlessly picking at my toenails. One persistent thought entranced me: *I hate him.* Occasionally, I glanced over at Dua Hyan, in another chair, his shoulders soft, his eyes glazed.

After a long period in the bedroom, Mama finally emerged alone. Her eyes sunk into shadows and only a sad stain remained of her lipstick. Dua Hyan and I both straightened up.

"What's wrong with him?" Dua Hyan asked. As an answer, Mama shook her head and ordered me out of the room.

"I want to stay," I protested. I dropped my feet to the floor one at a time—*slap! slap!*—emphatically expressing my indignation. First wronged, now excluded. I trudged toward the bedroom, but as soon as I was out of sight, I hunched behind the doorway to listen.

"He's broken," Dua Hyan snapped. He had found the right word. Baba was like a carefully pieced together eggshell delicately cupped in Mama's hands. One breath and—glue would be no use, the seams would open anew, and all of us would scramble to gather him up.

"Don't say that." Mama's pacing stopped and I heard her slide onto a chair.

"Look how tired you are." Now Dua Hyan rose. The clapping of his boots, strong and rhythmic, paced to and fro. "He's broken. He's broken."

"Shut up!" The words were damp and thick, clinging in her throat. She sniffed.

Dua Hyan stopped marching. "Are you crying?" Defiantly, he repeated his remark. "He's broken, Mama. You need to accept this."

"Dua Hyan, please don't leave." I stood in the doorway as he packed.

He smiled but his eyes looked sad. I wanted to grab his leg as I had when I was a kid and hold on. But I was eleven now. I had begun menstruating a few months before, and I restrained myself, as I thought an adult might. Though I wanted to beg and cry, I said, "Please stay."

"You really aren't a kid anymore, huh?" he said as if he were seeing me for the first time. His smile, directed at some point in time behind me, was pensive. Yes, I was taller. I had an itchiness in my chest too, and Mama had forced me to wear an undershirt. Maybe he wanted to swoop me up like I was still a gap-toothed and round-faced five-year-old.

"Stay with us," I repeated. With him gone, who would stand between us and Baba? Jie-fu was a son-in-law—he had to be polite. Dua Hyan was not afraid.

He lost his smile and turned back to his task. His shirts were meticulously folded, as if he creased paper not cloth. Mama had washed and ironed his uniform, and lustrous moons reflected on the toes of his black boots.

"Everything will be okay," he said. "Be a good girl and listen to Baba. Just listen to him."

The room stretched into a universe, and Dua Hyan became a tiny dot. "Okay, Dua Hyan," I said. "I will. I will be a good girl. I will listen to Mama. I will listen to Baba," but he was already too far away to hear me.

A couple of days after Dua Hyan left, two men came into the courtyard as I was gathering eggs. They wore drab sweaters and slacks, like men who rode pistachio-colored mopeds and roamed bookstores.

"Hello," they said brightly. "Is your father home?"

Unfailingly polite, these secret police. No more middle-of-the-night dragging away in one's underwear. No, in those days, they stopped a person in the market, one at either side, and guided him toward the waiting car, or they welcomed both husband and wife to gender-segregated trucks, holding their elbows as they climbed in, and toted the couple away in view of their neighbors. Fear grew more exuberantly in full sunlight.

I cradled three shit-speckled eggs in my hands. Small feathers clung to my shirt. Behind me, the chickens cackled. One of the men was young and had thick, beautiful eyebrows. Self-conscious, I blushed and rubbed my cheek against my shoulder.

"He's inside."

"Tell him to come out."

"Okay."

I shuffled into the house, careful with the eggs. I carried them to my parents' room, where my father was already standing in the doorway.

"Ba—"

"I'll be right out."

He had been waiting. Since the time he had first seen the men outside his window and in the fields; since the spies disguised as farmers riding atop oxen; since the men in the café and at the theater—he had been expecting them. Relief buoyed him. He ran his hands over his face and scratched sleep from his eyes.

Still carrying the eggs, I returned to the men. "He's coming."

"You have your hands full." The younger one smiled. He was so handsome, his eyelashes as thick as mink, and his milky skin and pink lips twisted my stomach.

I looked at the ground and didn't answer.

"Can I help you?" Baba's voice was clear when he stepped out of the house. His hair was neatly combed. He was even wearing socks and shoes with laces.

"Dr. Tsai"—the older man glanced at me—"can we talk inside?"

"Of course," Baba said.

I followed the three of them inside. Baba turned to me: "Make some tea."

Mama and my grandparents had gone to the Owyangs; Ah Zhay was in town, Jie-fu was at work, and Zhee Hyan was at cram school. If I left Baba, I was afraid he would not be here when I returned. If they threatened to take him away again, I'd toss the eggs at them. I'd cling to their arms with all my weight, grip their legs like I had with Dua Hyan when I was little. In the kitchen, my ears throbbed as I filled the kettle and lit the stove. I tried to hear what was happening in the front room, but the conversation was just tense silence broken by muted words.

Then Baba came into the kitchen and touched my shoulder. "Give me some of your school paper." His voice lacked urgency; he might have been entertaining old classmates.

"Yes, Baba. Do you need a pen too?"

In the front room, they sat at the table where my family ate our meals. Baba had set out a small plate of roasted watermelon seeds, which was untouched. I handed the pen and paper to Baba and glanced at the young man. I believed goodness could be read on a person's face. He looked like a good person. My criteria were slim: he had clear skin, a natural color in his cheeks, lush eyelashes, a mouth that turned up naturally at the corners. He smiled at me, showing his teeth, and I allowed a tremor of a smile in return.

"Write: *Honorable Su Ming Guo*," the older man began.

I stepped back and leaned against one of the two chairs set against the wall beneath a large scroll of peonies that my mother had painted. Its knotty wooden arm pressed into the small of my back.

"Start out chatty. Tell him you've been released from prison because the political climate has changed. Tell him about the freedom you have now. Tell him about"—the older man caught my eye—"about how wonderful it is to see your daughter."

At eleven years old, I thought too that I could read evil, like goodness, on a man's face. The older man looked evil: unruly eyebrows, pockmarked skin, wrinkles that cut too deep into his sagging cheeks. A yellowing, bloodshot eye framed his glances at me. I began to chew on the dried skin around my fingernail.

Baba sat on the side of the table facing me. He stared at me for a long time before he began. He wrote with a slow, careful hand; my mother had said he had the calligraphy of an artist.

"Encourage him to come home," the man continued. The younger man picked up the dish of watermelon seeds and tapped it gently, as if searching for a particular one. He put it down without taking anything.

Baba's pen hesitated. "Why?"

"As I told you, your only job is to help us with this one task. We need Mr. Su to come back to Taiwan."

Baba dug his fingers into his hair and pressed his palm to his forehead.

"Take a moment. It takes time to find the right words," the younger one said.

"I can't," Baba said.

The older man sighed and his wide, flat nostrils flared. "That's fine. A desk at our office might be more comfortable to work at."

Baba closed his eyes. He remained still, as if he had not heard either of them. The kettle whistled. I could not move. Both men looked at me expectantly.

"Sister, the water."

I shook my head. My mouth was stiff, my tongue dead against my teeth.

"Sister," the younger one said, "the water is boiling."

I could not move.

"Turn off the kettle," my father said, his eyes still closed; I could have been nothing more than a maid. Unseen, unheard.

I didn't want to listen to any of them, but I was afraid, so I ran to the kitchen and turned off the flame. My hands shook as I took the rag and lifted the kettle from the burner. I poured the water into a teapot and the steam singed my face. I was too careless and water overflowed from the teapot mouth and brought the leaves floating to the top in a clotted mass. I clapped down the lid and carried out the pot and three cups on a tray.

"Now tell him how much you are looking forward to seeing him."

Even the older man's ears were ugly: too small and splotched with brown freckles.

"Baba," I said. The younger man leaned back to allow me to approach the table. I set the tray down with care; even so, tea sloshed from the spout.

"Good girl," the young man said. "What a fortunate father."

"Yes, yes," my father said. "Tea?" Fatigue had crept back into his eyes.

"First, sign it."

Baba paused a moment before he scrawled his name. Exhausted, he put down the pen and his shoulders sagged. The younger man took the page and folded it carefully.

"I apologize, but we can't stay," the older man said. They stood up and thanked my father.

My father walked them to the doorway and watched them leave. When he turned back to the room, I asked him who they were.

"The men from the café."

I was not sure if I believed him. "Why did you have to write that letter?" They had been gone only moments. Steam still rose from the teapot, yet I began to doubt that they had ever been there.

"It was nothing," Baba said, "but don't tell anyone. Don't tell your mother. She'll just worry." He sat at the table. "Sit. Have tea with your Baba." He poured two cups.

"Will they come back?"

"No. They won't. Come sit. Sit with Baba."

I hesitated; I wanted to go to the door and catch a last glimpse of them. Whatever I saw, I would sear the picture into my mind and reassure myself it was true, not a play of light or imagination. Baba's suspicions were not fantasy; we were known.

"Sit."

I dragged myself to the table. Baba smiled and held out his cup. "A toast for us. Drink up," he said. The implied joy in the words did not touch his voice or his smile.

The cup was almost too hot to touch. The leaves had steeped too long and the tea was bitter.

Baba and I shared the secret of the visitors. As he gardened and I stood by, his waiting assistant, he spoke to me about his suspicions in low tones.

"They'd been watching me. No question," he said. "But there had to be someone closer by who had been paying attention for them. How else would the men have known to find just us at home that day? This is what I'm thinking. The nearest telephone is at Little Mouse's store, right? His store is on the road to town. Ah Zhay and Jie-fu had been in town that day. You see what I'm saying?" Baba asked, his fingers deep in the soil.

"You think Ah Zhay called them?" I asked dumbly.

"Keep your voice down." He glanced at the house. "Not your sister. The other one."

I squatted down beside him and answered in a dramatic whisper: "Jie-fu?"

"Yes. Exactly." Baba had fashioned a watering pot out of an old cooking oil jug. He scooped water from it onto the row of slender seedlings.

I considered this. My brother-in-law was funny. He made puns, told me silly jokes, and never snapped at me. Could a man like that possibly be a spy?

"Baba, Jie-fu is nice."

"Of course he is. Those men who came were nice too."

"But Jie-fu is your son-in-law."

"I don't know him and I don't know his family. He's a Mainlander. Mainlanders and Taiwanese will never be friends."

The Mainlanders had come when I was just a toddler. By the time I was old enough to keep a memory, the civil war on the mainland was over, and more than two million Nationalist soldiers and their families had fled to the island. The cities swelled with people. Many of them came to the island owning only what they carried. Fleeing made them orphans and bachelors. However, if not for my family's stories, I wouldn't know the difference. When my mother was wronged in the market or had a tense encounter on the bus, she immediately would point out whether the offending party was Mainlander or Taiwanese. If Jie-fu heard her, she would assure him, "I'm not talking about you."

To me, people were still just people. But I knew that my mother would tell me to not contradict Baba, so I said, "Okay, Baba." But my agreement, laden with doubt, patched together my memory of his sternness with me, a dozen of his other strange behaviors, and the evening at the movie. I suspected that Jie-fu-as-spy was no different from the other imagined dangers skulking at the edges of Baba's world.

"So you agree?" He ladled water into the furrow he'd made.

I hummed. He could take it as he wished.

"I'll watch him too. We'll watch each other."

"Okay." I worried about Su Ming Guo, the man Baba had pleaded with to return home. Baba's letter teased like a succulent delicacy in a trap. But a good girl obeyed. As I'd learned in school, when asked how to be filial, Confucius had said, *Never fail to comply.* I was a good girl.

"This is between you and me. Don't tell your mother."

My answer had the sober weight of a promise. "I won't."

17

"THE TIMES TEST THE YOUTH; the youth create the times. Obey."

"Exterminate the communist bandits!"

"Keep secrets; expose spies!"

"Long live President Chiang!"

I shouted these slogans in the classroom with spit-flecked zeal and found them printed on slips of paper tucked into cookie tins. Our teachers trained us to watch for enemy planes, to listen for betrayals and doubts, and to be good citizens in order to build a strong country.

The government had devised various programs to ensure we were all invested in this giant project called the "Republic of China." The Retired Servicemen Engineering Agency, partially funded by the United States, put old soldiers to work on construction projects, lest waiting for the retaking of the mainland drive them to other kinds of revolution. Through the agency, Jie-fu had begun working on the building of a new hospital in town. He left before dawn every morning and returned just after sunset. His skin turned brown and his arms whittled down to hard muscles.

Though the RSEA was established to occupy the tens of thousands of soldiers who'd come over from the mainland, it also employed civilians. Eager to win back Baba's love, Ah Zhay asked her husband to help Baba get a job. Jie-fu talked to his foreman, and one morning Baba woke up in the dark as well and left with Jie-fu.

Baba had been a doctor. Baba was ill suited to be a construction worker. Beyond the bamboo gates tied with strips of cloth, fluttering warnings that one was entering a work zone, dozens of bare-chested men worked with their stripped shirts hanging from their waistbands and their faces shielded by cone hats. They inched along bamboo scaffolding, lugged buckets of concrete, moved earth with ungainly machines, shouted, cursed, and grimaced. Baba, clad in Jie-fu's pants and shirt—both of which were at least two sizes too big—stood before the foreman. Baba squinted at the sun rising up behind the tarp-and-scaffold-clad skeleton of the hospital. The foreman was curt; he looked Baba up and down and assigned him the job of filling the buckets that came down via pulleys from the upper levels of the building.

I imagine it took, at most, until lunch for Baba to realize that only the camaraderie of one's coworkers made the monotony of such a job bearable. Jie-fu seemed to love the work of pouring concrete, but he also spent half the time (it seemed to Baba) bantering and sharing cigarettes with his friends. He came over to offer one to Baba and asked him how the day was going.

Baba said everything was fine. Jie-fu persisted, telling Baba to let him know if he had any problems. Baba gruffly agreed.

"I can ask the foreman to assign you another job if you don't like this one."

"No need."

"Are you sure? I—"

Baba cut him off with an angry wave and felt Jie-fu's hard stare.

Jie-fu dropped his cigarette into a pail of water and walked away.

What an actor Jie-fu was! Of course, the best informants were the ones who seemed most benign, Baba must have reminded himself, and he wondered how the secret police had approached Jie-fu. Outside the gate? At a restaurant on one of the evenings when a group of the men went for a post-work meal? What bothered Baba most was that Jie-fu seemed so untroubled. He joked around with such ease, as if his betrayal weighed nothing.

The realization was comforting. Now Baba knew how to proceed. He would have to be like his enemy. He would have to smile when he wanted to spit, laugh when he wanted to rage. Baba set about his work with renewed determination. They would see his righteousness in his efficiency. He had once been a doctor, but today he was a man who filled buckets with nails, and he had no reason to not do this with as much care as listening to a man's heart. And when it came time to fight, he would fight.

18

ZHEE HYAN COLLECTED BIRDS.

His reed cages filled the courtyard. Some cages dangled from the eaves; others rested on a little bench he had fashioned from scrap wood. Sometimes, I sat in my room and listened to him talk to them. All the words he no longer spoke to me spilled from his heart: his complaints about his teachers, his crush (it was the peanut vendor's daughter, Ah Lu, as I'd suspected), his concern about the health of one of their bird compatriots.

Thirty-nine birds, most of them various kinds of buntings with brown, yellow, or red breasts and a stern little white stripe above each eye. They spoke to one another in a clash of staccato tweets. Zhee Hyan soothed them with his clicking tongue. One escaped bird sent our whole family into an uproar. First, Zhee Hyan's shouting and flailing around the yard as he tried to capture it drew us all outside in a panic. Then, once he realized it had flown off forever, we spent days carefully tiptoeing around his sadness. "You don't understand," Zhee Hyan said. "That was Brownie. Will he even remember how to feed himself?" I didn't know how he learned to distinguish Brownie from Little Bird from Blossom, but I just nodded in sympathy.

"It's a bird zoo," our grandfather grumbled. Yet he sat among them, smoking the opium pipe his father had passed down to him but which now held tobacco, and basked in their song.

"You are like the last emperor of China," our grandmother said to Zhee Hyan. "I bet he had a room of birds. Only an emperor makes himself ruler of so many animals." She saved the burned rice scrapings from the bottom of the pot for his birds.

"Why do you like birds so much?" I asked.

Zhee Hyan scooped rice into tiny trays that slid in and out of the cages. He moved down the row, cooing to his pets. He even wore a shabby hat, formerly our grandfather's, and he reminded me of a worn old farmer who had forsaken the company of men for more trustworthy creatures.

"I don't know." That had been his answer for most questions recently. His voice had newly settled into a lower pitch and his words slurred softly together. He hushed the birds that fluttered around, alarmed by the intrusion of his hand into their space. "They're pretty."

I giggled. The idea that Zhee Hyan might find anything "pretty" was funny. The birds mostly were brown and plain: perfect for disappearing among the shadows and light of a field. At the market in town, I had seen pretty birds with brilliant colors. These birds were not pretty.

A few times a week, he went out with his net and stalked them in the field behind our house, driving them out with noise. He was not always successful, but he was patient. Every bird in the cage was a trophy. Occasionally, he had even allowed me to come along. I drove the birds out by clanging pots and Zhee Hyan would catch them in a net. He named me godmother of one, and I called it "Coffee." It was the only bird I learned to recognize among the others.

"I think you like catching them," I declared.

"I guess," he mumbled. I wanted to tease him about the soft black hair on his upper lip, but I held back. Mama was not around, but Zhee Hyan might tell, and I didn't want Baba involved. Mama's punishments were short and sharp; Baba made me kneel or hold a bucket of water over my head until my arms began to shake and the water splashed on the ground. My arms would be so sore that I could barely hold a pencil all evening.

The hospital neared completion. Baba had stayed on. He rose every morning and smiled at Jie-fu. He was so friendly, and the atmosphere of the entire house shifted. Mama seemed to even take pleasure in the chopping of vegetables. It was like a fist had unclenched. I didn't bathe for four days and no one said a word until the fourth day, but even then, the scolding ended in laughter as each person embellished the description of my odor ("Your head smells like stinky cabbage!" "No, her head smells like cabbage left in a damp pot for half a year." "A damp pot buried in the outhouse!" "Stop teasing me!"). We were like a government slogan painted on an alley wall: *Harmony of the Family*. At dinner, Baba told anecdotes about work, putting Jie-fu at the center of them, and Jie-fu beamed.

"And the hoisting rope had come loose and the cement bucket started to fall, but this hero"—a nod and grin at Jie-fu—"this hero caught it! Grabbed the rope just as it finally broke free and kept the bucket from knocking out a guy down below."

Another day: "And when the foreman asked who would go down into the hole—mind you, it was so dark I could not even see the bottom—can you guess who volunteered? My son-in-law. No fear at all."

And this: "We heard the cry for two days, but only my son-in-law thought to look at the top of the scaffolding. And there it was: a cat. He carried it down in a sack and we all cheered when it scampered off."

Then, all of a sudden, Baba was back. The Baba I had known, not the one Mama had loved or Ah Zhay had adored, or the one who had charmed us at dinner with silly anecdotes about the construction site. He came home in the middle of the day, globs of concrete stuck to his sandals, hardening on his feet, and speckling his pants. Only my grandparents were home, and my grandmother saw him approach as she tended the garden.

She called his name.

He kept walking, a hungry ghost deaf to the world.

She had a strange feeling seeing her daughter's husband stomp home in the middle of the day with his eyes dull as a dead fish. My grandfather was napping, and she decided to not wake him. She watched Baba go around the house, then stood up and followed him. He went to the pump, rinsed his hands, and dragged water through his hair.

"Son-in-law," she finally called.

He rubbed his hands beneath the water until they turned pink.

"Have you eaten?"

He scraped his fingernails against one another. The water darkened his sleeves.

"I'll fix some food for you. I'll go inside and heat some soup."

He seemed to notice her for the first time and he glumly assented.

She watched him through the kitchen window as she prepared his lunch. Baba sat in my grandfather's smoking chair. Only his hands were clean. He closed his eyes. All around him, Zhee Hyan's birds, agitated, chirped as if they suspected that his dark figure so close meant they would be fed. My grandmother went to the stove. Her grandson had used the word "broken"; reluctantly, she agreed. She stirred the pot. Bubbles broke through the surface, popped, and tiny splatters stung her arm. She could not decide whom she pitied more: my mother or my father.

She had been worried since the day he had shown up out of nowhere, saying nothing about the past decade. She was reminded of the old story of the man who drank the wine of the gods during a game of Go and fell asleep for generations. He had awoken and stumbled down the hill into another world, where children tugged at his long beard and laughed at him. Everyone he knew had died. She shook her head. It was a pitiful situation.

Suddenly, my grandmother looked up. A weighty silence had settled on the day. She went to the window.

All the cage doors were open. A stunned look in his eyes, Baba stood before the empty cages. My grandmother exclaimed and ran outside still holding the spoon.

The bare cages swayed. Not a bird left. She surveyed the courtyard, hoping kindness had ingrained some loyalty into the wild creatures. None remained.

"What have you done?"

Baba shook his head and his eyes filled with hurt.

"Your son's birds!" she cried. She wanted to jostle the fragments inside him until they settled into something like sanity.

"It wasn't right," he said.

"What's the matter with you?"

Who was this man who had come in her son-in-law's stead? This man who ruled the dinner table with his mood, who punished his children like soldiers, who set loose his son's pets. *What was recognition?* she thought. She had recognized his face the day he arrived, but she could not say she knew this man who moved without sense.

The house was quiet the way it was when it was going to rain and the birds nestled together in contented silence. I looked up but the sky was blue. Puzzled, I wheeled my bicycle through the gate. Zhee Hyan kneeled in the dirt in front of the empty cages.

I dropped my bicycle and ran to him. "Zhee Hyan! What happened?"

He refused to speak. Now, he looked not so much like a farmer as a weary old man. Dust dulled his black hair.

"Go inside," my mother ordered me.

Seven of us were in the courtyard, distaste and fear clearing large spaces between us. My grandfather had settled at my homework table and appeared to be leisurely smoking a pipe. Yet it was surely not incidental that he faced away from us, and his gaze traveled through the gate.

"Yes, Mama." I pretended to obey, but squatted in the doorway.

"What's your problem, old man?" Jie-fu snapped. His dark skin, inflamed with rage, appeared copper. Ah Zhay tugged at his arm. "Please, don't."

Jie-fu gestured toward the empty cages. "And this too?" When he turned toward my sister, she flinched. "You didn't see him—kicking the cement bucket, shouting nonsense. Now this?"

Go to Zhee Hyan, I thought. Please, Mama. But Mama didn't go to him. Whatever radiated from his curled figure was so intense that it repelled us. Mama took one step toward Jie-fu, then retreated. "Let's calm down," she said.

"Tell him! Tell your husband!" Jie-fu waved his arms violently. The energy of his frustration strained against his skin, made his muscles taut and his veins bulge; he was a beast ready to strike.

"Don't talk about my father that way!" Ah Zhay cried. She covered her face and turned away from her husband. Her stomach heaved with sobs that sucked the breath from her.

Baba watched the scene like an awkward child in a new classroom. His arms hung at his sides, just slightly away from his body, unnatural, as if he could not puzzle out the position of his limbs. His eyes darted between his anxious wife, his crying daughter, his livid son-in-law, and his indifferent father-in-law. Then he settled on me, the neutral observer. Clarity glittered in his eyes. I saw it. I tried to smile, but had to look away. I wanted to cry.

A deeper silence came over us when Zhee Hyan stumbled to his feet and began pulling down the cages from the eaves. Though the cages were delicate, the clatter as they crashed atop one another was horrific. He swept the rest from the bench. Then he stomped on them. Ah Zhay gasped and began sobbing again. The courtyard filled with the jagged sound of splintering wood. I covered my ears and pleaded with him to stop. Tremors in my throat turned to tears. He slammed his foot down a final time and shouted, "I hate you!"

The ruins lay like brown bones picked clean and trampled. Baba held up a hand. Silence. He offered no reprimand or apology. He pushed his way through the thick sadness between us and disappeared inside, leaving us wordless.

Zhee Hyan picked up a handful of splintered wood and, with an impotent cry, tossed it after him.

19

IN DECEMBER, my mother found Baba another job—this time, cleaning a doctor's office. Perhaps the feel of the medical equipment would dredge up the desire to work again, or sense memory would return ability. My mother was an optimist. Baba, who, after quitting the construction job, had drifted back into long daytime naps and had grown a beard, agreed to my mother's plan with no resistance or enthusiasm.

The night before his first day of work, my mother walked him to the kitchen—where we all washed on the far side, near the back door, using a basin of boiled water and a ladle to rinse—stripped him, and forced him to bathe. On a low stool, he let her wash him. She lathered up his hair, squeezing its thick soapiness between her fingers. He bent his head and covered his eyes and she poured water over him. She scrubbed his back in wide circles, and then urged him to raise his arms. His soapy skin was slippery and a low wave rose from her belly. She slid the loofah over his neck, down his chest. An ache radiated up the sides of her own neck, tightening her jaw and flushing her cheeks. She squatted down before him and looked at his face. A long moment passed before he lifted his gaze. She slid her hand up his thigh and toward his soft, apathetic flesh.

"You're still my husband."

He frowned slightly, his face drawn with guilt.

Her hand was wet and warm. His nostrils flared.

"Do you remember our trip to Alishan?" She smiled gently, but her face felt tight, her skin throbbing. Her mortality suddenly pulsed alongside her desire. Sudden fear of a life of celibacy unsettled her.

His lips still pressed tight, he nodded.

"I missed you," she said.

"I'll do a good job tomorrow."

"I don't care about that." Determination spiked her voice; her touch became more aggressive. He closed his eyes and held his breath.

She didn't know and couldn't have known how the days had churned away for him or how her touch singed his skin. For her, he endured it.

20

BABA BEGAN WORK at Dr. Sun's clinic. The structured days seemed to sort out the broken bits of himself. Just past dawn, we rode to school on our bicycles, and then he continued on to work. There, he greeted patients and prioritized them by ailment. He sorted out the pill cabinet, sterilized syringes, washed rags and bandages and hung them to dry on a rack on the sidewalk out front. Dr. Sun asked my father for his advice, or a second opinion. Sometimes they lunched together, but often my father ate the lunch my mother had prepared, drew the blinds, then napped through the noon siesta with his head on his desk. The afternoon was more of the same until it was time to meet me at the school gate again.

Riding home, he told me about illnesses and diagnoses: the girl with the infected burn on her arm, the woman with shingles, the man with the warts from belly button to groin. At the clinic, the human body became nothing more than another organism, an object. He spoke about the patients dispassionately and had no qualms about referring to menstruation or penises or bowel movements. I preferred this. His focus shifted away from me, and as I pedaled behind him, his voice intermittently washed away by the wind, I could just listen.

The New Year holiday ended, officially, with the Lantern Festival, on the fifteenth day of the first lunar month. My mother and grandmother made fresh sesame paste dumplings, and then we all went to town to watch the launch of the lanterns. I had a pile of new coins—booty from lucky New Year's envelopes from my grandparents and the neighbors—but this, the luminescent paper globes drifting in the black sky, was my favorite part of the holiday. Hundreds of messages carried up to heaven, bobbing slowly like small boats on an inky ocean.

I wrote two secret wishes in small script on my lantern. *I wish I would receive a record player.* Maybe some indulgent kindness would sweep over Mama and she would buy one from her own stash of savings. The other wish I scrawled on the other side: *I wish Baba would be normal.* Ordinary. A father who worked a real job, who drank tea and played mah-jongg with his friends, who, indifferent to his children, cocked his ear to the radio for hours on end. We lit our lanterns, and the heat lifted them into the sky, like hot air balloons, where they floated until they caught fire and fell to the earth as ash.

Dr. Sun's clinic was crowded—mothers held sniffling babies, men clutched newspapers, old women slumped in dazed fatigue—when the woman burst in, jabbing her umbrella like a sword. At first, Baba did not recognize the wife of one of his oldest friends. He had not seen her since before his disappearance.

But he knew her voice when she called him by his full name.

"You bastard! I'll kill you!" Her mouth could barely keep up with the force of her words; spittle foamed on her lips. "Traitor! Snitch!" The clinic fell silent. She banged her umbrella on Baba's desk, knocking over his teacup. Baba stood up so quickly that his chair fell over.

His neck throbbed. "What are you saying?" He glanced over his options. He could run through the examination room door, or perhaps push past her out to the street. Instinctively, he stepped backward and stumbled into a filing cabinet. Perhaps Baba thought his letter would not be delivered, or that Su Ming Guo would ignore Baba's urging to return home, or that Baba would remain ignorant of whatever happened once Su Ming Guo returned from his exile abroad.

But here was Su Ming Guo's wife, shaking her umbrella at the wide-eyed patients. "This man is a spy! A backstabber! An informant!" She turned back to my father. "Twelve years! They've sentenced him to twelve years! Why did you do it? What did they promise you?"

"I don't know what you are talking about," Baba said. He pretended he was the Dr. Tsai of half a year before: a body without heart or brain. He determined to feel nothing.

"You lied to him! He came home because of you!" Her coat was buttoned incorrectly and dark circles weighed down her eyes. Baba noticed how badly her hands shook.

"She's ill," he said plainly to the jury of patients. Somebody hissed in disbelief.

"Coward!"

What defense could he make? Everything she said was true. Yet, as a reflex, he denied it. "I don't know what you are talking about." Everyone heard the pathetic weakness in his voice. A whole chorus of accusing eyes: some bright, some bloodshot, others weeping pus, but all certain of his guilt. "You don't understand," he said.

"Mr. Tsai." Dr. Sun stood in his office doorway.

Baba said, "I don't know her."

"Go home," Dr. Sun said.

Su Ming Guo's wife's hand trembled as she wiped saliva from the corners of her mouth.

"Fire him," she said.

"This is a clinic, not a courtroom." Dr. Sun's voice was sharp. "Mr. Tsai, please go. Take the day off."

Baba grunted out some vague affirmation. He took his lunch tin, his hat, and his coat and slipped out under the glare of all those sick people.

As he pedaled home, the sun melting away the February chill, he thought of killing himself. He could strangle himself. He thought of the aborigine uprisings of his youth, of the hero Mona Rudao who had resisted even under the poison gas canisters of the Japanese. At the end of the siege, many of his men had been found in the forest hanging from trees. Better to die than surrender. Though the word "Savages!" had been splashed across the papers, Baba had found virtue—some deep, honorable machismo—in their deaths. In suicide, he saw the possibility of redemption.

He left his bicycle on the grass and made his way across the rocks to the river. In the distance, a turtle lifted its pointed snout, then dipped back under the surface. The water was slow, deep, brown.

He'd feared drowning once: one night, when soldiers had marched him by water that was already thick with bodies. The gesture was a threat, he realized later. But at that moment, cringing, waiting for the boom of a single gunshot that would drive the line of men—who were wired together at the wrist—into the water, he thought he would also be swallowed up by the dark. At the same time, he couldn't believe the stupidity of the killers: water reveals its evidence. Death floats. The soldiers would shoot only one of the men—the others, lashed to the first, would be dragged in after. He wanted to be the one who was shot. He prayed for it.

But they had kept walking.

He still feared drowning. He crouched, feeling warmth radiating into his soles from the rocks. He was a doctor; surely he could craft a better death, something more elegant. Bloodless.

On the other side of the river, a heron picked something out of the grass and jerked forward on its stalky legs.

He was six months out of prison. He had dreamed of the sky, and then discovered its endlessness a burden. He had imagined his children grown, and found, instead, these flawed creatures running through lives he would have forbidden. He picked up a flat stone and chucked it into the water. It skipped once and disappeared. He hadn't set all this in motion. He threw another stone into the water. The heron lifted its head and cocked an eye at him.

My father walked his bike toward the house. He had sweat through his shirt. He gripped the handlebars to steady his hands. He could not walk fast enough. At the pump in the courtyard, Jie-fu ladled water over his head. He must have seen Baba's shoes stop next to him. He shook the water off his head and warily greeted Baba.

"Stand up," Baba said. His hands, heavy with blood, felt like sledgehammers.

Jie-fu stepped back. Water ran into his eyes and down his neck, soaking his collar. His eyes skimmed around the courtyard—it would be just the two of them now.

"You've been watching me," Baba said. Every finger felt swollen. His fingertips throbbed and he barely noticed the fearful tick of blood in his throat.

"What?" Jie-fu blinked. He didn't wipe his face.

"I want you to leave." Joy followed the demand; he wanted to weep. Finally, he could say what he really felt. Wasn't it everyone's task to root out the enemy? Wasn't he following the government directive?

"I don't understand."

"Leave. Leave today." A good citizen. He had served everyone who had demanded it. Now he would scour away this final rat.

"I don't understand," Jie-fu repeated. He said it like a dare. Baba wondered if the man was pretending his stupidity.

Ah Zhay ran out of the house, her eyes wide and her hair loose. "Baba!" She rushed between her father and husband. "What's going on?"

"Your father told me to leave." Jie-fu's surprise spoiled into anger.

"What did you do? Baba, what did he do?"

"What did I do?" Jie-fu snapped. "He's crazy."

"Baba, he's my husband. If he leaves, I leave too. What did he do?"

"He's been spying on us." Finally, Baba admitted it. The burden slipped away; he felt free. His daughter should know whom she had married.

"Baba, no, he hasn't." Ah Zhay caressed Baba's arm. "Baba, if he leaves, I leave."

Baba didn't have to punch or pound. The steel in his bones entered his words. "Then you leave."

"Baba, I said if he leaves, I have to leave." Ah Zhay scanned Baba's face, waiting for Baba to realize his mistake and all the levels of loss he was enacting. Even when I had rebelled, or Mama had withdrawn, Ah Zhay had been there for our father, coaxing, yearning. She had been his only true ally. One quiet night, not long after Baba's return, I had seen her steal into the courtyard and present to him the pair of glasses she had chosen from the wagon that Mama had dragged to the secondhand market. Her face was expectant; it was a declaration of love. Baba had picked up the glasses, unfolded them and turned them around, then set them back down. "I no longer wear glasses like these," Baba had said, and I noticed how tightly Ah Zhay held them in her fist when she walked back inside.

Now, Baba again refused her love. "Then go. You all go." He could be free of all of them.

Mama's arrival interrupted them. She stumbled off her bicycle, her face swollen with tears, and staggered toward them.

"How could you?" she cried. "You lied." She turned to Ah Zhay. "He told Su Ming Guo it was safe to come home and now they've arrested him."

Baba saw understanding light in my sister's eyes, the gauzy veil whisked away.

"Traitor," she said.

Baba slapped her. The back of his hand on her cheek—so hard that he felt her teeth, so hard that her skin flamed into a scorned symbol that she bore for days.

Jie-fu shoved Baba, who staggered and fell. Baba glared at his foolish family—they didn't appreciate that his decision had been one of loyalty. The soft, soft scrape of the pen on the page as he signed his name—he had saved them all.

Standing over him, Mama whispered, "I don't know you."

I waited at the school gate until the crowd had thinned to just a few students who had stayed to sweep the classrooms and wash the blackboards. I became more worried. I searched for him among the crowds passing by, at the same time anxious that someone would say pityingly, "Are you lost?"

When afternoon darkened to dusk, I realized that my father wasn't coming, so I rode home alone.

The house was eerily quiet. No clanging in the kitchen, or my niece cooing away somewhere. I did not even smell my grandfather's pipe.

"Ma?" I called. I leaned my bike against the wall. A dark figure flickered at the corner of the house. "Hello?"

The figure hissed, "Come here."

I walked over to where Zhee Hyan was crouched out of sight of the door.

"What are you doing?" I expected the trouble was his. If Zhee Hyan was sullen and Baba was in a mood, the clash could send the house into darkness.

His damp hand grabbed my wrist and pulled me down. "Don't go in there. Stay here."

I curled my book bag into my lap and steadied myself against the wall. "What happened?"

He was still in his school uniform, his knees dusty and his shirt cuffs yellowed with sweat. He smelled like the boys at school: iron and dirt and a slight, bitter mildew in his clothes. His breath was sour, as if he hadn't eaten for a long time. "Ah Zhay left." As he recounted the fight, hot streaks of guilt burned my skin. I had brought the paper and pen to Baba. Just like Baba, I also had not refused. I was just a little girl, I told myself. Yet a man sat in jail because of me.

Afraid that Zhee Hyan might suspect me too, I spoke quickly. "Where did they go?"

"Don't know."

"And Grandma and Grandpa?"

"Inside."

I peered around the corner at the house cloaked in quiet blackness. We could have been two wanderers in a remote land happening upon a long-abandoned home.

"But it's dark." My protest came out like a bark.

"I know."

Something in my heart exploded. The men on mopeds had come because of Baba. I had brought the paper and pen only because Baba had asked. Baba had caused all this trouble. My face flushed and my ears throbbed. "I wish he had never come home."

Zhee Hyan flinched. I saw the pain of his missing birds flash quickly over his face, but he answered, "Don't say that."

"I hate him."

"Don't say that." Zhee Hyan, hunched and too tall, looked like a man forced to return to childhood in karmic punishment. "He's still our father." With Dua Hyan gone, Zhee Hyan should have been the one to save us. But he was just a silly boy.

"I'm not going to stay here," I said.

"Don't talk crazy." Zhee Hyan hugged his knees against a blast of wind. The moonlight glistened against the whites of his eyes. He would not look at me.

"This isn't even a family!" I shouted.

"Stop. You're just a dumb girl."

That was enough. I had no one but myself. Zhee Hyan snatched the hem of my skirt when I rose, but I tore it from him and ran to my bike. My heart was beating so fast that blindness laced the edges of my vision. Somehow I scrambled my way onto the seat and pushed off.

I had lost my father when I was two weeks old. I pitied myself, a fatherless girl riding along the black fields, past faraway homes lit like dollhouses. I didn't think about where I would sleep, only that I wanted to go away. I vowed to never go back.

Family.

I decided the word was meaningless, some dream sold to us by storytellers and government men.

1971

21

BY 1971, THE VOCABULARY of the world had changed. Some argue that 1968—the year of the student protests in France and the United States, Poland and Yugoslavia; the year Bobby Kennedy and Martin Luther King Jr. were shot—was the moment that the dictionaries were burned and rewritten, but this claim disregards the change that happens day by day, so incremental that it is invisible to us, like a snail sliming its way across a road. Somehow, we ended up on the other side of that road, in a world of two Germanys, two Vietnams, and two Chinas, one Free and one Red. The Republic of China and the People's Republic of China. I'd heard the battle cry for so long that I didn't even question it. The Nationalist government was stuffing tiny leaflets into tiny caplets for fish to swallow so that mainland fishermen would receive the KMT message along with their dinner. Toys bearing the flag of Free China were tossed into the ocean to be washed up on mainland shores. Armageddon was coming—always approaching, never arriving—in the guise of a showdown between communism and democracy.

I was twenty-four years old, working as a waitress in a restaurant near the university, serving mostly the American GIs who flew in from Jungle Survival School at Clark Air Force Base, northwest of Manila, to their new station at Ching Chuan Kang Air Force Base, in Taichung, Republic of China. Men of every shade with their Levi's and pressed shirts and aviator glasses and shorn hair. Word by word, I transformed my lexicon—

"Here's the skinny," "Foxy!" "How's it hanging?" "She's a piece of work"—learning English from the customers and from the class I took a few mornings a week that was taught by a young, red-haired Mormon man.

The restaurant, the Golden Rooster Garden, was a huge, open-air, shedlike building with a concrete floor that we sprayed down every night. During the summer afternoon thunderstorms, we unrolled the bamboo shades and lashed them to the pillars that held up the roof. People tried to talk over the rain clattering against the bamboo, but thunder was always followed by a moment of silence. The rain streamed in under the shades and streaked across the floor, such a relief from the thick tropical heat that no one minded.

The work was monotonous but fast; the hours passed quickly. I practiced my English as I served tall brown bottles of Taiwan Beer, bowls of soy-sauce-drenched fried noodles seasoned to the American palate, platters of salted shrimp and steamed crabs. At night, I rode home on my scooter with bags of leftovers dangling from the handlebars.

Other words had changed too. "Courtyard" no longer meant what it had when I was a child and chased hens across the banyan-shaded expanse of my grandparents' courtyard. Now it meant a cramped space twenty minutes away, crowded with motor scooters, drying raincoats, a birdcage still littered with seed that had belonged to my niece's long-dead bird. I lived with my sister and her husband and their three children in a house in the South River Veterans Village, where my brother-in-law had received housing for his service in the Nationalist air force. I stayed in the dark back bedroom that had a barred window overlooking the small weedy lot where we burned the neighborhood trash. The front room was paneled in a veneer of laminated wood. A large cross hung in an alcove alongside a mini plastic Christmas tree with tiny colored lights that stayed up year-round. My sister, lying in bed during her tough third pregnancy, had seen an angel hovering above her: a huge blue-faced angel with thick white wings that brushed against the sides of the room. The angel's words matched the blood beating in her ears: *He can save you.* The angel pressed against the mosquito net, mesh tight against its skin like a thousand cracks: *Repent and He will save you.* The voice was so loud that the world collapsed around her. Her fever broke, she went to church, and she had all her children baptized.

Jesus was also how she had reconciled with my mother. They went to church together on Sundays and Bible study on Wednesday evenings.

"Come with us," they urged in bright voices. Sometimes my mother said, more concerned, "Jesus will be good for you. I worry that you haven't found a path. Jesus can show you a path."

"I agree," I said. "Someday, Mama." But I never went. The remaining "sinners" of the family—Baba, me, Jie-fu, and my brothers—agreed on this matter: my mother's conversion had been strange. I found it less about faith than control. However puzzled, Baba treated it with respect and quickly hushed my sarcastic comments. Perhaps Baba guiltily saw himself as the trigger?

In Ah Zhay and Mama's church, everyone was a "sister" or "brother": Sister Chen, Sister Tsai, Brother Zhang, Brother Yu. When it was Ah Zhay's turn to host, they prayed and sang hymns in the living room while the kids played in the alley and I read magazines in my room and listened to the group's long murmurings punctuated by loud "amens." After they were done, I drifted into the room to share little plastic cups of Apple Sidra and munch on flaky Danish butter cookies from a tin. The sisters and brothers cooed over my niece and nephews and told me how wonderful it would be if I came to church too. I nodded, said yes, promised I would make it if I didn't have to work. They were always gone by the time Jie-fu came home, his clothes and hair steeped with spices and grease from his job as a dishwasher at a Szechuan restaurant. He brought food for us in plastic bags tied with pink string and we ate at the round table in the kitchen while Ah Zhay told us about everyone they had prayed for that evening. Every week, they prayed for Baba.

Ah Zhay had also started praying for our brother Zhee Hyan. He lived in a tiny studio in town and worked as a "houseboy" cleaning barracks at the air base. He said the GIs called him "Joey," which was, he said, better than the nicknames they'd given to the two other men who worked with him, "Donald" and "Mickey." Despite their jokes, they were kind to him. They bought whisky for him at the PX and, in return, he took them to "barbershops" and hostess bars.

"You're disgusting," I told him one night as I watched him polishing the handlebars of his motorcycle in the alley outside Ah Zhay's house.

"Why?" He chuckled. He twisted the rag around a finger and buffed a spot.

"Come on. Do they pay you?"

"Who?"

"The GIs. The bars. I don't know. Anyone."

"Well, it's not charity. Being a houseboy"—he crouched and began attending to the front forks—"is not a lucrative job."

"So drive a taxi! Become a mechanic! Do something else!"

He laughed again. "You're so naive. Do you want to meet some Americans?"

"No!" I exclaimed, and hoped it sounded sincerely offended.

"Come on. They're fun. We're going to the beach next weekend. I'll bring you."

"I'm not that kind of girl." I almost wished I was, but my whole being resisted it. I could not trust anything that easy or fun.

"Of course not. You're my sister. They want to meet nice girls. You're a nice girl. The nicest girl." He looked up at me with a placating smile.

I nudged him with my toe. "Stop. Ah Zhay is going to kill you. Corrupting your baby sister."

"What corruption? There's no corruption." He turned back to the bike. "I'm totally innocent."

My parents were concerned about my unmarried status and their nagging soon turned into action.

"Wei, the second son of Uncle Lin, is visiting." As soon as my mother started, I wished I had ignored the telephone. "He's getting a Ph.D. from Berkeley."

My parents had not forgotten how Uncle Lin had sent over Aunty Naomi with money for my mother when Baba was arrested. Aunty Naomi had held the matches when my mother burned the mementos of our life in Taipei.

Because of this, and their long history, Uncle Lin was the only one who had been exempt from Baba's strident ideas about friendship. Uncle Lin had been promoted to surgeon at the hospital in Taipei as the positions formerly held only by Japanese were vacated because of the war. However, like so many things masked under careful labels, he was officially a "research assistant," receiving no pay but prestige. Others envied him, but his wife worked as a Japanese tutor in the homes of rich Taiwanese in order to feed the family. When my father returned, just before the end of the war, he was disappointed to discover what he considered was Uncle Lin's betrayal—in a hushed, almost embarrassed tone, he referred to Uncle Lin as a "collaborator"—but he had not repudiated him as he did other friends.

Uncle Lin's acceptance of the hospital job was emblematic of his more moderate personality—the pragmatism that kept him out of danger when the riots broke out, that kept him from being arrested, that allowed him to prosper when my father was languishing away in a prison. And now his youngest son was earning a Ph.D. in America while Baba's son was cleaning rooms for Americans.

"Really?" I stared at the calendar. May fluttered in the breeze from the fan; somehow, we had made it to July without tearing off the months. "A Ph.D. in what, Mama?"

"In what? How do I know? He goes to Berkeley. I told his parents that they should come visit us. He wants to meet you. Be there at ten on Saturday."

I sighed. She did not ask; she demanded. "How old is he?" I squeezed the receiver between my chin and shoulder and reached toward the calendar; the cord stretched to its full length and I grabbed the two sheets and ripped them off.

"Thirty? Let me see, Ah Zhay was almost ready for school when Aunty Lin had him. Wei must be close to thirty."

"Ma, you aren't setting us up, right?"

Mama clicked her tongue. "Don't be a nitwit. It's just tea."

Despite my mother's denials, I knew this subterfuge too well. One by one, my friends had married similar men, graduate students in America who came back during vacations to look for wives. "Just tea" could turn into an engagement.

"Saturday at ten," she said again.

I sighed. "Right, Mama. Saturday at ten. Just tea."

I would not go. I told myself I would not go, even as I combed out my damp hair, as I swiped astringent on my face, and as I pulled on my jeans. I argued with myself: *But the Lins are driving down from Taipei for this.* The reluctant part of me countered that he was already thirty, too old for my tastes. The whole meeting was a waste of time. Again, I told myself I wouldn't go as I backed my motorcycle out of the courtyard.

The city now abutted my grandfather's land; the old dirt road along which so many visitors had trekked into our lives was sealed with tar and radiated like a stove in the July heat. I arrived with my face shiny and sweat rolling down my arms and between my breasts.

"Here she is!" my mother exclaimed when I entered. Indoors was only marginally cooler than outside. The electric fan mounted on the wall buzzed loudly. Looking unruffled by the long drive, Uncle Lin, his wife, and their son sat on one side of the low coffee table. My parents and grandmother sat in polished cherrywood chairs on the other side. My grandfather was in the corner, bent close to the murmuring television and ignoring us. Baba caught my eye for a moment. His mouth flattened into what a stranger would have read as a grimace but what I knew was a smile. Suddenly, I was eleven again, filial, compliant.

I said my hellos. My mother ushered me over to the remaining chair. I had seen the Lins a few times before, but their son had already been away at college by the time my parents had revived the friendship, and I had never met him. He wore his hair parted on the left side. His mouth was full and solemn. He wore socks and loafers despite the heat and humidity. He had no qualms about looking me over. His eyes traveled from the top of my head to my toes. His bold gaze embarrassed me. I blushed and focused on the gleam of his shoes.

Very quickly, his mother resumed what I suppose had been the earlier conversation topic: singing his praises. He was a Ph.D. student in physics at the University of California, Berkeley. He had received his undergraduate degree from National Taiwan University in Taipei. He spoke four languages fluently. He had a beautiful singing voice. He also had a hidden talent for cooking. I glanced at him. He raised his eyebrows and flared his nostrils, biting back a grin, as his mother broadcast his résumé.

I wondered what my parents would offer about me in return. I had ten toes and could blink my eyes at will. I could speak fluent Mandarin and could read a book. I could walk without stumbling most of the time, and I had very pretty hair.

Instead, my mother told them that I was a talented writer (was she referring to the single junior high essay that had been praised by my teacher?) and an expert homemaker and patient with children (many years of babysitting my niece and nephews). I glanced up once and caught Wei smiling at me. Mutual embarrassment bonded us. I let a smile flicker across my lips. Apparently—my mother claimed—I was also good with numbers (referring, no doubt, to my experience calculating bills for customers at the Golden Rooster).

My grandmother suggested that they leave us and visit a teahouse on the main road that had an air conditioner, a large, growling electrical unit wedged onto a windowsill and dripping condensation. All the parents pretended that this was a natural turn of events, and in a matter of minutes, after my grandmother forcefully clicked off the television and dragged my grandfather away, Wei and I were alone.

"More tea?" I asked.

"Thanks, but it's too hot."

I nodded. "Ah, I know." I went to the refrigerator that was set here, in the front room, near the door, not only because the kitchen lacked space, but also to show off this large, humming, status-laden machine. I found two popsicles in the freezer and gave him one.

He struggled off the paper wrapper and bit awkwardly. His nails were cut too short and the skin at the edges was bright pink.

We nibbled silently. I licked a drop off my wrist. Our parents' caravan had likely reached the teahouse, and they were just pushing back the sliding glass door and stepping into the chilled, damp room, battling the air conditioner's rumble with loud gossip about the two children left at home. I wondered how terrible it would be if I drove Wei to the teahouse and went to meet my friend at the department store. No, I had no choice. I'd have to endure it.

"Do you like California?" My voice startled him. He hurriedly chewed, then licked his lips and wiped his mouth with the back of his hand.

"Yes, quite a bit."

"Do you think you'll ever move back here?"

He shook his head. "There's nothing for me here. The economy is growing—no doubt about it—but despite what the economists say, this is still the Third World."

"Third world?"

"Technically, Third World means nonaligned, and we are, of course, with America, but we're also poor. Half the kids don't wear shoes to school." His voice swelled with something professorial and patronizing. He set the half-eaten popsicle on the table.

Annoyed, I told him he was wrong. "But there are so many factories here. There's a Barbie factory in Taishan. My friend Yi Chin went to work there. She says there're thousands of women working there." He had not lived in Taiwan for five years; he touched down in a Pan Am 747, stepped onto the sweltering tarmac, and lamented the sidewalks splattered with red betel nut spit, the street vendors with their sun-creased necks, the men pedaling tri-wheeled trucks laden with flattened cardboard, the cone-hatted women clearing rubbish from the streets, and the girls clad in long sleeves picking tea leaves. He didn't see the streets clogged with red taxis, the tiled high-rise apartments, and the factories running multiple shifts to keep up twenty-four-hour production.

"Factories are not doctors, scientists, inventors. Nothing original comes from Taiwan. We merely stamp out what others create." He emphasized his point by pounding his fist into his palm.

The popsicle melted onto the torn wrapper; the juice threatened to spill over the edge of the table. I watched its slow creep, fuming at his messiness.

He went on. "Made in Taiwan? It's a joke. Cheap toys, ashtrays, flimsy electronics." He threw his hands up. "Concerts for Bangladesh? You could just as easily put a picture of a dirty-faced Taiwanese orphan in the plea."

I continued eating my popsicle. I refused to let his tone incite me. He tore a piece of tissue from the roll on the table and wiped his forehead.

"In school, you learn the history of China as if it's our own. But we were a Japanese colony for fifty years. Their model colony, in fact. We were as advanced as any city in Europe. Then the Chinese came and treated this place like a temporary campground. Retake the mainland? Treating us like nothing more than a base camp for their final victory. Where is that victory now? The island looks like a shantytown."

"But at the root, we're all Chinese." Twelve years of school had taught me that, day after day.

He frowned. "If we are all Chinese, then why does the KMT send spies to America to watch us? Even in America, even in Berkeley, California, I must watch with whom I speak. Do you have any idea that people are coming together to talk about how we can take our island back? No, you don't, because there are only three television stations, and they are all owned by the government. This is a dictatorship. A dictatorship."

"You're wrong. We just had elections. Some islanders won." A viscous stream of juice trailed over the edge of the table. Smart but oblivious. I'd tell my parents how this careless gesture had revealed everything.

"Local elections. Agree to the rules and they let you play small stakes, just to make you think you have a say. Make your own rules and you go to prison."

Prison. We never said this word. In its place, my mother always held her breath, or found softer euphemisms: *He went away.* Baba had been away. Su Ming Guo had been away and had just recently returned. He'd sent a letter to my father—no doubt monitored—that said he'd forgiven Baba. It was the worst thing he could have said, doubling Baba's guilt.

Wei leaned forward. "Even your father—in prison for what? Ten, eleven years? And why?"

I said softly, "I don't know." I tossed the popsicle stick into the trash.

His eyes narrowed. "You don't know? Don't be coy."

"I really don't know." I kneeled next to the table and carefully lifted up his sticky discarded wrapper. It dripped across the table and floor as I carried it to the garbage. "I don't think we should talk about it."

He settled back and tapped his fingers together in a tent across his belly, signaling the start of the real sermon. "You need to know what your father did. After they broke him, he betrayed Su Ming Guo, but before that . . ." He sat up. "He wasn't arrested just because he spoke out. He was dangerous. He had ideas and, to the KMT, *that* was a crime. My father said he knew how to talk, beautifully, in a way that made people want to listen." His tone softened. "You should see that your father wasn't a bad man. For our fathers, that's why I—" He shook his head. "Oh, never mind."

"Good. Don't say any more." I slid back onto my chair. I inspected my fingernails. The buzzing of the electric fan grew louder. My mother had said Baba was a good man, but the claim slid in among all her other repeated phrases, uttered so often they lost any force. This was the first time I'd heard someone other than my mother call Baba good. But Wei did not know Baba; he knew only stories.

Wei cleared his throat. "In 1947, before the refugees got here, the islanders rose up for their rights. The KMT crushed them. Blood ran in the streets."

"I've never heard that," I rejoined, annoyed by his lie. "Where did you hear that?"

"I could go to prison for even mentioning it." He raised his eyebrow. Was that pride?

I wanted to crush his arrogance. "I don't believe you. I would have heard of it."

"Ask your father."

"That's ridiculous! Something like that, and I never heard of it?"

"Twenty thousand men died. Ask your mother."

I turned my head. I did not want to look at him. Spoiled by his American education. He was pompous. "No. It would be impossible to hide a thing like that. Be quiet."

"I was six years old. I remember that we hid." His voice softened. "They were raping girls. My mother smeared ash on her face. Ask your sister."

"No."

"Ask your brothers."

The first meeting should be light. We should be making small talk about recent events, hobbies, and pet peeves. The conversation had devolved. I would tell my parents how crass he was. I would say only that sentence: *He was crass.* I would not elaborate and let them draw their own conclusions.

"I'm tired." I rose.

"Ask your brothers," he said again.

"I need some air." I stepped around the table and past his chair.

He stood up. He touched my arm, a halfhearted gesture to soothe me. "I'm sorry. Forget it."

I waved him off and went out back, into the garden, and sat in a rusty folding chair. I looked at the furrows that Baba and I had tended years ago, which were gouged along the same paths year after year. My impatience turned into a rage that surprised me, and I found that I couldn't have spoken even if I'd tried. He thought he knew everything. He thought he knew my family, but he could not imagine what our lives had been like. I left him to swelter alone in the house until our parents returned.

That evening, I sat in the alley outside my sister's courtyard, cooling myself with a paper fan. My nephews were tangling and untangling a yellow yo-yo, while my niece leaned against her mother and tried to sidle into our conversation. Mei Mei was fourteen, with the same ear-length haircut her mother and I had been forced to wear as schoolgirls, the same heavy-lidded yearning in her eyes as her mother at that age, and the same deep gold complexion as her father. Her bare legs were marked with fading mosquito bites, and she scratched these as she listened.

"Don't lean on me. It's too hot," my sister snapped.

Mei Mei nuzzled her cheek on her mother's arm. "But, Ma, I love you." She flashed a conspiratorial smile at me. I grinned at her.

"Sweet talker!" Faux exasperation lightened my sister's tone. She asked me about Wei. "I remember him as a cute little boy. His brother and I dressed him up once in Mama's clothes. He was adorable."

"He's obnoxious." I slapped a mosquito, leaving a smudge of blood on my arm.

"Why, Ayi?" Mei Mei still clung to her mother's arm and looked up at me with bright curiosity.

"All he talked about was politics."

"Is he handsome? If he's handsome, it doesn't matter, right?" She smiled.

"Politics? He's really an American now," my sister said.

"He'd have to be a lot better looking to make up for his personality," I said, and Mei Mei giggled. Using Taiwanese, which Mei Mei did not know well, I said to Ah Zhay, "He told me about something else too. About Baba." I remembered how my parents had used Japanese for their private conversations around me; only Ah Zhay and Dua Hyan had been old enough to have learned it in school.

Mei Mei protested. "No fair! No Taiwanese. I want to hear the gossip." She pulled at her mother's arm.

Ah Zhay shrugged her off. "Quiet!" Her mouth tightened. "What did he say?"

I repeated what Wei had said about the massacre, about Baba's part. How he had stood up and been wanted for it.

"Why would he say this?"

"Is it true?" I countered.

Ah Zhay switched back to Mandarin. "Sweetheart, go play at the school."

"Why?"

"Just go. No, wait. Here's some money. Take your brothers for shaved ice." Ah Zhay dropped a stack of coins into Mei Mei's hand. The boys forgot the yo-yo—now a tangle of knotted string—and clamored for the money.

"But I want to stay." Her brow furrowed; she knew she was being excluded from the best parts of the conversation.

I smiled at her and drew on the privilege I had as an aunt—power without the stigma of an authority. "Go, sweetheart," I said.

After the kids ran off, Ah Zhay began again in a low voice, "I don't want to talk about it. But . . ." She sighed. "It started the night you were born. March first. I always remember your birthday because of that. The island was under martial law. I didn't really understand, except it meant we couldn't go outside, and the midwife wasn't coming, so I had to help Baba when you were born."

This I knew. It was family lore: I was born in the upstairs bedroom, at home, with Baba as midwife, Ah Zhay as assistant.

Ah Zhay went on. The Mainlanders were the protesters' first targets because after the Nationalists had taken over from the Japanese, they had been using the island to help support the civil war on the mainland: driving up inflation, causing a rice shortage, exhausting materials that might have been used to rebuild the cities destroyed by the Allied bombing. The Taiwanese were angry. Finally, Ah Zhay said, set off by a gendarme's beating of a street vendor, a young widow selling cigarettes, people took to the streets, protesting, picking fights, challenging passersby on the sidewalks with questions in Taiwanese, beating up those who couldn't answer.

"You have to understand how upset people were. Mama reminded us every night how lucky we were to have rice, because most people didn't. If you have nothing, at the very least you have rice, but people didn't even have that. Meanwhile, people said the KMT were hoarding. They were eating well, throwing parties. Worms eating an apple. Of course people were upset. I'm not saying it was right, but it was what it was."

At that time, some men still wore the Sun Yat-sen suit—it later became infamous as the "Mao suit"—but this identified them as Chinese, so they switched to Western shirts. Wooden Japanese sandals, a relic of colonial life, made a comeback.

"Why?"

"Because only Taiwanese women owned them."

It went on like this for days. The island was in chaos. School was canceled and students took up arms. The governor-general seemed anxious to know what people wanted. Community meetings were convened; people drafted up settlement demands.

"And Baba went?"

"Mama begged him not to go that day. She was sick. They had four kids at home, including a newborn."

"Me."

"Yes, you. I remember they fought about it all morning before he left. Mama cried, and Baba left anyway. All the men who went with him that day later disappeared."

A list of names floated through my mind—women I had heard about growing up, mothers without husbands.

"I don't understand. Wei said there was blood in the streets."

"Soon, the troops came to stop the protesters. Retribution. Even though things were already peaceful when they arrived. I heard the shooting. We didn't go outside for a week. We couldn't even go upstairs, but one day I snuck up there and looked into the street. There was a man, a body. How can you count them? There were no death certificates. Most of the time, there was no body. After Baba was taken away, we were certain he was dead. How would we know? People talk to each other; the story gets stitched together, piece by piece. We weren't the only ones. Su Ming Guo wasn't the only one. You have to assume we weren't unique. There were thousands like us."

"Then Wei was right?"

"I don't know."

A bird dropped a seed that skittered across the roof tiles.

"So, it was like that."

"Don't tell anyone." A well-worn phrase. Down the alley, a scooter rumbled and a woman yelled at her child. The streetlight slowly brightened and cast the alley in an eerie white glow. A mosquito buzzed against my ear and I batted it with my fan. "Don't talk about it," Ah Zhay said again.

"What did the body look like?"

"What?"

"The body you saw in the road." I was tired of not talking. Not talking had brought me—us—here. Silence, not speech, had been the problem.

"It was a man."

Maybe she had imagined it. A story drifts around, and everyone claims to be a witness. "I want to know what you saw. Old or young?"

Ah Zhay looked at her feet and hesitated. "I don't want to talk about it."

"What did he look like? I want to know what you saw."

She sighed. "He—he was on his back. His arm was over his face. His coat was torn and his blood was in the street around him."

She dreamed of the man for years. Not nighttime dreams, pregnant with symbolism, but drifting daydreams, as she wondered what had happened to Baba. She never told our parents, afraid they would be angry that she had gone upstairs. After Baba was taken, she wondered if another girl had pretended not to see our father's body, and had let the soldiers drag him away to an unmarked grave, or to the sea. For years, she uttered apologies under her breath to the fatherless girl.

She looked up at the bugs clicking futilely around the streetlamp; the light, like the chilled glare of a camera flash, made her face ghostly.

"That's just our life," she said.

"Don't say that."

The sound of the returning kids floated down the alley: their sandals slapping against the footbridge that spanned the benjo ditch, their voices layering over one another.

Ah Zhay smacked her knees. "I should make dinner."

After she left, I stared at the chipped stucco on the side of the house next door, whose back bedroom overlooked our end of the alley. Tiny little stars textured the window glass, creating a hazy vision inside. A shadowy figure crossed in front of a blur of light. A temple priest had recently been to the house after the construction of a new room had revealed human bones. He'd exorcised the home, and when the neighbor suggested that he come to our house too, Ah Zhay had scoffed. The city retrieved the remains, and the room was sealed in concrete, followed by a layer of brown-and-white linoleum.

Mei Mei and the boys ran down the alley in a whirlwind of noise and sweat, bug-bitten feet, ashy elbows and skinned knees, floppy hair and sugar-sour breath.

"Ayi, Ayi," they cried in voices that killed reverie.

On Thursday night, Ting Ting—a woman I worked with—and I went to the OK Bar to dance. It was one of a handful clustered within a few blocks that catered to the Americans and boasted grand and insinuating names: the Suzie Wong Club, King's Club, the Paradise Club, the Playboy. The OK Bar was the most innocuous among them—no "hostesses" or women wearing subtle lapel pins that indicated their occupation. A band of local kids played

Rolling Stone covers on a stage lit by red and blue lights. The area in front of the stage was mostly empty: just a few men clutching beer bottles and nodding to the music. Most people stayed outside the halo of the stage lights, lingering in the shadows along the walls and crowding at the bar. Ting Ting and I ordered beers and nursed them. We giggled and feigned misunderstanding whenever men we didn't like tried to talk to us.

Ting Ting was twenty-nine but she could still pass for twenty-five, or even twenty-one. She watched me carefully when we primped for our club nights and commented on the shininess of my hair or the texture of my skin. "Look how old I am," she'd wail, tugging at her eyes or the invisible lines by her mouth. She was determined to be married by thirty. She kept a diary of her exploits, which she showed me one afternoon. She called it her "American Tour": a man from each of the fifty states. By the end, she hoped she would have found a husband. Her colored pencil illustration of a map of the United States, with a third of the states shaded, embarrassed me. I was a virgin, but Ting Ting's candidness made me feel *virginal.* I smiled and handed the book back to her, and she said, "I hope you don't end up like me." I didn't know what to say—I hoped so too. So I just shook my head and said, weakly, "Oh, come on."

The androgynous lead singer, with floppy black hair and hip-hugging white pants, did a fair imitation of Mick Jagger. "I'd be his Marianne Faithfull," Ting Ting murmured. The singer shimmied across the stage with his lips pursed and his chin thrust out. A group of GIs near us snickered. Ting Ting shot them a dirty look. The singer leaped off the stage onto the empty dance floor and writhed into splits. A few women hollered, but his last notes faded into silence.

The stage lights dimmed and music came on over the speakers, coaxing people out to the floor. The singer, ignoring the lukewarm response, picked himself up, still swaggering. The band began dismantling. The beer was already warming my stomach and face, and I suggested we dance.

Ting Ting said she needed a shot of whisky first. "Sweetie," she called at the bartender, who had come to know us, "two shots of whisky."

"I have to work tomorrow," I reminded her.

"Don't be a killjoy. A shot. And then we dance."

It was the same routine. The one shot would lead to a second, and by the third I would be pulling her away from whatever man from whichever of the fifty states who was amused by her sloppy dancing. She would turn on me, accuse me of trying to ruin her fun, and she'd go off, not seen again until she trudged into work the next day, wan and abandoned. We'd done this for months now. I think she judged herself less knowing that a prig like me still found her worthy of friendship.

The bartender raised an eyebrow at me as he handed us our glasses.

"Come on," Ting Ting said to him. "I'm not forcing her."

"Completely by choice," I said. "I want to dance, she wants to drink. So we drink."

"Stop complaining," Ting Ting said. She held up her glass. "Cheers."

One shot led to a second, and soon the music was louder and the colored lights flashing brighter and the room was pulsing in my head. Dancers crowded the floor. Ting Ting had her arms around a short blond man in a purple shirt. I heard him say he was from Minnesota.

Ting Ting winked at me and shouted, "I don't have Minnesota yet!" as they danced away.

A man with dark curly hair leaned over and shouted in my ear, "Your friend left you."

I nodded.

"Me too."

I closed my eyes. Heat throbbed in my cheeks and radiated off the people around us. I opened my eyes and found him watching me. He had large brown eyes and long thick lashes. I closed my eyes again and let the room spin. He introduced himself, shouting, "I'm Sam!" in my ear. It was such a tidy name, and so completely without associations to me. I didn't know if Sam was a nice name or an old-fashioned name. I swayed to the music and softly repeated his name.

"It's hot. Do you want to go outside?"

I nodded. Alcohol always made me reckless. He took my hand and pulled me through the crowd and onto the sidewalk, where, beyond the noise, the world was muffled and the bass still throbbed.

"Ah. Fresh air," he said.

Various couples leaned against motorbikes and pillars, flirting, nuzzling, whispering. The street was still crowded with traffic. On every building, neon signs flashed and buzzed, announcing motels and furniture and jewelry. A man in a coned hat pushed his cart in front of the club and cried, "Stinky tofu!"

The sound of popping oil and odor of fermented tofu turned my stomach. My legs suddenly itched; I felt as if I were suffocating. I unzipped my boots and tugged them off and flexed my bare toes.

"Too hot," I said in English. I began fanning myself, trying to wave away heat and nausea. "Go away," I called to the tofu seller. He muttered and moved on.

"I can take you home. You look sick."

"No," I said, and kneeled next to my abandoned boots.

"Do you want me to find your friend?"

I waved my dissent just as the sickness washed up my throat. Sam squatted down next to me and held back my hair. I threw up again, simultaneously apathetic in my sickness and embarrassed by the stench.

"Let me take you home."

"I am okay," I said. My mouth was sour and tears ran down my face. Slightly more sober, my sense of shame had returned. I thought of how disappointed Mama would be. What if one of her church sisters or brothers saw me? I had become one of those girls who drank too much and acted like a clown in front of Americans. Like Ting Ting.

"Come on." He picked up my boots and helped me to my feet.

I told him, as best I could in my drunken, broken English, that I'd take myself home.

"I can't in good faith let you do that. You'll kill someone. Or yourself. My bike's over there."

The street trembled beside me, but a sort of tunnel vision had set in that muffled the noise of motorbikes and buses to a faraway place, and all I heard was the pressure in my ears and my own voice, pleading with my stomach for calm.

While islanders were content with their bicycles, upon which we managed to pile shopping bags, pets, children, entire three-generation families, the Americans went for old war bikes: Harley 45s, BSAs, and Triumphs. Ting Ting and I had spent hours parsing the significance of each type of bike—what it meant about a man's personality, status, ego. I would tell Ting Ting that Sam had a Harley, and she would tell me how to read the night's events.

Under normal circumstances, I would have tried to be modest and sat sideways, gripping the small bar behind the seat, keeping a polite space between Sam and me. But I was too ill. I collapsed forward, wrapping my arms around his waist, and dropped my head against his warm back. I closed my eyes and let myself relent to the speed of the bike, dipping into the curves and lashed by my windblown hair. So this is what an American smells like, I thought, even as I swallowed against my nausea. Inexplicably, I thought of Wei. *Look at me*, I said to him. *Is this Third World? Aren't you impressed?*

"Where are we going?" Sam shouted.

I called out directions with my eyes closed. I didn't have to look in order to tell him to turn at the dumpling stand, then at the shoe repair shop, then finally at the kindergarten with the plaster giraffe grazing against the mural. As his bike growled into the tiny alley-maze of my neighborhood, I suddenly realized what trouble morning would bring. Everyone from the main street to our dead end would hear the bike, arriving so late, so clearly American, and so obviously me.

He cut the motor and I hopped off. I mumbled thanks, too ashamed to look him in the eye, and hoped he'd make a quiet, subtle exit. The cooling engine ticked, almost keeping time with the crickets sawing away unseen in the dark. He wished me well, and I acknowledged him with a nod and a silent desire that he'd disappear. I waited behind the courtyard door until the sound of his bike faded, then I trudged to my room, where I curled up in my clothes, my arms slipped between the cool pillowcase and the cooler bamboo mat.

The sun never came into that back bedroom. The air base wall, the positioning of the house, and the bars over the glass all conspired against sunshine, so I woke according to clock alarms, noise in the front room, and, today, my sister screaming over me.

The stench of alcohol and smoke sheened across my skin and hung in my clothes. I turned away from her barrage of "hell," "Jesus," and "shame" and buried my face in my pillow. The room was still spinning and her voice slammed against my tender ears. Like a dream, she left the room, and I slipped back into a half-drunk reverie.

My memory was a line of punctuation and no continuous prose. Punctuation: Sam (was that his name? I could barely remember) looming over me; punctuation: the dark heat of the sidewalk, sheltered by the overhanging second floor of the bar, light glinting off rear lights and handlebars and baskets; punctuation: the rush of speeding through the streets cutting the summer heat. I barely recalled coming into the house.

Among those too was some vaguely articulated sense that he had been attractive. I had ridden home with my breasts pressed to his warm back. At the thought, lightness turned in my chest.

But now that I was awake, the illness returned. Hunched over, I ran to the bathroom. As I knelt in front of the toilet, my sister came to the doorway.

"I called Mama. What were you thinking? Don't you care about face at all? And was he American? An American? The only kind of woman who talks to Americans is a whore!"

I was too weak to argue. I soothed my hot skin against the cool bathtub.

"You couldn't have taken a taxi? Or walked? You have no self-respect."

"Thanks," I said. "Well, look, congratulations. Your sister is a whore."

She glared at me and disappeared.

I fell asleep against the bathtub and woke again to the bleary vision of my mother standing now with my sister in the doorway and muttering about the devil inside me. I closed my eyes again. Behind my dreamless sleep, I heard their prayers in the front room. Perhaps that angel my sister had seen had merely been a drunken hallucination, its warnings the utterances of overzealous family members in another room. When the shifting light woke me again, I found Mei Mei there, worry on her face. She whispered, "I need to use the bathroom," as if it were a betrayal.

I hauled myself up. I shook my head. I wanted to tell her I was okay, but I was too ill to open my mouth.

"I'm sorry," she whispered as I dragged myself past her. I crept out without glancing down the hall. I heard my mother say, "She's up," and the prayers began anew.

22

THEIR PRAYERS DID NO GOOD. Despite the vow to never drink again, I was just as unrepentant the next few days as I'd been that first sick morning. I did not speak to my sister except to tell her when I'd be home from work, or to ask where she had put the detergent. I did not want to see my mother, but on Saturday I went for dinner because even my mother's assertion that evil spirits had taken hold of me could not kill my filial guilt.

In the courtyard, the late-afternoon sun fell through the banyan as it had all of my life, and for a moment, nostalgia flashed through me as I remembered those painful afternoons of finishing homework in the dwindling light. Baba sat at the table that was now marked with thousands of pencil imprints in its soft wood. A pack of cigarettes and a red plastic lighter lay before him. He tapped his fingers against a jar thick with tea leaves and diluted tea.

I rolled my bike in and said hello, trying to hide my sheepishness.

"Come," he said.

I told him I wanted to say hello to my grandparents first.

"Come."

I nudged down the kickstand. Over the years, I'd developed immunity to my mother's hysterics, and even my father's explosions followed a familiar, if unpleasant, arc. Therefore, his measured tone scared me.

I sat across from him and waited for him to speak. If he had known how his calm frightened me, he wouldn't have bothered with yelling throughout my adolescence.

He looked directly into my eyes. His cheek pulsed; he was clenching his jaw. "How are you feeling?"

I could not tell if this was his idea of humor. "Fine, Baba."

"Your mother has said everything we need to say, so I won't repeat it."

The surface of the table, upon which I now concentrated my gaze, was a palimpsest of my childhood: word upon word, figure upon figure. I dug my nail into a fleck of bare wood and scratched at the peeling paint.

He stared toward the gate, his jaw hard, the creases by his mouth deep and placid. "Wei is in Taiwan for another month. You should spend more time with him."

"Okay, Baba."

"If he wants to go out, you go. No more bars, no more Americans."

I glanced at him. He was bathed in a familiar sweet, ugly smell of nicotine that reminded me of the men, dressed in white tank tops and shorts, who casually draped themselves on scooters at the side of the road while they blustered and chewed betel nut. The lost look in his eyes, as if he carried at every moment a wide and menacing world in his sight, had died over the years to a sculptured stillness. I was eleven years old again, being ordered to memorize my multiplication tables, and I could not say no. Baba picked up the pack of cigarettes and pulled one out.

Lightly clenching it in his mouth, he said, "That's it."

He clicked the lighter and I was dismissed.

Wei called me a few days later. He borrowed his father's car and drove down from Taipei. This time, I waited at my sister's house in the veterans village, and I wondered what he thought as he made his way through the laundry-strung alleys, kicking away dried cat turds and bits of loose paper that had not yet been swept up by a conscientious grandmother. He called through the screen door. I saw him—glowing in the sunlight, all slick-combed hair and sweat-glistening skin—before he saw me. His clothes were fashionable, but decidedly American—the colors and cuts slightly off. I felt a twinge of pity. I wondered if he felt like a stranger here in Taiwan, the place that should have been home.

Knowing he was too light-blinded to clearly see inside, I let him stare into the darkness for a moment before I returned his greeting.

When I nudged open the sticky door, he smiled and asked, "Is your sister here? I haven't seen her since I was a kid."

"She's out," I said. I locked the door.

"Let's make a fresh start." He smiled—a self-conscious and almost silly grin—and I noticed how uniform his teeth were. "Hi, my name is Lin Wei. I'm pleased to meet you." He offered his hand. I caught myself smiling and reminded myself: One date. This is punishment, not fun.

I took his hand. "Sure. Nice to meet you."

"No politics today, I promise."

"Swear." I pretended a searching look from the corner of my eye, and realized I had learned more from Ting Ting than I'd thought.

He held up his hand. "I swear."

We went to Sun Moon Lake, an obligatory tourist destination and a terrible choice on a sweltering summer day. The road to the lake was winding and rough past banana and orange groves and fields of pineapples. We rattled along with the windows down, no comfort coming from the hot wind blasting into the car. I'd spent all my summers in this heat, but I couldn't stop complaining about it.

"Berkeley has mild summers," he said.

For an hour, I'd managed to forget the reason for the trip, the weight bearing down on both sides, the hope from both our families that Wei would leave here in a month with a fiancée, but his comment reminded me.

"I'm just saying," he said to my silence. "As a comparison."

The lake came into view. "I've actually never been here," I said. I stuck my hand out the window and batted at the wind.

"You should see Lake Tahoe."

"Where's that?"

"It's on the border between California and Nevada. You've never seen water that blue."

"Oh." I offered the only piece of information I knew about Nevada. "My English teacher is from Nevada." I grabbed the leather strap above the door and gritted my teeth as we jerked over a series of potholes.

"Prostitution is legal there." He kept his eyes on the road, both hands on the wheel, a model driver.

I looked back at the lake growing closer and closer. "Oh." I didn't understand why he had mentioned such an awkward topic. I hoped he wondered the same.

Ahead, parallel to the lakeshore, a line of colorful stands bordered the road.

"I heard there is a good meat dumpling here," Wei said as he pulled over suddenly and lurched to a stop.

He was cheap also. I tried to be more generous and reframed my assessment: he was *frugal*. A graduate student in America, he most likely had become accustomed to living on a slim budget. That was the only explanation for our march across the road shimmering with so much heat that I felt my shoes stick, the explanation for the pink umbrella-shaded cart where an aunty said coarsely, "How many bowls?" and our subsequent squatting on the red plastic stools by the rickety folding table as we waited.

I offered Wei a tissue and we both blotted the sweat from our faces.

"I get cravings for this in California. There's no place like Nantou for this." Nostalgia numbed his gaze. I noticed tissue lint stuck to his forehead.

"Excuse me." I reached over and brushed it off, which sent an immediate blush up his cheeks. He reflexively reached up and swiped at his forehead again.

I looked over at the lake, reflecting the deep, rich green forest around it. Haze swathed the hills: Chinese watercolor paintings, I realized, were a genre of realism. A dock, ending in a pavilion, jutted into the water where people got on and off boats. A hotel and bus station ensured that the lakeshore was crowded. Could I marry this man, bumbling despite his spirited political pronouncements and apparent ego? I allowed myself a quick look at him out of the corner of my eye. I noticed his strong eyebrows, his clear eyes the color of tea, his wide, full lips. Today, he was almost charming. What did a young professor's wife do? Would Americans be kind to a waitress from Taiwan with halting English?

The aunty plunked the bowls down in front of us.

Hot dumplings on a hot day. I curbed my annoyance.

He ate with elegance—none of the slurping and sighing I would have heard from my brothers. I bit through the gelatinous skin and the steam rising from the meat and mushrooms scalded my tongue; I huffed the pain away. Wei wiped his forehead with the crumpled tissue, then touched it again with a self-consciousness that was almost sweet.

My grandfather had told me about the aborigine uprisings that had begun soon after the Japanese took over the island. The Japanese had adopted the American strategies for dealing with native peoples: reservations and decimation. For the first thirty or so years of the colony, the Japanese and the aborigine tribes traded horrors that stained the front pages of the newspapers: surprise attacks followed by beheadings at school events, poison gas bombings, hangings, burnings. Even as my grandfather narrowed his eyes and mimicked what he claimed were authentic battle cries, his expression betrayed a sense of irony that I read as sympathy. Today, the violence had ebbed away to nothing more than innocuous places similar to what we found along the lake: little shops built to look like authentic tribal homes where native people in native dress sold native weavings and beadwork, as well as cheap trinkets such as key chains cut from leather in the shape of the island or clay whistles molded like pipa fruit. I ran my fingers along a skirt of woven red and yellow thread. People who bought such things did not wear them. They tacked them to the walls as "folk art," or tucked them into drawers to be pulled out years hence when one wanted to reminisce about a particularly charming excursion.

"Interested?" Wei asked.

Glancing at the clerk, who wore a similar skirt as well as a woven head-band around her thick black hair, I told him in a low voice, "It's beautiful, but not something I would wear."

The clerk called across the shop, "A performance is starting in five minutes. Right outside."

Wei picked up a bottle of honey wine, marketed as a native specialty: "For the show." I winced with nausea at the sight.

We sat outside, shielding our eyes with our hands, as music howled out of a portable record player, and shirtless men performed a desultory dance before a small crowd of wilting tourists, many of them GIs, cooling themselves with leaf fans recently purchased from another shop. The dance ended to a smattering of halfhearted, heat-exhausted clapping. Wei tossed some coins into the tip basket, and then we caught a boat back to the other side of the lake, where we had parked. There, we wandered along the shore to a shaded rock. Wei offered me wine, but I told him I didn't drink. He unscrewed the cap and took a swig.

The drive to the lake had taken so much time that we felt compelled to sit there together even when many painful silent minutes had passed and I became too aware of the quiet to even sniff.

Purgatory on a rock—surely this erased my misbehavior. I had said yes to Wei's invitation. I had ridden hours in a car through the heat, made conversation, smiled. Because of our families' friendship, I knew I'd be compelled to see Wei for years. I had to be nice. I wondered what Ting Ting would say about him. "Bookworm," she'd surely sniff. "Good-looking but a bore." I defended him against her imagined accusations: *He's smart; he has opinions. Those are good qualities.*

Thick clouds gathered for the usual afternoon thunderstorm. Across the lake, a little boat appeared to redouble its efforts to return to the dock. However, people still roamed among the shops, holding concern at bay until actual rain touched their skin. I hoped the weather would free me.

"We should get back," I said.

Before we reached the car, the storm began—in typical island fashion—without prelude: a sudden lukewarm downpour. I shrieked as our walk turned to a jog. My cloth sandals began bleeding dye. Completely soaked, we collapsed onto the vinyl seats.

I smiled.

He reached over and swiped water off my cheek. His dripping hair was plastered to his forehead. I noticed the fine texture of his skin.

The honey wine on his breath was sweet. His gaze drifted around my face, as if he was carefully inspecting each feature in turn, mystified by a newly discovered creature. He gently tucked my hair behind my ear. My scared heart stretched and pushed against my ribs; I felt its beat throughout my body.

I waited for an utterance—*You're beautiful*—or for him to kiss me. Instead, he nodded slightly—an answer to an imagined question—and said we should go.

"Yes, it's that time." I fiddled with my seat belt so that he would not see the blush flooding my face.

We were far away from the lake when the pounding in my chest finally subsided.

23

MY FATHER ASKED ME to go to Taipei with him and told me not to tell my mother. Curious, on my next day off, I met him at the Taichung Railway Station. He stood in front of the gates, aloof to the taxi drivers who asked him again and again where he was going. He wore a white button-down shirt—ubiquitous pack of cigarettes in the breast pocket—and black slacks. He carried food in a little tote bag. He had already purchased our tickets.

We waited on the platform among men hawking saliva, and old women sitting among their stained, worn cloth bags, and mothers with babies strapped to their backs and bundles of fruit tied haphazardly with string into a contraption that could be carried in one hand. Baba lit a cigarette and paced, flicking his ash onto the tracks.

"Did you notice I didn't ask where we are going?" I had done him a favor by going on a date with Wei, and I was doing him a second favor with my complicity in his mysterious day trip. His debt made me feel free to be pushy, even a little mean.

He glared at me and continued pacing. His smoking was a meditative act.

I sat on a bench, determined to ignore him. I would be the good daughter and not speak until spoken to.

The train attendant, who pushed her tea cart down the aisle, offering her wares in a sweet voice that called to mind the ideal woman—elegant and professional, yet soft and delicate—must have been perplexed at the two of us, who stared straight ahead and ignored her pitch even when she paused beside our seats and asked, "Tea? Snacks?"

Baba's silence was a trigger. I saw him slipping down into the layers of his mind. He had the stoned stare he used to get years earlier when he lost track of the year, the place, us. After that, only the most nonsensical things made sense to him. I had the absurd thought that he was kidnapping me. I'd heard rumors that in rural places, desperate parents sometimes trapped unsuspecting men to be grooms to their dead daughters in ghost weddings. Perhaps I'd be met at the Taipei station by a cavalcade of robed men and women who'd carry me off in a palanquin to a place where I'd eat sweets with the dead and exchange vows with a stuffed-paper version of a man who was already rotting in his grave.

As the train left the station at Panchiao, closing in on Taipei, I couldn't stand it any longer.

"Where are we going?" I demanded.

My father blinked. He seemed to be mesmerized by the permed hair of the woman in front of us.

"I won't get off this train unless you tell me."

I was not even sure he heard me. I rolled my eyes and stared at the window, black in the lightless tunnel. I should have pleaded sick when he called the night before. He would drag me into some scheme. Three hours on a train, I was already a coconspirator.

The train pulled into Taipei. Baba stood up and joined the slow shuffle of passengers to the door. I stayed seated. He called my bluff and didn't turn around to check if I would follow. Embarking passengers started to push their way on before the car was fully emptied, bringing new baskets, bags, bundles smelling of the hot summer day: fruit going soft and over-sweet, train smoke, exhaustion and hunger.

"This is my seat," a somber little man with bloodhound eyes said. He held out his ticket as evidence.

I sighed and glanced out. My father waited patiently on the platform. I banged on the window. He did not look at me. I grabbed my purse, pushed past the people lifting their packages onto the overhead racks, and joined him as the station intercom played "Auld Lang Syne" to announce the train's departure.

I had not been to Taipei since my mother carried me out of the city as a baby. Even though it was summer, the sky was gray. Everything seemed doused in drab olive. The streets were a chaos of military trucks, taxis, cars, buses, pedicabs, and bicycles moving at cross-purposes. Baba pulled me through the people milling around the front of the station and flagged down a pedicab. The canopy was pushed back, and torn pieces hung down from the folds. Red paint flaked off the bike. The driver wore plastic sandals. As we moved through the traffic, the rhythm of the driver's callused feet mesmerized me. Baba elbowed me. The buildings rose around us: four, six, eight, ten stories high, each window boasting a treacherously balanced air-conditioning unit. On the sidewalks, pedestrians quickly avoided intermittent obstacles: a shoe shiner, a man chiseling stamps at a rickety little table, a woman with a face white with talcum squatting on a tiny stool as another deftly threaded off her facial hair with a piece of floss held taut between teeth and fingers. We moved away from downtown, past a shanty village of one-story buildings where women tended charcoal stoves out on the street and others waited for water from the communal faucet.

"We lived there," Baba said as we rolled by a Japanese-style house flashing like a zoetrope through a fence. I saw topiary, the pale figure of a person stepping off the porch in the stuttering motion of an old film. I craned my neck to keep watching. Baba didn't.

We kept going, up the wide boulevard shaded by trees planted in the median, past the looming Grand Hotel, built where the main Shinto shrine of the Japanese era had once stood and now owned by Madame Chiang and in the midst of expansion. Rumors claimed that secret air-raid tunnels that could hold ten thousand people ran beneath the hill.

Soon downtown was behind us, and the hills of Yangmingshan, formerly Grass Mountain—damp, luminous, and green—rolled through the skyline ahead.

We passed the Generalissimo's Shilin estate, but all we could see was the tall row of palms, their trunks hard as concrete, that lined the drive. Finally, we turned off the main road and rattled down an alley where homes sat behind metal courtyard gates.

Breathing hard, the driver stopped and wiped his forehead with a rag he pulled from his back pocket. We hopped off and my father paid him. The driver took a moment to catch his breath before he left.

It was early afternoon, Tuesday. The alley was quiet. Here, up the hill, things were damp and the air smelled of the sulfur springs on the mountain, and vines tangled around the walls and gates. Banyan trees dripped roots over us.

"Well?" I asked.

Baba walked across the street and sat on a small stone border surrounding a tree.

"Come eat," he said. "You must be hungry."

He pulled out a rice dumpling wrapped in bamboo leaves and string and gestured with it at me.

The non sequitur was insanity. He acted as if we were picnicking.

I crossed my arms. "I'm not hungry."

Baba shrugged and unwrapped the dumpling. He took careful bites, like a schoolboy afraid to make a mess.

At the cross street at the end of the alley, a woman gripping a parasol and dragging a rolling wire cart of groceries glanced at us as she passed.

"Baba, what are we doing?"

"We're waiting. Come sit next to me."

I relented. "What are we waiting for?" I could sense he was thawing. Reaching our destination seemed to have buoyed him.

He jerked his chin toward the house across the alley. "Su Ming Guo."

My stomach clenched. Peering down a stereoscope of memory, I saw the two secret police who had come to our house the day my father wrote the letter. One ugly, one handsome, two sidekicks in a terrifying dark comedy.

I had not realized that Baba had held it in his mind for so long.

"He came home last year." I remembered the letter Su Ming Guo had sent, and the line my mother had repeated to my sister, who then repeated it to me: *My friend, I forgive you.* My father had wept, but my mother thought it was a lie.

"Have you been here before?" Sometimes, when my mother was at church all day, my father was nowhere to be found. Had he been slipping off to Taipei for a year now?

"Just a few times."

Did they have an appointment or did he just sit here, eating his lunch and staring at the man's front door? Did they speak?

"He's really forgiven you?"

Baba cringed. I had watched him sign the letter that brought Su Ming Guo home to be arrested. Had he forgotten how I'd been his accomplice, serving tea to the secret police?

"His wife won't let me see him."

As I feared, he sat outside their door and waited, hour upon hour, uninvited guest, spy.

"Baba, let's go home."

"No!" Hands shaking, appetite chased away by anger, he hurriedly squeezed the damp leaves over his uneaten rice and dropped it into his bag. "I asked you to come as a favor. This is my errand. You leave. I'll stay."

I closed my eyes and tried to calm myself.

"I was the only one he would have trusted. I was his closest friend," Baba said. "I was the only one who could have done what I did."

Su Ming Guo was nothing more than a name to me. Three syllables I heard only on the worst days of my life. To Baba, the name had a history, memory, intimacy. In a way that I could not imagine, the name was a person.

"I'll stay." And then I'd tell my mother what we had done. But that would not stop his next trip. He was a blinded man: he could not see others' frowns, their flailing arms reaching out to stop him. Dragged by his heart, he bumbled along.

We waited. I found a stick and began carefully chipping away the dirt around a half-buried stone near my feet. I thought about Wei. Maybe I could call him and his neatly combed hair and reasonable voice would convince Baba to leave. The whole Lin family could gather around, urging and coaxing like police waiting beneath a man crying on a sixth-floor ledge. But that would surely draw Su Ming Guo out of the house. Thinking of Wei made me think of Sam, whose face I could barely remember. I wondered if I'd ever see him again. Or had he moved on to the next young, drunk woman? I felt a little slighted that he had never stopped by the next day to check on me.

Suddenly, the gate squealed. A man in a hat stepped through. My father straightened his spine. My stick froze, wedged between rock and brick. The man nodded at us, then paused to blow his nose with a crumpled handkerchief. He stuffed it into his pocket and turned back to the gate. His key ring clanked noisily against the metal.

"Baba," I whispered, "let's go. Don't bother him."

My father touched my knee to silence me and stood up. He strode toward Mr. Su with intention that could be mistaken, from afar, for menace. I couldn't help but call, "Ba!"

My voice startled Mr. Su, who immediately turned around. I couldn't see his eyes under the shadow of the hat, but I could see his mouth go slack in surprise and fear.

"Who are you?" His voice wavered. He sniffed.

Baba reached out his hands. "Please, my friend."

Mr. Su pressed himself against the gate and his heels caught on the hem of his pants. His eyes flashed toward me, sunlight catching the whites for a moment.

"Who are you?"

Baba stood right before him, entering a space that should have been saved for lovers, or strangers in a packed crowd. But the alley unfolded empty behind them.

"Baba, come here."

Baba gestured at me without looking, the kind of hand flick one might give to a dog to urge it to stay.

"Ah. It's you," Mr. Su said. Relief and annoyance replaced fear. He moved slightly away from the gate, which forced Baba to take a step back. "My wife mentioned you had come."

"She did?" I cringed at the boyish hopefulness in Baba's voice. "She sent me away. I told her you'd want to see me."

"Who is that?"

"My daughter. Did you greet Uncle Su?" My father spoke to me like I was a schoolgirl, and I responded automatically.

"Hello, Uncle Su."

"The youngest? The one Li Min was carrying when—" The last time he saw my mother must have been before all the trouble, when I was just an idea inside of a swollen belly.

I nodded.

"My wife will be home soon," Uncle Su said. "I was going to see the doctor, but I can wait. Let's go before my wife comes home." He pushed past my father.

Baba reacted the same way I did: for a moment, neither of us could move. We could not believe Su Ming Guo had decided to speak to us.

In the brightly lit coffee shop, I was able to finally see Su Ming Guo's face and I was surprised that such a plain man had been the focus of so much of our worry. His eyes were very narrow and half-moons of flesh sagged beneath each one. His lips were an odd purple shade. The hat had obscured a circle of baldness amid a U of thick gray hair. The heroes of revolution did not wear berets or belts of ammunition: they were stooped, middle-aged men with yellowed collars and nicotine-stained teeth.

I came back from the counter with pastries filled with cream and slid in beside Baba.

"Please, eat," I invited. They acknowledged me with a nod and continued talking.

Their conversation was just as pedestrian as Uncle Su's appearance: wives, kids, grandkids, what to do with one's free time. Every once in a while, he would pull his dingy handkerchief from his pocket and wipe his nose.

He seemed to be free of the obsessions that cycled through my father. However, I noticed Uncle Su did not show his teeth when he smiled.

"They told me I wouldn't see my children again," Baba said. "I tried to write in such a way that you would know it was not my voice. Didn't you sense it?"

Without lifting his head, Uncle Su looked up at Baba from under his lids. Nothing moved but his eyes, the light sliding over his damp, dark irises.

"I also had children," he said.

I wanted to leave. The café lights were obscenely bright, and the orange plastic tray beneath the untouched pastries was garish. Uncle Su's hands wrapped around his coffee cup so tight and still that they seemed like one object.

"I had been there already for eleven years," Baba said without energy. In the coffee shop glare, amid the students who had just come out of the nearby high school, and the other patrons who mysteriously had no work this Tuesday, intensity was masked beneath ellipses and vagueness. Spies, as everything from posters to gum wrappers to movie stubs warned us, were everywhere. It was our national duty to watch for suspicious behavior, to report unsavory words. Everyone in the café—the girl in the red-and-white-striped miniskirt pointing to the cakes behind the glass, the lanky boy with the American flag patch sewn onto his school bag, the young women with shopping bags piled on the seats beside them—they all could be spies. Even the old friend sitting before you.

Uncle Su rolled up a sleeve, exposing his wrist and forearm, and reached across the table. The skin was puckered and brown in places, scars like sunbursts and welts.

"This is only my arm."

"These mistakes—they were of the times. The past," Baba stuttered, his tone pleading with Uncle Su to believe him. The past. The past was dead, gone, irrelevant. His desperation made my chest tighten with pity.

Uncle Su wiped his nose. "I have given you a chance to speak, despite my wife's objections. Your burden is your own."

I lightly touched Baba's arm, felt his elbow twist beneath his sleeve.

"Please do not come see me again," Uncle Su said. "I have nothing else to say to you."

24

TWO WEEKS LATER, the streets were filled with smoke as the Festival of the Hungry Ghost began. Folding card tables covered in food and incense to honor our ancestors suddenly appeared on the sidewalks. Women stood over metal barrels and burned hell notes for the dead. Even my boss at the Golden Rooster put out a table: a fat and stinky durian, pyramids of steamed buns, bowls of chow mein and steamed shrimp, and a deep-fried fish on a platter. For a month, the world was thrust into danger as the door to the underworld opened and ghosts were free to roam among us. The living had to appease them with food, lest they cause harm. Swimming and traveling took on special dangers, and we were all careful of theft, of accidents, of arguments. Ah Zhay and Mama condemned the holiday as pagan and refused to take any part. Even though I knew it was superstition—just a way to urge the living to remember the dead—I still took care around water and while driving.

The Golden Rooster Garden was busier than usual, bright with the sound of clinking beer glasses and tapping chopsticks and male laughter. The weather report predicted a typhoon by the next day, and perhaps the Americans wanted to eat their fill before they were restricted to dining at the base. Already, the wind had blown out the heat and the bamboo blinds clattered against their moorings. I checked in with my boss and headed to the floor to take orders.

Ting Ting was scheduled to come in when I did, but I didn't see her. I asked another waitress, Yi Hua, what she knew.

"Sick. You know Ting Ting."

Another hangover, though she usually was able to drag herself to work. We hadn't been out together since the night I met Sam, but she had come in a few mornings since then winking about her previous night's exploits.

In the rush of the next hour, I forgot about her as I moved between table and kitchen in a flow that seemed more muscle memory than work. Tables of men ate, paid, left, replaced by more tables of men. The wind occasionally rose up, slamming the blinds and silencing the restaurant for a moment. My boss brought in the food he'd set out for the ghosts and called me over to help carry in the table.

As we were folding the legs, Ting Ting rolled up on her scooter, her hair tucked into her collar to keep it from whipping her face.

"Hey, Boss," she said. She nodded at me. She looked great: cheeks flushed, hair shiny.

"Feeling better?" he asked. He shook his head and barked at me to lift the other side of the table.

I raised an eyebrow at her as she followed us inside. She smiled.

"I'm going to fire you," our boss said, as he had said a dozen times before.

"I'm sorry," Ting Ting said. "I was really ill."

Our boss grunted his disbelief, but we knew he'd never fire her. Ting Ting was too pretty. When she wasn't there, customers asked for her.

"I'll be on time the rest of this week, I promise."

"And next week?"

"Next week too."

"Who raised you? You act like a girl, not a woman."

Ting Ting pouted and rubbed her stomach. Her cleavage quivered with the gesture—a move only Ting Ting could manage. "My stomach hurt. Don't bully me."

Our boss shooed her away. "Fine. Go. Work."

She was so easy with men. I could never be that way. I had brothers. Men had no mystique. Flirtation was awkward on me—my words and gestures came out stilted—and annoyance showed too easily on my face. I watched the sideward glances she gave to the customers and the way she jutted her hip and pursed her lips when they said something on the edge of inappropriate.

"She's nothing to be jealous of," Yi Hua said as she passed with a stack of dirty dishes. We both looked at Ting Ting across the room, laughing loudly as she poured beer for a table of pleased GIs. Yi Hua wrinkled her nose. "She's nothing."

We didn't get a chance to speak until the lunch rush died down. Already, up and down the street, shop owners were pulling in their sidewalk displays and taping and boarding up their windows. Our boss insisted that we work until the usual midnight closing.

Ting Ting beckoned me out back. The cooks had propped open the back door with a crate. She sat and lit a cigarette.

"You feeling okay?" I asked. I grabbed another crate and set it near her.

"How do I look?" She glanced over her chest. "Do I look different?"

"You look fine."

"That's good." She took a deep drag and exhaled. "I'm pregnant."

"What?" I could not imagine Ting Ting at home changing diapers. I saw her leaving the baby at home with her mother or husband as she went out with her girlfriends, with me. How could she have let it happen?

She nodded. "I'm pregnant." Holding the cigarette in her teeth, she squeezed her breasts. "Don't I look, well, *bigger*?"

"Are you sure?"

"I was at the doctor's this morning. It's true."

I scooted the crate closer to her. "Whose?" I whispered.

"The American. Eddie." I looked at her blankly, and she clarified: "Minnesota. We're going to get married."

"Oh, Ting Ting." We'd known enough girls jilted by Americans promising marriage and plane tickets. Two girls in my neighborhood had babies by men who had returned to the United States and left false addresses. The faces of their mixed-race kids declared their humiliation to everyone.

"We really are." Her voice was defiant.

I didn't know what else to say.

The back of the restaurant faced a field where a lone, abandoned house stood. Behind the lot was the ROC air base. From my perch, I had a clear view of planes screaming as they descended onto the runways on their return from sorties to Vietnam. Two months before, the Pentagon Papers had been published; now I wondered how much longer the war would go on, how much longer the Americans would stay.

Ting Ting crushed out her cigarette and stood up. She glared down at me and insisted, "They're not all the same." She left me.

War hovered at the periphery of everything. Not only in Vietnam, but in the continuing cold war across the strait, and the odd/even-day propaganda schedule agreed upon between the two sides. On alternating days, we sent—packed in buoyant Styrofoam—canned rations with labels reading OPPOSE COMMUNISM, bright color postcards with pictures of life in Taiwan guaranteeing fish, freedom, and singer Teresa Teng—the true emblem of liberation clad in sequins and hairspray—while the Chinese sent over leaflets with round-faced, smiling families that promised the beauty of the "ancestral land." On our side, newspapers had brought us stories of famine and terror from that same ancestral land. Mao was a tyrant. People starved to death in the streets. The sparrow population was destroyed under the Four Pests campaign: peasants swarmed the fields clanging pots and pans, driving the birds into the air, and kept up the racket until the sparrows dropped to the earth in exhaustion. But sparrows ate insects as well as grain, and without sparrows, the locust population bloomed, then burst into crop-decimating clouds that drove the country into famine. Antiques were crushed and scrolls burned, schools shut down and teachers tortured. Culture was dead. Or so said the papers.

My eldest brother, our link to authority, cast a strange sort of legitimacy over our family. Dua Hyan, stationed south in Gangshan, was soon to be a colonel in the air force. Over the last decade, we'd achieved a precarious balance between him and Baba and their two divergent lives. Even though Baba was an outcast, a criminal, Dua Hyan's position gave us some small security that we would never be truly adrift. It was unusual, my sister's husband reminded us, for a Taiwanese to rise in the military as Dua Hyan had, especially with our family history. What remained unspoken was the trade that must have taken place, whether of secrets or soul.

He had gone away from home, and though his life had followed convention most closely, he felt the most elusive. The routines of his life were mysterious: we knew he lived in military quarters, that he was somehow involved with the Americans who were using the island as a staging ground for forays into Vietnam, and that this arrangement was in exchange for some semblance of international support as the ROC's claim as the single government of a yet-to-be-unified China crumbled. We didn't know if he had a local girlfriend, if he lived as celibate as a monk or as libidinous as the Americans who flooded the island on R&R.

On leave, he had come to stay at Ah Zhay's. He accompanied me to our youngest nephew's baseball game—Ah Zhay and Jie-fu both were at work, and Dua Hyan and I were the sole representatives of our family. Little League fever had swept the island as it became more and more evident that Tainan's Little League team would be going to the World Series in Pennsylvania at the end of the summer, and, across the island, parents and siblings crowded the edges of countless baseball fields, squinting in the sun's glare, mothers shielded by parasols. Who knew which team might be next up for greatness?

Even in civilian clothing, Dua Hyan stood like his erect shoulders were still draped in uniform. Perhaps it was my imagination, but the people around us moved warily. He kept his eyes on the game, never shouting, even when our nephew Jia Lun cracked the bat against the ball and made it to second base.

"Let's eat after this," I said.

He nodded. He looked like Baba. If one had compared pictures of them at the same age, they might look like brothers, or even twins. But Dua Hyan radiated vigor and stability while Baba had shrunk in his late middle age. It suddenly struck me that Baba had once looked as austere and righteous as Dua Hyan. This is who Baba had been before I'd known him. And before Dua Hyan had become this man, he'd been the older brother who had protected me from the taunts of Zhee Hyan. He had stood between our mother and the rest of us in her moments of insanity, and had laughed when I was a little impudent girl and spat at him in frustration. I suddenly missed him.

Without thinking too carefully about it, I said, "You know Su Ming Guo is home."

He winced. "Mama mentioned that."

I wanted him to look at me. "Baba and I went to see him."

He snapped toward me. "In Taipei? What for?"

I regretted my confession. "Forget I said anything."

He glanced around. "We'll talk more later."

"It was nothing. Baba just wanted to say hello."

"Two"—he lowered his voice—"two criminals cannot meet up just to 'say hello.' What the hell was he thinking?" He crossed his arms. His fists clenched and the tendons in his arms pulsed.

I stepped away from him and hissed, "Baba is not a criminal."

"You are too naive."

A cheer rose as the batter on Jia Lun's team hit the first pitch. On cue, like an automaton, Dua Hyan clapped and whistled, a high-pitched, lip-biting whistle that he must have learned in the air force.

I could not move. Dua Hyan was angry at Baba, and Baba would soon be angry with me. Everyone, in fact, would be angry with me. Worry churned in my stomach.

"Dua Hyan." I touched his arm. "Please. Forget I said anything."

He pulled his arm away slightly, rejecting my plea. "If you thought that you shouldn't have said anything, then you should not have said anything. You're not a child anymore." He spoke without turning, seeming to address the baseball field.

The one person who would not be angry was Zhee Hyan, but only because he didn't care about anything except gambling, beer, his motorcycle, and women.

"Baba felt bad. He wanted to apologize."

"Baba has never thought about consequences. He can see only one step ahead."

"He just wanted to say sorry. He did. Then we went home," I insisted.

"Does anybody else know?"

"No."

"Not Mama? Uncle Su's wife?"

"I don't know."

"Why did you go? You can't feed his fantasies like that."

A moan floated over the crowd as a batter struck out.

"He's our father," I said.

Who was Dua Hyan? Where did his loyalties lie? With the Generalissimo, whom he had sworn himself to? Did that elusive, stubborn man with the too-wide smile, the tidy mustache, and the gleaming pate deserve a devotion greater than family? Of course, my niece and nephews and all the children of their generation, if they knew about their grandfathers' past, would side with Chiang Kai-shek. The lessons of their civics class were simple: Don't argue with your friends. Listen to your parents. Listen to your teacher. Chiang Kai-shek is great.

"Baba is deluded."

"Don't say that." I realized that I wanted to resurrect Baba in Dua Hyan's eyes. Couldn't he see how sorry Baba was?

"It's the truth. Someone needs to tell him."

"Dua Hyan. Please. Please don't say anything."

He stared at our nephew, who hunched at third base, his yellow-and-white uniform streaked with dirt and grass. "If they win, what happens?"

The conversation was over. A drop of sweat rolled down the side of his face and disappeared under his jaw. "They play again," I answered.

"And if they win that?"

"Another game." The bat cracked against the ball and Jia Lun ran toward home. The spectators screamed. A flock of colorful parasols bobbed as mothers clapped.

Dua Hyan whistled when Jia Lun slid into home. "How many until they make it to the Series?" he shouted against the noise.

"Dozens," I yelled back.

"Is it likely?"

"No. It's not likely."

. . .

Dua Hyan stayed at Ah Zhay's for one more night before going to my parents' for a couple more days. Despite Mama's attempts to coddle him, he insisted on washing his own clothes, on helping in the kitchen, on rebuilding the pigpen and slaughtering a chicken. Shirtless, blood splattered on his feet and chest, he plucked it in the courtyard. Small soft feathers stuck to his damp hands. His face showed no emotion.

Clenching feathers in his fists, what passed through his mind? Did he think about the moments that had made him, such as the time, years earlier, when he was a no-name young cadet, and he had watched with the same expression as his "buddies" strung up a stray dog they'd lured over with a chicken bone? They'd tied up the dog by its back legs and took turns beating it with a stick, its body clenching and swinging as it screamed. He hated himself for not speaking up. He had gone back to his bunk and cried. Later, he had reported on them to his commanders. The reports became a monthly occurrence, and if nothing happened, he made something up. The reports, above everything else, were the priority. These reports snaked throughout society: elementary school students reporting on their classmates, teachers reporting on their colleagues, neighbors reporting on neighbors. If one wanted a job, a promotion, a visa, this is what one did.

The chicken's body was still warm from the scalding water he'd dunked it in to loosen the feathers. Not twenty minutes before, this animal had been scurrying across the yard, jerking its head at him, murmuring. He suddenly felt the weight of its destruction, of the sack slowly filling with wet feathers.

Our father rolled his bicycle through the gateway. His shirt was completely unbuttoned over his undershirt. A cigarette hung at his lips. His chess game sat in a sack in the basket. He spent the afternoons playing with old men at the park. We weren't sure if he even knew their names, but he challenged them day after day. He never told us whether he won or lost.

Dua Hyan greeted him. Baba sat beside him and offered him a cigarette. Dua Hyan jerked his chin at his dirty hands, so Baba put a cigarette in Dua Hyan's mouth and lit it. Dua Hyan continued plucking the chicken.

"You kill it?" Baba asked.

Dua Hyan, his hands and mouth busy, grunted.

"Ah, the red one. She was sweet. Should have taken out that mean brown hen instead." Baba exhaled. He scratched his sideburn. His hair was flecked with gray and his hands mottled with brown spots. "Jia Lun win the game?"

Dua Hyan made a noise that meant *no.*

"Next time."

Dua Hyan gestured for Baba to take the cigarette out of his mouth so he could talk.

"You should have gone," Dua Hyan said.

"I was busy."

"Playing chess?" Dua Hyan ripped clumps of feathers from the bird. Baba cringed.

"Right."

"Or visiting Taipei?"

Baba smoked quietly for a moment, then laughed. "Your sister told you."

Dua Hyan did not lie. Baba took another drag, exhaled, paused as if he were going to speak, then, thinking another moment, drew again on the cigarette.

"Stupid girl," he finally said, his voice calm.

"It was a stupid thing for you to do."

Baba laughed again. "What a world. A son, eating his father's food, tells his father what is stupid."

"You'll ruin everything again. I could lose my whole career. Do you think they'll ever make the son of a criminal into a general?"

"They'll never make you a general anyway. You're Taiwanese." Baba dropped his cigarette on the ground and stamped it out. "Stupid boy."

Dua Hyan held his tongue. I knew what he was thinking because I had thought it too: he knew more about how to negotiate this world than Baba would ever know. He squeezed the cooling lump of flesh harder, digging his nails into the plucked skin, feeling the sharpness of broken shafts. This is what the military had taught him: to separate out rage from violence; physical acts come out of cool heads and hot heads should be followed by still hands. He was convinced that when the soldiers had sought out his father, it had been not a panicked reaction to the days of protest, but a methodical act, born of level heads.

. . .

At the end of his visit, we find this scene.

The train station is a relic of the Japanese era: red bricks and gray stones and a clock with a sooty face. In front of it stand a man and his grown son. They are relics too, mirror images separated by a generation, motionless amid the swirling chaos of the station. As their family looks on, the father puts his hand on his son's shoulder and, for the first time since their argument, looks him in the eye.

The son is surprised by what yearning arises: he wants his father to apologize, to wish him well, to tell him he loves him. He wants this to be the moment when all the scaffolding around the years falls away. Eight years old when his father left, the son was already away from home when his father returned. They met again as adults, two men warily eyeing each other.

The father says, "Safe travels."

The son exhales. He blinks. He glances at his shoes, which gleam. His father wears plastic sandals, house shoes, starting to tear. He looks at his father's eyes. The whites have yellowed from too much smoking, too much drinking. He thanks his father.

He has bought a ticket on one of the faster trains, a soft seat for the long ride south. He tosses his duffel bag on the overhead rack, then goes to the hot water dispenser at the back of the car. The city rushes away; buildings spread out to haphazard gardens—fences made of stripped mattresses and planters of rusty lard cans and old tires—to farms of glistening rice paddies and wide taro fronds, to fields and hills. Once he is settled again—his coat hung on the hook, a glass of hot water in the holder beneath the window, the curtain pulled partway against the glare—he begins his report.

25

THE NEWS THAT TAINAN'S Little League team was going to the Series marked the beginning of the end of summer. It was not my nephew's team, but we were all proud nonetheless. Paper jerseys and signs went up on shop walls and windows all over the island, proclaiming Nationalist Chinese pride for these little scrappy boys from down south. The end of summer also meant Wei would be leaving for California soon and he told me he wanted to see me before he left.

He took me to a fish market outside of the city. We walked past the baskets mounded with dried shrimp and flattened squid, among the trays of frozen-eyed fish laid upon ice and the tubs crammed with crabs scrambling over and under one another. The cement floors were wet and the place smelled like algae and glass. We bought a pink fish with wide, glassy eyes and a bag of writhing blue shrimp and carried them to a nearby restaurant, which prepared them.

I told Wei about Ting Ting. He frowned as I set up the story: her charm in the restaurant, the nights in the clubs, her journal. I thought he would think it was funny, mildly scandalous, but instead he said, "Girls like that make all Taiwanese women look bad. You shouldn't go out with her."

His response disappointed me. I glimpsed again the haughtiness of our first meeting. "She's not a girl. She's a woman," I said.

"She is just another plaything for the Americans. Doesn't matter if it's Thailand, Okinawa, or Taiwan." He bit a shrimp out of its shell and tossed the translucent carcass into a bowl. To him, this was such an obvious truth that it could be casually uttered as he spat shrimp legs.

"She likes it. You talk about her like she doesn't have a choice." I thought of my own encounter with the Americans. Sam. My cheek on his back, the wind tearing at my hair. His smell. Desire flickered in my chest. He was so different from Wei. Uncomplicated. Exotic. Would Wei turn his critique on me if he knew?

"I know what she likes," Wei scoffed.

"You don't even know her." I stifled an urge to kick him under the table. Even more than his words, I despised his certainty.

"She doesn't realize that she's just a cog in a larger system. What she thinks is choice is actually just— Never mind. I promised not to talk about politics." One by one, he sucked on his fingers. "Delicious. Very tender."

"Right. You promised. Anyway, she's getting married," I said triumphantly. Her search had been more successful than his. "The banquet is planned for October, and then they'll leave in November."

Wei said nothing. With his chopsticks, he lifted out the spine of the fish so that we could eat the other side. He picked at it slowly, methodically, clearly still brooding. He had a tall Roman nose, the kind I associated with Hong Kong men who had a touch of British somewhere deep in their bloodlines, and thick eyebrows—inherited from his Japanese mother—and the combination of his good looks and ego irritated me even more.

We left thin clean bones and broken shrimp shells.

By the time we reentered Taichung, the sky was dark and the city was a swath of lights.

"Shall we stroll the night market?" Wei asked. It was the first sentence of significance we'd spoken since dinner.

"Don't you have to get back to Taipei?" I asked.

"I'm not in a rush."

I remembered Baba's words. One more evening, and then my obligations would be fulfilled. I told him about the night market near the university.

It was early and the market was still setting up. Pedestrians were starting to trickle in. Carts selling fresh cane and watermelon juice and shaved ice and sweet sausage stuffed with raw garlic sat alongside booths—strung with dazzling white bulbs—of clothing, purses, and trinkets. Other vendors laid their wares across blankets on the ground or on simple folding tables, prepared to gather up everything if the police came to check permits. One whole aisle was devoted to games: pachinko, ring tosses, pans of small turtles with paper clips taped to their backs, and tubs of tiny goldfish. Children squatted before them with paper paddles, trying to catch a fish before the wet paper tore.

"Shall we?" Wei said.

I raised my eyebrows. "We're a bit old."

"Not at all." He bought a couple of paddles. We crouched in front of a pink plastic tub and watched the little orange fish dart beneath our shadows.

"The key," Wei said, "is to not plunge in, but skim the water." He smiled as he placed the paddle gently in the water and slipped it under a fish. Quickly, he flicked his hand and the fish slid atop the damp paper. He dumped it into a bowl of water the vendor had given us.

I tried, but I was too hesitant and the paddle tore. Wei bought another. He held my wrist, both our hands hovering over the water. His thumb pressed into my pulse. He spoke in my ear: "Wait." I could smell the beer from dinner on his breath, and it reminded me of the drunk men who showed up at the Golden Rooster late at night, flirtatious and loud. I liked the smell: thick, masculine, an entitlement that was frightening and sexy.

Wei parked on the main street: the alleys of the neighborhood were too narrow for a car. The flicker of televisions from inside living rooms illuminated the path. In the heat, people left their doors open and noise drifted through screen doors and open windows. I carried my two new pet goldfish in a plastic bag of water.

"I had no idea you were so skilled." I grinned.

"Hydrodynamics," he said.

"You must have a tank full of fish at home."

He laughed.

We stopped before the footbridge. Someone had set up a laundry line between the eaves of the two houses adjacent to the bridge and scrubbed white shirts dangled, smelling faintly of detergent and the sweet summer mildew that permeated nearly everything.

"I'm leaving in two weeks," he said.

"I know." A spasm tickled my stomach.

"Our families have a long history together."

"Your aunt must have introduced you to a lot of women," I tentatively probed. He simultaneously frowned and smiled, apparently amused by my obvious statement. His aunt had assumed the role of matchmaker, and my mother had warned me early on that he would be meeting other women this summer. That was how these engagements with overseas students went: a school recess, a whirlwind trip, a hasty decision based on three or four good dates, compatible family histories, and perhaps a horoscope reading.

"Don't say that." He laughed. "I like that you can't help but say what you think."

"Ah Zhay hates it."

He nuzzled my forehead. "Don't listen to her. Even when she was a little girl she was bossy."

A half-laugh jumped from me, sounding like a cough. I felt heat from the little triangle of exposed skin above the open top button of his shirt. I put a hand on his waist, holding him and pushing him away. He covered my hand with his. In this long, awkward moment, something shifted. In this new vision of the world, I glimpsed—just a brief, blurred peek—Wei not as a pesky sermonizer, but as a lover.

His lips grazing my ear, he said, "I like you. Would you consider coming to California?"

California. All I knew about it was artificial, stereotypes, ideals: sunshine, oranges, movie stars, Disneyland, and Steve McQueen.

I freed my hand from his and stepped back. "I don't know you."

"You know enough."

"You also don't know me."

"I've known you since you were born." His elegant nose. The divot at the base of his throat, between the ridges of his clavicles, glistening in the humid night. The weight of his fleshy palm. I fought to unsee my new life, to remember how grating he could be, how sure of himself.

"It's not the same."

"What are you waiting for?"

I was twenty-four, already quite old to not have a steady boyfriend or looming marriage. I figured I'd escaped serious intervention thus far because I was the youngest in the family, but my sister and mother had both warned me that after twenty-five, I'd be a spinster. I'd be Ting Ting, forced to marry an American.

"I don't know." I was not waiting to be swept away. My fantasies were humbler, even more romantic: the subtle, irrevocable plaiting of two lives.

"Think about it." He kissed my forehead. "Let's go."

We crossed the bridge into the darker end of the alley where it curved and ended at Ah Zhay's house. The red courtyard gate was locked, but I could hear the television in the front room and my nephews arguing. The cement courtyard wall was embedded with shards of glass. I'd have to knock.

"Go," I urged.

"Think about it."

I nodded. "Yes. Go."

I watched him walk down the alley, the light falling across his shoulders.

26

"**DID YOU KNOW** he had gone to see Su Ming Guo?" Standing in the doorway, Ah Zhay woke me the next morning.

Over a month had passed since the visit to Su Ming Guo. I had convinced myself that the whole incident had been forgotten—by Baba, by me, by Dua Hyan. I covered my eyes with my arm and steeled myself. "Dua Hyan told you?"

Ah Zhay's annoyance soared into rage. "Dua Hyan knew and I didn't?"

Once again I cursed my big mouth. I'd tripped into my own trouble here. Afraid to look at her, I stayed hidden beneath my arm.

"Baba's been called to Taipei for a meeting." The chopping of the fan blades sliced through Ah Zhay's words. A "meeting." We all knew this meant interrogation. Or worse. "Take the day off and go with him," she said.

"To Taipei?"

"This is your mess. You shouldn't have let him go see Uncle Su. Why didn't you say anything? He can't go to Taipei alone. You have to go." Someone needed to account for him, to bear witness if he entered the building and never came out again.

"I'll get fired," I whined. I clung to the idea of my meager job. This was just an everyday trip to Taipei. Nothing to lose a job over. Everything was normal. Friday morning, ticking fan, the faint shout of orders over the military base wall, the dying scent of the breakfast I had slept through.

"Find another job!" She turned off the fan and the room immediately swelled with heat. "Get up. He's leaving soon. And this time, don't tell anyone."

My mother had anticipated this day for years. One day, she knew, they would return for him, and their lives would fall back into the condition to which she had become accustomed: ignorance and desire.

When Baba and I left for Taipei that morning, Mama went to the big brick church with the red steeple and white cross that the Americans had built near the base. She carried a Bible with a dark green cover and gold ribbon bookmark stitched into the binding. This Bible had parallel English and Chinese text, and she had begun to learn English through stories of sons and fathers and sins.

She sat in a newly lacquered pew and stared at the stained glass—a cross set against a kaleidoscope of colors—behind the pulpit. The Bible remained unopened beside her. The church was empty except for an obasan who was sweeping. The rhythmic scrape of her broom echoed.

I imagine my mother contemplating time. It seemed to her like a train on a circular track. Passengers were lost in its seductive sway, in the present beauty of the scenery passing by, only to find, before they knew it, that they were stranded in the very place from which they had set out. Once the journey was over, it was as if it had never taken place. Had she moved? Had he come home? Or had it been a delusion and she would walk out to find that she had been alone for nearly twenty-five years?

God existed for us to serve Him, and she was deeply ashamed to ask Him for something so human. She wondered if it was petty to ask for His grace in this matter that consisted only of longing and fear. This wasn't about the greatest good, about the alleviation of poverty or hunger, or about the end of the war that burned so close by. This was one simple prayer, one tiny, deeply personal matter. Her husband.

The first few nights after his return, she'd been almost afraid to touch him when they lay in bed. Her tentative hand on his arm or chest startled her: he crackled with heat. She had grown accustomed to the blank crispness of the bed and suddenly here was this body, this man: his deep breathing, his murmuring, his restlessness.

She wouldn't speak her request aloud. Perhaps the arrogance of this prayer would be tempered by its silence. Staring at the cross, she spoke to God in her mind: He's a good man. Please. We've suffered enough. I repent for him. Never mind him. For me, Your humble servant. You are Goodness. I praise You. In my every deed, I praise You. Whatever You choose, I will praise You. But, please, let him be.

A wordless train ride, thick with guilt. I slumped against the window, cheek pressed to cool glass, and avoided looking at my father. I wanted to apologize, yet I couldn't bring myself to believe that I was entirely at fault. What did he think, staring off like that? Did he envision the past, the numerous interviews cycling through his years in prison, or did he think of the future, that afternoon, anticipating questions and devising answers? I thought of my mother's words as we left for the station: *Bring him home.* Neither Baba nor I had been able to answer her.

We left the train silently and flagged down a taxi. Once we told the driver the address, he joined our silence. The building was a nondescript celadon, as placid as a post office. I told Baba I'd wait at the cafe across the street, then watched him disappear through the doors.

I took a seat in a booth with a view through the wide glass front and ordered a cold tofu custard. The celadon building's only windows were high up, white, blinded by cataracts of sunlight. A steady stream of pedestrians walked by, enveloped in their own concerns and oblivious to what was happening behind the building's tranquil facade.

I remembered I hated tofu custard. I dug the spoon around, a pretense of eating as I sliced and smashed the soft gelatinous mass.

Baba did not come out.

A man and woman pushed through the doors, arm to arm, yet so narrowly not touching. It was a very hot day, but the woman wore a thin sweater over her dress and the peach shade of her legs betrayed pantyhose. Interrogated or interrogator? Neither smiled.

Red taxis rolled by, drivers slapping the horn and beaded tchotchkes swinging from rearview mirrors. A bus groaned past and left a cloud of black exhaust in its wake. The waitress took my uneaten custard and I ordered a Coke, which came in a bottle shrouded in condensation.

I nursed the Coke for as long as I could. The chill on the outside of the bottle cascaded off in the heat and soon the soda was warm. How long could I wait? How long would I wait?

Finally, three hours after he had disappeared behind the heavy glass doors, Baba emerged again. I left money on the table and ran out. I shouted at him from across the street and darted through the traffic. The flesh beneath his eyes seemed heavier and darker than usual.

"Can we go home?" I asked, then felt it was a stupid question.

He closed his eyes. He moved his mouth like he meant to speak, but no words came out. I took his arm. "Baba," I said. "It's okay." We merged into the flow of people. We were slower than most and they jostled and snapped as they rushed past us. By the time we reached the train station, the sky was dark.

On the train, still no words came to his mouth. Baba had tipped his head back and draped a handkerchief over his eyes, so casual, like he was settling in for a long, relaxing hot-springs soak.

Then he reached out and squeezed my hand; I stiffened in response to the unfamiliar gesture. When he relaxed his grip, his palm quaked against mine. Both yearning and pathetic, this act stunned me. Baba had not done more than clap a shoulder—or perhaps straighten my jacket or smooth a hair into place—in the last thirteen years.

On the motorcycle ride back from the train station, I was overcome by the thought of his vulnerability. I tucked my hair into my collar so it would not whip him as I navigated the roads home. He balanced with his hands grasping the bar behind him, and with every turn, I felt the shifting burden of his weight and tried to balance it with my own.

Mama sat in the illuminated front room, the Bible open in her lap. She had heard my bike shut off, and we both saw her eyes searching the dark courtyard for us. She called out: first Baba's name, then mine.

Baba sighed and I knew he saw what I was just noticing for the first time. How naive, how heartbreaking, how undeserved was her faith in us.

27

THE GOLDFISH LASTED a little over a week in the small, round glass bowl I had housed them in. First one rose to the surface, then I spent much of the next day watching the second fish struggle against the inevitable as it drifted zombielike toward the bottom of the bowl, then finally succumbed and floated. I took it as a sign, but soon my mother called to tell me that Wei's aunt wanted to arrange our engagement.

I looked at the poor fish listlessly bobbing around the surface of the bowl. Like a grounded ship wrenched from mud, I felt the slow movement of my life. Into the trough of its wake tumbled everything else: leaving home, a new language, new friends, children.

"What do you think?" Mama asked. I balanced the phone with my chin and tapped the fishbowl. The fish did not respond.

"What about love?" I asked. What would carry us through? Love, something less, or something more?

"Do you like him?"

I recalled the humor and goodwill that I'd seen at the night market, and the beer musk on his skin. I liked him. I blushed as I admitted, "Yes."

"That's good enough." She sounded weary.

"But Ah Zhay married for love. *You* married for love." I wanted a counterargument; a decision like this should come through struggle, torment, and tears—not a two-minute phone conversation.

She rustled against the receiver and finally answered. "It's not everything."

I pushed her. "What else is there, Mama?"

"The Lins are old friends. They are a good family. Wei will have his Ph.D. soon. What other chance will you have to go to America? Once you get there, you can sponsor your niece and nephews. This will be good for everyone." So she would not dissuade me.

Marriage was always for love, but sometimes that love was for family, not the lover. I remembered the phrase that had braced me that day in the garden when my father had sworn me to his secret: *Never fail to comply*. It was easier than defiance.

Riding around town, I'd always cringed at the outdoor banquets I saw in some alleys, festive but destined for sweaty brides and drunk guests walloped by heatstroke. I didn't like the striped awnings erected like circus tents, shading tables draped in pink plastic, the food doled out of huge steel pots. Even if our wedding had not been in the midst of the sweltering summer, we still would have held our banquet in an air-conditioned restaurant. And if any status is to be inferred from the size of the air conditioner, this one was as big as a refrigerator and as loud as a motorcycle.

The chairs were standard generic restaurant chairs in red vinyl with steel frames. I wore a gold silk dress embroidered with a beaded phoenix that rose up my side and extended across my bosom. My posture was impeccable, lest I burst either the side zipper or the front snaps.

My mother called my hairstyle—a tight, glossy bun—too severe and matronly; I called her old-fashioned. Our engagement party had elicited a couple of gold necklaces and bracelets and the pair of drop-pearl earrings that I now wore.

Wei and I were as comfortable as could be expected for two people who were freshly, tentatively *in* love, but not yet in the complacency of real love. I searched his face, hoping for revelation. He smiled and squeezed my hand. "It's too much, isn't it?" he asked. His buoyancy made me smile.

The banquet noise quickly overcame the gunning of the air conditioner: people shouted at each other across the tables, yelled at their children, tried to out-manner one another by offering the last bites of each dish, and offered to refill each other's glasses. Even before Wei and I began our round of toasts, most of our guests were boisterously drunk. Including Zhee Hyan, who had been baiting Dua Hyan all night.

Zhee Hyan loosened the first three buttons of his outrageous, large-collared, striped purple shirt and leaned his greasy, drunk face close to Dua Hyan, who looked smart and fresh in a somber black suit. Zhee Hyan's hair had escaped from whatever pomade he had rubbed in; it rose up on either side of his part like a bird extending its wings.

"Why don't you—why don't you get your high-and-mighty friends to—to strike Ba's file?"

Dua Hyan jerked his head out of range and batted Zhee Hyan away. "You stink." His tone was unperturbed, almost bored, and yet hardened at its core by a wintry distaste.

Wei's lips brushed my ear. To the rest of the room, it might have looked like a sweet nothing. He whispered, "Maybe we should seat them at separate tables."

"No, you—you stink," Zhee Hyan complained to Dua Hyan. Zhee Hyan was much more explicit with his emotions; he made as if to slap Dua Hyan, but stopped short and laughed. I squeezed my napkin and yelped.

Without a word, Baba left the table, probably going off to smoke out front. For most, smoking was a social activity—cigarettes and lighters shared, the smoke offering an easy respite between words. For Baba, smoking was his moment of escape, like his habit of pulling off and wiping his glasses, his instant blindness to the world. For a moment, we all fell awkwardly still, then Wei's parents busied themselves with the remaining scallops; his father tittered as he scooped them from the platter. Wei's older brother said, loudly, "Let me help," and took the spoon.

I wanted to run after Baba; I wanted to ask if he was okay, what he needed, how he felt about my marriage. I had done even more than he had requested—was he pleased? Instead, I walked around the table to my brothers, braced myself with a hand on each of their shoulders, and leaned over. Zhee Hyan's polyester shirt was damp. Dua Hyan was right—he did stink. Coated in lipstick, my mouth felt stiff. "Save it for another day," I hissed.

"Tell that to the one who insists on making a clown of himself." Dua Hyan's gaze wandered around the room. His disinterest hurt me.

His approval had become even more elusive than Baba's. "I'm talking to both of you," I said.

Across the table, across half-empty platters and dirty plates and the diminishing bottle of Johnnie Walker, my mother had slipped into her own idiosyncratic gesture—she held her head high, almost arching her neck as if her embarrassment could be overcome by an elegant and artificial nonchalance. She turned away from my gaze and I admired the swing of her gold earrings and the small light hairs coming loose from her upsweep in spite of the copious amounts of hairspray. Time's softening of her face made her look surprisingly vulnerable and even sadder.

"Look what you're doing to Mama," I whispered to my brothers, who watched as our mother rose from her chair and pushed her way through the crowded banquet hall to join Baba outside. Amid all the chaos, however, none of our guests had noticed the dissolution of our table. Wei's dad laughed again and his mother asked gently, "Should I follow her?"

I shook my head. "Please don't embarrass me," I pleaded to my brothers. Zhee Hyan stammered his protest, as I knew he would, but Dua Hyan silenced him by shrugging off my hand and storming away. "Dua Hyan," I cried. I thought he would follow Mama, but instead he took a seat at a table with our cousins who had come up from Tainan for the banquet, cousins I barely remembered except that their names all began with Ming.

My niece, Mei Mei, had been avidly watching the whole conflict, her bright doll eyes darting among all the players like a ravenous Ping-Pong fan. A teenager, she was lovely in that oblivious way of young girls, who are beautiful despite themselves, simply for the fact of their youth. My nephews—eager young Jia Zhe and the slightly less boisterous Jia Lun—were busy chatting between themselves, struggling in some boredom-battling game they'd made up with straws and napkins and an empty juice carton. I realized that my vows, my new promise to a near stranger, meant that I would not watch them grow up. I bit my lip.

Ah Zhay offered me a sympathetic grimace. "Sit," she said. "Enjoy yourself. Don't worry about them." Then, like a good older sister, she turned her attention to our remaining brother. "Don't make it worse. This is your baby sister's day."

Wei watched this all with amusement and, I think, a touch of annoyance. Back in my chair, I apologized. "Welcome to my family."

While my entrance at the start of the banquet, before the food had been served, had been announced with firecrackers and clapping, my change, just before dessert, into my second banquet dress—pink chiffon, with a scoop neck and puffy princess sleeves—went barely noticed, and the firecrackers disappeared in the noise of our guests. This was the sign of a good wedding.

Hoisting a bottle of brandy, the emcee led Wei and me around to each table for toasts. Wei guzzled; I sipped. When we reached his groomsmen's table, two of them flung their arms around his shoulders and insisted on a second shot. The whole table shouted and cheered as Wei drained his glass. I blinked and smiled demurely.

At another table sat my coworkers from the Golden Rooster Garden: my boss, who had pulled on a clean shirt though he still smelled of sweat and cigarettes, and the other waitresses, including Ting Ting and her American boyfriend. For the toast, she drank juice and winked at me. She was getting married in two months, when her parents could come up from the south. She said she hoped I'd still show up even though it broke the taboo of attending a wedding within three months of your own. "Oh, come on," I said, pointedly eyeing her belly, "who really believes that stuff?"

When we finally returned to our table, red-faced and woozy, a woman in a vibrant blue dress was in my chair. She clasped Wei's mother's hands in hers; the conversation looked earnest. As soon as she noticed me, Wei's mother—my *mother-in-law*—pulled her hands away. The woman in blue cocked her head at me and smiled. She stood up. "I just had to come over and say hello. Congratulations." She had the pristine enunciation of a person whose teeth aligned perfectly. I was tipsy. I could have listened to her talk all night. I didn't know two-thirds of the people there. Who was she? A family friend? A cousin? From my side or Wei's? She had liquid dark amphibious eyes. She was beautiful. Wei blinked quickly—I was afraid he was going to vomit. His face was red and shiny from our drinking tour of the fifteen tables, and he muttered a little thank-you. She squeezed my arm. "I hope he's being sweet to you."

"Of course," I said. She smiled again—yes, her teeth *were* perfectly aligned—and sauntered back to her table.

We tried to keep the liquor away from Zhee Hyan, but the Cousins-Ming-from-Tainan insisted on stealing a full bottle from a table of teetotalers and dragged him over. They forced reconciliation with Dua Hyan, and soon all of them were blustering and pointing in each other's faces in a sloshed debate about Kaoliang liquor. One cousin claimed he was going to get in a taxi and find a bottle and they would drink it to settle the argument.

Baba, seated again, fell deep into conversation with Wei's father. I often took their long friendship for granted. They had no need for show or polite conversation. Snatches drifted across the table: they were relating to their wives the story of some long-ago incident in Tokyo, some story the wives had no doubt heard five times before. My mother nodded: *Get on with it.* My father was the slowest storyteller, meticulous about the details. He often circled back around to revise what he'd earlier said. Listening could feel interminable.

The meal ended with a mochi soup—something auspiciously sweet and soft to begin our married life.

Finally, I changed into my last dress, a red minidress with little red-lace gloves. With our parents, Wei and I stood at the exit holding trays of cigarettes (for the men) and candy (for the women and children) and said good-bye to each guest and received their repeated congratulations. The woman in the blue dress appeared on the arm of one of Wei's friends. Her warmth as she spoke to Wei's parents was uncomfortably seductive. After she left, I asked Wei who she was. "Just an old friend," he said.

Wei had dismissed the idea of tradition. He had not brought his grooms-men to escort me and my trousseau to his family's home and also eliminated the ritual of sheltering me with a bamboo screen to stave off the eyes of ghosts. Instead, we scurried into a taxi and spent our first married night at the Mandarin Hotel, which was still fairly new. There, sitting on the bed in our fifth-floor room, we counted our red envelope money. I had changed into a modest, high-necked nightgown while Wei lounged in his underwear without a care. I tried to not imagine the rest of the evening. Ting Ting had reassured me that people were usually so exhausted from the banquet that the real wedding event did not take place until the next morning.

"You'll be a virgin a day longer than you think." She winked.

"Morning?" I had asked, incredulous and naive. She choked on her laughter.

Wei went to the tea table and poured a glass of hot water. He stood at the window, framed by black glass and the parted burgundy curtains. He blew the heat off the water. I ordered the bills by denomination and asked again about the woman in blue. He didn't answer. I looked up. His back was beautiful and strong. He didn't have the body of a graduate student, but of an athlete. Morning crossed my mind again and I blushed. Finally, he brought the glass back to the bed and offered me a sip. I declined.

"Actually, she's my ex-girlfriend." He folded one arm behind his head and leaned against the pillows.

"Oh," I said. I fanned the money. I was confused. "Did your parents invite her?"

"No, oh god, no. She tagged along as someone's date. She must have arranged it."

"She's still in love with you."

"No, I think she was just curious." He peeked at me out of the corner of his eye.

"She could have waited for the pictures." I didn't know what else to say. I wasn't jealous exactly. But how dare she come, even for a peek? A sour cast fell over the whole reception. I set the money on the nightstand, hugged a pillow and tucked my chin into it.

Wei rearranged himself, resting on the pillow clasped in my arms. The weight of his head pressed into my stomach. "We didn't date very long."

I hesitated and then put my fingers into his hair, struggling through the shellac. I raked his hair soft again and thought carefully about my tone. "How long?"

He exhaled. "Two years."

Two years. I'd known him less than a month.

"Obviously, if I was going to marry her, it would have happened." He closed his eyes and his face softened.

His carefully slicked hair was in disarray. I massaged his scalp. My husband. Even if I repeated the phrase a hundred times a day, it would feel strange for a while. "Why didn't you?" I asked.

"I went away to school."

"Oh. That's all?"

"Her parents didn't like me. They were old-school Chinese. I was too Taiwanese."

"And how did they feel about your Japanese mother?"

"That too." His eyes still closed, he grabbed my hand and kissed it, then pressed it to his cheek.

I pulled it away. "You should have eloped." I felt violated.

He laughed. "Then we wouldn't be here."

"Right, with all this cash." I scooped up the money from the nightstand. I tried to forget the woman in blue ghosting our conversation and clouding the glow between us. My stomach was sour. Afraid Wei would think me petty and jealous, I pushed back my discomfort.

He sat up and squeezed the stack of bills. "Not bad. At the current exchange rate, that's like three hundred US dollars. That's three months' rent."

"We still need to pay the banquet hall."

The conversation had eased into banalities; we truly were married. I put the pillow back in its place, tucked my nightgown under my knees, and yawned.

"I'm tired too," he said. "We should go to bed."

Afraid to see what he might be implying, I averted my eyes. I thought of the woman in blue and felt inexperienced and stupidly virginal. I put the money away in my suitcase, then crawled into bed and turned off the light. Wei kissed me chastely on the mouth and wished me good night.

"Did you love her?" I asked in the dark.

He rolled over and embraced me, pressing all his angles and softness to me. "It doesn't matter, does it?"

I considered this. "I guess it doesn't."

I lay awake for a while, listening to the traffic on Nanking Road and the revelers leaving the hotel nightclub and returning to their rooms. My husband held me and I knew he didn't sleep yet either. Eventually, though, we did.

In the morning, when I woke, I found Wei watching me. He smiled and caressed my cheek. "I'm scared," I whispered.

He kissed me, and then it was as Ting Ting had promised.

The week after Wei left Taiwan, as I waited for my visa to join him, the Tainan Little League team won the World Series. "A Win 'Made in Taiwan,'" cried the papers. Foreign newspapers called us the "Little Island That Could" and proclaimed the win "good for morale." The boys were heroes. If only that burst of pride could have carried us through the end of February, when Nixon went to China.

28

THE ISLAND BEGAN TO DISAPPEAR on October 25, when half a world away, the Republic of China lost its seat in the United Nations. An uncontestable reality, said the American ambassador, George H. W. Bush. The United Nations must reflect an uncontestable reality determined by land and population. Against all rules of the organization, the ROC was being displaced. Not kicked out, we were assured, though the draft resolution said they *wish to restore to the People's Republic of China all its rights and expel forthwith the representatives of Chiang Kai-shek*. The People's Republic of China would replace the Republic of China to strengthen the authority and prestige of the United Nations. Like a street hustler playing a shell game, the UN moved Red China to the Security Council and slipped Free China into the General Assembly. It had dismantled the symbol. And we, swindled pedestrians, overturned the shell and discovered beneath the Republic of China there was no China. We were an empty signifier. In disgust, Representative Liu Chieh left the floor, and Taiwan was never allowed back into the UN again.

But the news did not put a damper on Ting Ting's marriage celebration. She held a small banquet at a restaurant on the outskirts of the city that was attended mostly by Minnesota Eddie's American friends, who brought coveted bottles of liquor from the PX. By the end of the night, the party had trickled away to a few very drunk tables. I found myself sick on whisky, surrounded by American men, and absurdly confident about my English. I thought of my own banquet, tame in comparison, and then of Wei, so far away in California, and wondered what he might be doing at that moment. Sleeping, I chided myself. I thought of our good-bye at the airport in Taipei, and how surprising it was to feel that this stranger was now mine, forever.

I looked for Sam, the man who had taken me home that night in August, but Ting Ting later told me he had returned to Oregon, where he was originally from and where his wife lived.

Ting Ting wore bridal red that night—an empire-waist dress like the one Olivia Hussey wore playing Juliet in the film of the Shakespeare play that had been so popular a few years before. The dress hid her growing belly. I looked at her, my eyes bleary from drink, and I wanted to cry for her. When I finally left, nausea spinning in my chest, I hugged her tight and wished her a safe journey. She laughed in her carefree way and told me, "Don't let the boss bully you when I'm gone." A week later, she was on a plane to Minneapolis.

After Ting Ting left, I renewed my vow not to drink and began to prepare myself for my own departure. My visa finally came in February.

At the end of February, the *Spirit of '76* brought Nixon to China. He was a man with a face like a marionette's and a wife who looked like a brittle beauty queen. Wherever they went, he and his wife, with her bright red coat and blond hair, were the center of a crowd of people in drab blues and grays.

In Hangchow, his wife wears fur. They walk through a park with Chou En-lai, surrounded by curious onlookers in padded coats. Their translator is a young woman with bobbed hair pulled off her face with a clip and horn-rimmed glasses. She helps translate when Nixon bends over to shake a young boy's hand. The boy's sister is called over too, and when the American man talks to her, she presses her tongue into the space left by her missing front tooth and will not look at him.

"Where is your mother? Is she here?" the translator asks.

"In the city," the girl says, then tries to step away from the American and the cameras, but finds herself trapped by the ring of people.

After the girl comes the fishpond. Nixon stands against a metal rail and tosses food into the water with concentration and joy. He drops into a grinning reverie as if he has forgotten the entire world is watching.

"Dr. Kissinger," the translator says, "you can have a package if you want to feed the fish."

"Denmark, Denmark," says the Secret Service. "President feeding fish."

They stand here at this moment, three of them the most important people to the fate of Taiwan—Richard Nixon, Chou En-lai, and Henry Kissinger—on an overcast day in Hangchow, feeding fish.

I went to see my parents and grandparents for one last dinner before my departure. I had quit my job just a few days before ("So you're going too?" my boss said, and I swore I saw some regret in his eyes). My grandparents were taking their afternoon siesta and Mama was at church. I found Baba in the garden, a dead cigarette hanging from his lip, plucking snails from the plants.

I sank into a plastic chair that had a teddy bear decal peeling off the back.

"Have you eaten?" Baba asked.

"I'm waiting for dinner."

"Come help me."

I hunched down beside him and began searching for the tiny snails.

We worked together in silence for a long time. I wondered when I would see him again. What if my plane went down in the Pacific? More than that, I held a constant fear that he could just disappear. Thirteen years had passed since his return, and yet I still wondered each morning if that would be the day that Baba was gone again. If I had cut my knee, or even lost my leg, the wound would have healed already, but the mind and heart are trained in different ways.

"Ba," I said. "I love you."

I had never spoken these words to him—such words were for lovers. But maybe I had spent too much time watching American movies, where people loved their parents, their siblings, their pets, their clothing, and their cars. In our world, love was supposed to be unspoken and understood.

He traced his thumb over a leaf, slowly, as if he hadn't heard me. As he moved to the next plant, I watched his profile. His glasses were a decade out of style and his shirt, washed too many times, was coarse with tiny knots of fabric.

"I know. You don't need to tell me." He still didn't look at me. "You're a good daughter. Very filial."

It was the highest praise I could expect, and I felt grateful though I longed for him to say he loved me too. I stroked the leaves of the next plant, found another snail, and dropped it in the bucket. Baba thanked me.

At every stop, they hold a banquet. Nixon signals each joke and compliment to his uncomprehending audience with a smile and a nod. In Hangchow, he brings applause when he proclaims, "Now that we have been here, now that we have seen the splendor of this city, we realize why it has been said that heaven is above and beneath are Hangchow and Soochow." Smoke drifts around the room. Premier Chou En-lai stares grimly at the table as he listens, then claps politely.

The First Lady wears baby blue and smiles with her mouth closed.

To someone at the banquet table, as he eats, Nixon says, "I never have enough time to read the things I want to read."

The building where Wei's parents lived in Taipei was later demolished in the early 1990s and replaced with a cram school: six stories of classrooms stuffed with tense students weighed down with the pressure of exams. They come in their school uniforms—cheap cotton T-shirts with the contrast-color collars and polyester sweatpants, dirty after a long day—and sit in rows at long tables, by all appearances studious but secretly passing notes. During the breaks, they insult and smack each other. Their tables are crowded with textbooks and notebooks and cute novelty pens and empty snack wrappers and small cartons of milk tea.

I wonder if the ghostly imprint of my last night before I left for America still lingers today somewhere in a classroom on the third floor, where Uncle Lin's apartment had been. Do the students of this room, where the junior-high-level English class is taught—usually by an expatriate Canadian—find an inexplicable sadness among the exercises on subject-verb agreement? Do they sometimes see in passing, out of the corner of an eye, a family wearing old-fashioned clothes bickering and gossiping? And do they daydream of me, a young woman nearly the same age as their teacher, sorting through her suitcases as she prepares for a very long trip?

The apartment was the perfect size for a family of four, but my family added eleven more people, and for the duration of the evening, we stepped around and over and past one another. My two suitcases stood next to the door—a piece of waiting quiet in the chaos.

After dinner, I retreated to the Lins' bedroom to sort my luggage again; Aunty Lin had given me shirts and snacks to take back for Wei. I layered the packages among my clothes, wondering if Wei was really a secret fan of beef jerky and sour plums, or if his mother simply still clung to his childhood favorites even though he'd outgrown them. I would eventually find out. I had learned a lot about him through our correspondence since our wedding, but nothing as rote and banal as "favorite foods." I had not thought to ask.

Baba came to the doorway. "Almost packed?" He sat on the bed next to my suitcase. The Lins' bedspread was ornate: a blue peacock of silk thread burst onto a bright pink satin field. Baba ran a hand along one sapphire-embroidered peacock feather. I knew from the creases that they had brought this out just for guests and I wanted to tell Baba to be careful of his calluses.

"I'll be done soon," I told him. In the living room, my nephews were shouting and the women's voices rose in a separate conversation. "I think I've just crammed an entire dried cow in here."

"I have something else for you."

"Ba, I can't fit anything else."

He held a jar filled with what looked like coffee grounds. I leaned forward. The jar still bore strips of glue where the label had been washed away. I swore I would say no. I doubted it would pass customs.

"This is a godforsaken place. I sometimes wish that you—all of us—could leave and forget it. We're a cursed people," he said.

"Ba. Please." I slid yet another package of jerky between some shirts. Impatient, I was afraid to encourage another one of his flights of persecution.

"I want you to take this."

I pulled away from my suitcase and looked again at the jar. "What is it?"

"Soil from our garden."

The garden that my grandparents had begun half a century before; the garden that my mother had tended through my father's absence and that, now, my father still worked when he wanted to be alone. The garden where Baba had sought my complicity after the secret police had visited and where I had found refuge after my first meeting with Wei.

"I want you to remember." He set the jar atop my heaped clothing. "Don't forget."

Don't forget. His words were both an order and a plea.

Maybe, despite what haunted-house stories claim, ghosts aren't anchored to place. This must be true, for I carried that ghost across the ocean with me to California, where I heard it for years. Where I still hear it.

In his thick, black-framed glasses, Henry Kissinger looks younger than forty-eight. He steps up to the mic and waits for his introduction before beginning to speak haltingly, the "uhs" drawn out and deep. The communiqué between China and the United States has been released. He looks up as he speaks, thinking as he talks, clearing his throat, repeating, pausing. A bank of white men with cigarettes and pipes and gaiwans sit before him, watching and taking notes. The camera flashes sound like the slicing of scissors.

But there is no need to be cautious. The communiqué is filled with language about justice and freedom and liberation.

China says "it firmly supports the struggles of all the oppressed people and nations for freedom and liberation and that the people of all countries have the right to choose their social systems according to their own wishes and the right to safeguard the independence, sovereignty and territorial integrity of their own countries and oppose foreign aggression, interference, control, and subversion."

The Americans say, "The United States supports individual freedom and social progress for all the peoples of the world, free of outside pressure or intervention."

And then Taiwan. A thorn between the two nations, or, as phrased in the communiqué: "The Taiwan question is the crucial question obstructing the normalization of relations between China and the United States . . ."

And here is the declaration:

> *The Government of the People's Republic of China is the sole legal government of China; Taiwan is a province of China which has long been returned to the motherland; the liberation of Taiwan is China's internal affair in which no other country has the right to interfere; and all U.S. forces and military installations must be withdrawn from Taiwan. The Chinese Government firmly opposes any activities which aim at the creation of "one China, one Taiwan," "one China, two governments," "two Chinas," an "independent Taiwan" or advocate that "the status of Taiwan remains to be determined."*

While the United States "acknowledges that all Chinese on either side of the Taiwan Strait maintain there is but one China and that Taiwan is a part of China. The United States Government does not challenge that position. It reaffirms its interest in a peaceful settlement of the Taiwan question by the Chinese themselves."

Now it has been said. Words that will echo down the years.

A deep breath.

After the press conference, during the handshakes between both sides, Nixon says to an official, "Tonight I will not force you to Moutai."

And the Chinese official replies, "Quite on the contrary—we can drink more Moutai tonight."

Laughter.

We said good-bye in the airport.

The world was just as unsafe then, thick with potential death, but in those days we were still allowed to walk right up to the airport windows and watch planes depart. I crossed the tarmac, the straps of my over-stuffed purse cutting into my shoulder, and glanced back at my family behind the terminal glass. My niece and nephews waved; the adults did not move. My family was not the type to hug, but Ah Zhay had squeezed me and whispered, "I hope it's wonderful. Come home if it's not."

When I reached the top of the stairs, ready to enter the plane, I paused before the smiling stewardess and looked back one last time. In the days after our wedding, Wei and I had visited the hot springs at Peitou, avoiding the ones that were loud with GIs and their weekend companions. One night, in our hotel, lying in bed, Wei had talked to me about this day. "Don't turn around," he said. "Go up the stairs and leave. If you turn around, you'll never come. I'll be waiting in San Francisco for a girl who never shows."

For a moment, I doubted I'd actually step into the plane until the man behind me cleared his throat and nudged me with his bag.

By the night of the Shanghai banquet, after the release of the communiqué, Nixon is exhausted. The meal begins with the Chinese talking about how this banquet will stand up to the one in Hangchow, some friendly city-versus-city competition. Chou En-lai inspects the menu to see how it measures up.

The premier makes a joke about women in China no longer caring for their families, then laughs brightly and loudly with his hand over his mouth.

A final banquet speech. Nixon says, "What we have said in that communiqué is not nearly as important as what we will do in the years ahead to build a bridge across sixteen thousand miles and twenty-two years of hostility which have divided us in the past . . . Our two peoples tonight hold the future of the world in our hands. As we think of that future, we are dedicated to the principle that we can build a new world, a world of peace, a world of justice, a world of independence for all nations."

At a certain point, the land becomes patchwork. This is after the city has shrunk to the chaos of tiny crammed buildings and narrow alleys and minuscule scooters swarming the streets like ants. The land between the dark green hills and the gray tumbled-block city is laid out in haphazard squares of shimmering black paddies and chartreuse taro fields and marked by the red roofs of farmhouses. Motorbikes speed on singular roads as thin as thread, swerve past specks—oxen—that seem to not be moving at all. Cars grow slower; clouds intervene; mist envelops the windows. Sunlight replaces the overcast day. The world reverses, and through the breaks in the clouds and for hours and hours, the blue ocean.

In 1972, February had twenty-nine days.

BOOK III

BERKELEY

1979–1980

1979

29

MOST PEOPLE THINK they remember Jimmy Carter wearing a sweater when he made the announcement, but what serious president would not wear a tie when finishing the work Nixon had begun? He sat in front of gold drapes, flanked on both sides by flags. He wore a burgundy tie, and he tried to smile when he gave the news.

It's December 15, 1978, when he makes the announcement. His smile is cautious—this is good news, but he knows that his statement, in eight minutes, will delegitimize a government and turn a half century of history into a joke. That is why his people waited until the last possible moment to tell the Republic of China that today is the day. Messengers rouse Chiang Ching-kuo's men from their beds to hand them the notice, and they have barely enough time to craft a response that is anything more than disappointed.

Carter says, "The United States of America recognizes the Government of the People's Republic of China as the sole legal Government of China."

He says, "In recognizing the People's Republic of China, that it is the single Government of China, we are recognizing simple reality."

His smiles are random—notated onto the text of the speech?—before "historic," before "commercial," before "hegemony."

On January 1, 1979, the United States would assume relations with the People's Republic of China. Students in Taiwan—some say they are government plants—vandalize the American consulate. They hang signs that urge the boycott of Coca-Cola and depict a weeping Statue of Liberty and devilish Carter.

On February 28, 1979, the American consulate in Taiwan closes.

The students marched silently down Telegraph Avenue wearing paper bags over their heads with ragged holes punched out for their eyes. They bore signs reading **END MARTIAL LAW IN TAIWAN!** and **FREE POLITICAL PRISONERS IN TAIWAN!** Dressed like a student, I stood on the corner of Bancroft Way with my Leica and documented the protest at Wei's request. Across the street, a man I didn't recognize also took pictures. I tried to obscure my face with my camera. When Wei passed—I knew him by his clothes—he shoved the man so hard that the camera fell from his hands and broke on the sidewalk.

"What the fuck?" the man shouted. My own camera trembled in my hands and I resisted the urge to call Wei's name. Anonymity was crucial. Another protester ran up and threw himself in front of Wei: "No, not like this." He ushered Wei back into the group that was now crossing onto campus. The man, gathering up the pieces of his broken camera, continued shouting.

The group, nearly a hundred graduate students and young professors like Wei, drifted like scarecrows across Sproul Plaza and through Sather Gate. I followed. Since President Carter's severance of US relations with Taiwan, the newly rogue Nationalist government had become even more brutish. A young Pomona College professor, back in Taipei on summer break, had been denied an exit visa and interrogated. The morning after his interrogation, even though the police claimed they had escorted him home, his broken body had been found on the campus of National Taiwan University, a crisp hundred-dollar NT note tucked into his shoe as a traditional assassin's tip for the person tasked with clearing his body. Gangsters, claimed the government. Government, claimed everyone else.

Just the week before, someone had bombed the KMT offices in New York City and Washington, DC.

It had taken moving to America for me to realize what Wei had told me during our first meeting was true. American campuses were full of student spies who had been bribed with plane tickets and show tickets and other cheap trinkets by the Nationalists. Speak a wrong word in

New Haven and your cousin in Kaohsiung would lose his job. The chain of events could not be coincidence. In America, I had stopped calling myself "Chinese" and started calling myself "Taiwanese." In America, I had met my first Chinese national and discovered the gulf that separated us, despite the language we held in common.

But none of the terror could have happened without the tacit agreement of the American government, Taiwan's former and closest ally. Against it too, we protested.

A brown shingled house—four bedrooms, two and a half baths—across from a park, a short bike ride to campus. A swing set in the backyard crushing the grass. Two daughters, aged six and four.

The American Dream, and for a while, it was. Even to myself, my letters home sounded absurd, as if I had taken over another woman's life. I didn't feel like the girl who had grown up in my grandparents' farmhouse. I drove a station wagon, went to dinners with Wei's colleagues, gave birth in a sterile hospital coaxed along by women I'd never met before. And perhaps most strange was how normal it all felt, how easily I slipped into it, as if I had never watched movies under the stars, or played with chickens, or went to school barefoot. Yet, my story was an immigrant's tale told a million times over; in the everyday movement, it became pedestrian. I grew tomatoes and three kinds of lettuce. For dinner, I made taco salads topped with corn chips, or casseroles with Tater Tots, or Jell-O sculptures shot through with a vein of sour cream.

I had been born on the first night of the crackdown, in my parents' bedroom, guided by my father's hand. Old men who struck up conversations with me in the grocery store wondered if I was Vietnamese, or else called my homeland *Formosa*. It was a tiny island far away, almost mythical. I spoke to my parents three times a year. The first time I called home, after my arrival in San Francisco, I broke down in tears and wasted five whole minutes—a fortune—just crying. Now when I called, their voices were hollow and distant. I wondered how much of what I said they could imagine. They passed the phone back and forth, demanding to talk to the girls, who squirmed and said nothing, perplexed by these grandparents whom they had never met.

Taiwan was very far away.

30

I PICKED UP THE PICTURES the next Wednesday at the camera store on Ashby Avenue. The clerk, a college kid with a misshapen patch of scruff on his chin, had absolutely no reaction as he handed me the envelope. He was a modern-day priest, required to keep quiet counsel on all the hundreds of strange and banal photos he'd seen. My photos of masked men likely meant nothing to him.

In the parking lot, I sat in my car with the window cracked and riffled through the stack. Except for Wei, the protesters were unrecognizable. I spotted the man who had been taking pictures across the road from me. He didn't look particularly menacing. Boring, in fact, in a blue cable-knit sweater and brown slacks. A lock of hair hung over one eye. His shiftless appearance gave the impression of a man not anchored to any belief system, the kind of person who followed the scent of advantage. In the next pictures, Wei shoved him, they both looked at the broken camera, then the man glared at me as he picked up the pieces of his camera. The hatred on his face made me cringe.

A knock on my window brought me out of my thoughts.

A man smiled into my car. Black hair, translucent teeth, a sweater vest and tweed slacks. A birthmark in the middle of his cheek shaped like Illinois. He had a very square nose that matched his square jaw, and his skin glowed with the red-honey tone of a weekend at the beach. Panhandlers were common in Berkeley, remnants of the summer of love more than a decade before, or broken veterans, but he appeared to be neither. That worried me more.

"Can we chat?" he said in lightly accented English.

I glanced across the parking lot into the shop, where I could see the clerk behind the counter turning the dial on the radio and oblivious to us, and rolled up the window.

"What do you want?"

"I'll be just a moment. Come, let's get a cup of coffee," he shouted through the glass.

"I have to go." I shoved the pictures back into the envelope and put the key in the ignition.

"Milvia Street Preschool, right?" he said, still smiling.

I froze. He continued. "Stephanie gets out at one. You have plenty of time for coffee."

Stephanie. My mind stuck on my youngest daughter's name. *Stephanie.* My hand still poised at the ignition, I crushed the dangling key chain in my palm. Drive away, I thought. It can't be a crime to run over his foot. Bully your way to safety.

"Mrs. Lin? What do you say? Coffee?"

We crossed the street to a café full of old-men philosophers reading the paper and playing chess. I sat down and he brought us two cups of bitter coffee.

"My name is Lu Ai Guo." He handed me a business card, on which he was listed as a liaison for the ROC consulate, an institution that would soon disappear when Carter's Taiwan Relations Act took effect. His friendliness appeared genuine. He switched to Mandarin: "I'm sorry if I scared you. I had to get your attention."

His laughter was tinged with sheepishness. I tried to keep in mind that he was a professional, trained in psychology and manipulation and a dozen other skills I didn't even want to imagine. "Well, I won't be coy," he continued. "Let me speak frankly with you. I know who your husband is."

"Yes. He's a professor. Half of Berkeley knows who he is." Fear made my words sharper than I intended.

"I'm referring to his extracurricular activities." He scrunched his brow as if distressed by the thought.

I reflexively squeezed the purse on my lap. How naive we'd been to think we might have slipped by unnoticed. I blamed Wei; he had not been vigilant enough. Wei's political heart lay with underground activists trying to nudge the ruling KMT party, and the de facto one-party system, out of place. He wanted the dictatorship, martial law—all of it—to end. Like my father—I cringed—*like my father*—he wanted democracy and the island's self-determination, nay, its independence. The protesters' masks, Wei's "discretion"—all just false security.

"And I'm worried for you. I think that Professor Lin may be in over his head. I worry for his safety—and for yours and your daughters'. I don't think Professor Lin quite understands that this is not a game. Only Americans can play around like this with no repercussions."

"My husband *is* American."

"Then he has no business in Taiwan." His tone had teeth, but he quickly noticed his lapse. He smiled. "Please, don't be upset. I'm saying this to you because it's always the wife who is practical. I'm sure you know what I mean. While your husband is off dreaming of revolution, it is you who must remember to dress and feed the children. For practicality's sake, hear me out."

I was angry. Though I would never admit it, he was right. "You know nothing about my marriage. And what business is it of yours anyhow?"

"Forgive my big mouth. I guess I'm just a little old-fashioned. Now, I am only telling you this because I am concerned about you. I'm concerned about your daughters. I've seen too many husbands get reckless and hurt their families. I know it's a strange job, but now with the new status quo, we have a greater need to stick together, don't you agree? What's the phrase? We are strangers in a strange land here. Americans no longer care about Taiwan. Not like we do."

I stared at my coffee cup. The steam had gone away and oil sheened on the surface. I wanted to get up and run.

"So what do you want from me?"

"I don't *want* anything from you except your vigilance."

I suddenly felt my waistband cutting into my flesh, my collar choking my throat. As I picked up my coffee cup, I saw the tremor in my hand. The cup clattered onto the saucer as I set it down.

I had stood beside my father as he wrote a letter full of promises to his best friend and had watched the aftermath rip through him. Even I had despised him for it.

But this was different. On the clock behind the cash register, the long hand jerked toward the three; it was twelve fifteen. In under an hour, I would be at my daughter's preschool, set on a shady and windy street across from a nondescript apartment building where, I was often told, two famous poets had once lived in their pre-fame youth. The kind of place where people found it significant to remember the lives of young poets had to be safe. Behind the school's cedar fence, children galloped and screamed, and there was absolutely nothing to worry about.

The police would never arrest Wei. Spilling secrets would make him safer. The only price I'd have to pay was with my conscience. The torment would solely be my own.

"What kind of vigilance?" I ventured.

"Since you ask, the photos would be a nice start. You can make another set for yourself. My number is on my card. Call me if you need to. If you hear anything significant. And I'll do the same."

"You'll call me?" I asked as I tentatively pulled the bundle of photos from my purse.

"No," Mr. Lu said, "but I'll find you. Don't worry."

I sat in the car for nearly twenty minutes after Mr. Lu left. I watched people park, drop off rolls of film, emerge with envelopes of photos. None of them were accosted and forced to give up their mementos. I imagined them returning home, tossing the pictures on the table, getting around to slipping them into albums maybe this weekend, maybe during some rainy day devoted to long-neglected chores. Such easy lives. Maybe my fate had been set generations ago, Baba, then me, then my children, and so on merely discharging the ordained steps of our destiny. I pounded the passenger's seat and cursed Mr. Lu, Baba, and my jinxed forefathers.

It was nearly time to pick up Stephanie. I took a deep breath, smoothed my hair, and—my mind still wild with the unfairness of it all—returned to the camera shop and gave the negatives to the clerk.

"I need another set." I waited for him to meet my eye, to recognize me.

He scratched at his lame little beard and sniffed. He scribbled on the envelope. "Come back on Saturday." He handed me a torn stub. He was completely apathetic.

Stephanie was drawing when I arrived. Unlike the other children who looked eagerly through the door for whose parent would show up next, she didn't blink when I crouched beside her chair.

"Sweetie. What are you drawing?"

"A rocket ship." On the page was an almost-triangle with scribbles bursting from the bottom. Her lines were shaky and approximate. A person stood next to the rocket, the same size, with wildly different-shaped eyes and spindly stick limbs.

"It's lovely." I spoke to her in English. "Are you about ready to go?"

She ignored me.

I gathered her jacket and lunch box and returned to the table.

"I'm done," she declared, as if it had been her decision to leave. She passed me the drawing, then slipped her hand in mine. Stephanie looked like Wei; she had his high nose bridge and angular cupid's bow. "Stephanie": a name chosen from a book. Wei had argued for "Betsy." "It's patriotic," he claimed. I had told Wei that I liked "Stephanie" because it was multisyllabic, like a stream falling over three rocks, and because it was contemporary. And, besides, he had chosen "Emily," which he said was classical. The girls also had their Mandarin names, which I usually used when I was upset and my tongue stumbled over English.

She led me out, and when her teacher called good-bye, she responded coolly without a backward glance. She had even been an aloof baby, seeming to not need comfort, crying only in extreme situations—the opposite of her older sister, Emily, who had squalled at the smallest dampness in her diaper and like clockwork a few minutes before her scheduled feedings. Emily, who was silly and loud and the captain of every ragtag child army she formed.

In the car, Stephanie sat on the floor of the backseat.

"Stephanie, please sit on the seat."

"No." Her voice lacked defiance; her answer was simply a statement of fact: No, it was not negotiable.

"I can't drive if you don't sit in your seat." I felt as if I were in an enclosed tank of water, gasping for the final sliver of air at the top. I had almost nothing left. "Lin Yi Qing," I spat. "Sit in your seat." She pretended to not notice that I'd used my "serious" voice. She sighed and stayed a moment longer, then clambered onto the seat and I shut the door.

I clenched the steering wheel. Shouting was no use. My mother firmly believed that personalities were inborn, and you could know a child by her first few months. Stephanie had been born at Alta Bates, her tiny wrist strapped with a plastic band that read BABY GIRL LIN. Even now, when I told Stephanie I loved her, she would only look at me. Wei was much more tolerant of it—perhaps he felt a kinship with her because of their close resemblance. I held my patience most of the time. Today, it rankled me.

"I'm very upset with you," I finally said. I watched her through the rearview mirror.

She looked up and asked earnestly, "Why, Mama?"

"Because when I ask you to do something, it is for your own safety. The rules aren't arbitrary."

She frowned. "What's 'arbitrary'?"

"It means that I don't just make them up. I have good reasons. Besides, you're just a child. A good daughter listens to her mother." The words were like sand in my mouth. The rules *were* arbitrary. I was exasperated, as if she had forced me to this lie.

She kneeled on the seat and stared out the window for a moment. "Okay, Mama. I understand," she said finally. I felt an impulse to thank her, but bit my lip. I wanted her to feel the sternness of my silence, so I did not speak until we had arrived home.

That night, Wei asked about the pictures. "I thought you were going to pick them up today." He was in the doorway of the den. He rarely stood: his muscles were always half tensed, anticipating movement, like some sort of crouched cat sighting prey. Was he halfway in the room or halfway out? The lamp on the desk glowed; the room was a mess of stacked books and heaps of papers atop the thrift store desk and the frayed Oriental rug. Beyond him, a streetlamp illuminated the road and the park. Along the palisade of trees at the far side of the park, unseen, men curled in sleeping bags atop tarps, their arms woven through the straps of their backpacks.

Upstairs, the girls were asleep. I'd checked on them just minutes before: Emily's leg protruded from her nightgown. Sweat sheened across her forehead. Stephanie's thumb fell from her mouth, the indent from her teeth still glistening. My heart had seized with awe; I still had not gotten over the idea that they were my *children*.

I squatted in front of the television, clicking through the channels looking for Johnny Carson. The alternating hiss and chatter of the changing stations camouflaged the long pause as I decided how to answer. I didn't have the energy for the discussion that was sure to follow. I would tell him, I promised myself, on a day when we had the space for it.

"I went by, but the kid had ruined them somehow. He told me to come back."

"Did he let you have the ruined set? What did he do with them? Were they all ruined?"

"I didn't ask." The knob slipped off and I carefully positioned it back into the groove and turned it again. Dolly Parton was going to be on Carson.

"You should have checked. I can't believe—" He stopped. "It's probably fine but you should have checked. Just in case." He cracked his knuckles. "It's probably fine." I sensed him casting around for a relief from his worry. He yawned theatrically. "School's barely started and I'm already sick of it."

"Go to bed, honey."

"Already they're asking about the midterm."

My hand paused on the knob and I looked at him. "You'll feel better if you sleep."

"I'll have to grade all weekend. You sound like you're trying to get rid of me."

"I just want to watch a little TV. I'll be up in a bit."

The grating enthusiasm of a late-night mattress-king commercial filled the room, a glue for the moment in which we both decided not to acknowledge what we were ignoring. The jumping light made me blink; my pupils felt strained.

"I have an early class," he reminded me.

"I'll be quiet."

I waited until I heard him through the upstairs floorboards before I settled onto the sofa. The TV murmured; the studio audience occasionally clattered into applause. I could just tell him. I could just hand the card to him. Would he trust me more or less? We could construct stories together, shield ourselves with fiction. Together, we would feint. Wei could make up the stories that I would tell. And when the events we created did not come to pass, we would cry that we had been misinformed.

No, he wouldn't understand; every decision, starting from getting out of the car, had been wrong. He would tell me so in ten different ways.

My purse was on a chair in the kitchen. I found the card. I ran my finger along the thick paper edge and flicked it with my nail.

My father had sat at his own table and, with my pen and paper, had written a letter to his friend. That was deceit too. Fiction. And cooperation had not freed or protected him. When the water cried in the kettle, I had not been able to move. I'd watched my father sign the letter, all the weight of the gesture dragging down his face. Every burdened cell.

Not fate. Free will. Malleable. Choices burned to ash, new lives shoot-ing up from the devastation. Wasn't that why I had come to California?

I turned on the stove and watched the blue flames erupt one by one out of the burner. They hissed. I touched the corner of the card to the fire and the paper lit up. The edges curled, blackened, quickly eaten. When the heat seared my fingers, I dropped it in the sink.

31

IN THE MORNING, I had Nineteenth-Century American Literature and a James Joyce seminar back-to-back. I was one year away from finishing my degree in English literature. I laughed when I thought about it. I had come to the United States with a smattering of English, and soon I would have a bachelor's degree.

I'd been told that America was the land of equality, where the garbage-man had as much value as the president, but status had a place here too, which I discovered as the wife of a professor. Among the other faculty wives, I was the only one who had been a waitress. At faculty gatherings, I felt naked, my ignorance exposed and compounded by my frustrations with English.

"I love the delicacy of Asian women," one wife commented to me. "So *petite,* so graceful." Self-conscious with the language, I could only nod and smile while I railed against her silently in a string of words that were anything but delicate. *Cow! Tell me next how my culture has given me the skills to be an amazing house cleaner. An obedient wife. Ask me how many of my friends were prostitutes for GIs.* They were kind—too kind—as if I were helpless as a bald little newborn mole and they had to show how careful they could be with me, a testament to their generous and socially liberal natures.

I had to learn to speak. In the early days, though I had some rudi-mentary understanding from my lessons in Taiwan, learning the language was like puzzling out a code. I'd sit with my dictionary and piece it out. I learned roots and imagined histories extending down from each word.

I marveled that I could understand individual words, but putting them together in a sentence would transform the meaning of all of them. And when Emily started school, she brought home more words for me. And culture too, through the jump-rope chants and gruesome urban legends that are perpetuated in each generation as if they are recent creations. From her, I learned rhyme and pun and even double entendre, which made her laugh though she clearly had no idea what they meant.

"Miss Susie had a steamboat, the steamboat had a bell," Emily sang. "Miss Susie went to heaven, the steamboat went to . . . Hello, operator, please give me number nine. And if you disconnect me, I'll kick you from . . . Behind the 'frigerator, there was a piece of glass. Miss Susie fell upon it, and broke her little . . . Ask me no more questions, tell me no more lies. Miss Susie told me all this, the day before she . . ."

Emily stopped when she noticed I was both crying and laughing. She giggled. "Mom, what's so funny?"

I tried to catch my breath and wiped my face. "It's a funny song, darling. I'm not laughing at you. Go on."

Her laugh sounded like a bark of surprise. "You're silly, Mommy!" And then she fell into a fit of giggles too and continued the song.

After my seminar, I went and found Wei in his office hours. It was still early in the semester, and the halls were recently waxed and empty.

He had arranged his desk to face the door. Visitors squinted into the light of the window behind him while he sat in a halo. The books on the Steelcase shelves lay on their back covers, or up on their spines, no reason to their arrangement. Some weighted down stacks of unclaimed final exams. He had one hand thrust up in his hair and, with the other, tapped his chin with a pencil. He wore corduroys in neutral tones and some sort of thin sweater every day. This was his idea of a professorial uniform.

I felt a tightening from my throat to my chest. I knocked on the open door. "Professor Lin? I brought lunch."

He looked up and smiled. "Happy anniversary. I've been told this is our bronze anniversary. I hope you brought a sculpture."

We had married before falling in love, and I had made conscious note of all the subsequent moments. The night, six months in, when we brought home mangoes from the city and sex turned deeper than lust. The rainy day when he held an umbrella over me and taught me *ai ai gasa*, the Japanese term for lovers sharing an umbrella.

"No sculptures, just leftovers." I unpacked the mustard-colored Tupperware and peeled off the sunburst lids.

"How was class?" he asked.

"Good. I'm the oldest one in there. No one talks to me." I unwrapped chopsticks from their paper towel sheath and set them carefully across one of the bowls. He watched absentmindedly.

"They probably think you are a graduate student."

I shrugged. "Maybe. Come on, eat."

For the first year, we had lived in a studio on Shattuck Avenue, in a grand building with a canopy over the front door, rows of tiny brass mailboxes in the lobby, and an elevator with an accordion door. The bathroom had separate taps for hot and cold water, and its tiny single-pane window overlooked an airshaft and down into the window across the way. The small kitchenette had a California cooler where I stored produce. At night, our sleep stench filled the room, and every morning I opened the front window to the traffic on Shattuck. We had a television with foil-wrapped bunny ears set on an old dining chair.

During my first months in Berkeley, I didn't dress until the early afternoon. I watched TV all morning, then wandered the streets. I was shocked by the people who went to work and school in shorts and T-shirts, who grew thick beards and wore feathers in their hair. Soapbox preachers decrypted the Bible so that we would know how closely to the devil we clung and that the war in Southeast Asia foretold the Apocalypse. The young, earnest students around him cried, "Tell it, brother." Berkeley was nearly a decade past the Free Speech Movement and its tear gas and fire hoses; its reputation was firmly established. The war seemed endless and people spoke to me in loud, slow voices, some sympathetic, some angry, as if by virtue of my face I were directly tied to all their pain. When Wei came home in the afternoons, I'd be in my house clothes again, sitting at the dinette as if I'd never left.

Wei flipped through homework assignments as he picked at lunch. Years ago, a silence like this would have worried me. Now, I found it soothing.

He snapped the lid back on the Tupperware and wiped his mouth. "Let's walk."

"Are you taking me somewhere romantic?" I teased.

"It's a beautiful day," he said, but his eyes were on his crumpled napkin.

Students were strewn across steps and the lawns or walking briskly to class. Wei didn't like to be touched—no hand-holding or linked arms—on campus. It wasn't professional. With an appropriate space between us, we strolled to the oak-shaded creek at the bottom of the Faculty Glade.

He said, "I didn't want to talk in my office."

The anniversary glow was over. He knew. Mr. Lu must have come to him too. Maybe he wanted us to watch each other, but Wei—upstanding, moral Wei—was too loyal to keep it from me. Still, I was nonchalant. "About what?"

On a bench, two students necked. He gripped her cheek and she urged her breasts into him. I thought they were showing off. Wei watched them as he spoke.

"Tang Jia Bao left Taiwan." Tang Jia Bao, a friend of a friend, had been under house arrest for a year for speaking out against the government. He had become a default martyr of the Taiwanese democracy movement and we had been following his story.

"They've stopped their surveillance?"

"No."

"Then how?"

"It's not important. He's in Sweden now, and he's applied for a visa to come here. And if all goes well, he will."

I suddenly understood. "Stop. No. No, Wei."

He continued. "I want him to stay with us."

"Wei. Stop."

His eyes left the groping couple and met mine. "I want him to stay with us."

In the early days, I used to say to my husband, *Tell me something that happened when you were five.*

What's the worst thing you ever did?

In the dark, late at night, when the broadcasting day had ended and all the TV channels had turned to the monotonous night programming of a waving American flag against the backdrop of the national anthem, I asked him questions. *Who do your parents love more—you or your brother?*

What's the biggest lie you ever told?

His eyes hunted my expression for an answer. I looked again toward the couple on the bench. They pulled away from each other and the girl wiped the corners of her mouth with her fingertips. It was a delicate, sheepish gesture.

"For how long?"

"It might be days; it might be weeks."

I shook my head. "Don't tell me any more."

"Once he gets here, it'll be fine. It's all aboveboard. We just need to help him get on his feet."

"What about the girls?"

He twisted my hair around his fingers. It was a gesture like thumb-sucking, some childhood habit of comfort. "The girls will be fine. They won't know a thing."

I batted his hand away. "I don't care what they know or don't know. Will it be safe for them?"

"I told you, once he's here, it'll be fine. What are you worried about?"

"'Fine' like the man taking your picture last week? If it is 'fine,' why did you wear a mask? You know they are already watching us. You saw him taking pictures." And Mr. Lu, I thought. They are watching us carefully. "What makes you think that they don't know Emily's and Stephanie's school schedules?"

"They're children. No one will hurt them."

I wished I could believe him. I wanted to tell him about Mr. Lu, and his tone when he mentioned Stephanie's preschool. The memory of it brought out gooseflesh. A tiny girl was surely a nothing obstacle. I reassured myself: I had burned the card. It was over. It had never happened.

I clasped his shoulder, reassured by the curve of muscle. "How long?"

"Like I said, I don't know. You don't need to worry. You'll wake up one day and he'll be here and the girls will be fine."

That's how I wanted it. I wanted to wake up with the entire situation taken care of: all of us safe, all of us innocent. I didn't want the details. I wanted to be able to say with conviction—to Mr. Lu or anybody else—*I don't know.*

Early on, I'd wanted to know everything. I looked at the bottom of Wei's feet, searched for all his birthmarks. I kept him awake with questions.

What kind of student were you?

Who was your childhood crush?

Did your parents fight? About what?

What is your recurring nightmare?

32

JIA BAO CAME TO US late one night in mid-September, his face obscured by a thick beard, bearing a single duffel bag. He felt like a cousin or schoolmate I'd not seen since childhood, unknown yet familiar. The sense that we had met before was so strong that I had to comment on it when Wei introduced us on the porch, where I had been waiting as soon as I heard our car pull up.

"My wife," Wei said.

"Mr. Tang. Welcome," I said. I seemed to step through uncanny curtains of time as déjà vu washed over me. "Your face is so familiar."

"Well, he's been in every paper by now." Wei sounded embarrassed. He patted me on the back. "Let's go inside."

"We probably know a few people in common," Jia Bao said politely.

"Of course," I said.

"Of course," Wei echoed. "Now, let me show you around."

Not quite sure of what to do with myself, I followed as Wei led him through the house. Then Wei invited him to freshen up, and when he disappeared into our guest bath, Wei and I whispered in the kitchen.

"Is he okay?" I asked.

Wei kissed my forehead, squeezed my shoulders, and hushed me.

I worried about Mr. Lu. We now housed a brightly colored bird, highly sought and visible, and I wanted to cloak our home in drab cloth until he disappeared again.

The phone rang all night, people eager to know that Jia Bao was safe. Wei and I were restless too. I tried to read a novel. I scanned entire pages and could not remember a single word. I eavesdropped on Jia Bao's calls while Wei pretended to put his papers in order. At three a.m., Emily came downstairs, her hair damp on her forehead.

"I had a bad dream, Mom."

I pulled her onto my lap. "What was your dream? If you talk about it, it will go away." I pushed aside her sweaty hair and blew on her skin.

"So many bells were ringing. Like a house full of bells and I couldn't make them stop."

"Darling, that was just the phone. Remember I told you Uncle Jia Bao was coming to visit from Taiwan? His friends are calling to welcome him." Sure enough, the phone rang again, and Wei picked up the extension in the office. "See? Daddy just got it."

"I want to meet Uncle Jia Bao."

"It's late now. In the morning." I hugged her and she nestled against me. Soon, we both fell asleep on the sofa with the light on.

In the morning, when I came back from taking the girls to school, Jia Bao was barefoot and gazing at our small yard through the back door.

"Did you eat?" I asked. On the table, I'd left a pastry and coffee for him.

"It's beautiful." His enunciation was crisp. I could imagine his clean voice echoing in a lecture hall. Young redwoods lined the back fence and a patch of bamboo obscured our view of the house on the right. We were in the midst of an Indian summer, and the heat had wilted the lawn. In the far left corner, Stephanie and Emily's swing set gleamed in the sun. The yard was modest, but I tried to see it through his eyes. So much green.

"In the spring, I'll plant flowers."

I wondered what I would have to say to him in the hours until Wei came home. Should I treat him like an out-of-town guest, take him on a tour of the town? Or enclose him in a garret, sneak him pieces of bread folded into napkins? Was he safe now? Would he be like my father, glimpsing danger in every gesture?

He was wan from travel, his shirt crumpled from the suitcase. He was at least four inches shorter than Wei, small boned. A night in prison would crush him—and yet he'd survived much more, his figure belying the density of being, the will to revolution. Despite this, I pitied him. I knew what it was to land here, dizzy, the past wiped away by an ocean, the future unfurling like an unexploited continent.

"I'm going grocery shopping," I finally said. "Do you want to come?"

At the supermarket, he insisted on pushing the cart. He seemed pleased by the utter banality of the gesture.

He read everything aloud: the signs for the trading stamps that cus-tomers exchanged for sets of dishes, the price per pound of plums, the cuts of meat. His accent was light, his English fluent, and yet he read on. His narration of our trip was in a low voice, and I kept my head down, but I wondered if people around us gave second looks when he said, "Milk, a dollar sixty-three a gallon. Bread, fifty cents."

After shopping, we went for gas. The oil crisis had changed refueling from a casual errand into a major event. The station near our house was open that day, and we joined the line of cars waiting to fuel up. I shut off the engine. It was going to be a while. We cranked down the windows. I leaned against the door, an elbow poking out the open window. Just con-sidering the line tired me.

"How old are your children?" I asked.

He told me they were in middle school. He had uncharacteristically kissed them good night before he left and they had eyed him suspiciously. But in that kind of situation, I knew, kids learn to say nothing. We didn't acknowledge their uncertainty: whether or when he'd see them again, or who they would be when they did finally reunite.

"And what does your wife do?"

"She's a doctor." He watched the attendant pumping gas, then smiled grimly. "She was fired after my arrest, but she opened her own clinic."

"She must be so relieved that you're here." I noticed how bright I tried to make my voice, how I had widened my eyes in nodding encourage-ment: *Reassure yourself—and me—that this was not a mistake.*

He said nothing.

A gnat flew in and circled the dash. I waved it away.

"Were you scared?" The question burst out of me. I was embarrassed by my lack of tact.

Jia Bao took his time answering.

"I was more afraid of what would happen if I didn't leave. But I knew what it meant to people if I did." He tugged a pack of cigarettes from his front pocket. "Do you mind?" I shook my head and he lit one. I pulled out the ashtray.

"I didn't want to go back to prison. They would have sent me back. That government does not care about international censure. And the world does not care about someone like me. They would justify it as treason or some other scandal. I'd go away and my name would fade. There are already thousands like me who didn't leave. They've been shipped off to Green Island, and it's like they don't exist."

Green Island. The tiny place just off the eastern coast of Taiwan where Baba had gone. A beautiful name for the home of the Oasis Villa, the political prison. The writer Bo Yang had recently finished a nine-year sentence there. His crime: translating Popeye cartoons. One in particular had been read as critical of the Generalissimo. Popeye, with Swee'Pea at his side, surveys an island and says, "I'll be king of that island and you will be my darling prince." The dictator who cannot be named. Jia Bao was right: I'd forgotten about Bo Yang. I'd forgotten about so much in my time away. Looking at Jia Bao, exhaling smoke out the window and tapping ash into the tray, I thought of my father. This is what Baba had wanted to do. Leave. But he had been caught.

"What's the point?" I asked even though I didn't expect an answer.

He shook his head. "I don't know. Power." He took a drag on the cigarette.

"To what end?"

When he exhaled, the smoke melted from his mouth like a wave of fog. "Even power is overpowered by the desire for it. Assassinations, purging, massacres: all these inhabited the nucleus of every cell. Every decision tainted by fear. What else can account for the Generalissimo's statement: *Better to kill a hundred innocent men than let one guilty go free.* Not pure cruelty, but paranoia."

Only after moving to the United States had I begun to think of Chiang Kai-shek as a dictator, but the word "dictator" turns him to stone, a statue in a traffic roundabout, or a portrait on a wall. He was a man. A man who ate daily, who pissed and shat and made love. Jia Bao was right: the desire for such extreme power can be only selfish, only human.

"And why do you fight it? Can you fight it?"

The cars ahead had moved, and Jia Bao waited until I too moved forward and turned off the engine again.

"Your father did." When I heard his words, I felt as if the car was lurching.

My mouth felt sticky as I answered, "You know my father?"

"The island is small."

I wondered what he had heard: about Baba's imprisonment, or what had happened with Su Ming Guo, or all of it. To the new generation opposing the one party, was Baba a simple traitor or a complicated hero?

"He tried," I said. "He failed."

"I don't think so." He looked me in the eye. "Your father, all those men—I'm here, what we're doing, the opposition—they're here because of those men." Though he was not traditionally handsome, his compact assuredness was attractive.

I turned away. The woman in front of us dangled her legs out the open door and fanned herself with a magazine.

"That's kind of you to say." I felt ill. "God, it's so hot." I threw open my door, but it did nothing.

"Once you realize all our assumptions about power are created by the powerful, you understand it must be changed. You rethink power. Not the power that is desire, or dominance. The power that is strength."

He smashed out the cigarette. He smoked the same brand of Taiwanese cigarettes as my father, and the faint yellowish tinge of his fingers was pure nostalgia. An urge to smell his fingers struck me. I felt like crying.

"It matters," he said. "I'm sure it felt like it was for nothing. Maybe my children will feel that way too. But it matters." He looked out the window. A pair of college girls in peasant tops and long skirts walked by. They cut through the line of cars and their laughter floated over us. "It matters."

We ate BLTs on the back deck. We warmed our toes in the sun. The silence felt easy between us.

He reclined on the deck steps and stretched his legs out before him. Crows landed on the boughs of the redwoods and the trees shuddered.

I wondered how he had come to be sitting here with me, in Berkeley, eating sandwiches. He was too well known in Taiwan; his arrest had been splashed across the newspapers. Everyone knew his face. He was labeled a traitor, a man working to dismantle the foundation of the country. Most people knew better than to believe the stories planted in the paper, but truth or not, his face was known.

"How did you do it?" I spoke in a low voice, as if the retired nurse next door, rustling in her garden beyond the bamboo stand, would understand our Taiwanese, or even care. Had he followed the route of Peng Ming-min, who had been arrested for writing the Formosa Declaration of Independence? It was rumored that Peng had escaped house arrest—and the country—by changing his face. He grew a beard to an eccentric length that was meant to be a physical manifestation of his misery. He took long, meandering walks, pretending to be oblivious to the men tracking him. He erased all meaning from his actions. Then he shaved his beard and his head. Now he was smooth-faced and pert. He ironed and starched every piece of clothing before he left the house. After a few weeks, he let the beard grow again. Sometimes, he would go out to shop; other times, he would not leave his home for days.

He kept up his erratic behavior for months, until the surveillance team grew so weary that it paid no attention to whether he had a beard, no attention to whether his coat was bulky or he wore pajamas. The team pinned no meaning to whether he left at noon or midnight.

One cold night, Peng made his escape. He stayed in a safehouse for two days, then, under the watchful eyes of comrades posted along the route, he left the island. He arrived in Sweden a couple of days later with no papers and asking for asylum. After a few months there, he applied for a visa to the United States. I knew Jia Bao had followed a similar route, but *how*?

Jia Bao laughed. "I can only say it was like the song. 'I get by with a little help from my friends.' I'm sorry, that's all I can say about it."

"I understand."

He had the courage Wei had been seeking. But Wei could only circle around it, talking about it, yearning for it. I pushed away the thought. I reminded myself that my husband *was* sincere. Half of courage was opportunity, wasn't it?

The clock in the living room tolled. It was one—I had to pick up Stephanie. I asked Jia Bao if he wanted to come, but he declined. The weariness of jet lag drifted over his face, but he said he wanted to go for a run. How different it must have been for him to move through these wide streets unencumbered, to not appear as if he was running *away*. I found an extra key strung on an unmarked, flimsy metal-and-paper key fob in our kitchen catchall drawer and brought it to him. He squeezed it in his palm and leaned back onto the deck steps, where I left him in the sun.

33

IT TOOK FOUR SECONDS for a body to reach the water from the bridge. Seventy-six miles an hour. Dead on impact.

I had arrived in America on my twenty-fifth birthday. I passed through customs, nervously using my English for the first time in a real context to answer the agent's questions, then pushed my luggage cart through the gates to find Wei waiting for me, bouquet of daisies in hand. His voice sounded choked when he called my name and I smiled shyly. "Welcome home," he said. He handed me the flowers and took the cart, and we didn't hug until we had reached the car. We celebrated my birthday that weekend. Wei brought me to the Golden Gate Bridge. I had a plaid flannel coat. We didn't touch as we walked, and when we reached the midpoint, Wei told me to stop.

Some people survived the jump and died of hypothermia.

In the middle of the bridge, Wei took my picture. My eyes watered in the wind. Then we switched places and I took Wei's picture. This is what you did in the city. You took a picture on the bridge. The fog clouded around you, and you squinted as the wind whipped your hair. Then you walked back to your car and found a greasy spoon in Chinatown and ate dim sum off chipped melamine plates.

The picture on the bridge, two days after my birthday, was the first picture of me taken in America. I sent it to my parents. I counted off the days on the calendar: what day it would arrive, and how long until I'd receive their letter back. I asked for a picture of my niece and nephews.

The day after they received my photo, Ah Zhay called.

Baba had tried to kill himself. Some kill themselves out of despair; others commit suicide to save face. Baba had an old-fashioned idea of honor, but the gesture was a pathetic yearning for martyrdom too. He'd thrown himself into the river with a cinder block tied to his leg. But a man riding by on his bicycle had seen him and stopped. He dove into the water and, with a pocketknife, cut Baba free.

Jumpers who want to be saved leap from the side facing the city. Those who want to die face the open sea.

Baba was limp and distraught. Water spewed from his mouth, and the man cried, "Uncle! What's the matter with your life?" After Baba's color returned to normal, he told the man to go, but the man refused and they sat, in a stalemate, on the riverbank for nearly an hour as Baba's clothes dried. Finally, the man escorted Baba home and told my mother what had happened. Baba hung his head, an angry and scolded child.

I didn't tell Wei. I said good-bye and returned to the bed, which was our only large piece of furniture. Ah Zhay's phone call felt like a dream. I knew that later the news about Baba would clarify into something real, and I would cry—alone in the shower when Wei was at school—but, for now, I sat beside my husband as he watched *The Sonny and Cher Comedy Hour* and I laughed along even though I didn't understand a word.

Bundled up against the mist and wind, we walked across the Golden Gate Bridge. Wei carried Stephanie, and I gripped Emily's hand. Our cheeks were bright with the cold, our skin damp. Jia Bao walked alongside Wei, and I followed behind. The wind blew away their words. Children screamed, and the indeterminate snap of adult voices followed. Cars roared past, masking everything except our own breath in our ears and the ambient rush of the ocean below. Now here with the girls and Jia Bao, we stopped midway across. I tipped my head back and gazed up at the orange tower, the cables, the rivets. I crouched beside Emily and whispered in her ear: "Look." We grew dizzy gazing up.

Wei said, "I'll take your picture."

Jia Bao stood with the city behind him. The fog weighed down the headlands and the cypresses dripped into the wind. He smiled. Then he beckoned for the camera and said he would take our picture as a family. I picked up Emily. The four of us pressed together. The space between photographer and photographed was an invisible barrier that could not be trespassed. Other tourists swerved around the bubble between us, squeezing behind Jia Bao. I told the girls to smile.

We walked through the Dragon Gate of Chinatown and past the shops selling paper lanterns and tinkling metal balls that were good for your wrists but were rumored to have been passed on by concubines to improve other muscles, past the cheap T-shirts and fake ivory carvings, past tourists speaking in German and French and Italian and hunchbacked grandmothers in cloth slippers tugging along their reluctant grandchildren to the heart of Grant Avenue, toward a cacophony of honking cars. Traffic had stopped and the intersection was filled with old men clutching a long cloth banner that read KUOMINTANG: THE RIGHTFUL HEIRS OF CHINA. They faced off against a bank of young Chinese Americans who were waving communist flags and shouting, "Down with feudalism!"

"What's this?" Jia Bao asked.

Wei laughed. "The old KMT are still having a hard time with the new status quo."

"They've been doing this for years," I said.

Since the 1911 revolution, Chinatown had been filled with KMT supporters who thought themselves the torch carriers of Sun Yat-sen's republic. They ran the tongs and filled the rosters of the benevolent associations. Then consciousness-raising hit, and young, radicalized Chinese Americans began loving Mao and all things China. Once in a while, the old guard, the bachelors filling the residential motels who had lost families to the communists, feeling threatened, would shine their shoes, take out their signs, and step into the streets. To the younger generation, the KMT represented old-school elitism, something to be dismantled. Rumors too claimed that the KMT paid protesters. Last year, the police had been held up at another protest across town, leaving enough time for fifteen people to be brutally beaten by these paid hoodlums. It had killed tourism in Chinatown for a while.

Among the other tourist families, we watched the protesters, young men and women in their ringer tees and collared velour versus grizzled men—old, lonely bachelors owning nothing more than their principles—in their pressed white shirts, armpits scrubbed thin. If they hadn't fought for the KMT, then for what?

Emily covered her ears. "Mom, I'm bored. This is so boring."

A man came out of his taxi and screamed until his face turned purple. The honking and shouting masked his words, but we saw their force in the sunlight illuminating his spittle. He jumped back in his car and reversed suddenly, slamming into the car behind him, then charged forward and banged the car in front. Its bumper jerked into the crowd and a handful of people screamed. The students pressed closer to their opposition. The taxi thrust up onto the sidewalk, scaring people from its path. We were on the other side of the street, but Wei picked up Stephanie and pushed us to the window of the corner shop. Stephanie shrieked. My heart thumping, I lifted Emily and turned so that I stood between her and the street. People cried angrily at the taxi driver, and he turned onto California Street and sped away.

Emily said again, "This is so boring," even though she had thrown her arms around my neck in fear and excitement.

34

WHEN THE RUMOR of Jia Bao's escape to Sweden first broke, the authorities in Taiwan brushed it away as an impossibility. Rumor became news and, in a state of disbelief, they closed the harbors and airports and scoured the island. He was really gone, as a picture accompanying an article in a Stockholm newspaper attested. I spoke with my sister, who asked, "Can you believe it? Where has he gone?"

I answered, "I have no idea." I was afraid to tell her. It would only put them in danger to know. Wei had taught me the term "plausible deniability."

"If only Baba had been so lucky," she said.

And now Jia Bao was in America. The only thing that might silence him was dangling threat over his family: his wife's clinic was closed according to an obscure building ordinance; his daughter was denied entrance into one of the top middle schools, despite her scores; and a cousin had the imports for his store held up by customs and left moldering on the docks. Jia Bao's only weapon was fame. While the island government struggled to piece together a plan to smother this public relations mess—what stories this former political prisoner could tell!—we raised Jia Bao's profile by throwing a party.

Wei and I had gone back and forth about it for a week, whispering our argument in bed so Jia Bao would not know. We smiled all day, but at night, alone, we went over the same debate, day after day, getting nowhere. I was exhausted.

"You promised me you'd keep us safe." Frustrated, I pounded the bed. The blankets flattened the sound, making me feel even more impotent.

"This is the safest thing we can do," Wei insisted.

"How? Everyone will know he's here!"

"Exactly. No quiet disappearance will be possible. The American media would be all over it. They will keep him alive. If everyone knows, anything that happens to him will look suspicious. Do you think the KMT will risk losing face like that?"

"Do you think they care about face? You are so infuriating!" I grabbed a pillow and screamed into it.

Wei hushed me. "Stop. The kids will think we're doing something strange up here." He shot me a mischievous grin, then leaned over and kissed my neck. "This is the best way. Trust me."

"What are you looking for, Mom?" Emily asked as we stepped onto the porch. I held Stephanie, who, still drowsy, gripped my neck and rested her head on my shoulder.

"Please hurry. We're going to be late." I nudged her down the steps toward the front gate and she kicked her *Happy Days* lunch box with one knee and then the other as she walked. No wonder the Fonz was looking a little worse for wear when I'd packed her lunch the night before.

She sighed and said to the rhythm of her lunch-box drum: "Look both ways before you cross the street. Every morning, you look both ways like we're crossing the street. But we're not"—she banged her lunch box again—"even on"—another bang—"the street."

I opened the car door and urged her in, then lowered Stephanie onto the seat. "Come on, baby girl, you have to let go of Mommy now." She crawled in and slumped over, closing her eyes. "If you are this sleepy every morning, you're going to have to go to bed earlier," I warned. She let out a moan of protest and yawned.

I slid into the driver's seat, started the car, and watched in the rearview mirror as exhaust filled the air behind us. I thought about Emily's question as we drove to school. What did I expect to see each morning when I scanned the street as we stepped out at seven thirty, when the fog still hazed the neighborhood? An unmarked black car parked at a discreet distance, two men in mirrored sunglasses in the front seat? A man in a trench coat skulking around beneath our windows with a steno pad and a sharp number two pencil? I blamed Wei for my paranoia.

"Mom!" Emily wailed.

"What?" I snapped. I reflexively tapped the brake, ready to screech to a stop for whatever animal scurrying before us that I'd missed in my reverie.

"You passed my school!"

I glanced around. I'd overshot the school by two blocks. "Okay, okay. I'm turning around."

The drive to school was muscle memory, and my inattention alarmed me. Wei. Wei had set all this in motion. Outside of the house, every moment now seemed perilous. And now he wanted to open our house to the world with a party for Jia Bao.

"Jerk," I cursed as I swung back around the block to take my place in the school drop-off queue.

"Me, Mom?" Emily asked.

"What?"

"Am I a jerk?"

"No, honey, not you. No one. I'm just talking to myself."

Three weeks later, it was a rare warm Berkeley evening, and even with the windows open, the thick heat of fifty people crammed into our house—their breath and laughter and odor—was stifling. I threw open the front door. The party spilled out the back door, onto the deck and into the yard. Figures, scarcely lit by the tea lights flickering on the railings, shifted on the grass, far back in the shadows near the swing set.

The ambient sound track was tinkling glass and the surge of voices, flattened every so often by the collective, eerie silence that seems to fall innately on a group. We had a mix of university people, Amnesty International staff, and our Taiwanese American friends. They marked themselves off into cliques, and sometimes a quip at the wine table would lock strangers into conversation for an uncomfortable five minutes.

Jia Bao stayed on the sofa. The center of the celebration, he drew people to him. Everyone was eager to say hello, to ask of his escape, to commend him on his fight. I passed around a platter of Vienna sausages, cubes of cheddar, and manzanilla olives, each speared with a toothpick decorated in a frill of colored cellophane.

People lingered on the front walk and smoked, tapping ash onto the grass.

We depended on safety in numbers. The vigilance of the group. I didn't notice Mr. Lu slip in. Behind me, I heard his voice: "I agree. Mr. Tang is certainly a symbol of the power of democracy and freedom."

I jerked around.

He spoke calmly to one of Wei's colleagues. He acknowledged me with a nod and continued talking.

"Pardon me," I said, and put out my hand. "I'm Wei Lin's wife. You are . . . ?"

He smiled at my game and shook my hand. "Mr. Lu. I was just saying to Mr. Boyd here that this is a lovely party."

Wei's colleague agreed, said something generically kind about the food, then excused himself to refill his wineglass.

As soon as he was out of earshot, I muttered, "Why are you here?"

"I was invited. We have mutual friends, you know. It's a small community. I'm surprised—and a little hurt—that you didn't invite me yourself. This is a big deal, right? Tang Jia Bao escaping house arrest and making it all the way to California. In certain circles, this is cause for a huge celebration."

The room was hot. Someone had turned off a lamp. The dark was hotter. My hair clung to my neck. I searched the room for Wei—I'm sure Mr. Lu saw my frantic look.

"Please, enjoy yourself." I pushed the words out between my clenched teeth. Still carrying the half-empty tray of food, I squeezed between people, trying not to show my panic. At least the girls were at a friend's house. Wei was not among the smokers in the front or with the intimate shadows in the back. The kitchen too was as crowded as the living room, but he was not here either. I set the tray on the cold stove and waded back into the other room.

The door to the den was ajar. Wei stood at the bookcase next to a diminutive woman. At the sudden rush of noise through the opening door, they both turned.

"Helen," I said. "It's good to see you."

I didn't know her well. She and her husband, James, lived in the Berkeley Hills in a house much larger than ours. Our girls were close in age, and we had been to their house for dinner a few times. James and Wei shared political views and knew each other from their undergraduate years at National Taiwan University. Helen, also from their university cohort, was perfectly, blandly pleasant, with feathered hair and slim wrists that twisted like bird bones wrapped in muslin.

Her lips were wine stained, and her smile revealed purple-tinted teeth. "Great party. You worked so hard."

I deflected her compliment. "Hardly any work at all. It's an honor." I shot her a blithe smile and hoped she read it as sincere. I turned to Wei and, in a careful mock-chiding tone, I said, "Mr. Lin, I need you."

"Aha, someone hasn't been pulling his weight," Helen said. "Well, then, I'm going to excuse myself and get more wine." She waggled her empty glass. As she walked past me, I caught the scent of L'Air du Temps, such a chaste aroma, and I thought of the frosted doves that kissed atop the swirled glass bottle. She shut the door.

"We have a problem," I said.

Wei grasped both my shoulders and kissed my forehead. "What?"

"There's a man here who—who shouldn't be here."

Wei stepped back. "Who?"

"From the consulate. I don't think he's supposed to be here."

"How do you know?"

"I overheard him."

Wei sank into our old orange armchair, a remnant from our days on Shattuck Avenue. I'd stitched squares of brown cloth over its thinned arms. "Well, of course they know Jia Bao's here." He bit his knuckle. "Maybe this is good. He can't hide. We're not afraid."

"I'm afraid."

He dismissed me with a low hiss. "He'll look and leave. There's nothing he can do here." He asked me what Mr. Lu looked like. "We'll act like we don't even care. I won't even say hello. There's nothing to be afraid of."

I wanted to believe him.

The candles were extinguished and gathered, hard wax and singed wicks piled on the kitchen table. I'd decided to wait on the dishes until morning, and they sat in dirty but orderly stacks on the counter. Garbage bags of stained paper cups were heaped in the corner of the kitchen. We'd pushed some of the chairs back into place just for a semblance of order. The girls were sleeping and Jia Bao had gone to bed as well.

I stood in the doorway between the bathroom and our bedroom, rubbing lotion into my hands. In a commercial, standing before a woman dancing the hula, Don Ho had promised silky soft skin and I was Madison Avenue's perfect victim. I was nearly through with the bottle, had to twist off the pump, turn the bottle upside down, and shake and squeeze the moisturizer through the lotion congealed and clumped at the opening.

"I hate that stuff," Wei said. "It smells like I don't know what." He flung his arm over his eyes. "Why do you think he came? To scare us?"

I riffled through the vanity drawer, feigning disinterest. "I'm sure he had orders to check things out."

"He just wanted to see for himself," Wei affirmed. His eyes followed me as I walked across the room and slipped into bed. "How did you know who he was again?"

I leaned over and switched off the bedside lamp. "I heard him telling someone." I reminded myself I hadn't done anything. I hadn't even memorized the number on the card first, like some harried heroine.

"And he just introduced himself like that? 'Hi, I'm from the consulate'?"

I nodded. In the dark, he felt the gesture on the pillow.

"There has to be more. I'll talk to Jia Bao about it," he said finally.

"How long is he going to stay?"

"It's bigger than that." He answered curtly as if abstractions could muffle the danger.

"Wei."

My impatient, pleading utterance of his name hung in the room. I waited for his defense, though I could already anticipate everything he'd say. I ground my teeth. I wanted a vote in this time line.

"Wei?" I said again.

I caught the slow, deep drift of his breath.

He was asleep.

The shadow-leaves danced on the wall. A chair leg stuttered across the floor downstairs and then silence. I wondered how I could be so wound with tension while he slept easily. In the distance, a train whistle screamed and a dog barked. Finally, I took a book from the stack beneath the bedside table, found my robe, and crept down the stairs.

. . .

The den light was on; Jia Bao worked at the desk. He looked up as I approached. "Did I wake you up?"

I waved the book. "I need to finish this for class."

He stood. "I'll work in my room."

The perfect hostess, I backed toward the door. "No, no, I can read on the sofa."

"Please."

"No, stay there."

But reading did not calm me either. Just hours before, Mr. Lu had been in this room. He had touched my furniture, pissed in my toilet, wiped his hands on my towels. I scanned the pages of my book, but his violations obscured the text, and I remembered nothing, so I set the book down and went to the kitchen.

And had he stood here too, surveying my taste in dishware and choice of wine, cataloging and interpreting as a good spy should? As I filled the kettle, I looked at my reflection in the black window. Was it only sleeplessness dragging down my face? A blurred figure slipped in behind me. I turned off the faucet. Jia Bao stretched his arms and cracked his knuckles.

"You're a night owl like me," he said.

"Not usually." I set the kettle on the stove. The gas clicked and the flame hissed to life. "I'm making tea. Want some?"

He murmured some sort of affirmation and slid into a seat at the breakfast nook table. He drummed the surface, the energy of his racing mind expended through his fingers. "I want to write a book. My father died in the March Massacre."

"I didn't know that." I stayed by the stove and faced him across the kitchen. I thought of my own father, alive. I didn't want to talk about it, but he continued.

"I was just a child. I don't remember him. I vaguely remember the MPs coming to arrest him. They didn't bother wiping their boots before they came in. My mother was hysterical. She spent the whole night scrubbing the dirt from the floor, as if it would bring him back. I can't remember his face. I have to look at pictures to remind myself."

"I'm sorry." The words came out as a lame whisper. "Did you find out what happened to him?"

"We found his body in the street the next day. Shot in the chest and bled to death. Right outside our gate and we had no idea. My mother found him. She dragged him in and washed his body. A man from the American consulate came and took a picture." A scar along his chin like a fine white thread danced as he spoke. Something lodged in his throat—spittle or emotion—and he cleared it.

"What did they do about it?"

"What could they do? It was none of their business. An internal matter. The Generalissimo was an ally. You don't criticize your friends." The kettle started to cry and I quickly shut off the flame so the whistle wouldn't wake the girls. His voice was weary. "I don't blame Carter. He's right to turn the KMT into an international pariah. Their time has come."

I brought the tea to the table and he thanked me.

We sat for a while in silence, warming our hands on the cups.

The Generalissimo had died in 1975, but—befitting a monarchy—his son Chiang Ching-kuo had continued the legacy. I still try to make sense of Chiang Kai-shek. He was handsome really: a charming smile, kind eyes, that jaunty mustache. None of the sharpness of Hitler or the weightiness of Franco.

My family had been lucky. Baba had returned. But could our misfortune be measured on a spectrum? Were we thrown into a collective suffering for being Taiwanese—fate—or something more pedestrian like the ambitions of men working against us?

I thought of Jia Bao's wife. What was it like to be the wife of a national hero, a half-widow, every hardship lightened by the idea of a greater good, her experience so unlike my mother's? I imagined that if I were her, I'd hide in a kerchief and sunglasses like Jackie O, slipping between home and the clinic, notoriety both my burden and my security.

I felt Jia Bao's eyes on me—his gaze seemed to have a physical weight—pulling me from my thoughts.

He smiled. "What are you mulling over?" Unlike the grimace-smile he usually mustered, this was open, candid. I jiggled my cup and watched the bits of leaves swirl.

"You must miss your wife."

"I do," he said, and I admired him for not feigning stoicism.

"Do you have a picture of her?"

He retrieved a photo from his room. Their wedding banquet. She wore a red dress embroidered in gold thread and red lace gloves. Her eyeliner flicked up at the corners, thick, black, and exaggerated on her thin, pale face. He wore a plaid suit. His hair was carefully parted, varnished smooth, but a jagged tuft had come loose and hung over his brow, making him appear sweaty and unkempt. They stood side by side, mouths ajar, caught mid-toast.

She was tangible, and somewhere on the other side of the globe, she breathed. "She's pretty." I handed the picture back to him.

Modesty, I think, kept him from responding. He turned the picture over to its plain white back and covered it with his hand.

"I should sleep," he said.

I nodded. He carried his cup to the sink. Behind me, I heard the faucet, and then the scrape of the gritty, unglazed bottom against the porcelain basin as he set the cup down.

35

AS THE DAYS PASSED without incident, we eased into something that felt like security. It was easy having Jia Bao around. He made no demands, was kind to the girls, and thoughtful about his presence. He and Wei grew as chummy as brothers. I stopped looking around whenever I left the house. I began to believe Wei was right: we were safe; everything was going to be okay.

Through campus connections, Wei found Jia Bao a job processing incoming materials in the Department of Oriental Languages library. Each morning, they left together like two boys marching off to school with homemade lunches packed into their satchels. Some days, I met up with Jia Bao at the stone lions in front of Durant Hall and we walked across campus together to find Wei. The three of us ate in the shade next to Strawberry Creek, wedged onto a bench, our heels resting on the damp dirt. Wei sat in the middle. Wei always sat in the middle.

How does one reconstruct a life? This question, never asked aloud in so many words, hung over our conversations. The cataloging job could not go on forever. At the same time, Jia Bao could not drift into obscurity, or be expected to pass a quiet life. He did not know when or if he'd see his wife and children again. For the next few years, he could expect nothing but waiting.

He mentioned the book idea once more. Jia Bao had already passed into a realm in which only heightened notoriety would help. A semifamous man—with a name not immediately placeable but tickling the edge of your mind—found dead of apparent suicide elicits only pity (poor man couldn't stand the pressure). An *infamous* man found dead in his car, a victim of suicide (oh, *him*, yes, I know that name), inspires conspiracy theories, rattles trust.

During those lunches, as our Indian summer sank into a more proper and chilly autumn, Jia Bao and Wei planned the book. The story of the March Massacre, which had been discussed in a text by George Kerr and in a few eyewitness accounts by Westerners, was still forbidden to be spoken of openly in Taiwan. Jia Bao's book would start with the moment our difference was etched into history. That was how Jia Bao would later phrase it—*etching difference, the birth of the modern Taiwanese identity*. He would include his own father's murder of course, through martial law and the White Terror, then his arrest, imprisonment, and escape, making an ultimate argument for democracy.

"But the audience is limited if it's not in English," Wei said.

I was half listening as I watched a squirrel, at the base of a coastal redwood, gnawing on a scrap of something or other. I picked up a leaf and tossed it toward the creature. It scampered off.

"Will you do it?" Jia Bao broke me from my thoughts.

"Do what?" I leaned forward to see him past Wei.

"Help me translate my book," he said.

"Me? I can't do that." In my lit classes, I sometimes daydreamed about being one of the writers we were reading, spinning stories for others to get lost in, but these thoughts were only idle distractions. I never would have admitted my yearnings to Wei or Jia Bao.

Wei elbowed me. "You're being modest. Yes, she can do it."

Where had his faith in me come from?

"If not you, then who?" Jia Bao said.

I gestured at an imagined gallery of candidates. "Anyone else. We know a dozen people."

"But someone we can trust," Wei said.

Keep it within the clique. Mr. Lu's cocky smile came to mind, and I shook my head.

"Think about it," Jia Bao urged. His posture betrayed his easy tone. He was hunched forward, his elbows dug into his thighs, and his left hand fisted in his right.

Looking for an excuse, I glanced at my watch. "It's time to pick up Stephanie." I slipped on my purse and stood up.

"Think about it," Jia Bao said again. Too polite to say no, I nodded. I grabbed their discarded lunch bags, pecked my husband on the cheek, then strode across the glade toward Bancroft Way, where I had parked my car.

Despite the cool weather, the station wagon was hot. I rolled down the window, leaned across and did the same for the passenger's side. The arrests and killings, Baba's lost years—why dredge it up again? I thought of Jia Bao's despairing pose and something like pity flickered in my chest. No, no, no. I shook my head as if responding to their question once more. I shifted the car into reverse and edged out of the spot. Remembering didn't change anything. I didn't want any part of it.

When I arrived at school—a big yellow room with the rubbery, pungent smell of tempera paints and child sweat—Stephanie was in one of the tiny wooden chairs at a small table solemnly molding a lump of green Play-Doh. One cheek was an angry and alarming red. She offered a desultory wave and returned to her project.

Before I could look more closely, the teacher intercepted me beside the reading loft next to the door. "I tried to call you." Her name was Mary. She was a throwback: two vestigial blond braids fell over her sagging bosom, and bright calico appliqué flowers patched her high-waisted bell-bottom jeans. Her voice was breathy, like someone who had surrendered her attachment to base emotions and gazed upon humanity with the benevolence of a bodhisattva. Yet now, here, spikes of impatience poked through. She folded her arms and said, "Stephanie bit one of the girls in class and the girl slapped her."

"What?" I lurched toward my daughter, but Mary held up her hand and lowered her voice. "She didn't break the skin, but she bruised her." She glanced back at Stephanie. "We need to have a meeting—with your husband here too. We love Stephanie, of course, of course, but she's been acting up a bit lately, and . . ." She didn't finish, but I understood. We'd have to find a new school if we didn't get a fix on the situation. Our daughter was getting expelled from preschool.

I looked at my innocent and small daughter. Her fine black hair fell loose from the ponytail I'd made that morning. Flecks of Play-Doh glowed beneath her fingernails. Four years old. Children, still little beasts, react to the waves and impulses inside. Feeling, not thought, is the thing that is true and right.

I said as much to Mary. "She's just a kid," I concluded, but I knew it was a misguided excuse. Fighting was not in Stephanie's character.

Mary threw up her hands. "I know. I know. But we have to think of *all* the kids, you know what I mean?"

"Did you talk to her?"

"Of course."

"I don't understand. I can't believe it." I looked again at my daughter, now more shocked by the blazing red blotch on her cheek. "And what about the other girl? Look at that mark. That looks pretty bad!"

"Rebecca. Rebecca was simply defending herself."

Defending? I had nothing rational to say: I wanted to justify my daughter's conduct just because she was my flesh and blood. And to assuage my own concern.

"I'll talk to my husband. We'll talk to her. Call us about the meeting." I grabbed Stephanie's sweater and art from her cubby. Grimly, reluctantly, Mary nodded at every word.

In the car, Stephanie crawled onto the back console like it was a hobbyhorse and slung her arms over the front seat. Why was she acting out? She'd suffered no trauma that I could think of—our life went on as it always had. I thought seeing me worry would make her more anxious, so I slapped the steering wheel and said, "How about ice cream?"

"Really?" Her little hand caressed my collar absentmindedly.

"Yeah. Don't tell Em, okay? It's our special treat."

"Okay." She stood up and pecked my cheek. She was so sweet and even-tempered—how could she have *bit* Rebecca?

We went to Fentons, which beckoned with HAVE FUN AT OUR FOUNTAIN painted across the top of the building. Inside, amid the milk-and-metal ice-cream parlor odor, Stephanie pressed her palms against the cold glass and eyed the tubs of ice cream. She bounced on her toes and pointed at each one, declaring it the flavor that she wanted until she finally settled on rocky road. The girl behind the counter loaded it into a silver dish and we slipped into a booth. I had just a glass of ice water with lemon.

I watched her labor with the long-handled spoon. Finally, she used her fingers to push the ice cream onto it. I sipped my water and longed for a cigarette when smoke from a nearby table drifted over.

"What happened at school today?"

She shrugged and wiped her mouth on her sleeve.

"Stephanie, your napkin," I said.

She picked it up and wiped her mouth again and scrunched the napkin as she set it down.

"Nothing happened at school today?"

Thoughtfully, she licked her spoon. "Rebecky hit me."

"Why?"

"I don't know."

"She hit you first? Did you make her mad?" Under the bright parlor lights, I felt like an interrogator needling a recalcitrant suspect.

"I don't know."

I softened my tone and hunched over, trying to appear smaller. "Stephanie, Mary said that you bit Rebecca."

She nodded.

"You did? Why would you do that?"

"She's a bad girl. A very bad girl." With each word, she tapped the spoon against the ice cream and it splattered in a halo on the table.

"Stop that." I grabbed a napkin from the dispenser. "A bad girl? Why is she a bad girl?"

"I don't know."

I sighed. I reached over and wiped up the melted ice cream puddling around her dish. "It's very bad to hurt other people. You have to use your words. I'm going to tell your dad and we are going to punish you."

Her eyebrows shot up and she looked directly at me. "What's my punishment?"

"I don't know." I crumpled the napkin and reached for another. "I need to talk to your father."

She shoved her dish over. "No!"

I snatched her wrist. "Stephanie!"

"No!" she screamed. "Don't touch me! I'll tell the police!" Her eyes—wild, wet, and black—sparked like the eyes of a small feral animal seized in a trap. I grabbed her around the waist and her jeans squealed across the seat as I pulled her toward me.

"Let's go home." I struggled out of the booth with her in my arms. She writhed and screamed half coherently that I was a "bad mommy." The eyes of the entire parlor were on us. Despite the chill, I began to sweat. Stephanie's feet knocked against my legs and she wrapped my hair in her fist and tugged as she yowled. "Stop it, stop it, *stop it*," I said.

I heard someone hiss: *Those people.*

I shouldered the glass door open, and as we passed through, I felt Stephanie sink her teeth into my upper arm.

I let Stephanie cry herself out in the backseat and tried to ignore the horrible drag of her fingernails on the upholstery as she flailed and protested. I dropped my head into my arms, cradled over the steering wheel, and waited. I had almost slapped her. When she had clamped down in that hard and angry little bite, slapping seemed the only way to make her let go. And I wanted to punish her. I felt shame and relief in admitting it. I had wanted to punish her not just for hurting me, but for the judgmental glares from the other people in the parlor. Reflexively, I had tugged her hair—just enough to jerk her back into the moment—and she had let go.

Finally, she fell asleep, thumb in mouth, hair in disarray, and breath still shuddering from her tears. I looked at the bite on my arm. Blood speckled each tiny crescent. The entire bite was ringed in purple. She was only four, I assured myself. Just four. Every four-year-old throws tantrums. There was nothing remarkable about it at all.

Jia Bao had gone out for the evening with another local expatriate Taiwanese couple from our circle of acquaintances, and Wei and I found ourselves alone for the first time in weeks. After the girls fell asleep, we carried mugs of Carlo Rossi cabernet out to the girls' playset. The structure heaved as we settled onto the swings.

I laughed. "Are you sure this will hold us?"

"I'm sure. I built it."

I twisted one arm around the chain and nudged myself back and forth with my toes. Woodsmoke from someone's chimney, a bouquet of warmth amid the cold, drifted into the yard. Impending winter excited me; already, with glee, I had bundled myself into a thick gray wool sweater, hand knit, that I'd bought at a campus crafts fair a few years before. The wool had never lost its almost gamey barnyard odor. Yellow and orange lights from our neighbors' houses twinkled through the bamboo stand.

The bite on my arm ached. I'd cleaned it with alcohol and covered it with two Band-Aids and hadn't said anything to Wei. Like any proper procrastinator, I was waiting for the right moment. I took a sip of wine and rested the mug on my thigh.

"Do you think I'm a bad mom?" Admittedly, it was a leading question extending directly from my bruised ego.

"Where's this coming from?" Wei shifted and the whole swing set swayed. I gripped the mug to keep it from sloshing. I told him about Stephanie, and when I was done, he threw his chin up and laughed. He wasn't being mean-spirited, I knew—he was truly amused.

"It's not funny. I'm really worried, Wei."

"I know, but I can just imagine her face." He laughed again. He cleared his throat with a large gulp of wine and his voice shifted to solemn. "You're right. What's going on in that serious little head of hers? It's totally unlike her."

He remembered their birthdays, played Chutes and Ladders with them, read Dr. Seuss to them, answered their questions about the existence of giant squid or where thunder came from. He seemed to save all his patience for them. I longed to know where he found this reserve of composure. I thought of the bubble-bath commercial, the harried mother who begged to be taken away. The advertisers had touched on some universal longing. But there was no going away. When I woke up tomorrow, I'd yet again face Stephanie's preschool teacher and I would still have two bandages clinging to my arm, the edges rolled and the gum turning black.

From her mother's womb, untimely ripped. Pain urged me to expel this tiny beast. But the nurse, shaving me, told me to wait. She stood patiently—foamy razor held aloft—as another contraction traveled through me; when it had passed, she continued cleaning me for delivery. I couldn't see beyond the thin floral cotton kimono draped across my knees, but I felt her wiping away the shaving cream with a cold washcloth and then she inserted the enema. Wei had been pacing at the end of the bed; he cringed and moved up toward the head and clasped the rail. He hadn't been there for Emily's birth. Two years before, he had not even been allowed in the room. I wondered if he regretted the change in policy. He had no excuse now. The nurse flushed me out and then asked the question I had been anticipating.

"Epidural?"

I held my breath as I clenched up again. I would have taken a punch in the face.

I puckered my lips and exhaled. "Yes."

In a matter of minutes, half my body disappeared. My legs were not there; at the same time, they were an immense weight, heavy dense logs of clay. A useless bystander, Wei sank into the chair beside the bed.

"Don't push," the nurse said. I decided that I didn't like her. She was too thin. Translucent but not ethereal. Gray cast to her skin, too many freckles, elbows like dresser knobs.

"I can't tell if I'm pushing or not," I protested.

Her head disappeared behind my bent knees and the spread of my kimono as she checked my dilation. Her head popped up again. Over the hills of my knees, her green eyes met mine. "You're ready."

She wheeled me through the hall. I was anesthetized not only to the pain, but to the haze of light and faces I passed as we moved to the delivery room. Wei followed behind and then was masked head to toe in scrubs, shoe cozies, and a mushroom-shaped bonnet that looked like a shower cap.

My doctor, Dr. Brancusi, arrived too, shawled in the odor of coffee and tuna sandwiches (pregnancy had made my sense of smell sickeningly keen). Beyond the fresh blue drape that separated the still sentient part of me from the dull workhorse that labored and seized, he probed around and returned to me with blood on the tips of his gloved fingers. The baby was breech, he told me, curled up like a little Buddha, legs folded and butt nestled against my pelvic bone.

"I can try to turn it, but I strongly suggest a Cesarean."

"Stop pushing!" the nurse snapped.

Without pain, I felt my body rippling and struggling with the baby. It wanted out. I wanted it out. Yet we were in a battle. I felt trapped. "Whatever you think is best," I panted.

After I was swabbed and probed, Wei's face described to me everything that I couldn't see. The doctor took the scalpel and Wei's eyes widened and glistened and he gulped down his disgust. My blood spread down the sheets and he stepped back to me and touched my shoulder. "Like slicing open a fish," he told me later, describing how my flesh peeled back, revealing a white fatty layer and then our child in a secretive and dark pool of blood. Dr. Brancusi held her up, as if to verify there had, in fact, been an infant inside me, and I saw only the blue scrunched face before the nurses whisked her away so she could not be "contaminated" by me. I had a better view of my placenta, which the doctor displayed for me, expanding it into a veiny sac anchored by a lump of meat. I didn't know if he was putting me on. I nodded and closed my eyes—relieved, exhausted. The baby was healthy. I could sleep.

When I woke up again, Wei had gone home and the wound was stitched. A wide black mouth smiled beneath my now-deflated belly. A new nurse came in—at the start of her shift and fresh, with clean blond hair wrapped in a tight bun. She checked the stitches and declared, "No more bikinis for you. That'll be a mean scar."

I nodded drowsily. I could feel the pain throbbing its way up past the analgesic.

The nurse brought the baby, swaddled and wearing a little cap, in a rolling plastic-walled bassinet, and I had my first real look at BABY GIRL LIN, as the bassinet sticker read. Six pounds, three ounces; eighteen inches. I had forgotten how fragile newborns felt, like hollow rubber dolls, yet wielding so much power: I thought of the great stretch of time and energy devoted to creating her, how many people had been called into the room to bring her forth, how destroyed my body was in her wake.

The nurse told me that my colostrum was too weak; I'd have to bottle-feed formula. I wished Mama were there to tell her how ridiculous that was. When Emily had been born, the nurses had fed her sugar-water for the same reason, and after hearing this, Mama wrote me a long, angry letter. "You cannot let strangers tell you how to care for your own child. The American way may be the best way for an American child, but your child is Taiwanese!" She thought I should adhere to the one-month sitting period she'd followed (for every child except me) and could not believe that I had showered before leaving the hospital. "To not feed from your healthy breasts is an insult to your child and to God." With Stephanie, I would disappoint her again. I accepted the baby into my arms and took the warm bottle. I tickled the nipple against the roof of her mouth and she began to feed while my breasts wept into my robe.

The staff had waited three hours before letting me hold Stephanie for the first time. Their reasons were rational. The baby needed her vitals checked. I needed to be sewn up. We both needed sleep. Later, chatting with me about her own recent delivery, a friend told me how the doctor had informed her that she was considered a "good candidate" for post-delivery bonding. They had let the still-bloody baby warm himself on her bare chest. I was too ashamed to admit that no one had said such a thing to me.

I pushed off and the swing sagged and lifted, over and over, on its wheezing frame. I dragged my toe to stop and held out my mug. "More wine, please." Wei poured wine from his cup into mine.

"Well, Emily is doing great. So maybe we're not terrible parents?" Wei said.

"Yes, Em is fine." Sweet Emily, so good-natured—her emotions drifting across her face like clouds over a landscape—that one almost felt sorry for her.

With the mug held to my mouth, I whispered, "Sometimes I feel like I can't do it." For a moment, I was afraid he wouldn't answer at all and my admission would dissolve into the wide black sky above us.

Wei cocked his head and gave me a confused smile. "What's that?"

"Nothing."

"I didn't hear you. What did you say?"

"Never mind."

Wei shrugged. "Okay." He took another swig.

My hands were cold. I could see the faint cloud of my breath. I wanted him to ask again, to hear me, to comfort with logic. Instead, he said, "Ready to go in?"

I nodded and gulped down the rest of my wine. As we headed back toward the house, he put his arm around me and touched my cheek with his icy fingers. I pressed myself to him, seeking his warmth.

36

IN ORDER FOR STEPHANIE to remain enrolled in her preschool, we agreed to see a family counselor. "Americans!" I complained. Only Americans, I grumbled to Wei, would believe that talking about problems to a completely disinterested third party—a stranger—was a solution. "It's tacky. I'm almost ready to find a new school." As worried as I was about Stephanie, I wanted to stay suspended in this place of everything-is-fine.

Wei squeezed my shoulder. For once, I *wanted* Wei to make one of his dumb jokes. Instead, he was serious. "Hey. She's our baby. We need to help her." He pressed his forehead to mine. "We'll talk it out and everything will be fine."

The therapist, Dr. Matson, insisted that we call him Dave. Across a worn Persian rug, he sat in a papasan chair, his loafers, adult-sized Buster Browns, resting heavily on the floor. With the point of his pencil, he gently scratched the hair above his right ear as he waited for us to get settled.

Side by side on a tweed couch, Wei and I faced him. Stephanie had not come to this first session, which was, Dave explained, a chance for him to acquaint himself with Stephanie's "situation." All of our actions revealed something and I was conscious of every gesture; I feared that Dave would need to spend only this hour with us to know what brokenness our daughter had inherited. Therefore, I signaled how warm our family was. I sat so close to Wei that our arms touched and showed no disappointment when he subtly pulled away. Would this be the first note in our file?

Dave raised his voice at the end of every sentence, the sound curving up like a check mark, a nonthreatening question. No leading statements; we would damn ourselves. And what about the sandbox in the corner? Did he expect us to pay for our daughter to come play for an hour like a rat in a lab? Dave hummed as he wrote. "These are not judgments," he assured us. "I'm just tracking the conversation so I remember what I want to ask you?" He asked us how old Emily and Stephanie were, how they got along, how much time we spent with them per day and doing what.

Innocent questions, pure data. What could he possibly decipher from the fact that the girls had separate rooms, that Emily had decorated her room with unicorns and slept in a twin bed while farm animals pranced across Stephanie's and she laid her head in a transitional crib? As in a play, was everything in the mise-en-scène loaded with symbolism?

"And let's talk about your relationship?"

"With Stephanie?"

"No, your marriage? Let's talk about your marriage?"

I quickly said, "It's great," as Wei answered, "I don't see how it's relevant." I turned sharply toward him, surprised. Just as suddenly, Dave was there, squelching the spit of tension.

"One at a time? Describe 'great'?"

I felt my mother's instincts rear up. Proudly, we smeared clay into the breaches. A united front. "We never fight."

"Never?"

"Again, I don't see how this is relevant to Stephanie's problem," Wei said. "I'm here to find out how to help my daughter."

"I'm just trying to get a fuller picture?"

"No, we don't fight." Of course, I was visualizing my parents: the broken-glass comments sharpened by yearly iterations and the literal broken glass when words weren't enough. Wei and I had a two-story shingled house, dinner on the table every night at six. A Ph.D., citizenship, two lovely daughters. Again, the American Dream. What was there to fight about?

"Maybe 'fight' is a strong word. Argue? Bicker? Every couple has those few topics that get hashed out over and over. What would you say those topics are?"

I glanced at Wei, who was brooding. I knew he would not answer, so I made some harmless admissions. "I believe every couple argues about money," I began. Dave nodded. "Wei occasionally spends more than I would like to. And sometimes, I do not appreciate Wei's sense of humor. I think serious moments should remain serious."

"Wei, what do you think?"

"I don't think this has anything to do with Stephanie," Wei said again. His words darted out as if each quickening heartbeat paced his thoughts, and I realized how angry he was.

Dave shifted his tone. "Recent research shows that the parental relationship has a strong effect on children. In fact, some therapists believe that if parents focus on their own relationship, their children substantially benefit. I'll be happy to show you the journal studies next time?"

"Do that," Wei said.

"Would you two be willing to do some exercises at home together? Relationship work?"

"I'm here to talk about my daughter. That's what I'm paying for. That's *all* I'm paying for," Wei said.

Dave thumped the pencil against his notepad. "I need you to understand that this is a process? We don't just dive in; we get our feet wet first? I'd like one more session with just you two and then you can start bringing Stephanie?"

"I still don't think that it matters," Wei answered.

37

IN MOVIES, frustrated writers tore paper bearing only a few lame lines out of their typewriters, crumpled the sheets into tight, mad balls, and tossed them at the trash. This was the dynamism and excitement of the writing process. How else to externalize the racing, exploding mind?

It certainly wasn't visible in our den that fall as I helped Jia Bao translate his book. Just soft breath, a once-in-a-while sniffle, the shifting of paper, the sigh of a chair spring. The preceding shots of a revolution.

Jia Bao wanted to release the English and Chinese versions simultaneously, so I translated the early chapters as he polished the later ones. Even though the words were his, the deliberate choosing of equivalents and the careful parsing of meaning invigorated me. I longed to write stories of my own too, though I didn't dare admit it. So I sated my hunger transforming Jia Bao's words.

Jia Bao sat in the orange armchair and softly mouthed the words on the sheet I had given him. I sat on the footstool beside him, my arm folded onto the armrest of his chair, pretending to read along with him, but instead I watched his lips.

"Rather than 'oppressive,' how about 'brutal'?" he asked.

I straightened up. "'Brutal' is so dramatic. 'Oppressive' is much more measured."

"People need to be shaken up."

"But the wrong language may turn off some people," I argued.

Jia Bao read the line aloud again.

"It is brutal," he said plainly. "This is the most accurate word. Brutal." He jotted down the change.

"This situation must be so hard for your wife."

His head shot up and he looked at me as if trying to read my meaning. I was embarrassed; I wanted to withdraw my comment, but he said, "I don't think she realized what marrying me entailed." He bit gently at the metal ring girding the pencil eraser. His nails were trimmed at awkward, inconsistent angles, and tiny fringes of skin curled up at each base. He turned back to the page. "What is the next word?"

"How did you meet?"

He looked up again and, still drawing himself from another world, squinted at me. "What's that?"

I wondered if he found my persistent curiosity annoying. "Your wife. How did you meet?"

He smiled faintly. "In a ballroom dancing club."

I laughed. "You dance?"

"Passably." He tapped the pencil on the page. "It was a college club. My pal told me it was a good way to meet girls. And I did." He looked up at me. "And you? How did you and Wei meet?"

"Family friend. It was kind of arranged."

Since coming to California, I'd discovered what came to mind with the term "arranged marriage": exchanged trunks of gold and a veiled child bride who does not know her groom's face until the wedding night. Americans certainly didn't think of the casual dates Wei and I had shared, how we'd come to know how much we liked each other first. Our matchmaker could have easily been a mutual college friend—bubbly and meddling— who'd glimpsed some potential compatibility in us.

"You're a good match," Jia Bao said.

"Yes," I said, but wondered what he meant. Standing side by side, I barely reached Wei's shoulder. We would both be called slim, though Wei had some heft to his figure that brought to mind an athlete's body—a hockey player, perhaps. In Taiwan, it was considered a compliment to note that a couple resembled each other. What similarities did Wei and I share? A broad forehead? Attached earlobes? Or was our compatibility in the facade of unwavering support that I put up in front of our guest?

I tapped the page and said brightly, "Next sentence. I used the word 'demand,' but 'request' might be more moderate. It's polite."

"Less demanding."

"Yes, exactly." The corners of his mouth moved slightly and I realized he was teasing me.

"I'll trade you 'brutality' for 'demand.' That's fine. We want a consistent tone. Assertive but not strident." He had the pencil back between his teeth again. I looked at the page. His notations marked up my typing. Beneath this lay his handwritten original in characters, with my scribbles over them.

"You could do this on your own. You don't need me."

His eyes did not leave the page as he answered. "Sometimes the benefits of collaboration are more than . . ." He didn't finish.

"More than what?"

He laughed. "Oh, I don't know. It's nice to have a friend. This kind of work has always been about the group. There's no way to go it alone."

"Collaboration," "community"—all the key words I'd heard spouted at any gathering of earnest activists, whether in the middle of Sproul Plaza or on TV. What had I expected exactly? I blushed.

"I'm glad I can help," I said. My eyes drifted over the crammed bookcases where my and Wei's books mingled in rough alphabetical order. Work. It was always about the cause. I was not so earnest, but I had put up a good front for Jia Bao. "Wei is so passionate about this. I guess it's time for me to get involved," I said.

My duties as translator, it turned out, soon included driving. Jia Bao tracked down a retired KMT general living up north in Mendocino County who was willing to talk to him. Because Wei had classes to teach, the role of chauffeur fell to me.

"I don't want to," I had told Wei privately. Mr. Lu lurked in the background of my memories of the party, the last time I had seen him. Had he been satisfied by what he found that night? Or would this trip draw him out again? Already, I had the weight of the manuscript, which I could not deny knowledge of if he asked. Every escalation, I feared, would bring him closer to us; he'd catch the scent of it and seek me out. "I can't do it. The girls. Stephanie has an appointment with Dr. Matson on Tuesday."

"I'd go if I could, but I can't miss class," Wei countered.

"What about James?" Helen's husband had helped Wei organize the last campus protest against the KMT. Thinking of the protest reminded me that Mr. Lu possessed a set of those pictures. I crossed my arms against my turning stomach.

"He could, but he doesn't know about the book. You know it better than anyone—better than me. Even if I drove, I'd want you along."

"The girls, Wei."

"No problem. I have enough time before class to take them to school. I'll cancel office hours for Stephanie's appointment."

"I've never driven that far."

"It's not any harder than driving across town. Just takes a little longer. Any other objections?"

Reluctantly, I had agreed to the task and Wei, cupping my face, had kissed me wetly on the mouth. "Thank you. Thank you."

For a long time, Jia Bao and I cruised along Highway 1. Despite the gas crisis, I decided on the longer, scenic route, following the coastline, the gray sea blurring at the curved horizon. After the logging town of Fort Bragg, set on a craggy oceanside ridge rough and beautiful with hunched cypress, we turned inland. The general lived outside Willits, hours and hours from Berkeley. *The heart of Mendocino. Don't feed the hippies.* A small town where horses trotted on the roads alongside cars, and people smoked on the sidewalks in front of the liquor store. Embedded amid hundreds of miles of forest-dense hills all the way to the Oregon border, the area was warm and green and a perfect refuge for "recreational" gardeners. On our way into town, we glimpsed partially obscured gates leading down gravel-and-dirt drives, front yards with stacked wood and gutted cars and lounging dogs, and innocuous greenhouses. I'd heard a rumor that the elusive writer Thomas Pynchon lived here.

A monochromatic town too. I wondered what had brought the general, a military man from a tiny tropical island, to this landlocked place of cowboys and pot farmers.

Jia Bao and I checked into the Swallowtail Way Motel ("Where There's a Willits, There's a *Way*"), which boasted a funky and outdated neon sign that looked like it had been lifted off the Las Vegas Strip. Our keys came attached to large wooden squares branded with our room numbers; separate rooms in different wings of the motel.

The general lived in a raised yellow bungalow down a quarter-mile private drive off the county road. Two brown dogs—stocky and sinewy pitbull mixes—barked and splashed toward us through the mud thickening in the sun. The day was mild; a bearable winter bite hung in the air. At the end of the drive, inside a metal paddock, three horses, coats glistening with every movement, grazed. Beyond the pasture, trees were lost in the darkness of the forest.

"Horses," I said.

"I forgot to tell you. He raises them as a hobby," Jia Bao said.

As soon as we parked, the dogs stopped a few feet away, barking warily, but their tails wagging. On the porch, a man had been hidden behind the railing. Now he rose and waved at us—a gesture surprisingly warm. I had expected him to be aloof, cold—someone like my brother Dua Hyan.

Our shoulder bags weighed down by legal pads, pens, and recording equipment, we met the general and his wife on the stairs. He was a compact man, slim, bulked up only by his tan sweater. He still bore a military cleanliness: closely cropped hair and nails and a neatly shaven face. His wife too matched him in stature and tidiness, her hair short and silver, and her face brightened with coral lipstick. She told us to call her Lorraine. When Jia Bao introduced me as his translator, the general clasped my hand in both of his and his smile was so genuine that I almost forgot how practiced he must have been in the art of appearing sincere.

The house lay in a clearing, but the tall trees kept away the sun. From the porch, I enviously glimpsed the light in the pasture that warmed the horses and now the dogs, who had settled near the paddock gate. The chill was bright but not unpleasant, cut by the hot jasmine tea that the general's wife brought out.

I set the cassette recorder on the table. It was portable, ran on batteries, and had previously been housed in Emily's room, where it played stories for her at night. It had a mic embedded in the body, but I had brought a plug-in one too, and I began to unwind the cord.

"Please," the general said. "Notes only. I don't want my voice on tape." His eyes darted to his wife and she pulled her lips together in a way that told me they had discussed all of this before our arrival.

"No problem," Jia Bao said. I kept the recorder on the table, in the open, a gesture of honesty.

The general had beautiful slender fingers. I flinched when he picked up his tea. The water was freshly boiled—my own fingers had recoiled when moments earlier I had touched the cup. I could barely draw my eyes away from his hands as he began to speak. "First," he said, "I read about your escape. Very brave. That is why I agreed to see you. But anything I say must be off record. I cannot have my name associated with this. You understand."

Jia Bao nodded quickly. "Of course."

"You may not know that I'm *persona non grata* among the KMT. I'm sure if they could wipe any record of having known me, they would."

Jia Bao played it cool. "I hadn't heard."

"I retired. It was a forced retirement." He laughed. "Purely political. My enemies made it impossible for me to get anything done. My hands were tied. Nowhere to go but out."

"You can't get more out than here," I said. "Why this place?"

"Besides the horses?" He leaned back in his chair and his eyes traveled the tree line behind us. A twinkle of awe, or perhaps just the reflection of the sky, shone in his eyes. "Look at this place. Everyone knows everybody's business. Do you know what I mean? There are no secrets. There's no anonymity."

Hiding in plain sight, I took him to mean. A typical small-town eagle-eyed watchfulness pervaded beneath the sleepy exterior. The same reason we'd thrown the party for Jia Bao.

"In any case, never mind about me. Back to you," he said. "How can I help?"

Jia Bao described the laudatory books published by Westerners praising the Nationalists' goals and achievements, and the general nodded and grunted—he'd read them all. Jia Bao said he wanted to write the view from the inside, what lay behind the layers of carefully translated propaganda and official escorts. No Western account failed to comment on American-educated Madame Chiang's impeccable English. A beautifully tailored dress and fluent banter were enough to prove the government's good intentions.

The general closed his eyes and smiled. "Well, she is quite charming. No photograph quite prepares you. Go on."

"I want to write about 1947," Jia Bao said. I tried to read the tiny thread in his voice—aggression, maybe defiance. He had let the pen rest on the page and a drop of ink seeped from its tip.

Quietly, Lorraine slipped her hand over her husband's. Her nails were painted copper and a large diamond ring sat below a swollen knuckle.

The general opened his eyes. As a bit player, I had the luxury of watching faces. His look, settling directly on Jia Bao without a flicker, was almost hostile. Again, I asked myself if this was another skill from a career in politics: every weak emotion hidden beneath a mask of strength. He must have been veiling his surprise.

His delay was theatrical: a drink of tea, a lick of the lips and clearing of the throat. Finally, he spoke. I wrote as quickly as possible, blurring strokes into one continuous scribble, just enough for us to decipher it later. "I was a low-level officer then, you realize. We just cared about following orders. And to be honest, we also wanted to get the 'good boy' praise, maybe a promotion. To be acknowledged that we were patriots, willing to play the game. We had absolute faith that what our superiors told us was true: the insurrection had been planned by secret communist agents. We got the list of names. 'Just bring them in,' we were told. But what good would it do to put them on trial, or to jail them? Either way, they'd just become martyrs to the cause, which would keep the fight going. It was more efficient to shortcut the whole thing and wipe out the opposition. Exterminate them.

"So we did."

I flinched. "Them"—he meant men like Baba.

"Yes," Jia Bao said. His eyes narrowed, and he nodded, urging the confession out of the general's mouth.

"We shot them. Put them in rice sacks and threw them in the port. For efficiency, sometimes, we'd bind them together and use a single bullet. The whole line dragged down to their deaths. It was wartime. We were being economical." His smile was dry, without a trace of amusement. No, not a smile—a grimace. "We were simply being frugal." A life diminished to the price of a bullet; I felt ill. Needing some camaraderie or reassurance, I glanced at Lorraine, but her eyes stayed on her husband's face.

"Whose decision was it?" Jia Bao asked, and I finally understood his tone. He was nervous, a man finally sighting what he had long been searching for. What I initially heard as belligerence was actually anticipation and hope.

"The governor-general gets all the blame, but it was the Generalissimo who sent word. This went all the way to the top." Feeling like I was transcribing a line of noir dialogue, I carefully wrote down the general's words. *This went all the way to the top.* Maybe we all spoke in clichés, trying to elicit the drama of fiction to beautify the cadence of real life.

"No one has officially blamed Chiang," Jia Bao said. "Do you have proof?"

"Nothing but hearsay that he sent a telegram instructing that the situation be expeditiously taken care of. Now, however, one can't speak ill of the dead."

"Dictators are exempt."

"Ah, there's another funny thing. He was our president, fighting for democracy and freedom. A dictator? Who would call him a dictator? We don't use that language. That's for Westerners. If we say he was a dictator, then we will have to admit that we were duped."

To meet with countrymen in this remote Northern California town was a rare opportunity, and the general and his wife were eager to stretch our visit into the evening. Because of the forest, the light faded earlier than usual and an even deeper chill set in. The birds retired and the dogs sought warmth in the house. Beneath the yellow porch light webbed in dead bugs, our breath was as opaque as smoke. "Stay for dinner," Lorraine urged. I looked at Jia Bao for a signal of either yea or nay and found him searching my face for the same. I flashed a brief smile—*it's up to you*—and he answered, "We've bothered you so much already."

"My husband went fishing yesterday. It's fresh and there's more than we can eat. Unless you have plans."

"Are you sure?" I asked. "We don't want to be a bother." The back-and-forth etiquette dance—we all knew our roles. Next, the general's turn.

"Stay."

The general had spoken, and so it was done.

. . .

In the other room, a fire snapped and spit in a giant flagstone fireplace. The distant, low murmur of the general's and Jia Bao's voices reminded me of the conversations of people hidden in library stacks. I wanted to eavesdrop, but Lorraine and I made our own noise in the kitchen as we prepared dinner. I sliced ginger and scallions. She accidentally broke a glass against the sink and cried out. A dog curled near the kitchen door sighed and farted in its sleep.

In the window over the sink, I saw the kitchen open up behind me—streaks of light and glints of movement—and then that world disappeared when, outside, a deer pranced into the clearing, revealing itself with a flicker of white.

"Look," I gasped.

Lorraine dropped the glass into the trash and came to my side. Her shoulder pressed mine. Glimpsing us inside watching him, the deer froze. We too were still. Then he jerked his head and bounded back into the forest.

"He's a regular," Lorraine said. "It's all I can do to keep him out of my flower garden." She wiped her hands with a dish towel and set it crumpled on the counter. "Exciting, huh?"

"I saw a deer running down a street in Berkeley once, but this is . . . nice. It feels peaceful."

Lorraine spoke over the running water as she rinsed the fish. "It's wonderful." She nudged the faucet off with her wrist. She carried the fish on her two open palms like a tiny newborn and set it atop a paper towel. As she patted it dry, she said in a lower voice, "Actually, it's awful."

I was not sure I'd heard her correctly. "Awful?"

Her eyes darted toward the living room, gauging the men's voices, and then she smiled at me.

"Oh, I'm being dramatic." She arranged the fish onto a platter and stuffed it. "My daughter is in Taiwan and my son is in New York. I'm a little lonely." Her slick hands—speckled with tiny green scallion rings, knuckles inflamed and skin reddening in the creases—moved mindlessly. I thought of my mother's hands, too familiar to be beautiful. She ran them under the faucet; the water cascaded over her diamond, the careful manicure, the details that were useless, irrelevant here in the woods.

She hunched over to watch the burner as she clicked on the stove.

"A stranger in a strange land," she said in English when she stood up, then spoke again in Mandarin. "I moved to Taiwan from Fuzhou when I was thirty-two. It always felt like exile. But now that I'm here, Taiwan feels like home. Isn't it funny? The two of us here, so far away, brought together by the island?"

I understood what she meant. The names of people and places had meaning and memories; she could mention a street, a site, and it would bloom before my eyes: the direction of the afternoon shadows, the odor of charcoal and exhaust and benjo sludge, the commotion of horns and voices. The sound of Taiwanese jumbled with Mandarin. There, however, our paths would never have crossed. America—or was it exile?—had erased our differences.

After that, nothing else about the dinner stands in my memory except the word *copita*. We drank sherry after dinner. In detail, the general expounded on the benefits of the tapered shape of the *copita* and we sniffed appreciatively. It was after ten when we finally stretched and declared that it was time to leave.

As we backed out of the driveway, our headlights washed over our hosts, who stood waving from the bottom porch step. This was the image I would hold of my first and last encounter with them: lit up in an arc of white that swept over the house, streaked toward the paddock, then left them in darkness as the car turned away.

I grabbed Jia Bao's arm. "Navigate."

He picked up my hand and gently placed it on the stick shift: "Drive."

We found our way to the county road and knew it only when our tires hit the smooth blacktop.

"Left," Jia Bao said.

"Are you sure? I remember a right." The lingering taste of sherry soured on my tongue.

"I'm sure," he said as he hit the overhead light and unfolded the map. "What street is this?"

"I missed the sign." I realized that I'd had too much to drink. My face was hot. I reminded myself we'd likely be the only car all the way into town. Deer were the most dangerous thing I had to watch for. Out of the corner of my eye, I saw the mouth of another road and hit the brakes. Jia Bao found it on the map and told me to turn.

"It says 'private road,'" I protested.

"Look." Jia Bao poked the spot on the map and I followed his finger as it traveled the line to the one that would bring us back to the Swallowtail. "Turn right."

The road went on. Pavement turned to dirt. The road became a flue as it carved into the land that rose on both sides of us. Tree roots and shrubs slapped the car as we wound through. Then we rose again onto pavement. I didn't remember any of it from our earlier drive.

"Check the map again," I urged. Frustration sobered me. In the rearview mirror, I caught the glow of headlights far behind us. Relieved, I realized that this road wasn't totally untraveled.

"Thank god. Let's flag them down and ask for directions," I said.

Jia Bao grunted his assent without looking up from the map.

I began to veer off the road, but it narrowed to a dead end—a service road blocked by a locked gate and a sign punctured with bullet holes. "Perfect," I said. "They'll have to stop too and we'll ask them."

The car pulled over behind us, lights shining at our rear bumper and through the back window. When I looked back, I was blinded. I couldn't see the driver.

"I'll ask," I said.

Jia Bao glanced back at the screaming white light. "I'll come with you."

As we approached the car, two Oriental men—even in this moment, I heard Wei's exasperated reprimand: "*Asian*, not Oriental, dear"—got out. Average-looking guys in slacks and collared shirts. Here, in remote Mendocino. "Shit," I gasped.

Before I could tell Jia Bao to get back into the car and lock the doors, the men quickened their pace and had us backed against the station wagon.

"What's this?" Jia Bao asked, more to me. He knew. He had to know. I cursed his stupid question, this stupid trip. I cursed Wei for making me drive, for inviting Jia Bao to stay. My heart thrashed like a bird trapped in a box.

"We want the tapes," one answered in Taiwanese, and we knew.

"Tapes?" Jia Bao asked. I knew we had the same thought—I simply could not fathom that we had been followed all the way to this obscure road in far Northern California.

The man facing Jia Bao punched him in the jaw and his glasses clattered somewhere in the darkness. I squawked. Jia Bao staggered into me and I stumbled, but the other man caught me, embraced me for a moment before easing me back against the car. Jia Bao rose slowly, clutching his jaw. Blood dribbled from his mouth.

"The tapes."

Pain—broken teeth? broken bone?—muffled his voice. "Who are you?"

The one who had punched him now gripped him by his tender jaw and squeezed. Jia Bao grunted. His elbows banged against the car as the man nudged him back and said, "It doesn't matter." Jia Bao's blood shone on the man's fingers.

"I'll give you the tape," I cried. That was clearly the only solution. I pushed my way past my guard and—moving with deliberate slowness in a piteous attempt to appear sober—walked to the other side of the car. From the backseat, I pulled the recorder out of Jia Bao's satchel. I delivered it and let the man pop out the cassette himself.

"This is from today?" he asked.

"Of course," I snapped.

Anger crackled across his face, but he decided to not punish my impudence. He slipped the tape into his pocket and his partner released Jia Bao, who turned and spat.

"Stop fucking around," the man who had punched Jia Bao said. "This is nothing."

Still stunned, we watched as the two men returned to their vehicle, gunned the engine, and spun the car around in a cyclone of dirt. Even after we could no longer see their taillights, we could hear the engine's growl echoing through the woods.

Then, I think, I finally breathed. I searched for Jia Bao's glasses and found them unmarked. Exhausted, we collapsed back into our seats. I immediately locked my door. I rummaged through my purse for a tissue and, with one hand on Jia Bao's shoulder to steady him, leaned forward and blotted the blood from his chin. He closed his eyes and winced.

"We'll put ice on it when we get back."

His hair, I now noticed, was damp. How scared he'd been, though he hadn't shown it. I looked at the blood, bright on the tissue.

How smart too the general had been. The tape, of course, had been blank.

· · ·

Back at the Swallowtail, I bundled ice into a washcloth for Jia Bao. He lay atop the comforter of one of the beds in my room and held the compress to his swelling jaw. Even after we had washed away the blood, he looked brutalized: on his lip, a cut sliced through a black contusion and the bluish flesh on his chin had swelled into a freakishly misshapen lump. The bruise spread up his cheek, stopping just short of his eye.

I settled on the other bed and watched him. Between us sat a nightstand with two lamps and an illuminated flip clock, and I felt demurely American, like we were Rob and Laura Petrie. I'd forgotten to turn off the bathroom fan, and behind the closed door it whirred, white noise.

He had one arm tucked beneath the pillow. The other hand rested on the ice pack to steady it.

"Should I call Wei?" Guiltily, I realized I didn't want my husband to know yet: even from hundreds of miles away, he would wrest control—he'd tell me how many cubes to put in the compress, ask for details about the men and the car that I could not think about yet. He'd ask how old they were, what distinguishing marks they had. Could I really tell him that they seemed ageless, anywhere from twenty-five to fifty? Washed out by the headlights, their faces were bland—not a single freckle to identify them. I could not even recall the color of the car and certainly not the make.

"There's nothing he can do. We'll tell him when we get back." His injuries deadened his words. Speaking caused a spot of blood to erupt from the cut on his lip.

"You carried yourself well," I said.

He grimaced. "It's not the first time I've been hit." I had almost forgotten about prison. He had surely suffered worse. Wei had once regaled me with the alleged torture techniques of the secret police: gasoline poured up the prisoner's nose, electric shock, removal of fingernails, genital mutilation. It couldn't be true, I had said to him. If what he said was true, then my father had surely endured some of it—a thought too awful to accept. Finally, I had covered my ears and said, "Shut up, just shut up already." I could not think of Jia Bao there too, broken that way.

I kneeled in the narrow space between our beds. "Let me look again." Gently, I brushed the bruise with my thumb. It pulsated, hot. He opened his mouth and his jaw popped.

"Ouch," I said.

"Not broken," he said. "Just dislocated."

I took the towel to the bathroom and squeezed out the water. The row of bulbs above the vanity warmed away my exhaustion. It was one of those deceptive mirror-and-light combos that make you look thinner and clear complexioned. A much healthier, less haggard phantom existed on the other side of the glass. I wrapped more ice into the washcloth. The woman on the other side lived a very different life. She would have come for a lovers' getaway, not this.

Back in the room, I settled again on the floor next to Jia Bao's bed. His eyes were closed, but his breath was too shallow for sleep. I whispered his name and offered him the ice. He opened his eyes. Between us passed a realization of what we had both seen. The full weight of the day hit me. "This is real, isn't it?" I said.

"I'm sorry," he said. He gave me a funny half-smile and reached out to stroke my hair.

No, we could tell Wei in the morning. Even though I wanted to talk to the girls, I was afraid that my voice would break if I spoke to them. We could wait until morning to call.

This would never go any further, I told myself, as I crawled onto the bed beside Jia Bao. Fully clothed, I slipped my arm across his chest, my leg around his. He sank against me. I inhaled the musk on his nape. The Swallowtail Way Motel was nowhere in time. I held him until we both fell asleep.

38

GROGGY FROM THE SHERRY and sleeping with the lights on, I woke up before dawn. My arm was still folded around Jia Bao's chest and clasped in place by his hand. I was afraid that if I disturbed our configuration, we would never get it back. We smelled of sleep, and the ringing odor of blood still lingered over him. He must have heard me stir. He released my arm, reached back and stroked my thigh. I imagined he was lost in some dream where the warm body curved against him was his wife, but then he said my name and turned.

His puffy face, blackened with hemorrhaged blood, startled me. The laceration on his lip, now seamed together with a fine hard scab, had bled more in the night, leaving a brown smudge on his chin. I licked my finger and rubbed it clean. His eyes closed, and his grimace looked almost like the ecstasy of prayer. I slipped my hand under his shirt to his hot skin.

"Is this okay?" The words cracked out of me.

"I don't think my head is clear," he said.

"Me too," I murmured. I wondered if my woozy state—the previous night's adrenaline still seeping away and my energy drawn down by drink—would absolve me.

"What I mean is . . ." His nose pressed into the roots of my hair and his breath warmed my scalp. "What I mean is that I know how this goes." He lifted my hand from his skin and placed it on my stomach. "And I love my wife."

My face burning, I fell back and stared at the ceiling plaster. "I love Wei too," I said indignantly.

"Wei is a lucky man. But I can't be a hypocrite."

"Your political values include love too?" I said sourly.

As if racked with pain, he clenched the bedspread. "It's all love. Don't you see that? For me, it's all one and the same. I can't have one set of values on the street and another in the bedroom." We were lying arm to arm. I pulled away and he said, "I'm sorry if I misled you."

The hurt rose from the uneasiness in my stomach to a pressure in my eyes, but I held back my embarrassed tears. "But this feels real," I whispered.

When Jia Bao did not answer, I wanted to believe that honor held him back. In a surge of embarrassment, I realized that he understood me better than I did myself. He'd felt this before—the flush of adrenaline that turns the mouth to metal and burdens every choice as either eternity or oblivion.

"It's for another life," I said. "Like so many things. For another life."

There was no other life.

We didn't speak during the drive home. Exhaustion showed itself fully on Jia Bao's face; in the unfiltered sunlight, with broken black capillaries stippling his purpled skin, his injuries were monstrous, as if his skin was just a sack to hold the mess of his body.

"What the hell?" Wei asked as, laden with our bags, Jia Bao and I limped into the house. I shook my head, knowing that my tears would start at the first syllable. I reached for my husband. He embraced me, allowed me to hide my sobs in his chest. "What the hell?" he said again. "What happened? Are you hurt?"

Jia Bao pushed past us and washed his hands in the kitchen.

I cried harder.

"No," I gasped. "I'm okay."

Jia Bao returned, shaking the water off his hands.

"You need a doctor," Wei said to Jia Bao.

"Nothing is broken."

I shrugged out of Wei's hold. He said to me, "Why didn't you call? You should have called." His concern sounded like a rebuke.

"What would have been the use of calling? What could you have done?" Jia Bao's voice had an edge I hadn't heard before. "We're fine. She didn't do anything wrong." Shuddering with a deep hurt, I glared at him.

Wei saw something pass between us. Something he couldn't articulate, something intangible that triggered an uneasy pang. "You have no idea how serious this is. This isn't a game."

I heard the same man who'd lectured me in my grandparents' front room, the one who had looked at me and seen an uneducated waitress who needed the veil of her naïveté ripped from her eyes. He, of course, would be the one to do it.

"How dare you," I said.

"Wait. I'll tell you what happened," Jia Bao began.

"Yes, you tell him." My face was tender, my lungs fatigued. "I'm going upstairs. I'm exhausted."

"Right, go clean up," Wei said with an annoyance that he couldn't put his finger on raveling in his words.

I trudged up the stairs. I went to the girls' rooms first. They were at school, but their strong, sweet smells comforted me. Their pajamas puddled atop their unmade beds, and toys were strewn from bed to door in

Emily's room. I gathered them up and dropped them in her toy box. For this, right? For all this, I thought.

I remembered a moment from our first apartment. We had ridden the newly opened BART train into the city, to Sixteenth Street. The train smelled like a new car, with clean carpet and fabric seats. As we dropped into the Transbay Tunnel, I felt as if we were in a bullet shooting toward the future. In the Mission, the musk of all the fruit left in boxes in the sun reminded me of home. We brought back mangoes and papayas.

I had come out of the shower and Wei was at the table slicing one of the mangoes. He had stripped down to his undershirt. The curves of his golden arms were so beautiful, especially against his white shirt. The mango juice ran down; he raised his arm and licked it. I sat and he handed me half, cut the way my mother did it—scored in a grid and the skin folded so that the flesh rose in cubes. He ate slowly, his mouth grazing along the fruit, his lips glistening with juice. More juice trickled down his hands, down his arms. He caught it with his tongue. Juice ran down his chin. I wiped it with the edge of my palm and kissed the juice off his face.

This was around the time that Emily was conceived.

It seemed like so many years ago. As I left Emily's room, I heard the men arguing downstairs. I paused.

"It's the last straw," Wei said. "It's a declaration of war."

"We need to be methodical."

"I say strike. *They* have no method. It's just savagery after savagery. Why should we be civilized?"

"That's exactly why," Jia Bao said. "It's what they don't expect. What they can't imagine. They assume we will be like them."

"This is what I think we should do—" And then Wei shut the door to the den.

I wanted to run downstairs and stop their mad plans. *Look at Jia Bao,* I wanted to say. *Look at us. We can't win. Just stop. It's not worth it.*

Wei wouldn't listen. I knew it. Our tear- and blood-stained faces had made him only more strident and I was exhausted. Instead, I went to my room, where I took a long, hot shower and tried to pretend, at least for half an hour, that none of it existed.

39

REVOLUTION WAS IN THE AIR that autumn. The shah, sick with cancer, had come to America for treatment, riling up distrust that the United States would try to put him back in power, so on the morning of November 4, Iranian students broke into the US embassy in Tehran for a peaceful "set-in" that ended with the taking of more than sixty hostages. However, after the incident in Mendocino, Iran diminished for me to some murmured news report.

Wei, Jia Bao, and a group of their friends began gathering at a different house each week—was this pretense an actual strategy or some cliché pulled from a movie?—all men; the women had no role but to arrange the crackers or hush the children.

"What do you do every Thursday?" I asked.

"Bridge," Wei said. He had watched Jia Bao's bruises slowly turn from black to lavender to yellow before vanishing, and yet he still dared to continue.

"Don't you care at all about your family?" I fumed.

When Wei said, "It's just cards. It has nothing to do with you," I knew I truly had been exiled from their plan.

They never met at our house, and I could only suspect the numbers and names of the men who participated; if Mr. Lu ever questioned me, I could plead an honest ignorance. After it was all over, Wei would tell me that the group had planned to provide weapons to the activists in Taiwan in order to help nurture the native protests that had already begun to flare up: tiny explosions that the government quickly doused. Against the KMT's tear gas and truncheons and rubber bullets, the protesters had nothing but words. Martin Luther King Jr. was ten years dead and the oppressed were weary of nonviolent resistance.

I don't know the details. A few of them ran import-export businesses, and I suppose at that time, anything could be done for a bribe. Instructions were coded into invoices. With MADE IN TAIWAN still a ubiquitous sticker on many goods, this group of bridge-playing businessmen purported to be manufacturing golf clubs and patriotic sparklers.

A fourth force. Three fingers already jammed into the pie: the KMT, America, and China. Inspired by Graham Greene's *The Quiet American*, which I had read for a class and discussed with Wei one evening, they decided they would form a "fourth force." Four was an unlucky number, a homophone for death, but, as in tarot cards, death could be not an ending but instead a rebirth and change. Jia Bao was to be the liaison to the American media, his recent imprisonment and escape bolstering his credibility as a voice for human rights. But I did not know any of this until it had already all fallen apart.

40

FOR JIA BAO'S FIRST THANKSGIVING, I modeled our meal on the famous Rockwell picture, which I'd seen taped in the window of Andronico's market. I heaved a defrosted twenty-pound turkey out of the fridge, pulled a bag of giblets out of its body and set it aside for gravy, and crammed the cold, damp body cavity with stuffing. I rubbed the bird with seasoning and butter and wrapped it in foil and started baking. No rice noodles this year, no preserved duck eggs. Instead, I made a tomato aspic, corn on the cob, and mashed potatoes. In the grocery store Thanksgiving display, I'd discovered canned pumpkin, and made a pie according to the recipe on the label. Emily and Stephanie ran in and out of the kitchen, so pleased to not be in school on a Thursday. They stuck their fingers into the dishes, licked mashed potato off the beaters, and scraped the cans clean of pie filling. As a child, forced by Ah Zhay's and Mama's precise instructions, I thought preparing food was drudgery. I was happy that the girls still found it novel.

That evening, I pulled the turkey from the oven. It was beautiful: perfectly brown, crackling skin that split and revealed moist, thick meat. I called Wei and Jia Bao for dinner.

I made the girls and Jia Bao sit before I presented the turkey. The girls cooed and clapped; the whole event, done this way, was a novelty to them. I handed Wei the knife and told him to carve the bird.

"You see," Wei said. The knife sank into the meat. "Here we go, the American way. My wife has cooked all day, but I'll take the honors."

"No sarcasm, please. The girls are hungry." I realized I was still wearing my apron. I untied it and hung it on my chair. The smell of the kitchen was heavy in my clothes.

"What's the reason for this holiday again?" Jia Bao asked.

"Emily, tell Uncle Jia Bao."

"The Pilgrims were starving and the Indians helped them grow food, and when they harvested it, the Pilgrims and Indians came together to thank each other for not starving to death."

"Indians?" Jia Bao said.

Emily had used a literal translation of the word. "Indigenous peoples," I corrected.

Wei laughed. "Pilgrims and Indians. The explorers thought they had reached the Indies when they arrived." He lifted a chunk of meat. "Pass your plates."

We passed the dishes around the table the way that I recalled from faculty dinners, each person taking a share, unlike our usual practice of reaching into the common plates for whatever we wanted. Jia Bao hesitated over the quavering mound of tomato aspic.

"It's a savory gelatin," I said self-consciously. He shrugged and took a scoop.

Wei waved a drumstick. "I feel like a real American. Head of household." He took an exaggerated bite, like a lusty medieval king. His antics exhausted me.

"I want one too," Stephanie cried.

I hushed her. "Eat what I gave you."

"Oh no!" Emily cried. Her mouth formed a comic O of horror. "We forgot to say what we are thankful for. We didn't say grace."

"Grace?" Jia Bao said.

"She wants to pray," Wei said. "Ever since she went to that girl Amy's house, she wants to say grace all the time."

"Ah Ma would like that." My mother said grace before even a cup of tea. Suddenly, homesickness washed over me. I would call my parents later. "Should we talk about what we are thankful for?"

Emily closed her eyes and bowed her head. Wei raised an eyebrow at me. "I'm thankful for my family. Thank you, God. In Jesus's name, amen."

I repeated her "amen," and Jia Bao's and Stephanie's voices lagged a moment behind me.

"Me too," Stephanie said. "I'm thankful for my family. Thank you, God. In Jesus's name, amen."

"She copied me." Emily narrowed her eyes at her sister.

"Hush. She's not copying. We can all be thankful for family. I'm thankful that we can be together." Again, I thought of my parents, an ocean away, and I sniffed. "I'm thankful that we have so much to eat when children are starving around the world." I threw in a bit about kids picking up rice grain by grain from the sand, a visual for the girls to underline their privilege.

"I'm thankful to be safe among good friends who have shown me every kindness," Jia Bao said solemnly. He had closed his eyes too. I watched him suspended in his reverie. Then he lifted his head, opened his eyes, and smiled.

"Daddy?" Emily said.

"I'm thankful for television," Wei said. The girls giggled.

Nothing was sacred unless he declared it so. "How American of you," I said.

Wei threw up his hands. "That's what my passport says."

The girls and their little murmurings provided the sound track for our dinner. I took the silence as a compliment. Then after dessert, Jia Bao halfheartedly cleared his throat.

"I'm moving," he said.

Wei's expression revealed that he had already known. This declaration was for me. Emily let out a low, drawn-out *Aw*—the kind of disappointed six-year-old whine that threatened to be followed by a *No fair*. Stephanie's look darted between us; she understood that this was important but was not clear why.

"Oh," I said. A hundred thoughts ran under that deflated single syllable. I wanted to know whose plan it was and why.

"We found a place in South Berkeley," Wei said.

"You found a place." I made my face as unexpressive as my voice.

"South Berkeley. Prince Street. A little basement apartment."

"Already paid the deposit. Lease signed," I said, not question but confirmation.

"Lease signed," Wei affirmed.

"I couldn't trouble you anymore," Jia Bao said. He looked at Wei, not me.

"Of course you want your independence. Prince Street. Off Shattuck?" I almost said it once more as I tried to force the idea into my brain. "And the lease starts when?" I spoke so quickly that my throat felt choked.

"December first."

A week from now.

"Prince Street off Shattuck." I tried to picture the street. Residential, treelined, a little run-down, middle class. I stood up. "More pie?" Without waiting for an answer, I began clearing the table.

In the corner of my eye, I caught Wei and Jia Bao exchanging a glance. Jia Bao offered to help.

"I got it," I snapped. I let the plates clatter atop one another. An obedient, fearful silence settled over the girls.

"Help your mother," Wei ordered.

"Don't worry. I can do it." I forced a smile. I gathered the utensils into a noisy silver bundle that rang out against the plates. The girls scooted out of their chairs and skulked away.

In the kitchen, I turned the faucet on as high as it would go and watched steam float and the foam rising in the sink. Denied thoughts took a physical form: a constriction in the throat, a tension around a nothing that felt like an object, a ball, a knot, something lodged. I breathed hard, trying to loosen my ribs. My relief felt so strange. I suddenly thought of the previous winter, a spur-of-the-moment trip we'd taken up to the snow, the four of us, a family, in our inadequate winter coats and sneakers. We'd stopped randomly somewhere on Interstate 80; it wasn't even a snow park or anything, just a tiny turnoff with an open patch of snow. Wei had brought the garbage lid and we used it as a sled, skittering down the little hill and dragging it back up, over and over, all afternoon. We stopped at a diner in Truckee on the way home and feasted on burgers. The girls' cheeks were bright pink, snowburned.

No, I recognized with wonder, this is not relief. This is disappointment. I plunged my hands into the hot, soapy water. They tingled with pain. The trip was less than a year ago. Days you could count. I pulled the stopper and turned the water back on.

I turned my face into my sleeve. Behind the blast of the water, I could hear Wei and Jia Bao murmuring in the other room. No one came to ask what was wrong. And if someone had, I wouldn't have been able to answer.

Without a word to Wei or Jia Bao, I went upstairs after the dishes were done and put the girls to bed. After I tucked Stephanie in, she grabbed my hand and kissed my palm. She had become more physically affectionate since starting her visits with Dr. Matson.

"Mommy," she said. "Don't be sad." Her plea was a jab in my stomach.

"I'm happy," I protested, but I sensed that she knew it was a lie. "I'm happy that I have such a lovely daughter."

"*Two* daughters," she reminded me, holding up two fingers.

"Of course. *Two* lovely daughters." I smoothed the blanket and kissed her forehead.

From the phone in my room, I called my parents. It was almost ten o'clock Friday morning. No one answered.

I crawled into bed and it was hours before Wei finally came up. I pretended I was sleeping. He undressed in the dark and slipped in beside me. He was careful to not touch me—no toe accidentally nudging my leg, or an arm against mine.

My parents' eight-year anniversary, in the long narrative of their lives, was early in the story, before they'd even birthed their last child. Eight years was just the beginning: three years before my father's disappearance, fourteen years before his return.

Wei and I had been married eight years. We had made vows that promised a long arc, a life in which eight years would be just a few forgotten slashes on a doorframe marking out growing pains.

Maybe Wei was right to come to bed and not say a thing to me. Maybe what made the years bearable was to let all those bad feelings slip beneath the surface unacknowledged. We closed our eyes and dove in, ears muffled and holding our breath, and when we emerged again, a lifetime would have passed.

The next day, we drove to Placerville for the opening of the Christmas tree farms. The hills were dry and golden up Interstate 50 through El Dorado Hills until we reached Shingle Springs, where evergreens began to mingle among the oaks. We parked in a gravel lot. Everything about the day was bright: the sunbursts through the treetops, the crisp air, the crystalline voices traveling among the trees. We marched around engaged in debate about each tree's pros and cons: too tall, too wide, too sparse, too silver, and so on. Away from home, Wei and Jia Bao seemed to forget all the heaviness of their secret life. They joked and bantered, scooped up the girls and made them squeal. Wei threw his arm around me and nuzzled my cold cheek, and I glanced at Jia Bao; he was crouched beside Emily, discussing the differences between deciduous and evergreen trees.

We came down the hill at sunset, our six-foot balsam fir strapped to the roof of the car. We moved west toward the sinking sun. The sky turned a vibrant pink. Sacramento, a scatter of lights, opened up before us in its valley sprawl.

"Look," I said to the girls, and they offered a polite coo of awe. I thought of the discrete memories of my childhood—vivid moments rising above the vagueness of long stretches of unremembered time—and I wondered if they would recall this day, and the five of us together.

41

A QUIET LIFE. I wanted mulberry trees shading streets where children played. I wanted Jia Bao furiously typing away in his apartment on Prince Street, that simple, sad place full of dust and the stink of cats, a martyr's sanctuary. I wanted Wei, chalk on his fingers and clothes, lecturing in LeConte Hall to earnest undergraduates. I wanted Emily screaming across a playground in wild pursuit of her friends, and Stephanie curled up on a pillow in the reading loft of her preschool. I wanted all of that to continue, unbroken, through the winter and spring, punctuated by nothing but holidays marked by construction-paper snowflakes and hearts.

I met Mr. Lu at a restaurant in Oakland's Chinatown.

We ordered American style, each of us getting our own lunch special. I had no appetite. It was just after the noon rush, and the kitchen was noisier than the dining room as the staff ate. We faced each other like lovers at the end of an affair.

Once again, I marveled at the controlled menace in Mr. Lu's voice. His tone was friendly, but as taut as a piano wire being drawn across a person's neck, as he expressed *empathy*—as he called it—for my difficult position.

He said he had heard that Wei was involved in some sort of scheme with Jia Bao.

I wondered how my face had unintentionally betrayed me at our first meeting outside the photo shop. This man had trusted me not to confide in my husband, and I had not. He knew my own marriage better than I did. His colleagues must have profiled dozens of possible informants, and somehow they had settled on me.

"Jia Bao's gone now," I said. "So there's nothing more to say." A week before, I'd helped Jia Bao clean his new place, a basement apartment in a worn-down Victorian accessible through a side door behind the back-yard gate. Together, we had stood in the doorway and surveyed our task. An old turquoise refrigerator, dating back to the 1950s, stood behind the door and a rickety metal-frame bed with a thin striped mattress was visible in the gloomy bedroom. The odor of stale cat urine made me cough.

Mr. Lu asked me what I knew about Wei's latest scheme. I was a piss-poor source; why had he continued to pursue me? Because insinuation was enough to move me to action? Because an indirect chain of events was more effective on American soil, where assassinations and disappearances were frowned upon? Isn't that what I relied on—the protection of this land?

I told him the truth: I knew nothing. Wei had kept everything from me. All I knew—I gave this as a small token—was that Jia Bao would be speaking at a Unitarian church on International Human Rights Day. Mr. Lu smiled.

"I'm sure it will be well attended. Americans have a hearty appetite for the horror stories of other lands."

I took a bite of my vegetables, soaked in some sort of gravy that the menu simply called "brown sauce," and closed my eyes as I tried to swallow.

"Convince him to cancel. As you know, the island and the administration are having an image problem, and something like this will just fan the flames."

"I'll try."

"Please do. I know you are busy, with a lot on your mind. Not only a wife and friend, but a mother." He snatched up a piece of chicken and swallowed it. "By the way, if you need the name of a good day care, please let me know. One that won't make such strange demands on its parents. Customer is king, right?" He shook his head and laughed. "Therapy. Really!"

To stave off my nausea, I gulped down a few mouthfuls of ice water. I feared the glass would slip out of my shaking hand. I set it down carefully.

I steeled my jaw against my chattering teeth. "If you know so much, what do you need me for?"

My audacity, fearful as it was, amused him. "Here we have it. She finally speaks her mind. Because only one person can deal with Mr. Tang's manuscript for us."

"Manuscript?" My voice was monochromatic, fake.

"'Manuscript?' she says. Yes, the manuscript. I want to emphasize to you that it will be a disaster if it's published. A disaster for us, and a disaster for Mr. Tang."

"I don't know anything."

"The funny thing is"—he smiled a smile that was not a smile at all—"he was too happy to take the money we gave him to stop writing it."

I flinched. It's a game, I reminded myself. Still, the question rang, a sharp, shrill bell of doubt: He'd talked to Jia Bao too? I knew too well the twisted path of good intentions. No, Jia Bao was not a hypocrite. Yet anybody could turn. No: I would not be skeptical. Jia Bao was not like other men. Did Mr. Lu see my expressions dance through this debate before I finally said, "That's impossible"?

"Is it? It'd be best if there were a way I could be sure it would be destroyed. I'd ask you to destroy it yourself, but—well, I'm sure you understand. I need to oversee it myself. Do you think you can help me?" When I didn't respond, he set an envelope on the table. "A small thank-you in advance." I didn't move. He wiped his mouth and dropped his crumpled napkin on top of his uneaten food. He left a ten between our plates. "This will take care of the bill." He offered his hand and, pathetically, I shook it.

I waited until I was in the car before I looked in the envelope. Five hundred dollars. I rubbed the bills, wondering if they were fake. Could Jia Bao really have accepted their money? Perhaps the entire thing was a ruse; either way I'd lose. Sheepishly, I held the envelope up to my nose and sniffed. It had the distinctive smell of cash. I had taken it off the table; I couldn't have left it there. Perhaps I could find a way to return it.

I folded up the bundle and zipped it into my purse and thought of all the people I would please and disappoint.

42

DR. MATSON—DAVE—HAD A NEW RUG, this one woven out of rags, in all shades of red and orange. I was fascinated by its hideousness. He had also installed a small burbling plastic fountain that plugged into the wall. It sounded like a leaking faucet; I yearned to give it a hard twist and shut it off.

Wei and I sat at opposite ends of the couch.

Dave's eyes darted between us.

"How have things been since I last saw you?" he asked.

"Fine," I said.

"Any more to say about it?" Dave encouraged. Dave always wanted us to *say more,* to flay ourselves open, go beyond flesh to the guts. If that had been possible, we wouldn't have found ourselves here.

"Nope," said Wei.

Dave nervously shuffled through his papers. "Well then, let's talk about Stephanie?"

I squirmed. I was not sure I wanted to know. Every session—during which I had mindlessly flipped through magazines in the waiting room while Stephanie said god-knows-what to Dave behind the gloomy blank door—had made me less and less sure of everything. What kind of mother or wife was I? What kind of daughter had I been? Did the test of my existence come to this—the success of raising a child?

When neither of us answered, he continued. "So our sessions have been going well. She's a very thoughtful little girl. Very observant. Careful with her words. You know all this of course. She told me about her imaginary friend. You probably know about him. She says that he ran away from home and that he lives with her now."

"An imaginary friend? I've never seen her talking to herself," I said. "Are you sure?"

Stephanie was so phlegmatic, so sensible. Once she had learned that unicorns didn't exist, she had refused to draw them anymore. Even as a toddler, she had grabbed my face when I was talking to her as if to gauge my honesty. While Emily could be teased out of a bad mood, Stephanie didn't respond to coddling baby talk.

"Doesn't sound like her," Wei grumbled.

"Yes, let's see." Dave perused the paper. "She says his name is *Jaw Bow.*"

"Jia Bao?" I said. Our four-year-old had spent her therapy session talking about Jia Bao? The hard pump of my heart shot tension up the sides of my neck. I stiffened, afraid to betray my surprise. How had I not known?

"He's not imaginary," Wei cut in. "He's real."

"What do you mean 'real'?"

"She's telling the truth," Wei said. "A friend of ours, Jia Bao, has been living with us. But he's moved out."

Dave raised his eyebrows. "How long had he been there?"

I silently counted the months. "About two and a half months."

"Two and a half months is a long time." Dave drew the words out and his careful pacing was thick with implication. "It's interesting that neither of you mentioned him."

"Is it relevant? I thought these sessions were about us, my wife and I."

"Has it caused any tension between you two?"

Up rose the memory that I had forced from my mind: lying atop the faded comforter in Willits, Jia Bao's heart gently striking against my palm. Rooting against his hair for his most basic scent. I would recognize it again, the way a mother bird recognizes its nestling's cry. Earth and oil and the generic detergent-and-coconut hotel shampoo. I forced a laugh: "No. Jia Bao is incredibly considerate." Wei fiddled with the seam of the sofa arm.

"How did he come to stay with you?"

I waited for Wei to explain it.

"He needed a place to stay," Wei finally said. "He was down on his luck, you might say."

"That sounds like a lot of pressure on your marriage."

"Not really," I said, casting a glance at Wei's firm expression.

"It can be hard on children to have their routine disrupted."

But it wasn't Jia Bao, I wanted to protest. It was Wei, out of the house in the evenings at his mysterious meetings; it was me, scurrying around with blood money hidden in my purse. I suddenly saw our lives from Stephanie's point of view: the subterfuge so thick that the whole house was choked up with it. I was surprised Stephanie and Emily could even breathe amid all the dishonesty and wary glances.

I would speak up. We wanted to help Stephanie, right? "Maybe she talks about Jia Bao, but it's not his fault," I said. "It's our fault. It's you, Wei, talking about nothing but politics like the rest of us don't matter."

"Politics?" asked Dave.

"You could say I'm passionate about politics," Wei quickly cut in. I understood—I was not to say anything about it. Even American doctor-patient confidentiality laws were not confidential enough for this situation. Yet another secret to worry over and protect.

"Very passionate," I said. "When was the last time you were home early enough to tuck them in?"

Dave interrupted. "This is interesting and important, but maybe we can talk a bit more about Jia Bao, since that's where Stephanie's focus is?"

"Jia Bao is passionate about politics too." I barely kept the sneer out of my voice. "Believe me, this is relevant."

"I'm not interested in it for fun. I do what I do for the girls. You don't get that?"

"'What you do.' What is that exactly?" Dave asked.

"Yeah, Wei. What is it that you do?" I turned to Dave. "Do you play bridge?"

"No. Why?"

"Apparently my husband is an expert at it. He plays a few nights a week sometimes."

Wei rubbed his face and sighed. His voice was weary as he tried to dismiss my sarcasm. "I'm not having an affair, if that's what you think."

Did he really think I was so petty? "An affair?" I raised my voice. "Is this something else I should worry about? It didn't even occur to me. *Are* you having an affair?"

"I just said I wasn't."

"Then why mention it?" I no longer cared if Dave saw how ugly we were.

"If you think I'm . . . *interested in politics* just for my sake, then you don't know me at all. Do you think I want our kids to grow up like we did, without a country? Or like you, without a father?"

I flinched. "My father has nothing to do with this. The girls have a father now, even if he *wishes* he was rotting away in prison for being a martyr."

Wei stood up so suddenly that I recoiled. "I'm done," he announced.

Dave set aside his papers and beckoned to Wei. "Wait, wait, wait. Let's just cool down."

"I said I'm done."

"Wei," Dave said, "please stay to finish the session."

"No," Wei said. He struggled into his coat and his arm caught in the sleeve. "Fuck!" he shouted.

"What about Stephanie?" I screamed. "What about your daughter? This isn't about you."

Wei slammed the door. The fountain hiccuped and water splashed onto the floor. I wanted to follow him. All my veins throbbed, my throat felt crushed, my temples ached.

I loathed him.

Dave and I sat with the maddening burble of the fountain for too long. Finally, he asked, "How do you feel?"

My laugh was dry, almost a sob. "I feel awful," I said.

43

THE CHURCH ON CEDAR STREET was modest, the feel of colonial New England in its pale wood planks, with a simple meeting room for the congregation set up with folding chairs. The audience was a mix of young people with long hair and loose clothing and older, professorial types in the style of classic East Coast liberals: properly trimmed and tailored in tweed and corduroy. Except for me and Wei and a few of our friends, everyone was white. Wei had completely ignored my halfhearted suggestion that they cancel the talk. I bitterly thought of Mr. Lu's comment on Americans' voyeurism of international tragedy.

At my insistence, we sat in the last row where I could watch the door. A young woman from Amnesty International, in tight blue pants and some

sort of generic ethnic blouse—multicolored and stitched in a geometric pattern—introduced Jia Bao as "an asylum seeker from Free China,
which is neither free nor China." Wei snickered into his sleeve, masking it
as a cough. I exhaled loudly. Wei leaned over and whispered, "Don't mind
me." His frosty tone reminded me that he had not yet forgiven me for the
fight in Dr. Matson's office.

Jia Bao spoke for almost an hour, detailing his imprisonment and house
arrest, and the overall situation in Taiwan. He told of his less-famous colleagues who were still in prison, and the common citizens too, who had
lost their freedom for simply speaking their minds.

Jia Bao finished to impassioned applause. Questions followed: How
do you think the impending change in US-Taiwan relations will affect
the dictatorship? Is it really fair to call it a dictatorship? After all, Chiang
Kai-shek was an ally. Will you ever return home? Do you think you can be
more effective here than there? Do you call yourself Taiwanese? Would
unification with China be the best route?

Even after the questions had stopped, people crowded Jia Bao at the
podium. Alongside one wall, a table of cookies and Thermoses of hot tea
had been set up. Wei joined Jia Bao at the front—perhaps hoping to take
on some of the questions—while I wandered over to the snacks.

As I poured a cup of tea for Jia Bao, a low male voice said hello.

"This is quite awkward," Mr. Lu said. "I didn't expect either of us to be
here. I didn't expect there would be an event for us to attend. I thought
you understood what I had asked you. I thought you had agreed."

I pushed the guilt from my mind. "I couldn't do anything about it."

"Don't play the helpless female. You lied to me." For the first time, he
didn't bother to hide his venom.

Feeling a cold disquiet rise up my chest, I touched my throat. "I tried.
They didn't listen to me." Reflexively, I glanced at Wei to see if he was
watching.

Mr. Lu, who missed nothing, followed my gaze. "I'm looking forward
to meeting your husband. And seeing Mr. Tang again."

"Why him?"

"Do you think he's the only one? He just insists on being the squeaki-
est. What's that the Americans say about squeaky wheels?"

I didn't answer.

"Here comes your husband now."

I composed myself. I was placid. I was cool. "I was just about to bring Jia Bao some tea," I said to Wei as he approached.

Mr. Lu reached out to shake Wei's hand.

"Your wife tells me that you and Mr. Tang are close friends."

Wei answered with an ambiguous noise. "I'm sorry. I missed your name."

"Lu Ai Guo." He handed Wei his card. Wei's eyes drifted over it. His face hardened.

"Is that for Jia Bao?" Wei reached for the cup in my hand.

"Don't be upset. I'd like to talk to you. I've given your wife my card as well." How could he? My protest caught on my lips and I glared at Mr. Lu.

"Come." Wei tugged at my arm.

We left Mr. Lu at the refreshment table. On our way to the front, Wei asked me what I'd told him.

"Nothing!"

He clutched my arm. From afar—from Mr. Lu's vantage—it must have looked like a sweet gesture: a husband gently guiding his wife through a throng of people. Mr. Lu could not hear Wei spit into my ear, "Nothing? What's nothing? Everything is something. You should have known the moment you saw his card."

I had an impulse to confess everything. But I'd already taken it too far. I couldn't tell Wei. Never.

Once, driving on a freeway, we passed an accident in the opposite lane. The traffic coming toward us was backed up for miles. None of them knew what lay ahead—that a boat that had somehow jumped its towline had flipped over a car. We knew the disaster that lay, in a way, in their future. I mention this because on the same day that we sat in that little church, listening to Jia Bao narrate his escape, police in Taiwan's southern city of Kaohsiung—light scissoring across their black face shields— brought out the truncheons and celebrated Human Rights Day with beatings and tear gas.

I was there in the church on Cedar Street, listening to Jia Bao, while across the Pacific, Taiwanese echoed from a megaphone truck: "People in your homes, people on the streets, Taiwan is your home. Come stand together for your home. Police, you are brothers and fathers of Taiwanese. Come stand together for freedom. In three weeks, the United States abandonment will be complete. Taiwan will cease to exist. Come stand with us."

The loudspeaker mumbled and the voice of the crowd rose up in response:

"Human rights now!"

"Oppose arbitrary arrests!"

"Oppose torture and violence!"

"Oppose one-party dictatorship! Oppose one-party dictatorship!" The officers were three deep, and they completed their blockade with billy clubs. The loudspeaker called out for the protesters to join up with those waiting at the Tatung Department Store and the people cried back, "They've blocked us! We cannot move! The trucks are coming from the east!" The loudspeaker continued mumbling and then screams rang out: "Tear gas!" White smoke, reflecting the light of camera flashes, billowed out on the far side of the crowd. The panicked protesters waved their torches, trying to break through the police line, and the police resisted with their batons. A few hundred pushed through before the officers quickly closed up again, trapping inside the rest of the group who continued to cry, "We cannot get out. Stop the riot trucks!" But the trucks continued to roll on; they split the crowd and then were swallowed by it as the loudspeaker urged calm, urged the trucks to leave, urged the police to step aside.

Men in helmets, armored vests, kneepads, and black boots, wielding riot shields, ringed the giant crowd. Far off, the rumbling of a herd of trucks, an entire battalion, approached. The speakers resumed—histories of colonialism, of slavery; calls for the release of political prisoners—as the crowd started to disintegrate into chaos, as the police ringed in tighter and tighter, as fights broke out between the Anti-Communist Heroes (egg-wielding hoodlums wearing armbands printed with the Nationalist flag) and the protesters, as some tried to light the riot trucks on fire and begged for gasoline to be siphoned from the sound truck, as others urged for peace.

Canisters steaming out poisonous gas were lobbed into the group. A roar rose up, a collective *aah*. The officers swung their billy clubs, grabbing people by their napes or by their shirts and thumping them into submission. Gas, blood, sweat rained down.

Imperfect time travel for an imperfect world. Their December 10 happened before ours, and we learned of it when we came home that afternoon. One of our local Taiwanese friends called with the news. He had heard it from his brother, who was a taxi driver in Kaohsiung and who had seen it himself.

Wei, racked with guilt, sat down on the sofa while Jia Bao paced the room. I thought of the sweet church with its swept hardwood floors and the innocent plates of cookies and the welcoming crowd that had embraced Jia Bao and his words. Words, words, words—nothing but words and ideas—as heads had split open. While our friends were rioting, handcuffed and starving, in the yard, we were the ones banging on open cell doors, bellies full, crying for our freedom.

"I don't know what you've been up to, but you have to stop now," I said. "The situation is too dangerous." Martyrdom was paid for in flesh. Words from the man who lived happily ever after had the weight and consequence of air and Wei knew it.

"No, we have to move faster," Wei said.

"Faster doing what?" Anger and fear made my voice sharp.

Jia Bao was about to answer when Wei gestured for his silence.

"How well do you know this Lu Ai Guo?"

"Who?" I said.

"You've seen him before." Accusatory. Wei stood up. He turned in small circles, like a dog looking for a place to lie. So lost in his thoughts, he seemed to have no idea what his body did, then he sank into a blue armchair.

I protested, "He came to the party. I told you that."

"Who?" Jia Bao said.

My gaze darted to him—was he playing the same game?

"There was some snoop at the church today. She's talked to him." The weight fell on the pronoun—*she*—as if he ripped away my identity; I was nothing but a single-syllable generic pronoun. Wei turned to me again. "Did you talk to him before? Not at the party. Somewhere else?"

"I've never said anything." Blood shot from my heart to my brain; heat flared in my head. "I never said anything." The words collapsed, weak.

"She would never say anything." Jia Bao frowned. A grateful affection rushed through me. He continued: "She's your wife. You're being manipulated. This is how they destroy us. This seed of mistrust. She didn't say a thing." Jia Bao's voice was weary: this was a thing he'd seen a hundred times, the oldest trick in the book. I wanted to tell Wei everything, and what Mr. Lu had claimed about Jia Bao taking the money, just so I could say: *Look at him. He's no better than me.*

Wei gripped the armrests. His knuckles flushed red and white. He pushed "I'm sorry" through his gritted teeth. The urge to appear the reasonable intellectual kept his temper at bay.

Surveillance was the heart of it, Jia Bao reminded us. "Isn't freedom the ability to conduct our lives in privacy, without every action logged, reported, and punished? To ride the bus without wondering if the old woman clutching her purse is noting how you sit, whom you sit next to, what you mutter when the bus clatters over a pothole? Every banality jotted down in a huge file where every pedestrian action, beneath the glare of the investigator's lamp, takes on significance? The loss of freedom isn't a restriction of movement; it's the unending feeling of being watched."

I had to do something with my hands. I rearranged the trinkets we kept on the mantel: the brass monk's bowl, the ceramic kewpie doll that Stephanie loved, the misshapen cup Emily had made in school, the various cards left over from the year's holidays. "It's over, Wei. No more. I don't want to be a part of this anymore."

"It's not up to you."

"Go upstairs and look at your daughters and then come back down and tell me that. No more." Emily's cup fell from my hands and shattered. "Fuck!" I cried. I crouched down to gather the pieces.

Wordlessly, Jia Bao moved to the sofa.

Wei stood up. Restraint shuddered through him and he took his seat again. "You don't understand. We don't have to live small lives because of what happened to your father."

I turned and gestured with my hands full of shards. I'd cut myself and the blood trickled down my palm. "A small life? This is a small life? Everything you wanted, and you want to throw it away so you can play cowboy?"

The line of blood traveled to my wrist and a single drop splattered onto the floor. A snarl flashed on Wei's face, one brief reveal, and then his expression cooled. "Clean yourself up. You're hysterical."

Once I'd washed the blood away, all that remained was benign, not much bigger than a paper cut, and I covered it with a bandage. We arrayed ourselves again in the living room. Wei took up his place in the blue chair; I sat beside Jia Bao on the sofa.

"We're not going to run away like cowards," Wei said.

"This is the end game, Wei," I said. "It's over. What's the point? More violence? You think if you fight hard enough, the government will just give you what you want? You're not a naive student anymore. You know how it works."

Jia Bao sighed. "The fact is. The most important point is." He spoke carefully, a child leaping across a stone path through a stream. "What we need to remember now is that . . . something has happened. This is a moment. The pivotal moment, and all we can do is help as much as we can. Everything has been set into motion. The machinery has awakened. We have to keep it running. This is the moment when everything can change. I understand that—" He sighed again. "I understand that you two may not agree on this, but something bigger is happening now." Jia Bao's argument slowly turned on me. "We can't be selfish."

I stared at the ceiling. They were closing ranks. Cobwebs laced the light fixture. I watched a spider creep across the plaster. A small, drifting speck.

"I understand that you can't help but feel a part of it, against your will. And now the KMT have approached you and you have to decide what you think is right. But this is the moment." Jia Bao's voice was so soft, so reasonable. He spoke like a negotiator whispering to a person whose toes were already curling over the ledge. I resented it.

"I don't want to end up a widow."

Wei threw up his chin and laughed loudly.

"Go ahead, laugh. If this wasn't a life-or-death situation, you wouldn't want anything to do with it." My eyes returned to the moving speck, that industrious little spider trekking its way home.

Jia Bao cleared his throat. I hoped that he had felt the insult as well.

"You don't understand. In this place, even the smallest dissent can result in death. This is a looking-glass world without logic. Nothing is what it seems. Remember Professor Ong. Every gesture is a risk," Jia Bao said.

Professor Ong: dropped from a campus building by the secret police on a visit home to Taipei. For what? The opposition claimed his crime had been merely questioning party politics at a conference in California. A single question.

"Then say nothing." *See no evil, hear no evil, say no evil. Turn a blind eye.* I ran through the idioms I'd learned in my ESL classes, how I thought these trite turns of phrase, tossed into conversations, would make me more American. *Silence is golden.* Instead, these clichés, which came like blocks awkwardly tumbling from my mouth, had called out my foreignness. "Do nothing."

"It's not possible," Wei said.

I recalled the day we'd met, when Wei had first told me about the March Massacre and my father's role. Later that day, I'd gone home to Ah Zhay's, and we'd sat on the stone ledge in the alley and she had finished the story. The event had not even existed until I'd heard the story. It happened this way for each of us, one by one, across the island, a structure suddenly exploding onto the placid empty plain of our history.

"I just want peace and quiet," I said. I was losing. My words were listless even to my own ears. I wished none of it had happened. I wished Jia Bao back home and Mr. Lu back into the shadows. How far back would my wishes have to go to erase all of it? All the way back to February 1947?

"If only," Jia Bao said.

44

THE CHRISTMAS SEASON ARRIVED. Emily wrote a holiday card to the hostages in Iran and let Stephanie scribble a stick figure on it too. Across the country, schoolchildren put crayon to paper to remind these poor people that another world still existed, even as they were blindfolded and forced to sit in handcuffs for days at a time. In windows around town, American flags had appeared. Emily brought the patriotism home and muttered the Pledge of Allegiance as she colored.

"I don't know what to say," Emily complained. "My teacher said, 'Write something cheerful.'" Her crayons, all dumped from the box, splayed out in front of her. She gripped a chubby pencil, the stout kind made for children's clumsy hands.

"Well, you know you should start with 'Dear.'"

"Okay." She wedged her tongue into the corner of her mouth as she concentrated. Her letters were big and round. "Dear Mr. *La-i-n-g-e-n.*"

"Why don't you think about the kind of letter you'd like to get if you were—" I paused. If you were what? A hostage? "If you were away from home."

Emily tucked her fist under her chin and frowned, her eyes drifting in thought. Poor Mr. Laingen. We knew his face well from the news—Stephanie had mistaken him for Mr. Rogers. I understood how his family felt. Would it have been worse if we had known Baba was alive? If we had known that a blade of death—dangling by a thin, tenuous thread—hung over him each day? If we had known his life depended on the negotiations of dozens of strangers and the whim of angry students? If I could have written a letter, I would have told Baba he was not forgotten. That we thought of him every day. That his absence was a ghost in our home.

"I know!" Emily declared. She began writing.

I read over her shoulder: *I'm sorry you can't come home. What do you want from Santa this year?*

We miss you.

Come home soon.

An earthquake in Colombia, Soviets in Afghanistan, Mother Teresa winning the Nobel Prize. The world spun 'round and 'round with its usual mix of tragedy and triumph. Threading through it all, every day on TV, were the hostages. They lurked at the edge of everything, in every activity, a corner-of-the-eye twinge that something was out of place. I even dreamed of them.

On American soil, the Iranians, like us, had been vulnerable to the cooperative machinations of the CIA and their own secret police. As with the KMT, information was exchanged tit for tat with the shah's men, so that an American, bolstered by the promise of the First Amendment, was guaranteed to have his brother's legs broken in the homeland for the wrong words uttered so many thousands of miles away.

In my dreams, I sat with President Carter in a panopticon, while all around us, out of reach, blindfolded men were tied to racks, had their wrists bound to their ankles, and were lined up for firing squads armed with blanks that shot to scare, not kill. We pressed ourselves to the glass and called out for it to stop, but no one could hear us. I spotted Wei there, his face masked but his clothes recognizable. They tied his hands and removed his belt and let his pants drop in humiliation. He hung his head. *Do something*, I told the president. He smiled, ashamed.

I woke and gripped Wei's arm. All I wanted was to feel the realness of his muscle and bone under my fingers. I thought of my mother and how many times she must have woken up wanting the same and found nothing.

"Don't do it," I murmured to Wei.

The meetings continued. He stopped saying good-bye to me when he left. In frustration, I could not help but think that they were becoming a parody of themselves, as theatrical and self-important as the Weathermen or the SLA, their values disintegrating beneath ego. Though I had no idea what their plan actually was, I was sure of the impotence of their work against a machine as large as the KMT. Meanwhile, in Taiwan, the government had tightened its grip, bulldozing through magazine and newspaper offices and shutting them down, arresting writers, editors, teachers, thinkers.

Christmas was somber. We gathered at the tree on Christmas Day. The girls grabbed at gifts littered with dried fir needles. Wei and I smiled and cooed as the girls held up their presents—a mini Tupperware set, Legos, two dolls with matching black hair and blue eyes—but we could not look at each other. We stood the girls in front of the tree and took a picture of them cradling their new babies.

"Dad! The flash hurt her eyes." Emily nuzzled her doll. "She's crying. She wants her grandma."

Wei raised an eyebrow at me. "She means you."

Emily brought the doll to me and I brushed aside its nylon hair and kissed its plastic face. Its eyes rocked open and closed. "Don't cry, little baby," I soothed.

Emily smiled. "Much better." She planted a loud, damp kiss on my cheek and grabbed Stephanie's hand, dragging her back to their pile of gifts.

I watched them play. The recent progress reports from Stephanie's teacher had been positive: no more acting out, a generally more cooperative attitude. After our fight in Dr. Matson's office, Wei had refused to return and scorned the whole concept of therapy as hokum. He insisted that Stephanie would be better off if she wasn't made to feel "different" with these sessions and he pulled her from them too, preschool be damned. If Jia Bao had been the problem, he said, the problem was solved. There was nothing wrong with our daughter. I was the one forced to make a sheepish call to Dr. Matson to tell him to cancel our ongoing appointments. He asked why, and even though he must have known the reason, I lied and said with the coming holidays, our schedule was too busy to accommodate these extra hours a week.

Wei had been right—with Jia Bao out of the house, Stephanie seemed more and more like herself, as if she could finally relax back into the embrace of our once again complete family, even if her parents were barely speaking.

Jia Bao came over for an early-afternoon dinner. I could not look at him either. I vowed spitefully to be the dutiful wife. I served more food before they had finished chewing, poured more water before their glasses emptied. When the meal was over, Wei and Jia Bao disappeared on a walk and I took the girls, pushing their babies in tiny strollers, to the park.

The explosion happened that afternoon at the KMT headquarters in San Francisco, singeing the brass plaque black, shattering the glass door, and pocking the cement wall.

Wei was watching the late news and I was drying dishes. I leaned into the room. "What?"

"A bombing."

Plate and towel in hand, I came and stood next to the couch. Yellow police tape cut across the sidewalk to the street, wrapped around a trash can and back. Pulled from her Christmas dinner to weep in front of the damaged building and still dressed in a red-and-green snowflake sweater, a woman from the Coordination Council for North American Affairs— the new stand-in for the closed ROC consulate—said to the reporter,

"Thank god it's Christmas. Who knows how many would have died." She reached beneath her glasses and wiped away a tear. "There's too much evil in this world."

The police spokesman said, "This is obviously an act of intimidation. Even though there doesn't seem to have been an intent to harm, we will be fully pursuing this."

Shock was replaced by disbelief, then disgust. *This* was what they had been doing when "playing bridge"? *This* was how Wei planned to keep us safe? I saw nothing but reckless, selfish ego.

"I don't want to know," I spat. I wondered how much will it took for Wei to empty his eyes, as if his soul had gone slack. He clenched his jaw and his temple throbbed.

"I have nothing to tell you," he said.

The anchor turned and began reporting on Christmas traffic fatalities.

I went back into the kitchen and stood at the sink. Leave. Just leave. In America, you can leave. You can be a divorcée in tight plaid capris pushing a cart along narrow grocery-store aisles, a kerchief on your head and your fingers free of rings. My heart didn't beat. I didn't breathe. I was air. I set the plates in the cabinet and looped the towel through a drawer handle and went upstairs.

I was not really conscious of what I put into my suitcase—a couple pairs of pants, a few sweaters and blouses, a fistful of underwear. I carried the suitcase to the girls' rooms and tossed in a few outfits and their new dolls, then went downstairs and pulled their coats from the hall closet.

From the living room, Wei said, "What's the racket?" What did he care, sitting on the couch, musing over his handiwork?

Without answering, I returned upstairs and roused the girls. They were heavy headed and sleepy eyed as I struggled them into their jackets and buttoned them up.

"What?" Emily murmured. "I'm tired." Stephanie rubbed her fist against her eye and yawned.

"You can sleep in the car."

I carried them both down the stairs, carefully, my hip pushed to the banister as a guide. The girls dropped their heads into my neck, one on either side. I braced myself against the door and turned the lock and knob. My key ring dangled off one finger.

"Going somewhere?" Wei's interest sounded obligatory.

With my foot, I nudged the suitcase through the door. Stephanie wailed.

"Hush, baby." I left the suitcase on the porch and was down the steps when Wei, yelling, bounded to the doorway.

"You can't do this!" His voice echoed across the yard and against our neighbors' dark windows.

I hurried toward the gate and knocked it open with my shoulder. The girls slowed me down, and before I could reach the car, Wei was there, his hands up in protest.

"No, no, no. You're wrong. Stop. Stop."

"Move."

Wordless and now awake, Emily lifted her head and watched her father.

"Open the door," I said.

"This isn't right. Come here, Stephanie." Wei reached out for her. She tucked her face into me and said, "Mama." Her rejection pleased me, and I hoped it hurt Wei.

Wei's fist flew back against the car. "You're not going anywhere." Across the park, one of the transients rose, curiosity and tension in his dark outline.

"Get out of my way," I screamed. Wei grabbed for the keys and the metal ring cut into my skin. "Stop! You asshole! Stop!" A dog barked.

Wei threw his hands up again. "The neighbors," he whispered. His gaze drifted toward the lights coming up.

"The neighbors can go to hell!" I shouted. I lurched to the other side of the car. Wei watched me over the roof as I struggled to unlock and open the door, and finally dropped the girls inside. They huddled together and blinked at us through the windows. Wei slapped the car and the girls shuddered.

"Fine, go." He grabbed the suitcase from the porch and tossed it in the car. "Go. Go. I don't even want to look at you."

I refused to get in until he left. I waited until he slipped through the gate and back to the porch. In the doorway, he turned and yelled, "Go!"

I slammed the door and went.

Without a plan, I drove around for nearly an hour before settling on a motel near the bottom of University Avenue well after midnight. A horseshoe of two-story buildings in chipped blue and white paint ringed the desolate parking lot. I locked the girls in the car and went to the office. Checking into a motel is always the same pathetic experience: the sallow light, the bored overnight clerk, the clinging odor of old cigarettes and surrender. The woman handed over a key on a glow-in-the-dark fob.

The room was on the second floor. The girls trudged up the stairs and stood quietly on the cement landing as I opened the door and turned on the light. Room 203 smelled like the front office plus laundry detergent: a sad, failed attempt to freshen the place. A large black grease stain spread out from under the bed along the flat blue industrial carpeting.

"Get into bed," I urged as I shut the door. I set the suitcase against the wardrobe and pulled back the bedspread, hoping I wouldn't find bedbugs.

"It smells bad," Emily said. She wrinkled her nose. "It's gross."

"Emily." The weariness in my voice was warning enough; she pulled off her jacket and climbed in. Stephanie said nothing as I lifted her up and tucked them both in with kisses.

"Don't let the bedbugs bite." A wry joke as our pitiful situation settled on me.

"Really, Mommy?" Stephanie said.

"No. It's just a joke. There are absolutely no bedbugs." I waved my hand over them. "Poof. Gone. Sleep, darlings." I turned off the lamp and went into the bathroom. I sat on the closed toilet lid. The plastic shower curtain, edged with mildew, hung on knobby plastic rings and the small window above the shower sat crooked on its track. A watermark blackened the corner of the linoleum. My fantasy of the happy divorcée drained away within the beige bathroom walls. Every detail elicited self-pity: the ragged edge of the half-used toilet paper roll, the dingy drinking glass capped with a paper coaster, the remnant strands of hair ringing the base of the toilet.

We made a ritual of this faux vacation among hookers and down-on-their-luckers. A Styrofoam cooler served as our refrigerator: milk, bread, cold cuts, and a small jar of mayonnaise sat in half-melted ice chips. In the evenings, we ate at a diner close by, taking the same seats in the same black vinyl booth with the frayed tear patched with gray duct tape, becoming familiar with the waitress who had seen a dozen families like us: young mother and kids in limbo, fleeing or abandoned.

The rest of our long, empty days—the girls were still on winter break—we spent in room 203. The girls made forts with the chairs and blankets, while I, racked and splayed out by guilt, lay on the bed and watched TV.

I could already imagine my mother's shock if she found out where I was and how I had left. Ah Zhay might be more sympathetic, but she would certainly tell my parents. Besides, I was embarrassed: I looked around this ugly motel room and saw only failure. I wondered who I could confide in. Only Jia Bao came to mind.

I parked across the street and a few houses down, just enough to give me a discreet view of his place. Even having come this far, I still wondered if I could trust him. Turning off Shattuck, he came sprinting down the street. He stumbled to a stop in front of his house and then paced in circles as he cooled down. From so far away, I could not hear him, but I could see his panting: his breath flashed in bursts of vapor. He stretched for a few minutes, then disappeared through the side gate. I locked the girls in the car, warning them not to open the door or window for anybody—*not for anybody*. "I will be right back," I said. "Five minutes. I just need to talk to Uncle Jia Bao for five minutes."

"I want to see Uncle Jia Bao!" Emily shouted.

"Five minutes." I glanced back at Jia Bao's house, and then at the girls. "Okay. Let's all say hi."

When Jia Bao answered the door, he'd already stripped off his shirt. His hair was damp. Our eyes met for an awkward moment, and then his attention turned to the girls. "Emily and Stephanie! Come in." He stepped aside and they scrambled in, but he stopped me with a hand on my arm. "Where have you been?" he whispered. "Wei is worried."

"Never mind."

"Have you called him yet?"

"Not yet. I will when I'm ready."

He took a deep breath and let me pass.

He shut the door. "I have something for you," he said to the girls, who were poking into every nook and cranny and exclaiming to each other.

Emily turned from her snooping. "What is it?"

His apartment, without direct sunlight, was even colder than the street. "What happened to the heat?" I asked. I pulled my jacket tighter at the throat and crossed my arms.

He rapped on the radiator that was affixed to the wall. "I think it's broken. The landlady says she'll get it fixed soon."

"My god, this is unlivable." I sat down at his small kitchen table in one of the green vinyl chairs we'd picked up at Goodwill. "Girls, come sit down." I squinted at his bare chest. "Aren't you cold?"

"I was about to shower." From a drawer near the sink, he pulled out two sheets of paper. "I picked these up at the grocery store." He set one in front of each girl. Coloring sheets of Frosty the Snowman holding bags of groceries in his stick arms, part of a store promotion, "Color and Win!" along the bottom.

"What do we win?" Emily asked.

"I think the deadline has passed," I said, then curbed my tone. "Wasn't it nice of Uncle Jia Bao to think of you? What do you say?"

They thanked him and began squabbling over the crayons that he brought out.

"Do you want tea?" he asked me.

"I'm fine."

"Then I'll be right back." He disappeared into the bedroom. I surveyed the kitchen. A bit of cellophane tape held his wife's picture to the wall above the kitchen table. Next to it was a photo of the whole family, the four of them sitting stiffly on a white sofa. His daughter, in pigtails adorned with flowers and ribbons, had a theatrical smile, while his son awkwardly looked past the camera, as if posing miserably for a military ID card. Jia Bao had so few belongings that the place could not be anything but neat. A single cup and plate were drying on a cloth next to the sink. A shiver of loneliness and pity traveled through me.

He came back in a clean sweatshirt. "The other room is a little warmer. Why don't you two color in there?"

We helped the girls carry their crayons, and they settled on the floor at the foot of the bed in a sliver of sunlight. Jia Bao and I returned to the kitchen.

"I have nothing to say," I said. "I don't want to talk about the book, or Wei, or anything else. I just want to sit here with you."

"Sure." He slid into the chair across from me.

His hands rested calmly in his lap; he was so still I thought he might have drifted off into a meditation. My eyes darted from his face to the ceiling (a pipe system led from the unit upstairs to the sink; a spiderweb clung to it) to the table (I rolled a grain of salt back and forth with my index finger). I thought I should leave, but now that I had entered, leaving felt as large a gesture as my arrival.

"You know," I said, "I waited a long time to tell Wei I was pregnant with Emily."

Jia Bao frowned. His face had lost its post-run flush, but the straw smell of his sweat still hung in the air. He said nothing and I continued, feeling my mouth dry as I spoke.

"For some reason, I couldn't bring myself to tell him. I couldn't say it. I didn't know *how* to say it. An event like that seems too big for words—any way you say it it sounds like a cliché. You should be able to tell your husband something like that without having to say it.

"I went to the hospital without him. I found it on the map and walked there one day when he was at school. I spoke a little bit of English; I'd been taking classes at the adult school for a few months. I walked into the hospital—it must have been the emergency room—and I said something about a 'baby.' They were patient enough to figure it out. They escorted me upstairs to obstetrics to be tested.

"The doctor confirmed what I'd thought. I was ecstatic. I imagined having this little doll that would be all my own. That's what I wanted. I wanted her all for myself—yes, *her*—I was sure that the baby would be a girl. I didn't want to share her with Wei. Everything else I had was half his. I felt—I felt alone here, and she was all mine. So I kept her to myself, for weeks, until Wei got the bill. I hadn't expected it; I hadn't even thought about the money. I think a nurse helped me fill out the forms. It turned out that's how I told him. Bigger than words, right?"

"Why—"

I quieted him with my hand. "You want to know why I am telling you?" I brushed the stray salt off the table.

"No," Jia Bao said in his sure voice. "I understand."

"I know," I said. Finally, I met his gaze.

The light was always gray in that apartment, even on the sunniest days. It made life seem quieter, monastic, washed in dinginess. We sat there, paralyzed, like two figures in a Vermeer.

"Did you take the money?" The question shook in my mouth and came out as a whisper. I felt my pulse as a flicker in my throat as I waited for his answer. I suddenly realized that it was this question, sitting quietly unsettled in my thoughts, that had compelled me here, even though I'd had no conscious plan to ever ask him about it.

He leaned forward, his eyes black and serious. "What money?"

"The money from . . ." I swallowed. "From . . ." I couldn't say it.

Jia Bao's voice was hard and dismissive. "You need to call your husband. You need to go home."

I inhaled deeply. "Did you take money from them?"

His mouth drew up in an expression that was both closed off and sad. He looked beyond me through the doorway. I turned quickly to see what he was watching, but I realized he was trying to look anywhere but at me.

He spoke with his eyes trained on the far distance. "Wei was right."

"What does that mean? Right about what?" My voice was shrill.

"I can't have this conversation with you. This entire thing is way beyond you. Go home. Go home to your husband."

"If the answer is no, just say no."

"Go home." He looked toward the sad slot of a dungeon window that peered up onto the sidewalk.

I grabbed my purse and stood up. "Girls! Time to go!" I laced the strap around my fingers and squeezed hard. "Don't tell Wei I came over." Still he didn't look at me, but I knew that he wouldn't tell.

That was the last time I saw Tang Jia Bao.

I had $390 in the envelope. With it, we paid for the room. We paid Janet, the waitress at the diner. We bought milk and cereal.

The girls spread a blanket on the ground and had a picnic with their dolls, urging torn cold cuts into their closed plastic mouths and stuffing the tiny doll bloomers with squares of toilet paper meant to be diapers. The maternal urge struck even Stephanie, who was not yet five years old. Had it come from me? Even in play to reenact domestic duties? I wanted to stop them. I wanted to take away these dollies—"cousins," Emily pointed out to me—but lethargy held me to bed. I missed Wei. I called home, but when he answered, I handed the phone to the girls and watched their faces as they dutifully answered his questions: *Yes, Daddy. Fine. Good. Yes.* When they were done, he always demanded to talk to me. I didn't say a word as he told me what an awful wife and mother I was. He'd finish with a large sigh, which I took as my cue to hang up.

"When are we going home?" Stephanie asked. I told her I didn't know.

1980

45

WE CALLED WEI on New Year's Day. The girls went through their usual repertoire of answers—glancing at me as they spoke as if they were afraid of violating my trust and revealing too much—then Emily thrust the phone at me. I shook my head.

"Daddy says he *needs* to talk to you."

I rolled my eyes and took the phone.

"You there?" he asked gruffly.

"Yes."

"Your sister called. Your father has gone to Taipei again." A reflexive euphemism. Feeling weak, I sank onto the bed.

I twisted the cord around my fingers. Emily and Stephanie had gone back to watching TV. Stephanie's thumb drifted to her mouth.

Taipei meant interrogation. Baba was almost seventy years old. What could they want with him?

"When?"

"Yesterday. I would have called but you haven't given me your number. You see how ridiculous this is?"

I brushed aside his comment. We could fight it out later. "I have to call her."

"Where are you?" Longing was there too, amid his anger; I could feel it.

"I have to go. I'll call you later." I hung up and immediately called Ah Zhay.

The phone rang for a long time before she answered and accepted the call. Her voice was full of forced alertness; I realized it was past midnight in Taichung.

"Wei told me about Baba," I said as soon as she answered.

"They came for him two days ago. In the middle of the day."

My head felt light. It had been years since the police had last questioned Baba. Why now? Worry burned in my stomach—was this punishment for whatever Wei had been up to?

"What'd he do?" I asked.

"Who knows? What did he ever do?" Something shushed against the receiver. I waited for her to say more, but she couldn't. She couldn't trust the line.

"Where's he now?"

"Who knows?" I knew the defeat in her voice was fear.

"Did you talk to Dua Hyan?" As angry as Dua Hyan was at Baba, he surely would not let anything happen to him. I was not certain how much power Dua Hyan actually had, but I knew that he was discreet enough to never let us see the full extent of it.

"There's nothing he can do. He wouldn't anyway."

"How's Mama?"

Long-distance calls were hollow, as if sound traversed an actual distance. Even so, I could hear the saliva as she opened her mouth, then with second thought, closed it, a familiar gesture I could see. Finally, she answered. "She's fine."

Fine was fine. Secondary to whatever was happening to Baba. "What can I do?"

"Nothing." She paused. "Where are you?"

It would take too long to explain. "A marital spat. You know. It's nothing."

The words drifted past her, my troubles a small matter, brushed away. "I'll call you if I hear anything."

We said good-bye. I stepped over the girls, now sprawled on the floor and completely enthralled by Mighty Mouse, and stood at the window. In the parking lot, a woman, bony armed and dressed in nothing but a T-shirt and jeans despite the cold, danced erratically next to a car while the man leaning on the hood smoked. She cupped his face in her hands, pretended to kiss him, then spun away again.

I wondered what it was like to live in the moment, to be concerned with only your next meal and your next fix. A life in which everything else was either bodily pleasure or pain.

The desk clerk came out and slowly approached the couple. Her eyebrows rose in apprehension, and she spoke as she walked. The man shook his head.

The KMT hadn't gone after Wei or his parents directly, I suppose, because they thought that nothing could be more upsetting to him than to see me upset. He would willingly sacrifice himself, but not us.

The dancer twirled around the clerk, who held her arms defensively to her chest. I realized that the dancer was barefoot. Time did not exist for her. Living in the moment did not even apply. It was forty degrees outside and she happily wore no shoes. Mr. Lu had said he could help me. I thought of the envelope of diminishing cash—hadn't I already accepted his help?

Tit for tat, Mr. Lu had said.

The man ignored the clerk, who threw her hands up in the air and shouted at the dancer. She returned to the office.

The exchange of safety for information, he'd said. I realized Baba's arrest wasn't to punish Wei. It was for me. To scare me into giving up the manuscript.

He could help me, Mr. Lu had said. Now, I understood what he had meant.

"I'm hungry," Emily wailed.

A police car turned into the parking lot. Its lights flashed but its siren was silent. The dancer couldn't keep from tapping her feet and turning her wrists. The man dropped his cigarette and carefully stamped it out. The desk clerk came to the office doorway.

"I said I'm hungry, Mom."

I reluctantly turned away from the scene. "How about cereal?"

I poured three bowls but I couldn't eat. I dialed information and got the number for the Coordination Council for North American Affairs, and left a message with the secretary for Mr. Lu to call me at the motel. I sat at the table, listening to the cereal crackle in the milk, and stared dumbly at the television. If he called back, I would tell him it had been a false alarm. A mistake. The girls slurped at their bowls and kept their eyes on the television. It had to be a trap. He couldn't possibly convince the authorities in Taiwan to release Baba. Like Jia Bao had said, they were manipulating us. I decided I just wouldn't answer the phone.

My cereal turned to swollen mush. I poured it into the bathroom sink and pushed it down the drain with the end of the spoon.

When I returned to the window, the parking lot was empty.

The phone rang. Stephanie glanced at me.

"I'll get it," I said. I felt nauseated.

Mr. Lu's cascading voice greeted me. "I have a message that you called? What is this number?"

"I'm at a friend's."

"And you called because . . . ?"

"Mr. Lu, my father has been detained."

Was that a laugh or a cough? "I know," he said. "Two days ago now."

I faced away from the girls, as if not seeing me would keep them from hearing me. I cupped my hand around the mouthpiece. My breath in the receiver became a lusty feedback in my ear. "Can you do anything?" I whispered.

"Perhaps."

"What does that mean?"

"It means that I'll see what I can do."

"You will? Please tell me you are telling the truth."

"I've always been completely honest with you. But tell me what you will do for me."

I kneeled next to the bed to hide from the girls. "I don't know," I whispered.

"I see."

We both were silent.

Finally, dismissively, he said, "You know, my hands are tied. I can't help you unless you are willing to help me. I have given you quite a bit already and what have I gotten in return? This isn't charity. This isn't friendship. This is a business relationship. You know what they say about life—*there's no such thing as a free lunch.*" He uttered the last part in English. If I had not felt so awful, I would have laughed—he had an adage for every occasion.

"The manuscript," I said.

"Exactly." When I didn't respond, he continued. "Let me paint a picture for you. Your father's health isn't good—I'm sure your sister has told you that. He doesn't handle the cold well. Unfortunately, there are no heaters where he is staying. Perhaps, out of pity, they might have given him an extra blanket. If they have one. He will sleep in his soiled clothes. And—"

"Stop. I get it," I said. I thought of how perplexed yet resigned Baba had appeared the other times he'd been brought in. This time, his night-mare had come true. This time, they had actually kept him, as he always expected they would. My poor, poor father. Hadn't eleven years been long enough to get out of him everything they needed? "And you'll help him if I give you Jia Bao's book?"

"You have my word."

"But what will happen to Jia Bao?" My yoga teacher would have been proud. I was now folded up, my burning stomach against my thighs—an exquisite child's pose—the phone gripped so tightly my knuckles ached.

"You don't have to worry," he said. I listened for the tenor of real sin-cerity in his voice. I mulled over each word, searching for multiple mean-ings. I had to be certain his promise had only one interpretation. Seconds passed. "Hello?" His question was impatient.

"Give me two days." I told him I'd meet him at the restaurant in Oak-land Chinatown with the manuscript. Overcome by calm, I hung up. It was done. The only direction was forward. I called Wei back and finally gave him the motel number. For emergencies, I said.

I told the girls that I was taking them home for clean clothes. Wei was gone—I'd called before we left to be sure—but his smell had overtaken the house. This was his house now. The sink held a couple of dirty plates, and the sofa bore the imprint of a body. The bed was hastily made: the blanket stretched out but wrinkled and the pillows balled and lumpy. In the bathroom, rings of dirt colonized the sink and toilet.

I was disappointed. I wanted chaos: red-eyed fruit flies buzzing over garbage and stripped toilet paper rolls left on the holder—a mess to reflect the absence we'd left in his life.

With the girls upstairs choosing new toys to bring back to the motel, I went to the den. I had typed my translation on carbon paper, and the stack, each sheet doubled, was almost a hand high. I couldn't imagine all this work burned or shredded. Did Mr. Lu need both copies? Would he know? I went through and stripped each page from its smudgy double and separated the manuscript into two piles. I would think of an excuse for Jia Bao later. The whisper of the tearing paper was rhythmic, automated. Concentrating on it kept me calm. Nothing in the book was incriminating anyway. Just a simple history of oppression. *Brutality,* as Jia Bao would say. And it was all true—what would Mr. Lu find fault with?

When I was done, I bundled the carbon copy with a rubber band and put it back in its spot in the file drawer that Wei had set aside for me. I slipped the original in a grocery bag alongside a pile of Jia Bao's handwritten notes that I'd come across and went to fetch the girls.

Mr. Lu kept his word. The day after I gave him the manuscript, Ah Zhay—relief and exhaustion in her voice—called to tell me Baba had come home.

46

JANUARY 8 WAS A COLD, SUNNY DAY. The sky was bright blue, but you could see your breath in the air. Jia Bao had built his wardrobe out of donations and thrift store finds, and today he wore a blue Cal sweatshirt (LET THERE BE LIGHT, the scuffed gold seal on the chest declared) and faded black sweatpants. I tell you this because a thousand times I have forced myself to envision this scene in every minuscule detail, looking for the tiny gap, the slip, the one decision that might have changed everything. He wore a blue sweatshirt, nubby at the joints, no hood, a triangle of stitching at the throat, and still carrying the odor of its former life. He made a cup of coffee on the stove and drank it right there, too hot, heat seeping through the ceramic and almost burning his knuckles where they brushed the cup. Murky gray light fell through the narrow kitchen window and he stood in it though it did nothing to warm his cold feet. He softened a stale bun in the coffee and ate it.

. . .

He hadn't spoken to his wife in two weeks. Their conversation had been short and empty of real content; only the sound of their voices mattered. The words were merely vessels containing the timbre that said everything was okay, or wasn't. He imagined her in their apartment on the white vinyl couch with the brown piping, leaning over the armrest toward the phone table, chin tipped to her chest, trying for some privacy even though it was the phone line itself that revealed them. The building was under surveillance too. The police were obvious. She had said this aloud, to him and to whoever else listened. It wasn't a secret. He told her to be careful.

Brushing his teeth, he watched himself in the mirror. He was a small man, always shorter and slimmer than his classmates. What did his wife see in him? he thought. Did she regret it all? How many peaceful days had they had? He rinsed his mouth and scratched at the stubble on his chin. A few gray hairs had shown up. With his fingernails, he plucked them out. How much would she have aged the next time he saw her? When would that be? He thought of his children too, their time line moving faster than his, the difference between childhood and adolescence just a matter of months.

Truth be told, he didn't know what was the ultimate point. The fight had gone on for decades already; it would likely continue for decades more. Tens—hundreds?—of thousands of lives thrown into the cauldron; every life an inch of progress. What determined success?

Too impatient to wait for the water to warm, he splashed cold water on his face. Pink bloomed in his cheeks.

He sat in the kitchen chair and tied his running shoes, the only new clothing purchase he had made. Converse Trainers in blue and white. Laces pulled so tight that the nylon pursed against the blue suede eyelets.

He missed her. Despite the chaos of their days, they always had sought each other at night; in the dark, their bodies were a barricade against the world.

He decided he would buy a newspaper from the liquor store and then jog to Wei's house. Outside of the dim apartment, the sunlight was startling, and he stood next to the door for a moment, blinking.

It was a Tuesday. Except for a few cars parked under the bare trees, the street was empty. He walked down the middle of the street and felt the open space all around him. The glare off the windows kept the neighbors' homes private. A dog barked at him from its perch behind the second-floor window of a yellow house.

A car pulled out from its spot beneath an oak tree and crawled toward him. He moved aside to let it pass, but instead the car stopped. He glanced around; there would be no witnesses.

"Tang Jia Bao?" someone asked through the open window.

"Hey," Jia Bao confirmed. *Run,* he thought. *Run.*

Run.

Jia Bao thought of his wife, standing next to the sofa, phone at her ear, unable to speak.

If he made it to Shattuck Avenue, everything would be okay.

It would be early morning when she got the call. Before she went to work. She might not even be dressed yet. She'd stand next to the sofa, the phone held lightly to her ear. After she hung up, she'd sit for a while before she told their kids.

It's a gun, Jia Bao thought. *Run.* But his body could not move.

The man's hand was shaking. Jia Bao saw the tremor. *He's afraid.* If he had time enough to notice the twitch under the man's skin, he should have run.

Even the bullet didn't speed up time. It tore through his chest. He tried to duck, not fast enough, and the second bullet hit him in the shoulder. He heard the shooter grunt, or perhaps it was himself. A ragged cry, regret and surprise, congested with tears or maybe blood. This was how his father had died, he realized with irony and sadness: a few feet from home, in the street.

His wife wouldn't faint or collapse into tears. She would not believe it for hours. She would tell herself he was safe. She'd sit in the dark until the sun finally rose, and then she'd go to tell the children.

Every gesture was a risk, Jia Bao had said. The word "safe" did not exist.

Wei called me.

"Jia Bao, he . . . they . . . ," he began. As he told me what had happened, the world went hazy. I hung up the phone and hurried into the bathroom and shut the door and kneeled down and cried. It welled out of me with force, and when it subsided, I thought of Jia Bao again, reminded myself of what I had done and what had happened, of how I'd been betrayed, and I thought my tears would carry away the pain, but the grief was unending.

Our neighbor agreed to pick up the girls, and I went with Wei to identify the body in a room resembling a laboratory classroom with a round silver clock on the wall, bins of medical supplies, and shelves of binders. The coroner apologized as he led us in; they were waiting for new drawers and were forced to rotate the bodies through the few that they currently had. Covered corpses lay on the tables, and a chalkboard with names and times marked who was due to be cycled back into refrigeration next. The room stank of chemical cleansers that poorly masked the odor of death. Wei put his hand on my shoulder, as much to brace himself as to comfort me.

The coroner opened a drawer that groaned with its burden and cried on its tracks. Jia Bao's body was modestly covered at the waist, but everything else was exposed: his pale, bloodless skin; the soft hair ringing his blue nipples; the ragged wounds on his chest and shoulder that exposed thick, broken flesh oddly devoid of blood. Gravel still clung to his cheek.

I hid my face in Wei's shoulder.

"That's him," Wei said.

The drawer closed with a gentle clang.

Wei tried to tell the police it was an assassination. He tried to explain to the police who Jia Bao was and why the KMT would want him dead.

I sat, numb, in the institutional police station chair, a damp tissue balled and shredded in my fist while Wei spoke. He was pale. Though he'd lost most of his accent in English, now he stumbled over some of his words in his earnest attempt to convince them. "I don't think you understand. He's very well known in my country. He was under house arrest. The government wanted him dead. There's no way that this was an accident. The KMT men are ruthless. I am sure that they killed him."

"You said Thailand?" the officer asked.

"Taiwan." Ordinarily, Wei would have launched into a small sermon on the difference. Now, wearily, he said only, "Taiwan, Republic of China. Not Thailand."

What reaction did we expect? Outrage? That they would throw down their pens and their jaws would drop in shock? They betrayed nothing except, perhaps, a smidge of skepticism. Wei told them that he was certain they would find no evidence of robbery or conflict. Without that, what was left?

After we spoke to the police, we went to Prince Street, to a scene still marked and stained. We stayed in the car. A silent crowd had gathered to watch the clean-up crew scrub away the blood. Jia Bao's blood.

"Did you call his wife?"

"I did." Wei's voice cracked.

The light shifted, that subtle yet sudden transition from afternoon to dusk. One by one, people looked at their watches, gave a last glance at the glistening pavement, and drifted toward home. I felt nothing. I was gouged out and hollow.

"Will you come home now?"

Would I? In the motel, nothing had changed. I'd turn on the TV and it would still be on channel 36; the girls' clothes would still be scattered on the chairs; the milk in the cooler was the same milk from last night. It was in the same place it had been this morning when Jia Bao had been alive. At night, women's heels would again patter past our window and men would shout from the parking lot. It was wrong. It was wrong for it to have stayed the same, I decided, when everything was different.

"Okay," I finally said.

We drove to the motel and he sat on the bed as I tossed our clothes into the suitcase. I didn't bother folding anything. With Wei there, I suddenly noticed how ragged our lives in this hovel had been. The stale odor, which I'd ceased to notice, erupted again, along with the stains that had somehow faded during our stay. I saw how sun-bleached the old bedspread was, how dingy the carpet. I saw the dust in the pleats of the lampshade and the fingerprints smudging the TV screen.

"You were here the whole time?"

I nodded.

"How'd you pay for it?"

I shrugged, my stomach cramping with guilt.

"Okay, okay," he said. "We can take our time."

I kneeled and put my head on his lap. Tentatively, his hand settled on my hair.

"I'm sorry," I whispered. Sorry to him and to Jia Bao. I said it again and again and again until they became just empty, impotent words.

. . .

The Chinese-language papers in the United States put Jia Bao's murder on the front page; in the local English-language news, his death warranted nothing more than a brief note in the crime column. The newspapers in Taipei, of course, were silent.

We told the girls that Jia Bao had returned to Taiwan. Emily said that she would write a card to him.

"Why didn't he say good-bye?" Stephanie asked.

"He was in a rush," I said, my heart aching at every word. "He wanted me to say good-bye for him. He said you two were very good hostesses." Pleased by the compliment, even though she did not really understand the word "hostess," Stephanie grinned.

The funeral was well attended, but more than a few people, afraid of being targets themselves, stayed away. We all suspected who the culprits were—Jia Bao had not been robbed or beaten. This was not your run-of-the-mill South Berkeley crime.

I thought of his first day in Berkeley: how he'd reclined on the porch, eyes closed, warming himself in the sun. His glasses lay in a bag on our dresser, waiting to be carried back to Taipei.

Gently, I touched the urn. Silently, I told him I was sorry. *How dare you come?* I imagined him saying. No, Jia Bao was too rational. *I understand,* he'd say. *It was your only choice. This has always been about sacrifices.*

47

BECAUSE OF THE GIRLS, time could not stop.

Wei and I wanted nothing more than to close the shades and hide away, but these two small creatures demanded that the days cycle as they had before.

Routine numbed us. After sleepless nights, I forced myself to ready the girls for school, to attend my own classes, to make lunches and dinners and do laundry. Wei seemed to always be at some committee meeting or student conference. Long days on campus and short nights at home. He took up running too, some sort of homage to Jia Bao, I think. He wouldn't tell me he was going until he was out the door, and then, an hour or two later, he would be back, salty and damp, and go straight to the shower. We barely looked at each other.

I didn't mind Wei's absences. I hid the evidence of my broken conscience, the copy of Jia Bao's manuscript that I'd kept from Mr. Lu, out of sight in the attic, deep in a box amid my college essays. I needed the space to review my guilt, like a woman who must persistently count the cracks in the walls lest she go insane.

I'd had a conversation with Mr. Lu.

Baba had been taken in for interrogation.

I had collected the manuscript.

I would save both men.

Ah, that was the hitch, the point at which my imagination could not match the depravity of the state. I checked the details of the time line again, searching for other options, but everything circled back to now. I wept.

I suspected running for Wei was the same activity as my mindless work in the garden: a place where I could nurture my obsessive thoughts undisturbed.

My conversation with Mr. Lu.

Baba taken in for questioning.

Collecting the manuscript.

Would I have let Wei—if he had made the overture—pull me to his chest and, in that cradle, would I have felt permitted to cry out my pain? Hell yes.

In the end, what was intimacy? What could have been more intimate than our dear friend's death?

The first break in the investigation came when the car—noted by an old woman who had glanced out the window at just that moment, thinking she heard the mailman—was traced to a dealership in Oakland. The receipts were signed, two Chinese names, one illegible but the other stupidly distinct. He had come through the airport in San Francisco two weeks before, but there was no record of his departure from the same airport.

The investigators asked Wei who Jia Bao's enemies were, but still didn't believe him when Wei bitterly fingered the entire ROC government. They asked if drugs or gambling were involved. To them, assassination was for movies, not for humdrum Berkeley mornings.

Wei's friends demanded a federal investigation and began calling our congressmen.

I prayed they would find the killers. I prayed that these two men would turn out to be run-of-the-mill hoodlums, that this was a robbery gone wrong, a bad plan hatched in southwest Berkeley and not Taipei. Only then would I know that his death was merely coincidental with my surrender of the manuscript, and that I could forgive myself.

I called Mr. Lu from a pay phone a few times, but each time the receptionist said he was busy. I expected Mr. Lu to accost me with one task more as I came out of stores, or on the way to my car after dropping off the girls, but he was never there. "You lied!" I would have said with a feeling beyond rage. There was no word in any of the languages I spoke for how I felt when I found new pages in Jia Bao's apartment. He had not given up his work on the book. He had not been bribed. Rather, I was the dumb bird who had been lured to the chopping block, even with the glint of the ax blinding my eye.

Mr. Lu was gone from my life. I was on my own.

The pain of revisiting Prince Street was sharp and sweet, like teasing a loose tooth. I went back most mornings and parked in front of Jia Bao's place. My windshield framed bare asphalt and quiet houses. I willed myself to see Jia Bao, dressed in his running clothes, slip through the side gate.

He doesn't notice the two men in the car idling farther down the block, but I see them, and I want to warn him. They drive up to him and shout. I see in his face that he immediately understands everything.

I replayed it again and again. I watched the bullets burst through his body. I cringed when he fell to the ground, hard, cracking his elbows on the street. I realized the manuscript had been the only leverage he had in the bargain for his life. I almost believed the force of my regret would raise him. "I'm sorry." I tucked my face into my folded arms and sobbed. "I'm so, so sorry."

In bed at night, I begged my husband, "Talk to me. What are you thinking?" My mother had yielded to Baba's silences, but I was not my mother's daughter. I burrowed against his body to feel his heat on my back. I pulled his arm around me and kissed his fingers. "Please, Wei. Talk to me."

He would not speak.

The United Bamboo Gang. Begun in the 1950s as a group of street toughs, the children of high-ranking KMT, it had grown into a seething, powerful underworld organization, drawing money from gambling, nightclubs, and dance parlors.

The first link to Taiwan that the police found was United Bamboo, when they pulled over an olive '65 Ranchero for running a stop sign and the driver broke down in tears. He had an arrest warrant for a bounced check, but when they brought him in, he confessed to being the driver for the gunman.

"I didn't know he was going to shoot him," he cried. "I thought he just wanted to talk."

Within an hour, he had given up the name of the killer, who was hiding out in San Jose. The Frog. The more notorious the gangster, the more ridiculous his name: the United Bamboo was a veritable menagerie of Ducks, Dogs, Crocodiles, and Monkeys. We all knew The Frog, however. He'd been incarcerated on Green Island at the same time as Jia Bao, a common criminal rubbing shoulders with prisoners of conscience. Here was the motive, investigators concluded—it was a prison grudge taken to the extreme.

The police told us they'd made an arrest.

"It's not enough," Wei said. "He's not the only one. It's impossible."

We lay in bed, the only time of the day that we were really together anymore. I nudged my legs against Wei. He didn't respond. His stare remained on the ceiling, the hazy orange glow of the streetlamp outside our window reflected on the curve of his unblinking obsidian eyes. My husband ate meals with us, paid the bills, slept in my bed, but he was nothing but a body.

"Talk to me, Wei," I murmured.

"I want to take his ashes to Taipei." His voice was as unyielding as his body.

"You know you can't." Like many of our friends, Wei had been black-listed. He couldn't return to Taiwan.

"Maybe there's a way." He threw a sideward glance at me. For the first time since Jia Bao's death, I heard something lighter—almost hope—in his tone.

"There isn't." I whispered it. "You know there isn't." I stroked his shoulder.

"Maybe the police are right. Maybe it was just an old grudge," I continued. Please agree. Be complicit in my innocence.

Wei shrugged off my hand, turned away from me, and tugged the blanket to his neck. "Wei? What do you think? Maybe it was just that." I had almost convinced myself too.

Shunned by my husband, I began a journal. I was surprised by how much clarity ordering the words on the page gave me. I was forced to narrow down my chaotic thoughts to one adjective, one noun, one verb at a time. I liked the deliberation over language and began to think maybe this was a path I could follow. I brought it up with one of my professors. "Keep reading," he said. "Build up your language skills. Writing is not an easy business, you know."

I was embarrassed that he suspected me of naïveté, that I did not have a sense of my own limitations. "Of course," I said quickly. "But how could one get started in such work if and when she felt she was ready?"

He told me to try the *Daily Cal*, the school paper. We could talk more after we saw how that went, he said. I left our conversation resolute. I decided I would not tell him how much his discouragement had inspired me.

In writing, I discerned too the power that Jia Bao must have felt while working on his book, sorting out the mayhem of his experiences into a sane narrative. Understanding this, my betrayal felt doubled. Taking the manuscript had not been just theft, but emasculation. The nausea that surfaced when Jia Bao came to mind became a constant pall that I couldn't shake.

The trail stopped cold in Taipei. Despite The Frog's insistence that he had been paid by a colonel to knock off Jia Bao, and that the order had come from even higher—from Chiang Ching-kuo's gangster-consorting son—he had no proof. He'd been paid in cash. The government in Taipei disavowed any connection with him and offered his long record of arrests and imprisonment. Officials reiterated that it was a personal vendetta, most likely stemming from his and Jia Bao's time on Green Island. We heard rumors that on the US side, the government urged the police to solve the incident quietly and quickly in the wake of Taiwan's new status. It would be too embarrassing if it was known that the United States had allowed the KMT to run amok on American soil.

It was a mistake. The next year, a Carnegie Mellon University professor, Chen Wen-cheng, would die on a trip to Taiwan after a long night of interrogation, leaving behind a young widow and a baby son. In 1984, the KMT would come to California again to wreak vengeance. That time, it would be a US citizen, Henry Liu, shot in his garage in Daly City for an unflattering biography of Chiang Ching-kuo. That murder would make the *New York Times*. That murder would earn a congressional hearing. That murder would finally break open the truth.

Until then, Jia Bao was just another dead man.

48

WE GOT THE NEWS as we were eating the birthday cake that Wei had picked up for me at the grocery store. Shortcake, but he hadn't bought any strawberries, just strawberry ice cream in a box. Thirty-three years old. He stabbed two fat pink 3 candles in the cake. They leaned in opposite directions.

"Mom, look!" Emily tapped her spoon on the cold, spongy stew she'd made by furiously mixing the cake and ice cream.

"Don't play with your food," Wei said, jabbing his spoon toward her.

"Oh, let her. Who cares?" I said.

Wei started, "She's being—" The phone rang. He and I looked at each other.

"It's my birthday," I said, taking another bite of dry cake. Wei's spoon clattered onto his plate as he went to answer.

"It's good, Mom. Try it," Emily said. She slurped up more, and urged Stephanie, "Try it."

"Just eat up, darling," I said. The only wish I had made when I blew out the candles was that I wouldn't spray wax all over the cake. But when Stephanie asked what I had wished for, I smiled and told her it was a special secret wish.

I heard Wei hang up, but instead of returning to the table, he closed the den door. Emily and Stephanie, enraptured by their new concoction, hardly noticed. I hesitated to follow him. We'd had enough bad news.

Despite myself, I went to the den. He sat in the orange chair, elbow bent, his forehead resting on his fist.

I didn't want to ask. I didn't want to say anything. I wanted to retreat back to the table, but I forced the words out. "What happened?"

Wei pushed his eyes against his sleeve and looked up at me. His face was flushed, his eyes rimmed red. He told me that the twin daughters of the recently arrested activist Lin Yi-hsiung had been murdered the day before. Just a run-of-the-mill big-city crime, except for the date, the circumstances, the victims, and the perpetrators.

February 28. Broad daylight. Taipei City. Victims: seven-year-old twin girls and their grandmother. Girls barely older than Emily. Girls who no doubt owned the same kinds of toys: googly-eyed stickers, baby dolls with painted plastic mouths and nylon hair, wasp-waisted Barbies. Girls who sketched the same kinds of rainbow-framed drawings and made the same kinds of wishes.

Their father had been arrested after the December Kaohsiung protest and their apartment had been under surveillance ever since. After hearing that Lin had been tortured in prison, his wife had called a human rights organization. Later that day, Lin's mother and two of his three daughters were murdered in their apartment. Only the oldest one, stabbed in both lungs and found bleeding on her parents' bed by her father's former secretary, survived. She was eight years old.

"When will they decide they've taken enough?" Wei asked. He dropped his head again and squeezed the bridge of his nose.

My chest clenched, a burl of grief in my heart and lungs. I slipped out of the den and returned to the table. Emily and Stephanie, sensing that something terrible had happened, something so terrible that questions could not be asked, said nothing.

I stroked Stephanie's hair. "Are you done? Let's go upstairs. It's time to get ready for bed."

I trudged up the stairs behind them. I was tired of mourning.

I drew a bubble bath for the girls and let them play. I kneeled beside the tub, soaking my hand in the warm water, watching how quickly they forgot the crying adults in the joy of windup backstroking panda bears and plastic fish that squirted water.

I flexed my fingers and imagined a clean slice, blood clouding into the warm water. Billows of red engulfing the bath toys and encircling my daughters' limbs. A failure. Would they see my repentance for what it was?

I shook the water off my hand and tied up their damp hair. They were children, but I still thought of them as babies. My babies. They had flat androgynous chests. Their cheeks bloomed from the warm bathwater. Their small teeth were so white and their wet hair so black. The first time I'd held them, it seemed that they had always existed. I found it hard to remember the world before them, as if their being had been inevitable. *Of course it's you*, I had thought each time—first as I had cradled Emily and then, two years later, Stephanie. *You couldn't have been anyone else.*

I wiped my nose against my shoulder and chided my sentimentality.

They pushed each other, splashed water onto the floor, glanced at me to see if I'd say anything. I didn't.

How joyous it was to be free.

BOOK IV

TAIPEI

1982–2003

1982

49

THOUGH THE TRANSFORMATION had been gradual, I couldn't stop rubbing my growing belly. It had been six years since I'd last been pregnant and I had forgotten everything about it: the random little contractions, the swollen feet, the disturbances that felt like a small porpoise doing somersaults in the ocean of my body.

I was sitting on the floor of the den, newsprint spread around me, clipping articles to take home to show my parents. The summer before, despite my professor's doubts, I'd published a piece in a local free weekly about the attempt to turn a neighborhood park into a parking lot, with the requisite reference to Joni Mitchell's "Big Yellow Taxi." I had published two more pieces since then, and was starting to toy with the idea of finding work as a paid reporter rather than a freelancer.

Two and a half years after Wei had applied for the first time to take Jia Bao's ashes home, his visa had finally been approved. Wei thought the repeated denials had been a way of teasing us. We were not sure what had elicited this approval, at long last. After a decade away, I prepared to see my family again, and the girls would meet their grandparents for the first time.

I tucked a flimsy rectangle of newspaper into an envelope, which I would keep beside my and the girls' passports in my purse.

Wei would carry the urn. I looked across the room at the inconspicuous glossy black jar on a cleared bookshelf. That wasn't Jia Bao. I had a strange sense that he lived somewhere out in the world, because how could a man like that no longer exist? I squeezed shut my eyes and told myself not to think of it again. The edge of the tightrope cut into my foot: I reminded myself to keep focused on the moment before I tumbled again into reiterating my guilt. This was the precarious way I had rebuilt my sanity.

Wei popped his head through the doorway, as if he had just paused to tell me that we were out of eggs. I glanced at him over my shoulder.

"I want to tell you that I had an affair," he said, and walked away.

I had misheard him. Like a mechanical doll, I continued clipping. The scissors squealed, the blades resting flush. I was certain I had misheard him.

Gripping the arms of the chair, I hauled myself up. I found Wei in the hall, fiddling with the mail. The little being, in tune with my disturbance, danced inside of me. Massaging my stomach, I realized the acrobatics were my heart. I clutched Wei's arm.

"What did you say?"

He tapped the stack of mail against the hall table to align it and set it down. He didn't face me when he answered. "Can we talk in the den? You know, I don't want the girls to"—he lowered his voice—"hear us."

Wei followed me and shut the door.

"Say it again," I demanded.

He shook his head and I knew I had heard him correctly the first time.

"Why are you telling me this?"

"Because I love you."

I wanted to run out of the house and keep going, all the way down University Avenue to the marina, and baptize myself in sea spray. Instead, I eased myself into the armchair. I laughed meanly. "How long? Who? I mean, fuck, Wei, how could you?"

It hadn't gone on long, he claimed. He'd needed an escape after Jia Bao's death. I was distant. He'd thought I was in love with someone else. He was weak. The usual litany of excuses.

"Distant? Our friend was murdered. He was murdered, Wei!" I wrestled myself back to a pretense of calm. "And you thought it was about us? Are you kidding me?" I clutched my belly, seeking comfort from this other being and silently apologizing for flooding it with my sorrow.

I lifted my head. "Who was it? A student?"

"God no. Oh no. Are you kidding?"

"Who was it then?"

He sat on the floor, faced me, and gripped both my knees. "It was Helen."

I kicked his hands off me. "Don't touch me. Helen-and-James Helen?" We had just seen them the previous month at a mutual friend's party. I tried to imagine how it had started and what he had seen in her. The night at Jia Bao's welcoming party, when I had come across them alone in the den? A pat on the arm at Jia Bao's funeral? Some kinship in a shared glance? Where had they first made love? What had she looked like gazing up beneath him? Did he take off those stupid glasses with the purple tint or did she?

"Are you leaving me for her?" I whispered. "Is she leaving James?"

In the pause before he answered, my agitated nails dug into my palms.

"I don't want to leave you. I don't want a divorce," he said.

"Then why are you telling me?"

"I need to unburden myself."

"Selfish prick," I said. "Why did you? How could you?"

"Maybe I was still mad that you'd left," Wei said. He didn't sound defensive, but afraid.

"You mean with the girls?"

"Yes."

I thought back to the long runs that began after Jia Bao's death. The runs that I assumed were Wei's strategy to trade pain for exhaustion and, at the same time, keep in touch with Jia Bao's spirit. And the showers, washing away his guilty sweat before I could catch a whiff. All of it was an awful cliché. "How long did it go on? What about the running?" I asked.

He dropped his head, as if he had forgotten that his habit had been born out of that moment. Running had become a daily ritual, and he joked about his "addiction." Each milestone demanded another; he'd run two marathons since Jia Bao's murder.

"I was really running," he protested without much conviction. "Part of the time." He spread out his fingers and stared at his hands. "How long? A year?"

"A year?" All my strength drew out of my limbs in a shiver of revulsion. "Why are you telling me now?" I asked again, sickened. I felt like I was going to dissolve into a heap of boneless flesh.

"I need to be forgiven."

I turned away and hid my face again. *What was forgiveness?* I wanted to ask him, even as I realized my own hypocrisy: after all, I had never confessed to him about Mr. Lu.

But this was different. This was betrayal by heart and body.

"We can never see them again. Helen and James," I said.

"We won't."

I pressed my fists to my sore eyes. "How could you, Wei?"

"I know you can't forgive me." He touched my bowed head. "I'm sorry. I'm so sorry." I finally released my tears, feeling all the worse that the person I most wanted to seek comfort from was the one who had hurt me.

Wei and I barely spoke on the plane. The girls sat between us and we zeroed our attention onto them. After a long layover in Honolulu, we were on to Taipei. We would arrive in the early morning as the city was just waking up. In the last hours before landing, I tried to describe Taiwan to the girls.

"How hot is 'hot'?" Emily asked. She had turned the novel she was reading page-side down onto her lap and was nervously rolling up the sides.

"Emily, stop that. You're going to ruin it."

"I mean, is it like Death Valley hot?"

"It's a humid heat, not a dry heat. It's like a bathroom after a really hot bath."

She bit her lip and considered this. "You mean like a sauna?"

"What do you know about saunas?" Every day, I forgot how old she was, expecting her to open her mouth and still sound like the toddler she had been not that long ago. "Yes, it's like a sauna. Exactly. Great comparison."

Stephanie pulled on my sleeve. "What kind of desserts will we have?"

"Cakes, shaved ice, and some things you've never tried before. All tasty."

"And they have cars there?" Stephanie asked. "And toilets?" She was very particular about bathrooms. A number of times we'd had to rush home from the grocery store because she refused to use the public restroom.

Emily rolled her eyes. "Of course! Duh? You think people in Taiwan don't have to go to the *bathroom*?" Palpably proud, in the fall, she'd be going into fourth grade, one of the *upper* grades, with a playground separate from the younger kids. Wei and I had spent the last few weeks trying to restrain her ego.

"Watch it, Emily."

Wei caught my eye and smiled at me. I turned away. Principles were one thing, and I had some grudging respect for his honesty, but he was going to have to suffer for a little while longer yet. For days he had trod around me as if I were an invalid, cooing nicknames at me, on his best behavior, quick to help in the kitchen or with the girls, or to offer to serve me. All it did was remind me of his crime.

A few rows down, I heard a flight attendant ask someone to pull down their tray. Feeding time had come again for the penned livestock.

Wei elbowed Stephanie. "Don't eat the fish."

"Why?"

"Don't listen to your dad. He's being silly," I said. "He's not being serious." To Wei, I said, "If you have to explain a joke, it's not funny."

"What's wrong with the fish?" Stephanie looked back and forth between us.

"Nothing's wrong with it. In fact, your dad is going to have fish as well." I narrowed my eyes. "Right, dear?"

"Yes, I am going to eat the fish." He sighed. "And crow too."

I shook my head. He could joke and moon around, trying to convince me he was adorable and sincere, but I couldn't let it be that easy.

We showed our visas, filled out our arrival slip, which stated we'd be staying at Wei's parents' house, then pushed our cart with the crowd of fatigued travelers to the customs inspection counter.

"Please open your bags," the narrow-faced young man said. He looked as if he'd just completed his mandatory military service. Wei hefted our luggage onto the counter and unzipped each one while the young man slipped on a pair of gloves.

"We don't have—" Wei began, but I hushed him.

The girls were sufficiently sobered by the uniform that they said nothing, their wide eyes nodding up and down as the man flipped through our clothes, holding some shirts up to the light. Another man, with an older, war-weary face darkened with stubble and creases, strolled over and observed the inspection.

The young man held up my underwear for no reason I could discern except to embarrass me. Stephanie turned and put her small hands on my stomach for comfort. "Is the baby moving?" she whispered.

"Not now, darling," I whispered back.

He pulled out a few books that I had brought and called for a third inspector, who shuffled over.

"They're just novels," I said as the man carried them away. "Where's he going? They're just novels." I was tired, sore, pregnant, and angry. "What, you think I'm going to incite a revolution with Jane Austen?"

Wei squeezed my arm, urging me to shut up. Without raising his head, the younger man looked at me from under the hoods of his eyes. I decided to be patient.

Next, he pulled out the urn, which Wei had wrapped in layers of news-papers and sealed with duct tape. He showed it to the older man.

"What is this?" the older man snapped.

"It's an urn. We're coming for a funeral." Wei's tone was a dare. "Human remains. I have a certificate from the crematorium." He pulled it from his satchel and held it up for them.

The younger man sneered, set down the container, and rubbed his hands distastefully.

"Fine," he said. "Clean up your stuff and you can go." He marked our landing form.

"What about my books?" I asked.

"You can leave them or you can wait. Over there." He gestured past the counter.

Wei tamped down the disordered clothes and zipped, poking loose bits back in here and there.

"This is bullshit," he hissed to me in English as we finally passed through.

Our luggage again stacked on the cart, we lingered a few feet away.

"Why can't we go?" Stephanie whined.

"Because we have to wait for Mom's books, stupid."

I couldn't blame Emily for being snappy; we'd been traveling for twenty hours. Wearily, Wei stepped in with just one effective word. "Don't."

Stephanie climbed atop the suitcases and sat swinging her legs, while Emily wandered in tiny circles and sang softly to herself. I leaned against the cart, wishing I could take the shoes off my swollen feet.

"Forget it, Wei. Let's just leave them. I can buy new copies when we get home."

"No. We'll wait. I won't let them scare us off." He eyed the customs agent like he was preparing for a bar fight. "Assholes."

Twenty long minutes later, the man returned with the books. I thanked him and slipped them into my purse without another glance. I couldn't wait to get out of the airport.

"What a waste of time," Wei said after the inspector had walked away.

In the terminal, among the anxious people waiting for relatives they hadn't seen in years, Wei's parents hopped up and down and waved when they caught sight of us. My annoyance lifted away and I waved back.

"Look at you all!" Wei's mother exclaimed.

Stephanie grabbed my hand and swung back, half hidden behind me, but Emily shouted, "Hi!" and ran to hug both of them. Wei's father patted her back.

"Okay, okay, enough," he said gruffly, but I saw his sheepish pleased smile. I wiped my eyes.

"You're much further along than we expected," Wei's mother said.

I rubbed my belly, felt the slow, watery movement of a foot or elbow sliding under my flesh, and thought of the movie I'd taken the girls to the week before we left, and the telescope-necked alien reaching out his finger to promise, "I'll be right here." We had all cried. The entire theater had cried.

"I want a brother," Emily said. "One sister is enough."

"Emily," I warned.

She had some notion that charming adults meant saying terrible things about her sister. The thing was she was right. Most people laughed and thought it droll. It was a habit Wei and I were trying to break.

"Boy or girl—as long as it's healthy," I said. For now, the baby was both real and abstract; it might as well have been an alien. It's becoming. It's still *becoming*, I thought. There was something uncanny about it.

"Enough chitchat. Let's get out of here," Wei said, his teeth still clenched from the inspection.

The city planners had made the road from the airport the grandest in Taipei: broad and treelined. The white-helmeted Garrison Command patrolled the streets; pedestrians wordlessly parted before them. Stopped at a light, I stared at one sentry. Specifically, at his rifle, which looked like a toy, too much to be real. His eyes latched on to mine. Even behind the window, sheltered by my family and my pregnancy, my neck felt ice cold and chicken flesh broke on my arms. I quickly looked away.

After a full day driving around from meal to meal in this city we had not seen for a decade, that evening we finally settled around the dining table with a bottle of whisky—glasses of tea for me and Wei's mother—while the girls, knocked out by jet lag, slept.

Wei's father, whom I no longer called Uncle Lin, but *Lin Baba*, cleared his throat.

"So, you're going to see Tang Jia Bao's family?" he asked.

"We are going to deliver his ashes."

Lin Baba refilled his and Wei's glasses, then toasted his son. Wei mirrored the gesture. "Bottoms up." Lin Baba set down his empty glass and wiped his mouth with the back of his hand. "Now, don't look for any trouble."

Wei slammed down his glass. "We just got here. You really want to get into this?"

I touched his arm. "Wei."

Wei's outburst failed to ruffle his father, who said, "Taiwan and America are different countries. Remember that. Look, even America wasn't safe enough for Jia Bao."

"Do you want to check my bags? I already went through customs, but you're welcome to inspect them again." Wei stood up. "Come on, I'll show you."

"Sit down," his dad said.

"Enough, enough, enough," his mother said. "Let's put the alcohol away now. We're all tired."

"Sit down, Wei," I echoed in English. "Just sit down."

The two men ignored us. Lin Baba continued. "I just want you to be careful. Big fish, small fish—they will take them all. Don't forget that."

"I know!" Wei snarled. Under our parents' roof, even with our own children here, we were turned into children again. Wei had always skated on the edge of filial, not quite brainwashed by Confucianism like the rest of us, and I envisioned dozens of past fights of the same ilk. Easygoing Lin Baba let Wei get away with it. My own father never would have.

"Enough, enough," Lin Mama said. "You should thank your father for his concern."

Wei sat down. "Thank you, Baba, for your concern."

"Honey," I said in English, "I think it's time for bed."

Wei continued on in Taiwanese. "I just want to pay respect to my friend and have a nice visit with my family. I'm not looking for trouble."

"Enough, enough," Lin Mama said. "Let's change the topic."

We moved on, and Wei and his father continued to drink, but the mood had soured; disquiet hung over the table, and any topic might lead back to what we were avoiding. Obliged to play our roles, we forced the conversation until the whisky was done.

50

ON OUR SECOND EVENING in Taipei, Wei announced he was going out "shrimping" with some old friends. Shrimping—catching shrimp from huge, artificially abundant cement pools seeded with shrimp and then grilling them on-site—was not his style. It was too blue collar for his tastes. I was suspicious.

"You promised you'd behave," I said.

"This is not misbehaving. I'm just catching up with some old college friends."

"Wei." I sighed. I wanted my hurt to be enough to make him stay. The baby poked me near my rib; I winced and pressed back in greeting.

"I swear to you these are nothing more than college friends. Just the guys. Beer, shrimp, and old friends." He exhaled sharply; he was already impatient with my distrust. "You're right. I won't go. I'll stay home with you."

Was I shrill? Was I unreasonable? Feeling strangely guilty, I urged him to go.

In the metal echo of the iron-roofed shrimping hall, Wei and his buddies discussed the recent death of a criminal by drowning. He had escaped,

the police claimed, and jumped into a river and drowned. Wei was outraged by the obvious lie. But even if no one believed the lie, they could
do nothing but shut up and take it and write thinly veiled poems and
make thinly veiled films and write thinly veiled songs. The whole country
existed in metaphor.

At the Lins', waiting up for Wei after everyone had gone to bed, I
curled on the sofa with a notebook. I had an assignment to write a first-
person introduction to Taiwan—a story I myself had pitched—something
light for armchair explorers. Something even a child could understand. I
recalled a fight I'd had with Emily as she worked on a family tree report
for school. She was assigned to interview a member of her family and she
chose me. She wrote on the worksheet that I was from China.

"I'm not from China," I had said.

"But the boxes of clothes we get from Ah Ma say 'Republic of China'!"
she insisted.

"Yes, Republic of China. That's not China."

"But it says *China.*"

"We are from Taiwan."

"Then why do they call it *China?*" Her nostrils flared. She furiously erased the worksheet and the dark litter perfectly expressed her
frustration.

It was too complicated to explain, so I said, "For mailing purposes,
sure, it's China. Well, the *Republic* of China. But you know, and I know,
it's Taiwan."

For some reason, she was convinced I was lying to her and she burst
into tears. She could not believe she was wrong. She had seen the word
"China" with her own eyes.

Nothing was as it seemed; everything was subterfuge: me, Wei and
Helen, Wei and his friends, the name of the country, the label Free
China—ironies cascading over one another like a toppled heap of dis-
carded pages.

I did not include any of this in my article. Instead, I created images of
ruddy-faced children, paddies full of water buffalo, cities teeming with
stylish men and women. I fell asleep on the sofa clutching the legal pad.
Wei came home late smelling of smoke and beer. His kiss woke me.

I wrinkled my nose. "Stinky."

"See, I really went to the shrimp pools." At his careless use of the word "really," I cringed, reminded of his confession, just days old.

We went to the bedroom. While Wei showered, I lay on the bed, now wide-awake, my limbs splayed in the heat, upset anew at the cunning of his timing. We both knew that I would not leave him with this baby just months away.

Wei crawled into bed. The girls slept on the floor on a pallet of blankets and made little grunts at the disturbance of the light but did not stir. Drowsy from drink, Wei fell asleep right away.

My head throbbed with the thoughts of the last two days. How wonderful and unsettling it was to be bathed again in the sound of my most familiar language, the barrier of ignorance gone and every conversation intruding on my thoughts. When I'd first arrived in the United States, trying to make sense of the babble around me, my mind started to transform the conversations into sensible nonsense.

Love shield that fish two who yes.

Tired brother, endure ah big hello?

I'd felt like I had discovered an eccentric hidden language. It took months for me to parse the syllables, then the words, then the meaning.

Tomorrow, I would finally meet Jia Bao's wife. If, to hide my remorse, I was too friendly, it would strike a false note with everyone, but if I was too reticent, that would also seem strange. I decided not to think of it. I told myself that everything that came before today no longer existed.

Oh god, I realized. Just like my father. This must have been the mantra that allowed Baba to endure the days.

I felt light-headed. The baby squirmed, jostling my organs. I made my way out of the dark bedroom and into the living room. I eased myself onto a wicker ottoman in front of the fan and closed my eyes.

Nothing could calm me. In the throes of full-fledged insomnia, I grabbed *Gorky Park* from the stack returned by the customs agent. As I tried to find my place, I noticed that pages twenty-nine to thirty-four were missing, sliced away close to the binding, nearly undetectable save for the gap in numbers. I flipped through. Page seventy-three/four was gone too. I leafed through the other books. Jane Austen was completely intact, but John Fraser's *The Chinese: Portrait of a People* was shredded.

I thought to keep them as a memento of the trip (*Look*, I'd tell my friends in Berkeley. *This says everything you need to know about the situation in Taiwan.*), but the two ruined books were unreadable. I tossed them in the trash, where I knew they would end up in some riverside rubbish heap, burned to black smoke.

It was nearly two a.m. I shuffled back to bed, where I lay until morning in some stunned, jet-lagged space between wakefulness and slumber.

The next day, we went to Jia Bao's house. His family lived on a small alley across from a little park made of cinder-block paving and a few trees that smelled like orange jasmine and carambola. Their apartment was on the fifth floor.

The four of us trudged up the stairs. Wei carried the urn, which we had swaddled in white silk.

Jia Bao's wife, Qiong Hua, stood only as tall as my ear. Her hair, cut like the gamine heroine of a French New Wave film, emphasized her petite bone structure. I tried to imagine her ballroom dancing with Jia Bao in the school club where they had first met. She must have been a tiny music-box ballerina. Nevertheless, she radiated strength, and I could tell that no amount of threat could terrorize her.

"Please, come in," she said. Over her shoulder, her children watched us expectantly.

The house smelled like Jia Bao. Yet years had passed—how could it be? For a moment, the night in Willits exploded before me: my fingers were fragrant with the smell of Jia Bao's sweat, my nose buried in his musky hair. I squeezed Stephanie's hand.

Wei had rehearsed with me what he would say when he handed over the urn, but in this actual instant, with lunch steaming on the table and Jia Bao's children's eyes wide upon us, he could not say a word. He presented the urn to Qiong Hua and she received it without a lip quiver or tear. This kind of stoicism, which I'd seen with my own mother, was heartbreaking. For sure, in seclusion, she'd likely gnashed her teeth and wailed and pulled her hair. Who knew what private sorrow her children had witnessed to carry around in their hearts and memories.

"Thank you." She placed the urn beside an offering of oranges, incense, and a cup of wine that had been set in front of a picture of Jia Bao mounted on the wall. I had never understood why people chose the worst, most bureaucratic pictures for these memorials, the same photos on ID cards and in official files. Did anyone consider when they posed that these rote and standard photos could one day be their funeral portrait? Here was Jia Bao, looking stupefied by the camera's flash. Who would want to remember him this way?

Ceremony completed, Qiong Hua clasped her hands together. "Come, let's eat while the food is warm."

At the table, while Wei and Qiong Hua caught up on the people they knew in common, I searched her children's faces, willing Jia Bao's features to reveal themselves. Their daughter, unlike both of her parents, was unusually tall. She was in her second year of high school, and was enthusiastic and authoritative in a way that mesmerized Emily and Stephanie. She announced that her English name was "Melody" because she wanted to be a singer. She was the cool older girl; for an afternoon, at least, the girl they wanted to be when they grew up. I saw a hint of him in her eyes and in the way she moved her mouth. But her face was light, happy, while Jia Bao's had carried a perpetual uneasy cast.

His son, Jia Lung, on the other hand, was awkward—as adolescent boys are—a little angry, a little sullenly obedient, nothing exactly you could pin on a specific action but a general sense of bitterness and maladaptation about him. He did not engage with anyone. When Wei tried to speak with him, he barely opened his mouth, as if his lips were afraid to form around words, lest anyone see that he moved and lived. In short, he was utterly paralyzed. Even though he seemed so unlike Jia Bao, I saw his face superimposed on the bones of his father. Yes, Jia Bao was in there too.

I dropped back into the conversation. "After Jia Bao passed, I stopped all interaction with the movement," Qiong Hua said in a way that let us know she actually hadn't. Was this admirable or stupid? Did Wei feel the same? So committed that no fear could drive him away? And for what? An abstract principle that had no bearing on whether the kids had rice to eat each day? I politely kept my mouth shut.

Qiong Hua reached over and poured more tea for us. "After I lost my husband, my patients stayed away. They were afraid to see me. Now, my friends have become my patients. Even when they're healthy, they still come see me." I was moved by her friends' simple, sympathetic lies. Without the imagined ache or phantom sore, she and her kids would have nothing to live on.

She and Wei continued on, and the girls chatted with Melody, but I, like Jia Lung, could not bring myself to speak. After lunch was over and we had moved on to a platter of chilled sliced pear, all I could do was poke at the fruit with my toothpick and smile whenever Qiong Hua caught my eye.

Then Jia Bao walked in. The colors of the room, the sounds, everything grew brighter and louder and blood pounded in my cheeks. When I opened my mouth, only a dumb little exhalation emerged. He slipped into the chair between his wife and his daughter, grabbed a toothpick, and snatched a wedge of fruit. I saw the saliva glistening on his lips, and the dots of light reflected on his glasses.

Wei slipped his arm around my shoulders. "Hey, are you okay?"

I couldn't catch my breath long enough to answer.

Emily asked, "What's wrong, Mom?"

Jia Bao was gone and all that was left was a table of staring faces. In my wrists, in the crooks of my elbows, and in my throat, my pulse throbbed, my skin was feverish.

"Come, lie down for a bit," Qiong Hua said. "In the bedroom."

Wei helped me stand and the two of them escorted me to the bedroom, where Qiong Hua pulled the curtain shut and turned on the air conditioner. She left the lights off. After I settled onto the bed, Qiong Hua asked Wei to leave the room. She brought a folded damp washcloth and laid it on my forehead.

"Everything's been normal with this pregnancy?"

I nodded. "It must be the heat."

She picked up my wrist and took my pulse. "Nothing to worry about here. Just rest."

Rest. Just rest. After she left, I gazed around the room. This was Jia Bao's life right here: the laminated white dresser, the vanity stool upholstered in rose print fabric, the framed pastoral print on the wall, and, next to it, another picture of him, this one a casual photo blown up to portrait size, the pixels glowing black, magenta, cyan, and yellow. Where I now lay, he too had once lain scheming about revolution. He had spent his house arrest in this very apartment, pacing from corner to corner, gazing out the window at the police posted below.

He had been as real as the rest of us sitting around the table.

There must be a word for a person there but not there. Something more concrete than a ghost and realer than a memory.

Qiong Hua gently jostled me awake. "I'm so sorry, but Wei wants to go home."

It took a moment to place myself. I caught sight of Jia Bao's portrait and recalled where I was. "How long have I been asleep?"

"Two hours. How do you feel?"

"Much better." I struggled up, still trying to catch my bearings.

In a surprisingly intimate gesture, she sat on the edge of the bed. She frowned and pursed her lips a few times, readying to speak. I was afraid of what she would say.

"You were such a good friend of Jia Bao's."

"We did what anyone would have," I insisted.

She smiled. "Please, don't be modest."

I blurted out, "I'm so sorry that we couldn't protect him."

"You saved him. You gave him freedom."

I bit my lip. Freedom?

She read my expression as survivor's guilt. "Nothing would have been different if he had stayed," she assured me. "They wanted him and they got him. They would have gotten him either way. At least he got to taste freedom. And he got to write his book. I'm grateful for what you did for him. Grateful. I was hoping that you could have brought the manuscript back, but I know you couldn't. Maybe someday I'll come to America and see it. Tell me, is it good?"

A pang of guilt struck me as I answered. "It is. He said everything he wanted to, without apology. It is powerful."

She pressed her knuckle into her eye and smiled. "I miss him."

"I do too," I said, surprising myself with how natural the words sounded. The admission lacked the desperation of the lovestruck or guilty. It was simple empathy.

I do too.

51

WHEN THE TAXI STOPPED at the gate to my grandparents' courtyard, Mama ran out to greet us. She looked over my full belly with nostalgia for the two pregnancies she'd missed, then turned to Emily and Stephanie.

"Who are these pretty girls? Your mother wrote so many letters to me that I feel like I know you."

"Did you greet your grandmother?" I nudged.

"Ah Ma," they said in unison, and I was pleased that they sounded just like dutiful Taiwanese children, obligated to state the title of every relative who crossed their path. Grandmother, second paternal aunt, maternal uncle's wife, paternal uncle's daughter—through greeting, they contextualized their position in relation to everyone else in the family.

Baba followed, instantly triggering my anxiety about coming home for the first time as a mother. Would he criticize my parenting the same way he'd criticized my homework? Would he take my authority for granted, or would I revert back to my childhood self, as Wei had before his father?

"Hello, Baba," I said. "Girls, did you greet your grandfather?"

Even the normally outgoing Emily was suddenly shy in the face of this man in the big black-framed glasses, his white hair combed in the style he'd had since his middle age.

"Hello, Ah Gong."

"Have you eaten?" Baba asked.

"We ate on the train," Wei said.

"Let me take your bag," Baba said. For him, there was no time for cooing over the missing years; it was important that we immediately plunge into normalcy as if only yesterday I'd boarded the plane for San Francisco. Couldn't he spare five minutes for sentimentality?

When he reached for my bag, I snapped, "Ba, Wei will get it."

"Well then, why don't you and you"—he jerked his head at the girls—"come meet the chickens."

I released the breath I'd been holding. The girls fell in line behind him and marched into the courtyard toward the chicken coop. The dirt beneath the banyan tree looked raked clean, and this small touch made me regret my impatience. Baba clicked his tongue to call the chickens, and the girls squealed as the birds darted over in their jerky, prehistoric way. Mama and I exchanged a look.

"Your father is very happy that you're home."

"I know, Mama."

"You can stay in Ah Zhay's old room."

She led Wei and me inside. My grandparents were both dead, and I felt their absence. Other than that, the house had not changed except to grow more decrepit. It held all the same old furniture that I had grown up with, now scuffed at the arms and the base of the legs, the basketry of seats and backs torn. "We send you money; why don't you buy new furniture?"

She didn't answer.

"Ma?" I understood her silence. "Ma, are you giving the money to Zhee Hyan?"

Wei cleared his throat. We had suspected as much, but even so, I could not stop sending them money, even if they threw it away on scam antiques aged like buried treasure in the dirt of someone's yard or—as it were—gave it away to my deadbeat brother.

"His wife is having a baby," she protested.

"A baby?" Wei said diplomatically. "That's good news."

We arrived at Ah Zhay's old room and I tossed my purse on the bed. "He's married? When did he get married? And you didn't tell me?"

"His girlfriend. His girlfriend is pregnant. But she might as well be his wife."

I shook my head. "Ma, that money is for you and Baba. Zhee Hyan has to take care of himself. He's older than me."

"He's your brother."

I began to complain, but Wei touched my arm. "I'm going to get some fresh air."

I nodded. "See if the girls are thirsty."

After Wei left, Mama raised an eyebrow at my belly. "Tell me, has everything been fine?"

I sank onto the bed. Her question seemed to imply more, and I wondered if I should let her know about Wei's affair. "Perfectly normal." I wouldn't mention the spell at Qiong Hua's the day before, or the specter of Jia Bao that I'd seen. Nevertheless, she searched my face skeptically.

"Take a rest. Baba will watch the girls."

After she left the room, the girls' excited voices drew me to the window. Baba embraced one of the hens and the girls reached out, squealed, and snapped their hands back.

"Gently," Baba said. "And not so loud."

"Look. Like me." With more courage, Stephanie reached out again and stroked the bird.

"Right. Good girl," Baba said, and I was a girl again, barely older than Emily, under the same banyan. Where was the ruler to strike their hands? The eraser to efface their work? The stare that would silence them?

We are different people now, I reminded myself. Wei crossed the courtyard to them, barking at the chickens that scurried toward him. "I have nothing for you, birdies." The chickens squawked and lifted their wings and doddered away.

"Dad! Look!" Stephanie rested her hand on the hen's head. "I'm petting a chicken!"

"Amazing!" His voice was full of kindness. I thought of Helen again. A whole year? Four seasons? Did he call her on Christmas? Did he give her a gift?

The last time we had seen them, I had offered to help her with the dishes, but Wei had cut in and said he would do it. I had read it as love for me; now I understood I had been wrong.

Outside, Baba smiled at Wei. My daughters, showing off to their father and grandfather, beamed. In the trees around the house, cicadas buzzed. This scene. Exactly and only this.

I found out that Mama was making money through piecework for a small local doll manufacturer. "Every living room a factory," some politician had proclaimed when I was a child, turning Taiwan into an economic dragon, and now my mother, trained in fine arts in Tokyo, painted faces on generic dolls. She opened a sackful of doll heads, to the delight and horror of the girls. When she offered to repaint their dolls' faces, they ran to pull them from the suitcase. Stephanie wanted her doll's blue eyes painted over in brown.

We watched as my mother, her glasses propped on the tip of her nose, pinched a blank doll head steady. With a very skinny brush and extremely noxious paint, she colored the irises brown, enlarged the black pupils, and added a dot of white light to each eye.

"Ma, you should ask Zhee Hyan to come help you do this. He can earn his pay," I pleaded.

"Oh, shush."

"Why don't you come to California and stay with us? We have an extra room."

She pulled Stephanie onto her lap and let her paint one of the faces. Stephanie's dexterity was good for a six-year-old, but still the eyes were lopsided, strokes sloshing out of the preform eyeballs.

"Too far. Even Taipei is too far. What kind of life could we have there?"

"You have us. You could walk the girls to school. Try it out?"

"America. America. That's a whole other country. I don't even speak English." She returned her attention to Stephanie. "Good, now let me rinse the brush and you can try painting the mouth."

"I want my turn," Emily said.

"Be patient, Emily. One at a time. Ma, you can get by with very little English. Chinatown is just a train ride away. Try it out. For a year?"

"Chinatown? What do I want with Chinatown? Wow, she has a very big mouth! Let's wipe it off and try again." Mama twisted the end of a rag and dabbed the sloppy, oversized mouth that Stephanie had painted, and I understood the discussion was over. I was sure they would be happy if they only gave it a chance. They probably imagined isolation, swathes of suburbs, and had no idea how diverse and lively the Bay Area was. They would learn to love thick chewy bread and red wine, the open sidewalks and cool weather. I had.

And I needed them. What if I left Wei? Or what if we continued on "for the sake of the children," two mildly invested people sharing, by force, a life? Perhaps I could move back to Taiwan with the girls. They would hate it at first, but they were young enough that those unpleasant memories would eventually recede and they would barely recall the time before they belonged.

After dinner on the second night, I walked with Mama around the neighborhood that had sprung up in the years since I'd left. The Owyangs had sold their place; the paddies had been filled in and large tiled houses built. The city had inched up to us, bringing the glare of streetlamps and constant drone of scooters. Tonight, though, the main road where I'd first met my father was empty. I linked my arm through my mother's.

"How have you been? I want the truth."

Was it the tension in my breath, or did my arm tremble against hers?

"What's wrong with you? Speak up."

"Ma." I uttered one syllable before I began crying too hard to speak. We continued to walk, and she squeezed my arm as I let myself free the tears I'd been holding back.

I wiped my nose on the back of my hand and caught my breath. "Wei had a mistress." I had chosen the wrong word—it made him sound like some fat-bellied patriarchal landowner. I thought of concubines, wives two and three. "Affair" seemed so breezy, more American. I said in English, "Wei had an affair." I found the distance created by language comforting. I waited for her to curse him, to tell me to leave, to offer me her home. Instead of Mama moving to Berkeley, I could move back to Taichung. "Well? What do you think? Look at me: six months along with a cheating husband."

"How did you find out?"

"He told me."

"And you never suspected?"

"Never." I caressed the curve of my stomach, while sweat slid down my other arm onto the crook of my mother's elbow.

"Ah, so he's more clever than I thought."

I suppressed an instinct to defend Wei, and instead accepted the insult as a gesture of solidarity.

"And so what are you going to do about it?"

"Leave him?"

"Why?"

"Because he lied to me!"

"And you have never lied to him?"

My pause gave me away. I recalled handing the manuscript to Mr. Lu and the undisguised triumph in his smile. I wished I had thrown it down and burned it, right in front of him. A scene. In the parking lot of the Longs Drugs, spectators gathering around us (A dysfunctional marriage?

An ending affair? Who? Why?), and us staring at the tidy bonfire both surprised by my stunt. If only.

"What is your marriage for? Just love?" Mama asked.

A stray dog ambled toward us; we stepped aside, but it paused a moment to sniff us before moving on.

"Isn't it?"

"Love is love, but do you think your daughters want a mother without a father? Does the child you are carrying? Do you want them to envy their friends?" Where our skin touched, I felt her pulse moving fast. "This is a small matter. It all fades away. Forgive him."

"How can I, Mama?"

She didn't answer. We reached the intersection of the road that led directly into the heart of the city, so we turned around and headed back home. I pulled my arm out from her grip and rubbed it dry against my shirt. Our ideas of love were clearly different; where I saw devotion, she saw duty. I cared how one *felt,* while to her what one *did* was what mattered. I wondered if I should pity her. Or perhaps my abstract concept was the more hopeless one.

The next night, my entire family sat around a huge round table in a restaurant in central Taichung. The restaurant was on the seventh floor and looked out at the multiplying high-rises, the infinite gray rows of narrow windows that promised industry and growth, a view I found both dystopian and hopeful.

Ah Zhay, in her midforties, had—for some reason—returned to the same schoolgirl haircut we'd been forced to wear more than thirty years before. Jie-fu looked strong, but marked with thick pouches of exhaustion under his eyes. I marveled that there had never been a sign of discord between the two. My niece, Mei Mei, had come with her husband and her daughter, Yaru, who squirmed on her lap, grabbing for the chopsticks at every chance until Mei Mei had cleared an arc of empty table in front of her while her husband ate contentedly, oblivious to the struggle at his elbow. When Yaru occasionally patted her father on the arm, he would look up with a mouthful of food, smile, and return to eating. I didn't know him well; in fact, I couldn't remember his name and just called him "nephew." I caught Mei Mei's eye and raised an eyebrow.

"You have your hands full with her," I said across the table.

"Yeah, she's a naughty one," Mei Mei's husband said proudly, and stroked his daughter's hair. He reached for more shrimp. Mei Mei shrugged.

Mei Mei's two brothers were in their twenties now. Both politely called me "Aunt" and chatted with Emily and Stephanie.

"Your Taiwanese is good," they said to the girls, who exclaimed in response: "We're Taiwanese, that's why!"

Dua Hyan had come to dinner too, and I was pleased. He cast his critical eye around the table: who drank their beer without waiting for a toast, who held their chopsticks lazily and dropped food on the table, who took too much of one dish. I waited for him to rebuke Mei Mei's husband for his selfishness, but he said nothing either.

Stephanie had taken to Dua Hyan. She sat between the two of us, and something in the tone of his questions made her feel respected and adult, so she carefully answered as if she actually were the young woman he seemed to think she was. She sat up and pondered her answers so seriously I wanted to scoop her up and cover her with kisses.

"What do you want to be when you grow up?" he asked.

"A car," she said.

"What?"

"A car."

"What is she saying?" he asked me, certain that she had misspoken, or he had misheard.

"It's true. Stephanie wants to be a car when she grows up. Wei told her she could be anything when she grows up and she has decided to be a car."

Dua Hyan pressed back his laugh when he saw that she was not joking. He matched her earnestness.

"What kind of car?"

"A truck. A red truck." She emphasized "red."

"Why?"

"So I can carry things. I can go anywhere and carry things, and you can't crowd me with too many people, so they won't make a mess." She switched to English. "It's practical." I translated for her.

"She's special," Dua Hyan said to me.

I covered her ears and agreed with him.

They continued on about the specifications of Stephanie's future; with the obsessive focus of a first grader, she could discuss horsepower and mileage and tires.

I glanced over at Zhee Hyan's girlfriend, who was even further along in her pregnancy than I was. At twenty-six, she had two children already. She was incredibly beautiful, on the edge of unusual: she had a long face and a long, slim nose, but something in her mouth, the way her top lip perked up, made her look insolent and alluring. Why had she chosen Zhee Hyan? He overcompensated for his average looks with overdone hair and loud clothes, yet she somehow found him attractive—perhaps because he expected she would. She was the third or fourth girlfriend he'd brought around whom we thought he might marry. With the baby on the way, however, this time he surely would. At that moment, I realized my brother was the kind of man so in love with his own masculinity that he would end up with a lot of children. There was something proprietary about it, which wasn't about legacy, or some dream of family, but pure strutting cockerel.

Her name was Ching Ching. She called me "big sister" (I was nearly ten years older than her) and stood up to reach across the table and put food on my plate. Her kindness felt almost aggressive.

"Please, I'll get it myself," I protested.

"I've never met a professor before!" she said brightly to Wei. "I feel so honored. You must be so smart."

She was inane, and while Wei might banter back and forth with Mei Mei, who was nearly the same age, he was cold to Ching Ching. He answered all her exclamations with a single-syllable grunt. It seemed he couldn't even bear to look at her. Pregnancy had made us both voluptuous, but I noticed that while I hid my curves under a loose, flowing top, she wore a shirt that slipped down to reveal her full cleavage; once in a while, she tugged her collar back up, drawing attention to what she purported to hide.

Maybe Wei wasn't annoyed. Once the thought crossed my mind, I couldn't lose it. When he answered her, his eyes didn't meet hers. What was he looking at? Had I ever looked so beautiful, like an adman's perfect vision of pregnancy? My hair was frizzy, my face swollen, and my skin waxy. I had no "pregnancy glow." And there was Ching Ching, with her legs still slim, her ankles narrow. What did I really think? That Wei would take her into the bathroom and make love to her, her pregnancy hiding the evidence of the deed? I knew the idea was completely irrational, but I watched Wei's eyes again follow Ching Ching's hand as she lifted the neckline of her blouse and concealed the shadow of her cleavage.

"I need to go to the bathroom," I said.

Wei grabbed my arm as I rose. "Are you okay?"

I barely spat out the word "fine." I hurried past the bathroom and out the front door into the vestibule in front of the elevator.

I went to the window and squeezed the sill. The overcast day looked deceptively cool, but no amount of rain would wash away the tropical heat. Would my blood thicken with jealousy every time we encountered a new woman? How could I trust that he wouldn't find another excuse, and then another, to justify his infidelity? Mama had told me to forgive him—but how could I listen to a woman who had chosen misery, it seemed, at every opportunity? I did not want to martyr myself to some ideal of marriage.

I thought of all the ways I could hurt him: his pride, his heart, his life. Leaving him—divorce—was what he feared the most.

Feeling mean, I decided I would tell him just as he had confessed to me: offhand, through a half-open door, as if it meant nothing to say.

But I wasn't so casual. I looked forward to revealing my decision. That night, we lay beneath the mosquito net. The girls had been sleeping in my old bedroom, so it was only the two of us. The moon, and a yellow light Baba had installed in the courtyard, shone through the open window. The clacking of the standing fan that Mama had set up near the door provided a shield of white noise. Curled on my side, I reached out and touched Wei's arm. He pulled my hand to his lips, kissed my knuckles, and turned to face me. He brushed the hair from my temple and tucked it behind my ear.

"I decided what I want us to do," I said.

"About what?"

"About us."

He knew. He knew from my preface. His eyes traveled my face. I thought back to our date at Sun Moon Lake, both of us drenched, finding refuge in his car, me holding my breath for a kiss that never materialized.

Had this moment always been inevitable, from the very beginning etched into the DNA of our relationship?

"And what do you think?" he asked.

As much as I wanted to be cruel, I found I couldn't. And I found I couldn't say the word "divorce."

"I want a separation."

"A separation." He sounded relieved, as if giving me everything would make me change my mind. "Just temporarily, right? I get a place nearby, give you your space, we work it out?"

"No. Permanently."

"Permanently? You mean a divorce?"

I pressed my lips together and nodded.

He sat up. "That's a mistake. You haven't had time to think about it. What about the baby? What about the girls?"

"I don't think you were thinking about the girls when you and Helen—"

"This is different," he snapped.

I felt a little sorry for him, but more than that, I was relieved. Another, brighter life appeared before me, without the melancholy cast of my stay at the motel two years before.

In his breath, I heard him sorting it out. He left the bed and paced the room. I wanted to comfort him, but instead I waited.

"Three kids by yourself? Have you lost your mind?" he finally said.

I didn't answer.

"You haven't thought about this. In just two weeks, you can make a decision like this and just toss away ten years of marriage?"

"Eleven years," I corrected.

"I won't let you. I won't agree to it." He sat on the edge of the bed. "Please don't."

With pity, I reached out and tugged the corner of his shirt, wrapped it around a finger. "I won't tell anyone. Not now. We can finish our trip and talk about it more when we get home. Let's just make the best of it for now."

"You'll change your mind."

The spell of sympathy was broken. I let go of his shirt. Now, the other details of our early meetings came to mind: how he had patronized me, lectured me, judged me.

"Yes, exactly. I will change my mind. I'm just saying this for laughs." I curbed my anger and said firmly, "I'm not going to change my mind, Wei."

Still he did not face me, but his shoulders sank, and I did not know if I was sorrier for me or for him.

52

WE SMILED THROUGH our last two days in Taichung. I believe that my parents never suspected a thing. In fact, Wei and I were even closer than ever, affectionate, touchy, as if we were determined to draw the most out of our remaining time. Mama assumed I had listened to her advice and that we had reconciled. She caught my eye once and offered a grim, approving smile. She could read the news in a letter, later, once everything was settled and we had made the living and custody arrangements.

We even made love, our last night in Taichung, his body scooped around mine, and for a few moments, I forgot our trouble. Maybe Wei started to believe too that I had changed my mind. Afterward, he nuzzled under my hair and kissed the back of my neck and said he loved me. I did not answer.

We had three more days in Taipei before our flight back to California. We returned to Wei's parents' house. His mother took me for some last-minute baby clothes shopping—she was determined, it seemed, to send me home with one extra suitcase full of gifts for the baby, despite my protests.

In Wei's old bedroom, Wei and I worked to organize the baby clothes piled on the bed. I kneeled on the floor next to the open suitcase, while Wei folded and handed me the small bundles. Already, I had decided that we should wait to separate until at least the baby was born. Wei deserved to see the birth. But as we moved through progressively larger sizes, from the zippered, hooded sacks for newborns to the two-piece sleep outfits for an eight-month-old, I imagined how the next year would look in our house without Wei. How strange it would be to see his shadowy figure behind the stained-glass front door panel as he rang the doorbell to be let in. So many real and imagined boundaries would spring up from a decision encapsulated in one word.

"What is this?" he asked.

"A jumper."

He shook it. "It has no butt. There's a big hole here."

"Your mom says that's the best way to potty train. Just let the baby go. She says I'll get attuned to the baby's signals and the baby will be potty trained before he or she turns two."

"Are you serious?"

"That's how my mom potty trained me."

Shaking his head, he doubled the jumper, handed it over, and said he had a surprise for me.

I raised an eyebrow. "Oh yeah? I hope it's better than the last one."

He frowned, but ignored my remark. "I want you to take a trip with me. Just one night. I asked my parents to watch the girls." Like the naughty child who charms his way to forgiveness, Wei seemed to expect me to share a strange amnesia for his misdeeds. His knitted eyebrows and earnest stare seemed to ask how I could possibly carry my anger from one day to the next. It offended me.

I put my hand on his knee. "What are you thinking? One night is not going to change my mind."

"I've made the reservation already," he said. "My parents will think something's wrong if we change our plans."

I returned to the suitcase, mindlessly tidying the already tidy stacks of clothes. "I don't want to go. I just want to spend time with the girls—maybe we could take them to the zoo. Is Lin Wang still alive?"

"That old guy? He must be dead. How long can elephants live? He's been around since before I was born."

It occurred to me that the iconic elephant would be a great addition to my article—an elephant born in the early twentieth century, who had worked for the Chinese troops in Burma, then had come over to Taiwan with the Nationalists in the 1940s. "I want to take the girls to the zoo and see if he's still there."

"I made a reservation already," he said again. "My parents are going to watch the girls." He dropped down next to me. "Please. One night. Why won't you at least give me a chance to make it up to you?"

. . .

I imagined Alishan, where my parents had honeymooned—that we'd ride the rickety colonial-era train and watch the sunrise from the top of the mountain—but we stayed in Taipei, at the Mandarin Hotel where we had spent our wedding night. Wei could be playful, flirtatious, and ironically romantic. But this gesture was sincere. The surprise he had promised had actually surprised me.

"I couldn't get the room we stayed in," he said.

"Do you even remember the room we stayed in?"

"Yes. Don't you?"

"No. Somewhere on the fifth floor, I think?"

This time we found ourselves on the sixth floor. The rooms had been remodeled, but we had the same view of Nanking Road. Wei sank into a paisley armchair. "This is new," he said.

"That was some night, wasn't it?" I turned to the window. I smiled, but nostalgia—some hazy feeling of loss and longing—surged through me. I gripped the edge of the curtain.

"There's a good Sichuan place close by. For dinner," Wei said.

"I can't eat spicy." I locked my fingers beneath the curve of my belly. I was tired of thinking of us and what we had lost. I didn't want to play-act anymore, and I didn't want to argue either. I didn't want dinner or fabricated romance. I just wanted to sleep. "What about the place downstairs?" Something easy.

Wei must have read my suggestion as a kind of thaw. He grinned at me. "Whatever you want, babe."

The hotel restaurant was a trap for travelers. Tables spaced so that one could walk by without knocking someone's chair or purse or elbow. Tablecloths. Subdued lighting. It was mostly empty. I felt like a tourist, and I liked the feeling. My mood lightened.

"We've never done this, have we?" I asked.

"What do you mean?"

"I mean been tourists somewhere. I almost feel like a foreigner. Eating mediocre Chinese food by choice. We haven't had dinner like this, just us, since Emily was born."

"I never thought about it," Wei said.

"Neither did I," I said.

We ordered more than we could possibly eat, just choosing whatever looked good. The food wasn't awful. Not great, but not bad.

Wei's questions were polite and overly formal in a way that reminded me of our first dates.

"How's your article?" he asked. "Is it coming along?"

"I have an outline. And now I really do want to write a story about Lin Wang. It's amazing, right? An elephant that old? It must be some sort of world record."

He laughed. "Maybe a children's book?"

I found myself echoing his civil tone. "That's a great idea. Em and Stephanie could help me."

He put some noodles on my plate. I smiled at him.

"Is grumpy old Professor Green going to be around this semester?" He was Wei's least favorite colleague, a man who made it clear that he resented every minute he was teaching at Berkeley and not Oxford.

Wei groaned. "Don't ruin dinner."

"I sort of feel sorry for him."

"Don't. He's a pompous ass. Do you know what he said at the end of the semester?" He was piqued now. He kept a running catalog of Green's offenses—his snubs, insults, and vain declarations.

"Don't obsess," I reminded him.

"You're right. We're having a nice dinner."

"Good job, dear."

I blushed. Reluctantly, I realized that Wei's plan was working. It was as if he had taken his strategy from those screeching women's magazines that advised rekindling love by re-creating the early days of a romance. I almost felt twenty-four again. I looked at his face warmed by the low yellow lights; with a pang, I understood what Helen had seen in him, but I wanted to forgive him.

When we left the restaurant, he put his hand on my back and I felt myself lean into his touch.

Back in the room, we kicked off our shoes and slid into the complimentary hotel slippers. Wei turned on the television, but when I said, "Don't, please," he turned it off.

I complained about the heat and he cranked up the air conditioner. I settled into the armchair. Thinking of something Stephanie had said, I giggled.

"What?" Wei asked.

"The other day, Stephanie referred to Zhee Hyan as a 'whippersnapper.'"

Wei threw his head back and guffawed, a laugh I hadn't heard for a long time. My anger washed away for a moment and it felt good.

There was a knock at the door.

"Another surprise?"

"I'll get it," Wei said.

He was still smiling when he pulled open the door and found two uniformed men from the Garrison Command. I couldn't move. Sweat prickled my fingertips.

They spoke before either of us could find the words to ask why they were here.

"Hello, Mr. Lin. We'd like you and your wife to come with us." As one spoke, the other stared over Wei's shoulder, surveying the room. I held his gaze until he looked away. Had he noticed the fear in my clenched teeth and the disgust in my eyes?

"Why?" Wei demanded. *Stay calm,* I pleaded silently. I watched him restrain himself. "I mean, can I ask why?"

"This is a question we can't answer. We're here only to escort you."

"My wife is pregnant. She can stay here."

"No, she will come too."

How could Wei fight while wearing those ridiculous slippers? He still held the doorknob, and he twisted it as he decided what he could do. I stood up. "Let's go."

I now understood the look that had crossed my father's face whenever he was called in. The panic was all consuming, the unrelenting tug of an undercurrent, and yet I moved normally, calmly even, toward the door. I gripped Wei's elbow as I put on my shoes and then he put on his own. He took a moment to turn off the light and lock the door behind us.

One man for Wei and one for me. We walked in slow motion down the hall. In the elevator, no one spoke, and I wanted to laugh at the absurdity of it all when I saw the four of us lined up in the mirrored walls and multiplied back into infinity. The elevator door opened and we strode across the lobby. People turned and stared. They all knew. When I caught the front desk clerk's eye, he quickly looked down at his ledger. Like gentlemen, the officers pushed open the doors on either side of us, and the muggy night greeted us. A car waited.

The city sparkled behind the car windows like a dark glimmering ocean.

"Will we get a lawyer?" I asked Wei. "I mean we have to, right? We're American citizens." A thin panel of glass separated us from our guards. Did they understand English? Did they flinch at the word "American"?

"I don't know. They held that American professor, Big Beard, the one they accused of killing Lin Yi-hsiung's twins, for twenty-four hours before they told the AIT." I recalled the false accusation meant to throw everyone off the scent of the government's wrongdoing. It was an absurd allegation; the professor had been a friend of Lin Yi-hsiung's family. The AIT, the American Institute in Taiwan, was a "private corporation" that had replaced the US consulate after the end of relations—another ruse of nomenclature. "But that was two years ago. It depends what happens. Are they really asking questions? Or are they arresting us? If we're accused of sedition, we can be held for two months incommunicado. New law. Does it apply to Americans? I don't know."

"Sedition? Wei?" What had he done? I could not risk asking right now.

He squeezed my hand and said pointedly, "There's no reason to think that. It's probably about Tang Jia Bao."

One of the men up front said loudly, "These Chinese don't even speak Chinese. Just like foreign devils." My eyes widened. If he'd had the vocabulary of American racism, I'm sure he would have called us "bananas," or "whitewashed."

"So you think we'll go home tonight?" I continued, as if the man had not spoken.

"I'm sure. Don't worry." But now Wei didn't look at me, his brow furrowed, and he stared straight ahead.

A soldier pulled open a gate and the car rolled through. It had started to rain lightly, and our two guards opened the car doors. One held an umbrella for me.

"Thank you," I said.

We bypassed a few lit buildings, then stopped in a room, one of many in a long row, that faced a cement courtyard. At the far end, I saw the menace of an iron-barred door, which undoubtedly led to the cells. The rain pattered on the metal roof, and occasionally a disconcerting cry drifted across the yard.

There was a green sofa and, facing it, a desk. On the wall, manacles and hooks hung from chains.

"Have a seat," one of them told me.

I sat. My obedience surprised me. And then they were leading Wei out of the room, and I hoisted myself to my feet again and cried, "Where is he going?" One guard turned to grip my shoulders. Wei glanced back at me. *It's okay,* he mouthed.

Now my panic rose to the surface and my hands began to tremble despite the heat. The guard gently eased me back onto the sofa. Sweat beaded on my forehead. It rolled down my face, over my collarbone, and down between my breasts. I wiped it away and dried my hands on my dress. I didn't cry.

A new man came in. He was barely taller than me and wearing brown slacks. He was close to my age, with a wide and round white face, eyes like two dashes of ink, and slick hair tidily parted on the left. He carried a brown accordion file.

"Hello, Mrs. Lin." He dismissed the guard and sat himself at the desk. The clock on the wall read five past nine. Though the room was sweltering, and the man's white shirt had gone translucent in certain spots, he made no move to turn on the fan bolted to the wall above him. "How are you?"

"Am I under arrest?" I asked.

He laughed. "No. Not at all. We'd have to call the AIT if you were. You came voluntarily, didn't you?" He suddenly looked serious. "They didn't handcuff you, did they?"

"No," I said. Their scheme was suddenly clear, the convolution of words and legalities. They had never said "arrest." They had requested that we come, and we had. It might as well have been an invitation embossed on hundred-pound linen paper with a gold foil–lined envelope for the way we practically leaped up and strolled away with them.

He opened the file he had brought and scanned it as he spoke, half distracted. "No, no, no. We just want to ask some questions."

"And my husband?"

"They are interviewing him in another room. You know how these things work. We can't interview you together. We need to see if your statements corroborate each other."

"I understand." I didn't know how I could be so calm.

"Then let's begin."

"Will you tell me your name first?"

He smiled. "No one has asked me that before. You can call me Mr. Ping." He asked me questions that I knew he knew the answers to—my date of birth, my husband's name, the address of my childhood home. Jia Bao had told me that interrogators never say what they want. Your uncertainty means that you reveal more than you intend. I reminded myself to stay vigilant.

He asked me about Jia Bao—when he had arrived, when we had decided to house him, how he had spent his time there. He was already dead; I thought there was no harm in recounting the facts of that time. Nothing incriminating was left, and no one to be incriminated. I spoke deliberately. Some things I did not say. Memories arose that I didn't mention—Jia Bao's wire-framed glasses, the secondhand clothes that we donated back to the thrift store after he died, the cleft at the center of his chest that I felt rise and fall as he slept that night in Willits.

The clock on the wall now showed nine thirty-five. I was tired. I wanted to go to bed.

Another man entered the room with a fastidious bearing that put me on instant alert. I sat up a little straighter. So did Mr. Ping. "Good evening, Mr. Yang," he said, phlegm quavering in his throat.

Mr. Yang raised an eyebrow and settled beside me. He tugged at his white cuffs and adjusted his watch. He and Mr. Lu were of the same genus. The near calm that Mr. Ping's soft manner had elicited in me now receded.

"Read," he commanded, and Mr. Ping thumbed through the sheaf. The consideration that had been in Mr. Ping's voice when he interviewed me was gone. His tone plummeted into monotony, and it was several sentences before I realized with horror that what he read was a letter Wei had sent me years and years ago when he was in California and I was still in Taiwan waiting for my visa. Our innocent, blossoming love was made dirty and ridiculously naive in his colorless voice. They had been reading our mail. Not just reading it. Copying it. Keeping it. I closed my eyes against the humiliation. My cheeks burned.

Mr. Yang said, "That's enough. Let's be serious now."

Mr. Ping folded the letter and picked up his pen again.

Mr. Yang crossed his legs as if we were settling in for a cozy chat. "Why are you in Taiwan?"

"To see my family."

"That's all?"

"Yes. I wanted to see my parents. And wanted my daughters to see them too."

"And what about your husband?"

"We came as a family, of course."

"What other business did he have here?"

"Business? He had no other business here."

"And what about his meeting with Huang Ying Cheng on August tenth?"

"What meeting? My husband has been with me the whole time."

"August tenth, August tenth. It was a Tuesday. The day after you arrived." He bared his bottom teeth as he waited for my response.

I tried to remember August tenth. What had we done that second day? The girls were drowsy with jet lag. We had lunch with Wei's parents, and then roamed the Mitsukoshi department store, relieved by the air-conditioning. And then . . . and then Wei had gone out. With college friends, he'd said. My temples tensed and my ears began to throb.

"You remember something." He smiled.

"I don't remember anything."

"You were with your husband the whole day?"

"I was." He had said he was fishing for shrimp at the pools. His face had been red from the alcohol. I'd smelled the smoke and beer on him.

"I understand. He is your husband. My colleague Mr. Lu has spoken highly of your loyalty. But I have my own loyalty. I love my country. I want to protect it. Your husband is a person who wants to destroy it."

"He's not," I said, like a sulky child.

"If you say so." My interrogator turned to Mr. Ping. "They can start."

Mr. Ping capped his pen and picked up the phone. Time revolved around me, slow. Even the second hand of the clock seemed to dawdle. It was nine fifty-two. I watched his pale lips say, "Go ahead," into the receiver.

A long, terrified moan came through the wall. It was not human.

I flinched. "What is that?" A gray fog pulsed around the edges of my sight.

"What is your husband's plan?"

Through the wall came multiple dull thwacks, the sound of a baseball bat hitting a leather punching bag. So that is the sound of beating flesh, some more rational part of me noted. The poor man cried out again. Horrified, I recognized my husband's voice.

"Please don't hurt him," I whispered.

"He says he has nothing to tell us—it's as if he has no interest in saving himself."

My husband wailed again. "Stop it!" I cried. To hear the voice I knew so well distorted in pain made me sick. I drummed my feet against the floor. "Stop it!"

"August tenth."

"I don't know anything about it!"

The third time Wei cried out, I vomited. I tried to hold it in and cover my mouth, but it spilled out of my hands and spewed over my dress. Mr. Yang lurched back as I convulsed. I wiped my hands on my ruined dress and rubbed my mouth against the crook of my elbow.

He stood up. "If he won't tell us what else he's been up to, then you should. Save your husband." He turned to Mr. Ping. "Clean her up, then let her see him."

Mr. Ping's anemic face shaded toward gray as he approached. He marched through the vomit splattered on the floor and helped me to my feet. His hands were strangely soft, as if he lacked bones.

Ten o'clock.

We weren't due back at Wei's parents' place until noon. No one except the people in the lobby even knew we were gone. The Garrison Command had fourteen more hours with us.

There would be consequences, I assured myself, as Mr. Ping led me toward the courtyard. If they harmed us, the AIT would investigate. It would be an international incident. Then I remembered Jia Bao, murdered on American soil. Chen Wen-cheng, the Carnegie Mellon professor who never came back from interrogation. Wei had told me a gentler era was encroaching upon Taiwan. Brutality belonged to the previous decade. Does brutality ever get old? I wondered. Each generation brings a new group of men who have not yet learned the guilt of the last. They need to feel bones breaking under their very own fingers to know for sure how they feel about it.

Mr. Ping's soft hands on my arm. In the courtyard, I stood at the center of the prison block, within view of all the cells circling around. Faces, made spectral by the moon, appeared in the dark cell windows. Mosquitoes buzzed in my ears and bit my face, my arms, my ankles. Mr. Ping's white face grew more wraithlike in the dark; with his white shirt and dark pants, he looked like the apparition of half a being. Behind him, incongruously, loomed a broken basketball hoop.

He sprayed me with a hose and my heart seized from the cold water and I shrieked, then worried that Wei would think I was crying from pain and do something stupid. The water soaked through my dress, through the pads of my bra, wet my flesh. It washed over my sandals and swept away the odor of puke.

And then what? I thought. Mr. Yang said I'd see Wei. Was it a lie to urge me forward? Was I to be delivered, sopping wet, to the couch to continue answering questions, or would I see my husband? I tipped my head back to squeeze out my dripping hair and saw the moon haloed by a cloud. Emily and Stephanie would be asleep by now. I felt linked through the years to Baba by this moon, which had witnessed it all. Had he stood here too, under its gaze, thinking of his sleeping children? I longed to say to him: *Baba, I understand.*

The examiners had stripped Wei. They had spread his legs wide apart and chained his feet to bolts in the floor. Trickles of blood ran down his legs. His ribs were mottled black. At the sight of me, he strained against his manacles.

"Wei!" I cried. I moved as if to run toward him, but Mr. Ping was fast, and he grabbed me. "Let him go!" I could not catch my breath.

The walls had softened and chipped, and mold speckled the paint. The air smelled damp and singed. Mr. Ping pulled me to a chair and apologized as he handcuffed my wrists in my lap.

"You can't do this. He's an American citizen," I said, even as I knew "citizen" had no traction here in this place where no one who mattered knew where we were. I wondered what they could do with me as witness. My presence would not stop them. I shuddered as I remembered what had already happened. Car "accidents." Murder-suicides. Or we could just disappear without a trace. There had been plenty of those too. What did those five words—*"I am an American citizen"*—matter to these men caught up in sadism, enrobed in the moment of inflicting pain on my husband, who had lost his humanity in their eyes? He was just a piece of meat—if that. In fact, his suffering did not exist for them at all. And even if Washington were to find out, official relations between the two countries were nearly dead—would the US government jeopardize what was left for two lowly citizens like us?

With Wei were three men: one to ask the questions, one to hold the prod, and the last to control the voltage. I thought of a nursery rhyme—*and this little piggy went wee wee wee all the way home.* When the second man touched the prod to Wei's testicles and the third man turned on the voltage, Wei unleashed the beastly scream I'd heard from next door. He twitched and pissed himself.

"I'm sorry," he blubbered to me. I closed my eyes.

The man tasked with asking questions turned and snarled at me, "Keep watching, you bitch."

I knew his insults were meant only to rile Wei, and I prayed Wei would not be provoked. Of course, Wei was hotheaded even at his best, and he found some reserve of spirit and snapped, "Leave her alone."

"Now, now," Mr. Ping said. Greenish circles had emerged under his eyes; he sounded weary and strangely sheepish.

The interrogator ignored both of them. "Answer me and I won't have to rape your wife." He was tall and extremely thin, and as he strode toward me, he resembled a giant insect coming to suck the sap from my veins. Empty threats, I reminded myself, but all the same, I felt a hot, sour liquid rising in my throat. I was determined not to retch again and I choked it back down. Uttering a barely audible apology, Mr. Ping stepped aside to allow the man to stand behind me. He cupped the back of my neck with a cool, dry hand.

"There's no plan," I said. "Wei, there was no plan. Don't lie for my sake."

The man's hand slid down over my collarbone and onto my breast. He squeezed, pressing my nipple into the center of his palm. I cringed but shook my head at Wei. "There was no plan," I reiterated. Whatever Wei had done—whether he had met with this man Huang Ying Cheng or whether the accusation was just for intimidation—Wei had always been discreet. Wei would never name names. I was invested in my image of Wei as an idealist, stubbornly—naively—devoted to his beliefs and his vision of himself as a hero. I didn't want this destroyed by some lout's hand on my breast. It was just flesh.

"Huang Ying Cheng," Wei began.

The man's hand relaxed and slid out of my dress back to my shoulder.

"Stop, Wei."

"Chen Hsin Je."

I screamed and I jerked the man's hand off with such force that I fell out of the chair. My elbow slammed into the cement and my whole arm reverberated with pain. My hair stuck to my face, and I couldn't keep the spit in my mouth. I tasted blood. I felt every fleck of grit scrape my flesh as I tried to crawl toward my husband. The thin man leaped toward me and seized my ankles. The cement abraded and seared my skin as he dragged me toward the door feetfirst. Mr. Ping tried to be kind. He grabbed my bound arms and lifted me from the ground.

They put me in a cell with a cracked wood floor, a toilet, and a blanket. My dress had dried stiff. I imagined I heard Wei crying, but it could have been anyone in the cells around me. The heat was even more stifling in this windowless cell, and I uselessly batted away mosquitoes. Their bites turned into welts. In frustration, I scratched until blood washed away the itch.

We were innocent, I told myself. And then I recalled how innocence had done nothing for others. What was *innocent* when it was up to the Garrison Command to decide the definition of terms? Too upset to sleep, I pressed myself to the wall to wait for morning. They wouldn't kill him, I told myself over and over. And they couldn't keep us here indefinitely. A lawyer must come at some point.

I felt my concept of time evolve. How long time felt waiting for rescue. Was it absurd to think there might be someone who could or would rescue us? To think that our fates were out of our hands and that there was some conquering hero who might swoop in and find us? Jia Bao had told me how interrogators were careful to use techniques that wouldn't leave marks—beating the bottom of one's feet, for example, or just internal injuries. Their carelessness with Wei—I'd seen the black burns and the bruises—worried me. They were not concerned about evidence.

. . .

The heat of the rising day filled the cell. I rinsed my arms and splashed warm water on my face from a spigot next to the toilet. What a decadence to have a cell to myself when I knew the ones around me were crammed, no room to stretch out or do push-ups for sanity. I was *blessed*!

I suddenly saw my gratefulness as a kind of insanity. What would eleven years do?

I heard footsteps in the hall so I returned to my station with the wall safely at my back. The loud, strident tone outside the cell sounded like English. The window in the door opened and a foreigner's face appeared. Then a key clanked in the lock and the bar squealed as it was yanked back.

In a short-sleeved baby-blue button-down and clean black slacks, framed by the grimy doorframe, the American was almost incandescent.

"Mrs. Lin? I'm Mark Jenson from the AIT. I'm so sorry about this. I'm here to take you home." His nostrils flared in disgust as he looked around the cell before entering. He stepped toward me and reached out two hands to raise me to my feet. I struggled up. I had not eaten and had been given just one cup of bitter water that tasted faintly of tea.

I gripped his arm as we walked down the hall. "What about my husband?"

"He'll come with us too."

I glanced at all the shut doors I passed and thought of the people behind them who would not be going home.

Wei sat on the sofa in the room where I'd originally been taken. Though he looked haggard, true to Jia Bao's statement, his face showed no obvious sign of abuse. I hurried to him and pressed my face into his neck. He stank of sweat and urine. My relief was so sudden and overwhelming that I began to sob. I felt tremors in his chest as he tried to hold back his own cries.

When we finally pulled apart, Mr. Jenson introduced us to his colleague Benjamin Sutton, freckle-faced and slouching next to the door, looking as if he was on his first foray outside of the AIT compound.

"We'll be leaving in just a moment," Mr. Jenson said before he excused himself from the room. Mr. Sutton's eyes ricocheted between us and the door.

"How are you?" I asked Wei.

He squeezed my hand and didn't answer. He had not said a word to me. I began to fear that if he opened his mouth I would see broken teeth, a lacerated tongue.

Through the wall, we heard Mr. Jenson yell, "I understand, but what the hell were you thinking? You should have called us right away. This was way, way out of line. You better believe we're calling this one in. Your goons have created a real fucking serious situation. Fucking amateurs."

I wondered if the man receiving these words even understood the word "goon." No, I thought, fuck him. Fuck them all.

A cramp shot from hip to hip. I moaned and doubled over.

Wei gripped my shoulder. "Are you okay?" he asked, and I was relieved to see his teeth were intact.

I did not want to tell him how much it hurt. I nodded: *I'm okay.*

Mr. Sutton tapped his watch. "As soon as Mr. Jenson is back, we'll go see a doctor and have you both checked out."

The cramp receded slowly; a shadow of pain lingered on the spot.

When Mr. Jenson returned, he exhaled loudly and wiped his palms on his pants. I swore I saw him sneer. We stink, I thought.

"Shall we?" he asked.

I wanted to tell him that I had noticed his contempt and remind him: *Our kids could go to school with yours. I make a mean macaroni casserole. We are Americans like you.*

They didn't take us to a hospital, and instead called a doctor to the AIT office. Wei suspected that they were trying to be discreet. The doctor said Wei's burns would heal without long-term damage. There could even be a baby number four. He gave Wei an ointment for his bruises, noted a possible cracked rib, but no broken bones. He asked no questions about where the injuries had come from.

My and the baby's heart rates were slightly elevated—adrenaline and dehydration, he said. Drink water, rest, check again when you get home, he advised.

The two men took us back to the hotel to gather our things. There, Mr. Jenson told us we had twenty-four hours to leave. We were being deported. He could free us, but he had no control over deportation.

"Can we ever come back?" Wei asked.

"It depends on how the wind blows. I wouldn't rule it out."

"And what recourse do we have for what happened last night?"

"Of course we'll make a report to the State Department." Mr. Jenson squinted. "But to be honest, there's so much on our plate that I can't see much happening after that. The men who interrogated—"

Wei cut him off. "It was torture."

Mr. Jenson sighed. "The men who interrogated you will probably be reprimanded to save face, maybe be moved around, but I can't see much more than that happening. I'm just being honest."

"I understand," Wei said, his face dark with anger.

53

WE FOUND OUT Wei's father had called the hotel when we were two hours late coming home, and the man at the front desk had whispered the story to him. He had immediately called the AIT.

We told the girls the police had just wanted to ask questions, no big deal. Emily, seeing us rumpled and dirty, glared as if we had betrayed her.

"Then why did the police take you for so long?"

I reminded myself that she had grown up thinking the police were the good guys, there to help if you were lost, or you couldn't find your puppy. Only real criminals earned the ire of the police.

"They made a mistake," I said.

Stephanie balled up a section of my dress and tugged on it. I dug my fingers into her hair, comforted by the heat of her small head.

"Why did it take them so long to figure it out?" Emily insisted.

How could I explain it? "It was a mistake," I snapped. "They made a mistake. Even police make mistakes."

Her eyes drifted over my greasy hair and reeking dress, then she jutted out her chin and stomped away, dragging Stephanie with her.

On the plane, my body felt completely still, completely numb. Shaken to tranquillity. Would a doctor have called it shock? The baby did not protest my exhaustion and lay motionless, a boat floating on a placid lake.

I recalled how, before we left, Emily had walked into the room as I was rubbing ointment on Wei's battered chest. He hurriedly threw on his shirt.

"You lied to me," she wailed.

"I'm fine. Look at me." Wei stretched his arms and popped his back. He clenched his teeth and forced a smile. "Come here, Em." He tried to hug her, but she struggled out of his grip and threw herself into a corner, crying against the wall, suddenly an inconsolable toddler again, provoked by a force far larger than she could comprehend.

Even this memory exhausted me. I didn't dare think about the rest of it. We had left the country and were in the air, we would be home soon, and I finally felt safe enough to sleep.

An hour before landing, when we were still miles out over the Pacific, I awoke. I stretched and rose. Stephanie joined me and we paced the aisle, then gazed out one of the back windows at the clouds tipped gold and pink by the setting sun. She pressed her palms to the window and marked it with her breath. She dragged her finger through it, drawing an X of clean glass.

"It'll still be light when we get back," I said. "We'll have dinner, and unpack and take a nice hot bath and go to bed. How does that sound?" The normalcy of it was surreal. Which was the dream—the interrogation, or the sheltered life we were returning to?

She turned from the window. "Can I watch TV?"

I ran my fingers through the tangles in her hair. "Of course."

I tapped my stomach. I tried to remember when I'd last felt the baby move. During the questioning? When I'd returned to Wei's parents'? Before I boarded? During our layover in Honolulu? I rubbed small circles. *Baby, wake up.*

During the next hour, I waited for the baby to turn itself around, to knock a joint against my flesh, to assert itself. When we felt the subtle shift of descent, the baby still had not responded to my moves to wake it.

Waiting at the baggage claim, Wei nudged up against me and put his arm around my shoulders. "It's nice to be home."

I stared at the luggage dropping onto the carousel and circling past. "The baby hasn't moved all day."

"What do you mean?"

"I mean usually she—he—she—is usually restless, but I haven't felt anything the entire flight."

"You were sleeping most of the time. You were too tired to notice," Wei said.

"Maybe." I wanted to believe him, but the way his eyes darted around the terminal made me doubt that he believed it himself.

The city greeted us with fog, cool and white, a stark contrast to the bright sun and unrelenting heat of Taipei. The fog lifted somewhere on the Bay Bridge and the East Bay was warm. On the radio in the cab, we heard that while we were in the air over the Pacific, the last of the three communiqués between the United States and China had been announced. There was a sense of finality to it. America reiterated its position on Taiwan. We were too tired to care.

Closed up for weeks, our house had a stale odor, but I could smell us too, our family. I could detect both Emily and Stephanie in it, Wei, and then the deeper bones of the place, the seventy years it had existed before we moved in, years and families before us deep in the paint and wood. I went around and opened the windows.

In our bedroom, as the girls watched TV downstairs, I sat on the edge of the bed, picked up the phone, and held it in my hand so long that the dial tone became an alarmed flashing cry. Wei came to retrieve our laundry and found me.

"What's going on?"

"I need to go to the hospital. It just doesn't feel right."

He took the phone from my hand and returned it to the receiver. "Of course."

"Now. I need to go right now." I saw his shock as he registered the exhausted green smudges beneath my eyes, my face drained by nausea and fear.

"Let me tell Pam that the girls are home alone. She can come check on them." A few minutes later, I heard him outside knocking on the next-door neighbor's door and her exclamatory hello, followed by the murmur of polite exchange about the trip, and then the tone lowered and grew more serious. I remained on the edge of the bed, afraid to lie down. I felt like nothing inside.

. . .

The ride to Alta Bates was short, but we couldn't get there fast enough. *Wake up. Move.* I found myself pleading with the baby so often that it became a mantra before I realized it. I bargained. I waited for a tiny knee to reach out and kick me, to make me cry out with relief.

In the examination room, wearing paper pajamas, I waited anxiously for the doctor to begin. I stared at the posters taped next to the lights on the ceiling and thought of the other women who had lain here, dozens a day, gazing at these same inane images, slogans in comic-book fonts encouraging us to eat cheese and broccoli, or to HANG IN THERE, BABY! My rage at the men who had interrogated me was so consuming that I felt dizzy and my limbs driven to a numbness indistinguishable from apathy. I did not know this doctor—Dr. Sloan—the only one available; luckily, she emanated competence. Her black hair was streaked with gray and twisted into a bun, and she spoke with a trace of New York in her voice.

She gasped when she saw the bruising and scrapes on the side of my body and glared at Wei.

"I know what it looks like," I said. "But I fell. I really did. He's never laid a hand on me."

She looked directly into my eyes and I met her stare. I saw that she believed me. She slid the wand over my belly. I reached for Wei's hand. Where there should have been the rapid *whomp whomp* ocean rush of a liquid heartbeat, there was nothing but white noise, something too close to silence. I waited for the doctor's explanation—the machine was broken or the baby was elusive. Something other than the reality that was forcing itself upon us.

Dr. Sloan looked at the nurse as she said, "I'm sorry." Her eyes darted over to Wei before she finally made eye contact with me.

Wei squeezed my hand. "What do you mean?" he asked. "Do you need another machine?"

"We're going to have to induce you."

"Induce me? I'm only at twenty-six weeks. The baby will be too small." I saw a slug of a baby, hooked up to wires and tubes, in a huge plastic incubator. "It's too soon." So, there is something to save, I thought. I allowed some relief to creep in.

Dr. Sloan still held the wand midair. "There's no heartbeat." She left a space between each word. "The baby has passed. I'm sorry."

"Impossible," Wei protested. "The baby was fine yesterday."

"No, it's gone," I said. My gaze tracked back up to the ceiling toward the inspirational posters, then drifted across the expanse of pocked asbestos tiles. "She's right. The baby is gone."

I found there are memories too painful to recall in detail, so my mind slides over them: the cramps unlike the contractions I'd had with Emily and Stephanie, labor without pain, the eerie silence of waiting for a wail that never comes. He. A boy. How the nurses still suctioned the liquid from his nose even though he didn't breathe.

They wanted to take him away—my son—like he was medical waste. Though it was not protocol, the doctor relented to Wei's forceful pleading that we be given time with him; Wei's face was warped with pain and anger, and no one would have dared to say no. The nurse wiped our son down, wrapped him in a blanket, and slipped a small cap on his head. He was small enough to be cradled in two hands, but I held him in the crook of my arm.

He had eyelashes.

If his eyes had opened, what would they look like? Amphibian, glossy and black? Or some milky-gray not-quite color? In a chair pulled up against the side of the bed, Wei hunched with his elbows on his knees.

"We have to give him a name," I said.

"No," Wei said.

"Then how will we refer to him? The Baby? Will we never talk about him? He needs a name."

I understood Wei's reluctance, how naming him would make this real instead of some bad experience we could push aside.

We had discussed names over the last few months but had settled on none. I wanted to name him for the other recent loss in our life. Not Jia Bao exactly, but something that would resonate with it. The two characters of Jia Bao's name meant "family" and "treasured," or "precious." I thought of an uncommon character, more formal, that echoed the meaning of the second character: Yu. A character that combined the gold and jade radicals.

I suggested it to Wei.

"Just one character?" he said.

"Yes, like your name. One character. Simple. Yu."

I could see in his eyes the baby taking on this name, this history. No longer nameless, our son was Yu. I could see what he might have been. I could see already how he would have Wei's nose, but my chin. I imagined him fighting with his sisters. I imagined him at five years old, wedged between them—Emily already a teenager and Stephanie close—posed in front of our door for a first-day-of-school photo. Wei was right to be afraid: naming him had turned him into a real person.

I began to unwrap his blanket. Wei asked what I was doing, turned away and said he didn't want to see.

"I want to remember just his face," he said.

But, allowed only one encounter, I wanted to commit our son's entire being to memory. Despite himself, Wei looked too as I inspected his tiny fingernails. His body was covered in black downy hair, and a blue "Mongolian spot" spread across his lower back and butt. Emily and Stephanie had been born with this birthmark too; it had faded by the time they started school. I was gentle with his limp body. The creases at his wrists and elbows and ankles indicated where he would have grown plump once he started breast-feeding.

The nurse returned after an hour. I could not give him up. I wanted one more hour, and then another. Carefully, I swaddled him again. I pressed my nose to him and smelled him. He smelled of my blood. I handed him over, and then Wei held my hand and we both cried.

Our son's death was something we couldn't come back from. Wei stopped apologizing at random moments for what had happened with Helen. He stopped his flirtatious pleas for my affection. We were both somber.

I realized that this was what Mama had meant by love. A shared experience, a shared history, a shared trauma: this is what made us a family. No one else could understand it. I knew that for as long as Wei and I were married, even if my head was turned by another, the other man and I would not share this one critical thing—this one summer—and that would be enough to unmake any potential love affair. I thought of all the moments growing up when I had disliked my family—my resentment of my father, my disgust at my mother, my anger at my siblings. *Of all the families in the world, why was I born into this family?* I'd thought. As if just dumb fate had brought us together. Now I understood there was something stronger than fate. Choice. It was ugly and quotidian and lacked romance, and that was exactly what gave it its strength.

So, like my mother, I chose to stay.

2003

54

EXCEPT FOR A FEW random reading lights, the plane was dark and mostly empty. The flight attendants, dressed in lavender, murmured in the galley. Occasionally, a flipped magazine page rustled. I rose and paced the aisle to soothe my swollen legs. On a more crowded plane, this would have brought anxious glances and a request to stay seated, seat belt fastened, but this hollow dark body was a respite from the chaos below and no one stirred beneath their thin microfleece blankets.

A few old men gathered in the small vestibule near the emergency exit. They swung their arms and stretched, and smelled of sleep and body odor. They nodded and acknowledged me with grunts. In another world, tanks were rolling into Baghdad. We didn't talk about the invasion or the epidemic. The roar of the jet was peace.

When I returned to my seat, the woman across the aisle had awoken. She fanned herself with the laminated emergency landing instructions.

"What bad luck, right? Descending right into hell."

I hoped my smile would deter her. My throat was sore and dry and I didn't want to talk. I buttoned my sweater, pulled up the blanket, and closed the air vent.

"Did you hear about the old man who came back from China with the disease? I mean the doctors don't know if it's bird flu or swine flu or god-knows-what flu."

"They are calling it SARS," I said. "It's not that bad. They say it's like pneumonia. If you're healthy, you should be fine." Instinctively, I knocked on the armrest as if it were wood. We moved against the exodus; the US State Department had issued a travel warning to Taiwan, and nonessential expats were encouraged to leave. Some mysterious illness with flu-like symptoms—a quick death, the new Spanish flu—was speeding through Asia. Whole buildings, thirty stories high, were cordoned off in Hong Kong and their residents bused to recreation centers to wait out their quarantine. Feverish salesgirls led to department stores shut down for disinfection. Panicked American newspapers blamed the dirty Chinese and their markets of rusty cages and crying birds, of civet cats mewing before slaughter, of strange culinary tastes and unwashed hands. In my own suitcase, I carried a box of surgical masks.

Wei had been worried about my trip. We no longer had to fear the government—martial law had ended in 1987, and the country was now under the administration of the first non-KMT president. In the end, on the issue of democracy, Wei's side had won. Taiwan had full enfranchisement and freedom of speech. Now, it could focus on the kind of contemporary concerns brought on by freedom, like global epidemics.

"Just wait and see how your mother does," he had said after my sister's call. "It might be a false alarm. Do you really want to throw yourself into that situation? Even the State Department is advising against it."

"She's ninety years old," I had insisted. "There are no more false alarms. I have to go home. She's my *mother.*"

"It's bad." The woman drew out the word. "I wouldn't have come if I could have avoided it. Wouldn't you have canceled a wedding? What kind of bad luck start is that?" She grabbed a water bottle from the seat pocket and unscrewed it. The plastic crackled in her fist as she gulped.

"I'm sure we'll be fine. The news exaggerates everything."

With the back of her hand, she wiped her mouth. "Oh god, I hope so."

We landed in Taoyuan just past dawn. The plane emptied quickly, and we trudged in a haphazard line over an antibacterial rug, then past a temperature scanner. My body appeared on-screen in a rainbow aura, technology illuminating my chakras: red at my core and a milder orange radiating outward to yellow, an indicator of health.

The airport hallways were lined with photos of a Taiwan as Portuguese sailors might have seen it more than four hundred years before: emerald isle and azure sea, marble gorges and tattooed, nubile native women in woven dress. Sprinkled among these were posters advertising an exhibit for bodies preserved with plastic in various athletic poses. I'd heard a rumor that all the cadavers came from unclaimed Chinese prisoners, and I had to turn away from the face, stripped of flesh to red-and-white muscle, that grinned at me from behind glass.

I stood in the line for US citizens, my blue passport in hand, once again aware of the strangeness of returning to my country as the citizen of another. The customs official, a man in his thirties with a trim haircut and angry eyes, looked me up and down and asked if I'd had a fever in the last two weeks. Had I been to a farm or near livestock? Where in Taiwan would I be staying? When I answered in Mandarin, he seemed even angrier, as if I were an outsider pretending to be one of them. The slam of his stamp on my passport sounded like a gavel. He waved me through.

Beyond the frosted glass doors that separated transit from arrivals, I found the bus counter and bought a ticket to Taipei on the Flying Dog line, which sounded like a knockoff of Greyhound. All the buses into the city were two-story mammoths with padded reclining pilot chairs, personalized video screens, and speakers embedded in the headrests. The air outside was startling, thick and hot, but the driver, with a surgical mask hanging by its elastic strap from one of his ears, refused to turn on the air-conditioning, claiming it increased the risk of infection. I pulled open a window. On the freeway it made no difference; we moved so slowly that the heavy air merely mingled with the congested smog on the road.

Again, the island had changed in its constant cycle of creation and destruction, but a few old monuments still stood like stolid warriors among the streaking traffic: North Gate, the train station, the temples. Around them, new condo high-rises, new karaoke parlors, new cram schools, new restaurants and cafés: a hundred thousand earnest entrepreneurs who'd have a new venture by the time I next visited.

I was unfamiliar with Taipei, so I disembarked at the railway station and flagged down one of the hundreds of yellow taxis that seemed to be hungrily trolling the place. A mask obscured half the driver's face, and he gazed at me warily before he hopped out and helped with my luggage.

"You gotta be careful," he said as he heaved my suitcases into the trunk. "One sick person and—wah—it's over." His cautiousness was the typical mood of the city, but he made this declaration with a light tone and I assumed he was smiling beneath his mask. His black hair flopped over his forehead. I had no idea how old he was. Maybe forty? Or a robust fifty-five? His toes peeked out from velcroed sandals—a generic version of the hiking sandals that were the rage in Berkeley—but they betrayed nothing except an ingrown nail on his left foot.

A carved wooden goddess hung on beads from his rearview mirror. He rubbed her with a rough thumb and said, "Most Americans are leaving, not coming. Maybe it's a good time for a vacation. You must have something important to come for. Business?" I let him continue his speculation without responding, and after a brief monologue, we arrived at the entrance to Ah Zhay's alley. He claimed his car would not make it through, so he unloaded my bags there.

"I'm not really scared," he said as I handed him cash. "It's just a flu. I change this mask every day. But you be careful. You've been away awhile, I can tell." I smiled at his concern and thanked him, then dragged my bags down the alley.

Ah Zhay and her husband had lived in the veterans village in Taichung until moss grew on the mounded roof tiles and weather had cracked the window frames of the decrepit plaster house. They never repaired the flaking walls because they always intended to move. The government had promised to relocate them into a new high-rise; they just had to wait for the slow, rusty bureaucratic wheels to creak into movement. The letter would come any day, Jie-fu claimed. Their endless waiting took on the feel of a magical realist story: my brother-in-law's insistence that the letter would arrive before they died was almost comical. However, the government's patience outlasted my sister's. When they left, the land for the new development finally had been cleared—an open-air market was bull-dozed and the vendors resurrected their tables among the rubble until a fence was erected around the site.

Ah Zhay decided she wanted to move to Taipei where Mei Mei lived. My parents, at the time nearing their nineties, and dependent on my sister, had no choice but to move as well. Now, on quiet Lishui Street, behind the Normal University where my niece worked in the library, they lived in a three-bedroom apartment in a modest building clad in gray tiles. The small sunporch, where they kept the washing machine, looked over an empty lot. They had come to Taipei with only suitcases and bought everything new: a pretty green refrigerator and a Sanyo washing machine, cheap imitation Scandinavian-style furniture in blond wood veneer, bedding from Ikea. After forty years in a house, the only things of value they had that were worth moving were their clothes.

I rang the intercom and Ah Zhay exclaimed when she heard my voice. The building door buzzed as it unlocked. I yanked it open. I heard the apartment door on the third floor scream open and the shuffling slap of slippers hurrying down the stairs. I had just dragged my suitcase through the door when Ah Zhay met me.

"Little sister!" Her hot hand squeezed my arm. "You never change. How was your flight?"

Ah Zhay was in her midsixties. She looked entirely like the sister I'd always known, and yet I was not sure I would recognize her if I passed her in the street. Her figure had thickened and her hair was chopped short. Extra weight cushioned her features. She must have looked at me with the same wonder at the passage of time.

"Pretty empty, but smooth," I answered.

Her smile faltered and she frowned. "I'm sorry you had to come home now. I wish . . ." She sighed. "Never mind. Come, let me help you." She grabbed the top handle of my suitcase and lugged it up the first step, where she paused and gathered momentum for the next stair.

"Ah Zhay, let me!" I tried to take it from her but she elbowed me.

"Don't be silly."

She made it up one flight before yanking her hand off the strap and laughing. "Okay." She exhaled and dabbed the sweat off her forehead. "You're younger than me. It's all yours."

"How is she?" I asked Ah Zhay as we sat before my open suitcase. I'd brought an assortment of vitamins and supplements, as well as some expensive antiaging lotions for Ah Zhay. We were in Baba's room. His smell clung to the walls: menthol oil and nicotine and a particularly pungent aftershave that I was sure only men of his generation wore. The next room was my mother's: a narrow single bed, a desk piled with sketch pads. Now, at the end of her life, she had finally returned to her original passion, art. She drew street scenes—vendors squatting next to crates, people strolling under trees. Every drawing, I noticed, had one subtly positioned out-of-place figure: a woman at a desk under the shadow of trees, a child building a tower of blocks in the middle of the sidewalk, a man washing his dog next to the entrance to a store. I wondered what it revealed about my mother.

"I'm tired," Ah Zhay said. Her blue cotton shirt crept over her belly, exposing a wedge of skin. The flower appliqué on her shoulder was coming unstitched and two of the petals curled up sadly.

I was afraid to ask for details.

"You'll see yourself," she said to my silence.

"What did the doctor say?"

"Nothing more than I told you."

Certain questions can't be asked. Was this a long demise, or an acute illness that would strike quickly? Had I returned for Mama's last moments of coherence, or for the real good-bye? *Hope springs eternal*—a truism for jilted lovers and for the children of dying parents. We convince ourselves the inevitable isn't, and when it is upon us, we rail and plead. Or deny. Busy with preparation and travel, I had pushed away my worry; now that I was here, at midmorning in Taipei, when less than a day before I'd been in the chilly Bay Area, my new reality struck me.

I tore open the box of masks I'd brought. This box was precious, almost contraband. Recently, a woman had been arrested for falsely advertising cheap masks as the coveted N95 respirator, which were in short supply at the moment. Her online selling handle had been "squirellygirl," and now headlines were emblazoned with the evil deeds of squirellygirl, and outraged letters to the editor complained about the decay of morals in the younger generation. Even the police were looking for her. She had become the vessel for every fear sweeping the country.

"Thank you. Did you wear this on the airport bus?" Ah Zhay asked.

I shook my head.

"You should have." She took one from me and slipped it on. Her tired eyes and the mask's strange white muzzle and exhalation valve transformed her into an alien.

The hospital had multiple buildings: one, in red brick with white trim, had been built during the Japanese colonial era, and the other was a more modern cement high-rise. A walkway connected the two. The hospital was near New Park, which was now called 2-28 Peace Park in commemoration of the March Massacre, which itself had been renamed the "February 28 Incident," as if the weeks of disappearances could be narrowed down to only the episode with the cigarette vendor.

At the door, nurses in quaint pink uniforms zapped our foreheads with infrared thermometers. When the thermometers beeped at 37 degrees Celsius, the nurses thanked us and waved us through. The plastic chairs in the lobby area, punctuated by unattractive but hardy plants, were filled with people in surgical masks. Rows of dull black eyes without joy or fear.

In the room, Baba napped in a vinyl armchair, a faded peach hospital sheet draped over him. Mama slept too. Amid all the machinery, I could see very little of her—just her thin white hair clumped to her forehead and her gaunt arms. A thick plastic ventilator that clouded and cleared with each breath dug into her cheeks. Her hands were wrapped in mitts and strapped to the bed. Various lines disappeared into her veins, and a urine bag hung off the bed rail.

"My god. Why didn't you tell me all this?" I whispered to Ah Zhay. I felt sick. I sat on the empty bed that lay on the other side of the curtain. Was this how my mother was to die—half machine? I covered my eyes. Even the last time I'd seen her, she had moved with the exquisite posture that I had admired as a child. She had still gone to have her hair washed and set every week. Now, she seemed so exposed—she would have despised her own vulnerability—unbathed, unveiled. I wanted to weep for the shame that I imagined she would have felt.

"The nurses weigh her diapers to see how much food she's absorbed. Did you really want me to call you about this?"

"And Baba just waits with her?" I whispered.

"He watches TV when she sleeps," Ah Zhay said. She was inured to it; she had no more energy for horror. "I'm here every day."

"Why is she tied down?" The sight of my mother strapped to the bed like a Victorian-era lunatic frightened me the most.

"She tries to pull out the IV every chance she gets."

"Mama?" I could not imagine my mother doing anything but acquiescing to the doctor's orders.

"She wants to come home. She doesn't want to be here."

"Oh god, so let her."

We heard someone stirring on the other side of the curtain, then Baba croaked, "Daughter?"

We both came forward.

"Ah, you've come," Baba said. Still groggy, he gripped my arm in greeting. I covered his clammy hand with mine, no word except "Baba" coming to me.

I helped him sit up and handed him a cup of water from the tray next to my mother's bed. He held it with both hands, like a child might, and cleared his throat. "Your mother is very sick."

"Baba, don't talk like that," Ah Zhay said in the loud, over-enunciated voice people reserved for the elderly and foreigners.

"Don't talk to me like I'm a child," he growled. I was relieved; he had not changed.

"Okay, okay." She backed off. "Let's just try to be optimistic, Baba."

"Everyone dies," he said.

"Ba, please." Ah Zhay and I exchanged a glance. What else could he do? Cry all day? He was as scared as the rest of us. Anger hid his hurt, as it always had.

The PRC government called the virus on Taiwan an "internal matter" and wouldn't allow the World Health Organization to come to the island. The talking heads went on for hours dissecting the decision and the implications. Like a snake eating its tail, they talked in circles, working up to a fever pitch. All complaints and no solution. The answer was not in our hands, but in Beijing's. Some claimed this was Beijing's warning against Taiwan's president, the first elected from an opposition party and a congenial loose cannon with a big mouth who edged closer and closer to an official declaration of independence. *Slap on a surgical mask, hunker down, and shut up*, Beijing seemed to be saying in response.

Weary of the relentless noise, I clicked off the TV. Baba had gone home with Ah Zhay to clean up and have dinner with Jie-fu, and I had stayed behind with Mama. She was sleeping, but a faint greenish bedside light—a thin fluorescent bulb that emitted a tiny insect buzz—illuminated her face. The respirator clouded, cleared. The machines rose and fell and clicked and beeped.

In the downstairs lobby convenience store, which sold crutches and bedpans and syringes and pills cups, I bought a sports drink and a Styrofoam bowl of dried ramen, then perused the fashion magazines that had already been torn from their cellophane wrappers.

Reading one article, I caught my breath.

It was a profile of a pop singer who went by the stage name Melody. *Your parents*, the article said, *may recognize her as the daughter of murdered opposition party activist Tang Jia Bao.*

Jia Bao's daughter. To many of her fans, this detail must have been an abstract piece of history, secondary to the fizz of her pop songs about love, motorcycles, and candy.

To me, they had always remained as they had been that afternoon we last saw them in 1982. His wife—the kindly doctor—and the son and daughter on the cusp of adulthood. I had imagined them forever inhabiting, as Jia Bao did, that bygone world.

In the photos of the collage accompanying the article, she wore outrageous costumes—fuzzy pink gloves, platform boots with oversized socks, a skirt made of feathers—but I could still see the ghost of Jia Bao's face in hers. She was on the older side of pop stardom; however, after four midmarket albums, her latest had been her breakout. I eagerly scanned the article.

The magazine asked her about her father's death and she said, "For a long time, I was angry—at my mother for letting my father go, and at my father for leaving. I was angry at his murderers, of course. But I hated America the most.

"After years of bitterness, a good friend said to me that anger is an ember, and the one who holds it is the only one who is burned. This advice woke me up. I realized we all have a chance to remake the world. We don't have to hold on to the world as it came to us. We can have a vision and make the world anew. Every day, we have a second chance. This is what I hope to pass on with my music."

I closed the magazine. Were these her own words, or focus-group tested and churned out by her management? Her optimism devastated me. The wrenching pain of that awful winter when Jia Bao died—and everything that followed—grew vivid again under the cold convenience-store lights.

Upstairs, I filled the ramen bowl at the hot water dispenser near the nurses' station and sat at Mama's bedside table to eat. It was nine in the morning in California. I dug out my calling card and called home.

No answer. I tried again, dialing the international calling card center, then the calling card number, then finally entering my home phone number. One wrong button and I'd have to start again. It was like a recurring nightmare I had of misdialing, over and over again, long-distance on a rotary phone. Still no answer. I wasn't ready to tell Wei about Jia Bao's daughter, but I wanted to anchor myself with his voice.

I tried to settle into the vinyl chair that Baba had napped on, but it was like sleeping on a table. I stood at the window and looked toward the faintly lit park below. It had once been a meeting spot for gay men; now Filipino and Indonesian workers gathered there on Sundays to spend their single day off among countrymen. On other days, families strolled the paths, old men and women sunned on the benches, downtown workers cut through from corner to corner, and tourists wandered. Maybe one day I'd go down for fresh air. Maybe I could bring Mama. Once she was better. I leaned my head on the glass and closed my eyes. As if.

The 2-28 Memorial Museum was down there too. Depending on one's politics, the event was known as the "2-28 Incident," the "2-28 Massacre," or the "2-28 Uprising." It had a logo. There was a movie, a CD, books. There were T-shirts and hats. It had gone from a national secret to a branded industry. I had never visited the museum. I wondered if Mama had and if she had thought it strange to see a life she recalled encased and retold as history. Would she even associate herself with the stories inside, or was her life too singular to be linked to the rows of black-and-white pictures and dioramas of disaster?

The first night I spent in the hospital, taking Ah Zhay's place beside Mama's bed, I could not sleep. I kept the television on, muted, and the same images cycled through the night: tanks rolling into cities and exhilarated citizens toppling statues of dictators with nooses, then clips of closed schools and stores, and people thronging railroad stations and airports and drifting through the streets with white masks that revealed nothing but their frightened, suspicious eyes. Half-empty subway trains ghosted through the city.

Mama had not woken since I arrived. Her sleep was induced and artificial. I wondered what—if—she dreamed.

For a moment, I had the eerie feeling of seeing my mother through a stranger's eyes. She was suddenly alien to me. I recalled Jia Bao's funeral, which I had not thought of in such a long time—how I'd seen him transform through the eulogies: each speaker revealed a new person, one I hadn't known in my limited view.

To one man, whom I didn't recognize, Jia Bao had been funny, a real crack up. He said you never would have guessed. To his library supervisor, Jia Bao was humble, someone overqualified for the job he'd been given, but who did it without complaint. Wei called him an uncommon man, someone who "made all of us strive for higher ideals." I didn't speak at the service. My ribs girded my pain, constraining all my grief. I could not cry.

The machines around Mama flashed meaningless graphs and beeped like neglected digital pets, begging, *Feed me, groom me, love me.* In death, who would my mother be revealed as? And Baba?

The East Peace Street Hospital was the first in the city quarantined. In desperation and panic, a nurse threw herself from a window, adding coroners and police tape to the barricades. News crews created another buffer between the hospital and the world. Even though it was only a mile away, it felt like another country.

I finally reached Wei.

"How are you? How is your mother?"

"Wei, it doesn't look good." Speaking it aloud made it real; I realized the words were true. My mother was dying.

55

DUA HYAN DROVE UP from the south that afternoon and took Baba and me to a graveyard in Liuzhangli. I had missed Tomb-Sweeping Day by three weeks and most of the graves on the hillside were already cleared of weeds. The oranges left as offerings were sunken and wrinkled, flowers had toppled on their dried stalks, and mountain rats had eaten away the other food, leaving empty bowls and torn wrappers.

Wei's parents' neglected plots stood out among the tidied graves. I thought of our baby boy's grave in Oakland: a smaller marker, with no picture embedded in the stone. Just one name and one date. It was almost strange that I loved someone so much who had never been. I had never seen him move, or cry, but I thought I knew who he would have been, and I mourned him for that.

I set out a foldable stool for Baba, and then Dua Hyan and I began pulling weeds. I had brought a bottle of cleaner and rags, and I wiped down the graves. Because of my parents' disdain for the old superstitions, I had hesitated to bring offerings, but some tiny part of me, the girl who had grown up among clouds of burned dead money in the streets, feared that the baby, and my husband's parents' ghosts, would be starving and neglected in the afterworld, so I set out a vase of artificial flowers and a few packages of ramen. Glancing briefly at my cynical brother, I bowed to the graves and gestured with my hands folded in prayer. Dua Hyan scoffed.

"Baba, you don't mind, right?" I asked.

Baba had not said a word on the drive, or on the climb up the hill. I'm sure he tired of our anxious hovering, as if we expected to fight the Grim Reaper off him at any second. But perhaps he had spied death too, and that was why he had insisted on visiting his oldest friend's grave.

He waved away my question impatiently, not deigning to speak, and I smirked at my brother.

Dua Hyan jutted his chin at the ramen, which I'd arranged in a pyramid. "Rat poison."

"Better the rats than us," I said. "Baba, shall we eat?"

Baba sighed, which I took as a yes, and we spread out a blanket and I offered the bento lunches I had picked up from 7-Eleven. I opened Baba's, separated his chopsticks and sawed them together to file away the jagged edges, and set it before him. He ate slowly and meticulously. Dua Hyan, despite his military training, or because of it—too many mess hall meals and young men tussling for portioned servings—ate noisily and quickly.

The weather was mild and the empty graveyard felt like the safest place in the city. On the other side of the hill, builders worked on the tallest skyscraper in the world, which was stacked like a tower of take-out boxes. A light wind moved among the graves and a plain white butterfly, almost blinding in the sun, danced past us.

Dua Hyan was a bachelor, a retired major general, and from the few times a year that we spoke and based on what I heard from Ah Zhay, he spent most of his leisure time training his two corgies and tending his garden. He kept his life so private that I did not know if he'd ever had any lovers, or even if those lovers would be male or female. We certainly didn't talk about the past, as if we shared none beyond the intuitive sense that we had known each other a long time, so we talked of what we loved in common.

"How is Stephanie?" he asked. "What is she studying again?"

"Ethnic studies. She studies global immigration patterns."

"Is there work in that?" He actually looked interested.

I laughed. "I'm not sure. But that's what American kids do—study whatever their hearts desire. Knowledge for knowledge's sake."

"She's always been brilliant," he said. "And Emily?"

"She's working for a union. Organizing. She has the perfect personality for it."

Dua Hyan smiled. "I see it. She really can talk. What kind of union?"

"Food service workers." Emily had majored in anthropology, so I was surprised by this job, which she had fallen into after a summer stint, but her extroversion and energy suited the work well.

Baba's cough interrupted us, and I leaned over and pounded him on the back while Dua Hyan snapped the seal of a water bottle.

"Drink, Baba." I grabbed the bottle from Dua Hyan and urged it to Baba's mouth. He struggled for a few moments—we all could hear the phlegm rattling and dislodging in his chest—and finally, he cleared it. He was red and shaken.

"Ah Zhay didn't say anything about your cough," I said.

"It's nothing."

"You don't want to pass anything on to Mama."

"Just went down the wrong pipe."

"You sure?" Dua Hyan asked. Authority entered his voice and Baba responded as he usually did.

"Quiet down. It's nothing. Stupid rice." He nudged away his empty tray and the dirty chopsticks rolled across the grave.

"Dua Hyan is just worried." I gathered up our garbage.

Dua Hyan helped our father to his feet. Baba was weaker than I had realized. His hands shook as they clasped my brother's arms. I walked beside the two of them. I would lose both Mama and him soon, I suddenly understood.

We returned to the car and drove back into the heart of the city, to the hospital, where, for the first time since I'd arrived, Mama was awake. With her eyes open, she looked more robust, to my relief, even though her black irises had faded to milky blue. I went to her.

"Look who's here," Baba said. I touched her hand. From inside the mitt, her fingers tried to grip mine.

"You look good, Mama." I hoped she did not detect the sadness beneath my smile.

She wanted us to unstrap her hands. "Of course," I said, but Dua Hyan said no.

"She's stubborn. She'll rip everything out." He tapped his fingers over the machines next to the bed, as if inspecting them. "It'll be a bloody mess." He settled into a chair. "Right, Ma?" His voice rose and his words slowed when he spoke to her. She closed her eyes, offended or defeated. I glared at him.

I slipped the breathing apparatus off my mother's face and gave her a moistened large cotton swab to suck the water from. After she'd wet her mouth, she said, "No filial piety."

"Who? Dua Hyan?" I looked back at my brother, who now stood at the window with his arms crossed.

"It's for your own good," Dua Hyan said.

Meanwhile, Baba had retrieved a bottle of vitamin E oil and began massaging Mama's swollen feet. He stroked Mama's waxy skin, his thumbs pressing into her soles, his fingers pinching her toes. His hands trembled on her flesh—this act was an effort. *They still love each other*, I noted with awe. *After everything.*

For a while, we basked in our own meditations while Baba rubbed Mama's legs. Dua Hyan found the remote and flipped through the channels, moving through the entire listing three times before shutting it off.

"When's Zhee Hyan coming?" he asked. "He should be here. You came all the way from California. What's his excuse?" Zhee Hyan was a long-distance bus driver for the Aloha bus company with a schedule that we had trouble tracking. Of course, even when he was unemployed, he was hard to pin down.

"Ah Zhay says this weekend," I answered.

Dua Hyan snorted. "We'll see." He settled into a chair and crossed his arms.

"Ma," I said, "can we get you anything?"

She blinked wearily and shook her head. I suddenly realized why she looked so much older than the last time I'd seen her—her dentures had been taken out. Her mouth had collapsed on itself, destroying her grace.

She had come in for her lungs, developed and recovered from septicemia, only to have the doctors discover a previously undiagnosed heart condition. Baba, Ah Zhay said, had maintained himself with the same stoic bearing that had carried him through my youth, but I saw his worry reveal itself in his tenderness with Mama and in his impatience with us. For the past few days, every answer from his mouth had been a bark, but as soon as he turned to Mama, his voice would soften. He was more attentive than the nurses: he checked her pills, scanned her chart, applied balm to keep her lips from cracking.

Touched, I said, "Baba, let me take over."

I slipped Mama's hand from the mitt and began rubbing her palm and squeezing her fingers. Like scored clay, her soft skin bore the imprint of the velcro straps.

"Thank Jesus," she murmured, and I realized she was praying. She had assumed Ah Zhay's prayer style: her prayers were usually long strings of barely audible words followed by a loud utterance of "Thank Jesus."

Her lips moved softly, almost no sound coming out until the next "Thank Jesus." We carried on with the afternoon punctuated by the soft moan of Mama's prayers.

56

AND FINALLY, after hopscotching across the city, the quarantine reached us. The announcement, preceded by a pleasant three-note tone reminiscent of a doorbell, came over the loudspeaker. The woman spoke with the calm and clear attitude of an airport boarding call.

"Attention all guests. Do not leave your room. Do not exit the building." At first, her requests sounded mild, temporary, as if a minor incident had taken place in the lobby. A hush fell over the entire hospital for a moment. That's strange, I thought, then all those late-night news reports that had echoed in my sleep coalesced into meaning.

I opened the door. The halls filled with people—faces all obscured by cheap paper masks—clamoring at the nurses and doctors, pushing for the elevators, rushing into the stairwells. I stood in the doorway in disbelief.

"What's happening?" I called out to a woman pushing a slumped old man in a wheelchair.

"Quarantine! Somebody's sick. You better get out." She edged the chair into a crowd of people waiting in front of the elevator.

I knew immediately that she meant SARS. Quarantine, as the people stampeding toward the exit would attest, was a death sentence. I shut the door and locked it.

Baba had been dozing in the chair next to Mama's bed.

"Huh?" he asked.

I went to the window. The police cordons were already up. Anticipating the reaction, they had erected the barricades before the announcement. The police wore white hazmat suits and their usual white helmets. Through an electronic loudspeaker, one officer's voice rose in an incoherent buzz. I imagined the people pressed against the glass doors downstairs, their slaughterhouse eyes pleading with the officers.

"They've quarantined the hospital." I was stunned.

"Which?"

I turned back to the room. "This one."

Baba stared at me as if he still didn't understand. Then his ear caught the tumult outside.

I turned on the television and found . . . us. The anchor was on the phone with a breathless woman who spoke from inside the hospital.

"It's a madhouse," our fellow prisoner said. Her tone was firm, confident, as if she had prepared for this moment: to be the clear-voiced spokeswoman for the doomed.

The reporter leaned forward on her elbows, her pink sleeves creeping back; she looked into the camera: a deep gaze into all of our captive eyes. "Which floor are you on?"

"I'm on the third floor. I've locked the door. I'm wearing a mask. It's mayhem, I'm telling you."

"Tell us how it feels." Voyeuristic curiosity—the relief of sidestepping tragedy—passed beneath her concerned frown.

"I am afraid," our spokeswoman said simply. "This may be a death sentence for us. We may die here. This will be blood on the government's hands." It was the declaration of a true martyr.

The anchor nodded sympathetically. "Just a moment—we have another view from outside the hospital." The camera zoomed its grainy eye to the torn pieces of paper crying I'M NOT SICK! and SAVE THE INNOCENT! that were held against the windows, the telescoped image of ghostly white-coated and white-masked doctors struggling through the crowded halls, the glare off a fifth-floor window where a gray-haired woman, a mask obscuring everything but her moist, stunned eyes, pressed her palm to the glass in a gesture that looked like desperation.

I had to tell Ah Zhay, Wei, my daughters. Someone. I picked up the phone. A tone identical to the one that had preceded the quarantine announcement rang out and a recorded woman's voice followed: "Apologies, the network is temporarily out of service. Please wait and try your call again."

Later that afternoon, CNN reported that an American had been caught in the quarantine and the surreal sight of my picture flashed on the screen. A snapshot of me laughing with Emily. Blown up, it was grainy, our faces bleached by the flash, our irises slightly red, the kind of photo shown ten times an hour when a person goes missing on a canyon hike with her dog, her car found unlocked in an obscure parking lot, or something like that. Was that the best photo Wei could find?

"Ba, look. It's me," I said, bemused. As if the quarantine was not surreal enough.

Baba frowned. "So it is."

"I'm famous."

"Infamous," Baba said, and I was relieved to hear that he still maintained some humor in this situation.

"Internationally infamous." I laughed drily. CNN debated whether the United States would intervene to release me, or if it would try to negotiate with China to allow the WHO into Taiwan now that American citizens had been roped into the drama. The talking heads spoke by satellite to an expert on cross-strait relations, who sat in front of a green-screen image of a generic city skyline. The pundit declared me too unimportant for such a move. Viewer e-mails expressed fears that if I were released, I might be the next Typhoid Mary.

The outer hallway had settled into quiet, but I still had not opened the door. I picked up the phone again. No service. According to the news, some people on the fifth floor had tossed a bag of coins and cash, along with a note of food requests and their room number, from their window, but their plan for take-out was squashed when a first-floor patient darted out and stole the bag of warm bento box lunches that had been kindly deposited just inside the barricade by a cameraman. A young nurse, convinced she had been given a death sentence, threw herself from the roof in a copycat of the previous week's attempt, and an ambulance had to be called from another hospital.

I made lukewarm ramen from the tap in the bathroom.

"You'll have to open the door eventually," Baba said.

"Why?"

"The doctor needs to check on your mother."

"Ba, the doctors aren't coming. The nurses are killing themselves. Mama is safer in here with us." Even as I spoke, the words seemed unreal.

"Her pills come at five o'clock. If the doctor doesn't come, I am going to look for him."

I checked the phone again, hoping to call Wei. He must have been panicked. The line was still down. Silently, we watched the recursive news stories, which all circled back to the quarantine—now one subway station had been closed for disinfection—and every few minutes, Baba checked his watch.

"They won't come," I said. Hysteria rose in my chest. "Haven't you been watching the news? We're imprisoned here."

Baba closed his eyes. "When I was in prison, we'd take walks around the world. One man—he was a doctor too—had been to New York City, and he walked us block by block through the city. All the grocery stores, laundries, delis, the women on the stoops, the taxi exhaust, the racket. I have been to that city." He opened his eyes. "The doctor will come at five, or else I will go look for him."

"What happened to him?"

Baba shook his head and looked at his watch again. "Four forty-five. In prison, we never wanted their doctor to come. You went with him and you came back with Frankenstein scars. I often had to fix his work. We had no tools. We urinated on the wounds to clean them."

My mother stirred and Baba went to her. I stared at the TV. My father had never spoken of prison to me, not once in my entire life. Maybe in the diminishing light of a long lifetime, no secret is worth taking to the grave.

"Four fifty. Come help me," Baba said.

Mama, softly moaning, relented to us. We leaned her forward. I supported her while Baba thumped gently on her back to get her circulation going.

"The doctor will be in soon," Baba told her.

"Ba." My tone was an admonishment. He should tell her the truth.

An old vigor flared up in his eyes and I knew to stop. He wouldn't be corrected.

He rearranged her pillows, and we eased her back. He curled his fingers onto her pulse and closed his eyes for a few seconds. "The doctor will be here soon," he said again.

"No, he won't!"

"You be quiet!" He said I had a crow's mouth, harbinger of bad luck.

Mama was too tired to respond to our fighting. I collapsed into the chair and wondered if we'd die from a weeklong diet of instant ramen.

Then a knock on the door rattled me out of my anger. I looked at Baba. He gestured for me to answer.

It was the doctor. He wore a flimsy paper mask over his mouth and nose.

"How is our patient?" All business, as if the quarantine had been a momentary disruption to the day. He said hello to my father, took my mother's hand and asked her how she was. He checked her chart and the machines. "I'll ask the nurse to give your mother more morphine and bring her pills."

I felt sheepish asking, but I could not help myself. "And what about us?"

He shrugged. "The chance of transmission is actually quite low. You should just make the best of things. The government is only being cautious."

"What about the nurse who . . ."

He shook his head. "People always get hysterical in these situations.

We're no exception." He sighed. "Let me know if you need anything. The courtyard is still open if you want fresh air. They'll probably reopen the convenience store once the clerk calms down. Otherwise, we might end up breaking down the gate." He chuckled. He reminded us to wash our hands thoroughly, and then he was gone.

After cleaning my hands according to the multistep chart posted in the bathroom, being sure to scrub my fingernails by rubbing them in soapy circles in the palm of my hand, I returned to the window. The sun was low, and bright spotlights beaming from news cameras revealed all the reporters below. The stigmatized street was otherwise dead.

A wild-eyed nurse came in, her eyes darting, and briskly urged Mama to take her pills, which had been crushed and mixed with warm water in a tiny paper cup.

"You're the American?" she said.

"Yup."

"Your family must be so worried. But at least someone cares about you. I saw it on the news." She clicked her tongue. "Two thousand Taiwanese stuck in here, but they only worry about the American."

The thunder of trucks woke me. Bearing huge tanks of disinfectant, they moved slowly down the street. Men in white suits stood on the running boards spraying down the blacktop with misting hoses. We had left the TV on mute, and the news had shifted back to the situation in Iraq. President Bush had declared the incursion over and successful—mission accomplished—but the conflict still lingered. I'd already been relegated to a once-hourly ticker update. "American still quarantined in Taiwan hospital." And, in the PRC, the Chinese government was threatening to execute those who broke quarantine.

Baba was asleep. I showered and dried myself with a washcloth and a fistful of paper towels.

The hospital was quiet. The nurses had apparently organized themselves into shifts, and half of them slept on wheeled beds lining the halls. A few, still on duty, dozed at their stations. I took the elevator to the lobby. As the doctor had promised, someone had broken down the gates to the convenience store—or else the clerk had surrendered and left it for us in a gesture of compassion. It was open and unmanned. Many of the food shelves were almost bare. I took a few bottles of barley tea and some tuna sandwiches. I also found a bag of almonds that had fallen behind the rack of disposable underwear. I felt entitled to what I'd found, but I left money in a drawer behind the counter anyway.

Through the hospital front doors, I could see the news trucks parked in a row across the street; however, except for the police pacing in front of the barrier, no one else was in sight.

We sat on the edge of a planter in the courtyard; Baba's sandaled feet barely touched the ground. From some secret stash, he had brought cigarettes, and we smoked together. I hadn't smoked since the middle of my first pregnancy, back when doctors did not warn against the habit, and when smoking was one of my few solaces during those hard months. Three decades later, it felt good. I understood how old addictions crept up and latched on.

I didn't want to say anything because the cigarette seemed to have loosened Baba's tongue. Again, he had begun to talk about his eleven missing years, about the Ankeng Military Prison where he spent the early part of his imprisonment and then the prison on Green Island, which now was open to the public as a memorial. At Ankeng, cells so crowded that the men had to sleep in shifts, then on Green Island, for a period, where solitary confinement was served in a hot, padded, coffin-like room, and men were damned by frivolous charges like "discontent with the status quo" and "criticized the KMT." Later, a portion of the prison had been named—ironically or cruelly—"Oasis Villa."

"You have no idea. You cannot imagine. Thirty-seven men crammed into a room for six. You ever seen rats crammed into a cage? They start biting each other, claw out their own eyes, chew on their limbs. Men too. Sometimes when you were sleeping, someone would stomp on you in your sleep. Bang. Break a limb. You go out to the infirmary and there's a little more space for the others. One man was stomped so hard, his bladder burst."

"And then what?"

"And then what? He died." Baba shook his head. "It was better on Green Island. At least we got our own tatami then. And we could go outside. It was an island—where could we run? But in Ankeng." He shook his head and took a draw of his cigarette. "Tuberculosis was rampant. That's how they wiped us out the cheap way. Put a few sick people in a room—don't have to pay for a bullet later, right?"

Our conversation was interrupted by a twentysomething man in pajamas who bore a railroad of crusty stitches across his shaved head and a black chest tattoo peeking out the top of his shirt. I was wary, but Baba said hello immediately and introduced me tersely by saying, "My daughter."

"The American?"

I nodded.

"I saw you on TV. My cousin lives in Los Angeles. Wong Bin Lao. You know him?"

"California is pretty big."

He sat on the other side of Baba and lit his own cigarette. "Can you believe this shit? Ah, excuse my language, Grandfather." His laugh had a sour edge to it. "I thought I was coming in for surgery, not prison."

A patch of blue sky, inaccessible freedom, taunted us. Around us were the shadows of the old red brick; parched, scraggly grass; and halfhearted palms. Some "experts" claimed that SARS, like the old viruses of yore, died in fresh air.

"Which one of you is the sick one?"

"We're here for my mother."

The man laughed. "Well, that's bad luck."

A doctor stepped into the courtyard through the French doors. He nodded at our odd crew, pulled off his mask, and asked for a light.

"No problem, Doc." The man hopped down and lit the doctor's cigarette.

A relaxed silence fell between us. The doctor paced the courtyard, his exhalations weary and almost thoughtful.

"Doc, what are the chances we're going to die?" The man scratched at his stitches.

The doctor sighed. "Nil. But it makes everyone feel better to keep us here. We're lepers."

"Lepers. Ha! I was a leper before I came here."

The outside world was quiet. We could not hear anything beyond the courtyard, as if the city had come to a standstill. I'd heard that the subway trains raced past nearly empty platforms and parents were going mad trying to calm their cabin-fevered children now that the schools were closed.

The image of the virus circulating through all the cracks and vents came to me. Tiny, sneaking specks of illness. I wanted to go home alive. Like a gesture against superstition, I decided that when I returned to our room, I would wet a towel and stuff it against the gap under the door.

We had nothing to do but wait.

57

FEARING FOR THEIR LIVES, healthcare workers quit en masse at two of the city's hospitals, causing angry politicians to rail against their selfishness and threaten jail. Two new declarations came out from independent researchers—one that said the virus was spread from unwashed utensils and the other that declared civet cats as the definite culprit.

It made little difference to us. A week of identical days passed. Our dangers were not dirty forks or civet cats, but each other. The news crews maintained their post outside even when the dramas of our more hysterical fellow prisoners stopped. Bored patients and their families gathered in the common areas to stare gaping at the mounted televisions. Sometimes scuffles broke out among the frustrated internees, drip bags swinging on their poles, tubes entangling.

Mama was weakening. The color was almost completely gone from her face; she woke less often, and when she did, she cried out that she was in pain. More and more morphine dripped into her; the doctor called this "comfort care" and neither Baba nor I commented on the euphemism. She existed now. I would not imagine a moment beyond that.

Baba stood at the window for long periods. Occasionally, he'd comment on what he saw as the streets came slowly back to life despite waves of panic that rolled through with each newly discovered infection: the office workers again cutting across the park, lovers kissing behind trees, taxi drivers playing chicken with pedestrians. What did he think about as he gazed over this city he had known? His boyhood in the narrow streets of Twa Tiu Tiann, the shudder of the ground against his straw-soled sandals as he ran past the tea merchants, the rice flour grinders, the apothecary with his jars and drawers full of fragrant herbs—that moment in life before one becomes aware of himself?

I thought of all those times past when it was just Baba and me, like this, Ah Zhay and Dua Hyan wishing they could find the center of Baba's attention as it had been before he left. Had he spoiled me precisely because I had no memories? With me, he didn't have to be the father they remembered, the one who was certain and moral.

I washed his shirt in the bathroom, and when I came out, I found him at the window in his undershirt, his bare shoulder pressed to the glass: this short, thin, old stranger whose body my father—enigmatic, overwhelming, fearsome—somehow occupied.

The compassion that I suddenly felt for him surprised me. I joined him at the window, trying to understand what he saw. Buildings, the haphazard jumble that betrayed the city's turbulent history, obscured the horizon, but I imagined I saw the curve of the earth, a smash of life gradually thinning out at the edges, sprinkled into the dark green hills, empty to the sea, an island, shaped like a yam, or perhaps a leaf of tobacco, with a black spine of dark mountains and knobby strings of twinkling lights cascading down the edges.

"I feel like I have been thinking about death my whole life," Baba said.

I didn't know what to say.

"I thought your mother would live forever. She was always going to outlive me." His eyes, blue with age, sparkled in the sun's glare.

I tried to think beyond my own meager personal memories to something more primal. A planet amid deep black space, still cooling from whatever blast or collision or universal hand that has created it. This planet is not just a lump of dumb rock. It is alive; it moves, shakes, slides. Two plates collide. Four million years ago, two plates collide and an island erupts. This island. Our lives were so minuscule in comparison.

THE WORLD DOES NOT HAPPEN the way we lay it out on paper: one event after another, one word following the next like a trail of ants. The rocks in the field do not preclude the flowing river fifty miles away; a man sneezes and at the exact same time a woman washes her feet, a child trips and blood oozes from the broken skin, a dog nips at a flea on its hindquarter, and a bird swallows a beetle. Past, present, and future too swirl together, distinguishable but not delineated by any sort of grammar beyond the one our hearts impose.

I want to believe that my parents found a way to bypass time that night, to compress and expand their lives together, to live out their whole lives again in their good-bye.

The shades were drawn. His daughter had fallen asleep, but he didn't want to wake her. This moment was for the two of them: he and his wife.

This was the night, the moment. She was already halfway there, dragged down by morphine, which was the boatman of her voyage tonight. He brushed hair off her forehead. If their places were switched, he knew, she would be praying for him right now. Though the gods changed, she had always prayed for him. He had no prayer, believing only one thing from the thousands of Christian words she had said to him: *earth to earth, ashes to ashes, dust to dust.*

This night felt so broad, broader than the years that had preceded it. He wondered how the decades condensed like this, disappearing into a blink, while one moment unfurled almost endlessly.

How quickly it all had passed.

That year, the cherry trees on Grass Mountain bloom in late February.

He sits on a blanket beneath a tree that is thick with flowers. The girl sitting beside him bats away a petal falling slowly toward her. Five of them are arrayed here sharing snacks and cups of cold sake: he; his sister, who has asked him as a pretense for inviting his friend Su Ming Guo, of whom she is fond; her classmate; and her classmate's cousin. This girl, the classmate's cousin, who has just caught him watching her, has blushing white skin the same color as the drifting petal. Her name is Jeng Li Min. He tries to return his attention to admiring the sakura, but his eyes keep being drawn to her creamy throat and the darkness of her hair against her skin.

Mono no aware. The bittersweet of transience. He tries to concentrate on this feeling. They come here not for mere beauty, but to think of the brief, brilliant flash of their own mortality reflected by the sakura. But he is a doctor, not a poet.

She, however, is a painter. He wants to ask her what she sees when she looks at the trees, if she sees them like he does. But amid the chatter of the picnickers around them, the question seems too earnest.

"I skinned my knee here," his sister cries, and pulls up her skirt to reveal a light brown scar etched on her skin. He cringes at her blatant attempt to charm his friend and his friend's indifference, though Ming Guo dutifully rolls up a sleeve to display a puckered line on his elbow.

"And you, Li Min? Any scars?" his sister asks.

Li Min blushes, but her expression doesn't change. He's curious about what she will say. Will she play the game or demur?

She tilts her head up and touches a finger to the underside of her chin. "A dog nipped me once, when I was three."

His sister leans forward to inspect, then calls him over. "I can't tell if it's a scar or a birthmark. Dr. Tsai, you look."

"Why would she lie?" he says.

"You're the doctor. Look. It looks like a birthmark to me."

He sighs, takes off his glasses and wipes them with his handkerchief.

"He's very serious," his sister's classmate says, and giggles.

"Always," his sister says.

He puts his glasses back on and leans forward. His sister gives him a mischievous smile as she moves out of the way.

This close he can smell Li Min's hair, sweet with artificial roses. She holds herself very still. Right below the scar, her skin pulses.

"What kind of dog was it?" he asks.

"A street dog."

"Ah, my brother's bedside manner in action," his sister says.

He leans back. "Definitely a scar." This jagged scar against her pale throat fills him with the sort of clenched awareness that the sakura is meant to elicit. He swallows heavily and his eyes grow moist. He chides himself for this sentimentality. "Who's next?" he says.

His sister claps her hands. "Now he plays."

The sky is perfectly blue. In two days, it will be March. Because of a light breeze, the usual sulfur smell of this mountain is faint. His sister and her classmate have escorted Ming Guo to walk among the trees. He swore he saw his sister wink at Li Min as she left.

He knows his value. He is a doctor. Staring into the mirror as he shaves, he has moments of objective observance, noting that a passing stranger would likely consider him attractive. Yet, sitting on this blanket beside this girl, empty cups and crumpled paper between them, he feels that he has nothing to offer her.

"Look at how the flowers crowd together," she says.

His gaze follows hers. On each gnarled branch, blooms cluster in bouquets. This is something he has both known and never noticed. He sees how the filaments burst like fireworks from the centers. Of course, these parts have names, but he cannot recall them.

"To the distant observer / They are chatting of the blossoms / Yet in spite of appearances / Deep in their hearts / They are thinking very different thoughts," she says. Her forthrightness startles him. Her eyes have not left the blue sky or pale flowers. "A poem," she says. "Ki no Tsurayuki."

"Did you study poetry as well?" His words come out too fast.

She laughs. "I couldn't study painting without studying poetry. Words and images are inextricable."

He admits this is true.

"However, I mainly studied Western painting. Only pictures. No words."

"Why?"

She looks at him. Her eyes are so dark that the reflection of the sky has completely obscured their original color. "For the same reason you studied Western medicine."

He considers this.

"I'm not sure you are right," he says finally.

She smiles. "Then why?"

"I think you expect I will say that Western is modern, and that our culture is old-fashioned. But I don't believe that. I don't believe the West equals modernity. The idea is colonialist."

She glances at the Japanese family beneath the tree next to them and hushes him. He switches to Taiwanese. "We are curious creatures, we Taiwanese. Orphans. Eventually, orphans must choose their own names and write their own stories. The beauty of orphanhood is the blank slate."

These words are blasphemy. He is sorry as soon as he is finished. Only a man as clumsy as himself would express such sentiments on such a beautiful day beneath such a beautiful sky. He notices that she has been fiddling with the hem of her skirt. He wants to tell her how she has struck him. On a day with a sky so blue and air so crisp, how can he be held accountable for what comes from his mouth?

"I understand," she says, and then she quotes Du Fu: *"The country is broken, but the mountains and rivers remain."* Her eyes flash; he catches sight of the fire in this modest woman.

"We are the mountains and rivers," he says, impressed. "No matter what the country is called."

"Dr. Tsai!" his sister calls. Her arm is looped through Ming Guo's and they march toward him. Her face is lost in the shadow beneath her hat.

Li Min glances at him and smiles. "Back to flowers and wine," she says.

59

A LONG, SHRILL TONE startled me awake. Baba held Mama's hand, his head tipped and his eyes closed as if he didn't hear it.

"Oh no!" I exclaimed. I stumbled out of the chair. "Baba, call the nurse!" My finger jammed at the call button, but the nurses were already bursting through the door.

They swarmed my mother, checking wires and tubes and punching buttons on the machine, and a moment later, the doctor entered.

I paced around the periphery, moving from one side of the bed to the other. "Is she okay?" I asked, hoping the answer would surprise me. "Is it a malfunction? Is she okay?" My voice grew tighter at every iteration of the question. "She's okay, right?"

The doctor called out the time to a nurse, who jotted it down.

"I'm afraid she's passed," he said.

I pushed past him and my hands shook as I wrenched my mother's hand free of the stupid mitt. "Mama," I said. "It's me. Come on."

The doctor gently touched my arm. "She's gone. Would you give us a moment to clean up, and then you can say good-bye?"

I reluctantly let go and went to the other side of the bed. Baba still had not opened his eyes. I kneeled in front of him and spoke to him in Taiwanese. "Baba, they need a moment. We can come back, they said."

I cried as I pulled his hand from hers and helped him to his feet. We left the nurses bustling around the bed and I guided Baba toward the empty waiting area. My hands shook. I walked too fast and I had to remind myself to slow down to his pace. The TV played on mute. I helped Baba into one of the hard plastic chairs and sat beside him. He still had not said a word.

"Baba," I whispered through my sobs, "you don't have to be strong for me." I needed to see him cry too.

A torrent of platitudes spewed from my mouth: *She's at peace now; it's in God's hands now; she's with Jesus now, Baba.*

"Daughter, please stop talking," Baba finally said. His shoulders slumped and he covered his face.

Hurt, I said, "I should call Ah Zhay and Dua Hyan. I'm going to find a phone."

When I stood, I was disoriented. I saw the nurses' station, brightly lit, behind us, but I couldn't remember where Mama's room had been. I caught sight of the bathroom sign, so I pushed open the heavy door and vomited into the sink.

I sank onto the mottled tile floor and wailed.

What would Baba do without her? Maybe the doctor had made a mistake. I would ask him to check again. Newspapers were full of stories of people who had been thought dead until the moment that they shifted or groaned during their own funerals. Doctors were not always right, I thought bitterly.

Drained, I held on to the lip of the sink and pulled myself up. In the bathroom's greenish light, the mauve stall doors as my backdrop, my face looked terrible: red, blotchy, my lips and nose swollen. I splashed water on my face and wiped it with my shirt.

In the hallway again, I stopped a nurse and asked if the phones were working. Above her blank mask, her brow furrowed.

"Not yet," she said, and this nudge of frustration was enough to make me cry again.

I found my way back to my mother's room. The nurses had put down fresh sheets and carefully folded back the edge beneath Mama's arms. They had removed all the machines and wires, turned off the overhead light and left only the soft yellow bedside lamp on, switched on a fan, and spritzed the room with a menthol freshener. Baba was back in the bedside chair, Mama's hand clasped in his. I thought I heard the susurration of prayer.

Baba lifted his head. More than grief—*defeat*—showed itself in every part of his face: his bloodshot eyes, furrowed brow, and pursed mouth. "Did you call your sister and brother?"

I shook my head.

I went to the other side of the bed and pressed my palm to my mother's smooth gray forehead. Her serene face revealed what a violence her illness had been. I kissed her eerily cool skin.

Because of the quarantine, my siblings could not come into the hospital, so I said good-bye for all of us, her children.

60

WE STUMBLED OUT of the hospital blinking into the sun and the glare of camera lights. Police guided us down the path. The quarantine had ended the way it had started—with a three-tone ring and a restrained announcement: "Guests, the quarantine has now ended. You are free to leave the building."

Earnest reporters still clad in surgical masks greeted us, shouting questions and thrusting microphones over the plastic cordon. Baba and I walked together, his arm in mine. Mama's body lay in the hospital morgue, waiting for the funeral. We hobbled past a woman who was repeatedly asking an official from the Ministry of Health if he was sure that we were not contagious.

We moved slowly past the barricades. A man in a bright purple tie shoved a microphone in our faces and called Baba "Grandpa" and me "Aunty," as if this false intimacy could mask his hunger.

"Grandpa, Aunty, were you afraid? How did you pass the time? Was your family worried?"

I pleaded with him to leave us alone. Baba did not look up.

Finally, beyond the reporters, in the crowd, we spotted Ah Zhay and my brothers.

On such short notice, plane tickets were too expensive for Wei and the girls to come for the funeral.

"I can't do it without you," I said to Wei.

"I'm sorry." I heard the guilt in his voice, as if he was apologizing for everything. "I love you. Hold on, Emily wants to talk to you."

Emily came on the line. "Mom, I'm so sad. Tell Ah Gong we love him." Her voice was choked and I heard her tears start as she handed the phone back to Wei.

"I miss you," Wei said. "Come home soon."

His words unstitched me all over again and I cried silently into the phone, finding small comfort as he uttered, "Hey, hey, hey. It's okay. You'll be home soon."

What is home? I wanted to ask. *Haven't I already come home?*

Mama's funeral was held at the Second Municipal Funeral Home in Taipei, a large complex of ceremony rooms. My siblings and I wore traditional hemp robes and bowed before her casket, then followed it out to the crematorium. After Ah Zhay, Jie-fu, and my niece and nephews and their families left, my brothers and I waited in the parking lot for my mother's ashes. Zhee Hyan smoked while leaning on the hood, and Baba sat in the passenger seat of Dua Hyan's car with the door open. He was too exhausted to cry. I had heard him the night before, in his room, underneath the sound of the television, weeping. I had been staying in Mama's room, trying to disturb as little as possible. I didn't even touch a pencil on her desk. It was a diorama of her last days. In so many ways, she was still there. I opened the wardrobe. After all these years, she still wore the same perfume and it had seeped through all her clothes. I wondered how long it would linger.

When we collected her ashes, I was numbed by the notion of this pile of soft dust and bone debris. In the backseat of the car, I clutched the urn in my lap as Dua Hyan drove and Zhee Hyan finally shed his tears.

61

BEFORE I LEFT TAIPEI, I still had a few more stops. The first was 2-28 Peace Park, which was now a memorial. Not to the dead—that would be too controversial. Like so many memorials of atrocities, it was a monument to peace, a promise to never forget. A three-diamond sculpture with an antenna of geometric shapes rose out of a reflection pool. A plaque declared HEAVEN SHALL BLESS THIS ISLAND OF TREASURES, FORMOSA, TO PROSPER FOREVER. And in the former Broadcasting Bureau building, where anxious announcements had gone out the night of my birth, sat the museum memorializing the victims of the massacre that had forever changed my family.

Could we call this success? The country had exploded into a robust democracy with the end of martial law in 1987; the press burst forth in tabloid excess in an effort to fill up twenty-four hours of news, willing to cover any and all complaints, small and large. Voter turnout was sometimes as high as 75 percent. People celebrated this as a "bloodless" transition to democracy, ignoring the quiet revolution that had taken place for decades and the tens of thousands who had died in the streets, by the interrogator's hand, or in prison for this victory.

Inside, the museum had re-created the scene of the cigarette seller's conflict: a cart, cigarette cartons spread across the ground, a raucous city as the backdrop. From a photo, the widow gazed across six decades. She was young, her hair pulled back tightly off her forehead. This was the "old widow" whose pleading with the Monopoly Bureau agents had become the originating myth of this whole history? This woman who was not more than forty?

Upstairs, the faces of the dead, dozens of men in black-and-white photos, stared at me. Lim Mo-seng, Su Shui-mu, Wang Kui-liang, and on. And Jia Bao's father, setting forth on the same fate that would curse his son. Before I even read the name, I knew it was him. Jia Bao, but for twenty-five years.

My father's face was not among them. No memorial was built for the men who had survived by selling their souls. The thousands who had disappeared over the years, stained as criminals, who emerged back into the light as neighborhood pariahs for nothing more than the desire to claim an island as their own. No memorial for the men more complicated than martyrs—or for the families who'd had to relearn the hardships of the everyday.

Number 183 Nanjing West Road was the "flashpoint," where the widow peddling black market cigarettes was pistol-whipped, the moment when discontent tipped into violence.

A waist-high marker indicated the spot. The incident had taken place in front of the Tian-ma Teahouse, but that was gone. The current businesses on either side of the plaque, the MEN'S TAILOR, SINCE 1948 and BEAUTY PARLOR CLUB, were both closed—and the latter was a charred hulk of a building gaudily marked with a dusty pink neon sign.

The only light in this gloom was an apothecary shop, where three men stood behind the counter—evenly tall, solemn mouthed, and eyes meditative—quickly measuring herbs on tiny handheld scales; a flick of the wrist moved the herbs from balance to counter, the scale rocking like a sloshing bucket, the herbs dropping softly as daisy fluff onto sheets of tissue paper.

The plaque was easily missed. Cars parked beside it, pedestrians walked past it without a second glance, businesses opened and closed before it. Something had happened here once, but other things had too, and life went on.

We have to remind ourselves to remember.

I gave my respects to the widow, beaten the night that my mother had gone into labor with me—neither woman aware of the other or how their fates were tied, however tenuously. Maybe this is what it meant to be a citizen of a place—bonded to each other by the histories thrust upon us.

I ordered noodles at a vegetarian stand across the street from the plaque. Old men at another nearby stand ate and talked loudly. A woman with a shriveled arm sold scratch-off lottery tickets. The proprietress flipped through a magazine. I would fly back to California the next day, and I was not ready to say good-bye to Baba. My next visit home would likely be under similar circumstances. I pulled a handful of tissues from the box on the table and wiped my eyes. A week ago, I'd spoken to my mother; now, her lifetime—spanning from colonialism through a world war, nearly four decades of martial law, and then democracy—was diminished to dust.

"Too spicy?" the proprietress called with a grin.

I nodded and said, "Yes, too spicy," and blew my nose. I left my dirty dishes in a bucket of water near the street and wound my way back to the train station.

EPILOGUE: *MEMENTO VITAE*

A FEW WEEKS AFTER my return to Berkeley, I went to the attic and rummaged among the boxes. Wei had stored copies of old academic journals, manila folders crammed with duplicates of his articles, and, inexplicably, a few years' worth of final exams. I was no better—I had stuffed my clippings into unlabeled envelopes and, in some cases, had kept the entire issue of the publication that my story had appeared in. We had the girls' childhood drawings and essays. I'd scattered packets of silverfish repellent over everything, but that hadn't prevented years of humidity from puckering the pages. I wondered if everyone's attic was as loaded with nostalgia and narcissism.

Finally, in a yellowed bankers box, I found what had drawn me up there. As soon as I touched the rubber band, it broke limply, too desiccated to even snap. After Jia Bao's murder, the thought of looking at the manuscript again nauseated me and I had put it away. Now, I sat with it on my lap for a moment, my palms pressed to the front page. He'd been gone for more than two decades. I had moments when I didn't think I would survive, the pain so deep it sent me clawing for air.

Carefully, I laid aside the first sheet. The Courier font looked old-fashioned, each letter woolly with time. The lines and spacing too lacked precision, and hearkened back to a world in which everything had the giveaway touch of a human hand.

I cringed when I began reading. The grammar mistakes that had been invisible to me then were now too apparent. I saw language filtered and trying to break free from crudeness into something approaching elegance, and I saw all our youth and earnestness.

In another life, I'd once told him. I meant it too, bolstered by a notion that I could take an eraser to my life and scribble it anew, as many times as it took. Had Mama suffered from the same illusion? Was that why she had decided on baptism, only to find a Christian rebirth was metaphorical, and she was still stuck in the one existence she had?

I read in the attic until sunset, and then I carried the manuscript downstairs. Over the next few weeks, in the same office where I'd first worked on it, I rewrote it. It is common practice among writers to let a manuscript sit awhile before revision. In this case I'd waited nearly a quarter of a century. I had been too close before; as translator, I had pieced it together word by word, thinking only of the flow of sentences. Now I could see, clearly, the subtext—the struggle and yearning—that had lain beneath. During my edits, I finally sloughed away my illusions of romance and regret and grazed the sharp edge of who Jia Bao—and I and Wei—had been.

Lost children. How young thirty-two looks from the vantage of fifty-six. And yet I had only a few more answers than I'd had then. How could I find forgiveness for all of us—Baba, Wei, Jia Bao, me? After Baba came back from prison, my parents had forty-five more years together. Had it been enough to wash away the scars of those eleven lost years? Had they ever lain in bed and whispered, *I'm sorry,* an apology for the decades, one single utterance of regret that would atone for it all?

I published two versions of Jia Bao's book: one in characters, in Taiwan, with the help of my niece, and the other in English. I found a small publisher in Southern California that specialized in East Asian texts, and it agreed to a printing of five hundred copies.

I asked Emily to pass it out among her—as she referred to them—"comrades" in the union, and Stephanie to leave copies in the graduate student lounge. *What is this?* Emily had asked. *A book by a good friend,* I had said. Emily faintly remembered Jia Bao but Stephanie did not, so I told them about his escape and murder, but nothing about the other turmoil of those days—not about the trip to Willits, Mr. Lu, or the foundering of a marriage. Nothing about how my parents' life had echoed amid the chaos.

I gave away copies at community meetings and cultural festivals. I sent copies to professors and human rights groups. I *disseminated*, like a Johnny Appleseed of revolutionary text.

Whenever I opened the book, felt the strain of paper against the binding, Jia Bao's voice was there—distinct, alive.

Two distant points now touching, the word and the page a bridge and amends.

My father wasn't executed. He was arrested. He disappeared. He came back, not a saint, but a man. He was angry, sad, on occasion happy. He scolded us, cursed us, loved us as best he could. My mother did the same. Life was not a beautiful thing, not swathed in tulle and glitter, strapped with angel wings. Nothing sublime hid in the pain we found in one March decades ago, a month that went on and on beyond the boundaries of the calendar. It was more than a commemorative hat or T-shirt, or a picture on a wall in a museum. It was more than a story.

It was like this, wasn't it?

ACKNOWLEDGMENTS

After spending fourteen years on this project, I have accumulated quite a list of people, places, and sources to whom I owe thanks. The following is my best attempt to express my appreciation to the many, many people I encountered on this journey. I apologize to anyone whose name I might have missed.

I want to thank the Institute of International Education for funding my initial research trip to Taipei in the form of a Fulbright grant in 2002. In Taiwan, the following were especially giving of their time and stories: Chen Yao Ji, Ho Cong Ming, Li Rong Zong, Li Shi De, Liao De Zheng, Liao Ji Bin, Liu Ke Xiang, Ruan Mei Shu, Su Feng Fu, Xiao Jin Wen, Zhang Liang Zhe (Jeffrey Chang), Linda Gail Arrigo, Jerome Keating, Mark Harrison, Paul J. Mooney, my hānai family, the Yus, and my family, the Yangs.

The Bay Area Taiwanese American community was extremely supportive. Ho Chie Tsai, founder of TaiwaneseAmerican.org, was the first to reach out when he heard of my project, and warmly welcomed me into the community. Because of him, I was able to find a number of first-generation Taiwanese Americans who generously allowed me to interview them about their lives. I was deeply moved by the stories they shared. *Green Island* is also dedicated to this generation, who grew up under the shadow of martial law but never lost their faith in a vision of a better world, and who continue to fight for recognition of Taiwan: Jeffrey Chang, Leon Chang, Cheryl Chen, Mrs. Fred Chen, Hsiu-li Cheng, Ma-Chi Chen, Muh-Fa Chen, Sue Chen, Yi Ming Cheng, Ching-Wen Chenglo, T. K. Chu, Thomas Ho, Tammy Hong, Edward Huang, Meina Ko, Rocky Liao, Rebecca Rose Reagan (Li-Ching Liu), Pam Tsai, Ming-Tzang Tsay, Stella Wu-Chu, Liwen and Fan-Chi Yao.

Love and appreciation to friends and family: my sisters, Christina, Annie, and Emily; my parents; Jackie Bautista; Jeffrey Boyd; Carley, Jia Yn, Limon, and Ming Tzong Chen; Jia Ching Chen and Mona Damluji; "Groop"; Eva

ACKNOWLEDGMENTS

Guo; Seth Harwood; Akemi Johnson; Sean Kim; Tony Lee; Kyhl Lyndgaard; Zachary Mason; Heather Moore; Rob Pierce; Jennifer Sime; Gary Snyder; Spring Warren; and Andrea Young.

Thank you to the English Department at the University of Hawai'i at Mānoa for research and peer support, and the remarkable students at UH, from whom I have learned so much about passion. Thank you to the staff of the *MĀNOA Journal*—Frank, Pat, Sonia, and Noah—for giving me a second home in the department. Thank you to the *Asian American Literary Review*, which, many years ago, published an early version of the first chapter. I continue to be grateful to John Lescroart and Lisa Sawyer for the Maurice Prize, and to my first press, El Leon Literary Arts, and its publisher, Thomas Farber, who has been a mentor and inspiration for nearly twenty years.

For his unabating support and love, Hugh Sutton-Gee.

I am deeply grateful for my amazing agent, Daniel Lazar. Over the years, he and his assistant, Victoria Doherty-Munro, both patiently read and gave feedback on endless drafts. I'm honored that my editor, Carole Baron, believed in the book, saw its potential, and wanted to work with me. She and assistant editor Ruth Reisner guided me through extensive revisions and gave careful comments on each iteration. I am awed by their enthusiasm, energy, and wisdom.

Though elements of this novel are loosely based on actual events, and a very real political situation, this is a work of fiction, and I have changed some facts in order to maintain the integrity of the fictional story. However, I want to credit some of the books that informed this novel in large and small ways. For example, for Jia Bao's storyline, I drew on the experiences of Peng Ming-Min, Henry Liu, and Chen Wen-cheng to understand the various legal and extralegal mechanisms the KMT government used to control its challengers, particularly from abroad. This is not an exhaustive list, but it is a good place to start for a reader who is interested in finding out more about Taiwan and the themes explored in this novel.

Linda Gail Arrigo, *A Borrowed Voice: Taiwan Human Rights Through International Networks 1960–1980*

Edward I-te Chen, "Formosan Political Movements under the Japanese Colonial Rule 1914–1937"

Leo T. S. Ching, *Becoming Japanese: Colonial Taiwan and the Politics of Identity Formation*

James Davidson, *Island of Formosa, Past and Present*

Mark Harrison, *Legitimacy, Meaning and Knowledge in the Making of Taiwanese Identity*

David E. Kaplan, *Fires of the Dragon*

Paul R. Katz, *When Valleys Turned Blood Red: The Ta-pa-ni Incident in Colonial Taiwan*

George Kerr, *Formosa Betrayed* and *Formosa: Licensed Revolution in the Home Rule Movement, 1895–1945*

Faye Yuan Kleeman, *Under an Imperial Sun: Japanese Colonial Literature of Taiwan and the South*

Sylvia Li-chun Lin, *Representing Atrocity in Taiwan: The 228 Incident and White Terror in Fiction and Film*

Tsung-yi Lin (editor), *An Introduction to the 228 Tragedy in Taiwan for World Citizens*

Peng Ming-Min, *A Taste of Freedom: Memoirs of a Formosan Independence Leader*

Owen Rutter, *Through Formosa: An Account of Japan's Island Colony*

Tehpen Tsai (translated by Grace Hatch), *Elegy of Sweet Potatoes, Stories of Taiwan's White Terror*

Shawna Yang Ryan
Honolulu
May 2015